◙　　◙　　◙

"Engine Arm to ascent…" Shepherd read off, and instantly Lucas flipped the toggle. "Program 99…" He counted down. "3…2…1…" Shepherd pressed the final button on the computer keypad. "Proceed…!"

A rapid succession of muffled pops sounded, and a slight, sharp vibration struck beneath their feet as explosive bolts detonated, severing all electrical and physical connections between the upper and lower stages of *Starlight*. Unaware that he was doing so, Lucas held his breath and braced for the sudden, upward rush.

And waited.

Nothing.

"Manual!" Shepherd called, but Lucas' hand was already on the way. He jammed his thumb into the round red button before him, jammed it hard.

And again.

The hush was deafening. The stillness was brutal.

The ascent engine, the only part of the spacecraft with no possible backup system, was silent.

ICE

SHANE JOHNSON

FOREWORD BY GENERAL CHARLES DUKE, APOLLO 16 LUNAR MODULE PILOT

ICE

THE GREATEST TRUTHS HIDE IN THE DARKEST SHADOWS

WATERBROOK
PRESS

SCF
F
JOH

ICE

PUBLISHED BY WATERBROOK PRESS
2375 Telstar Drive, Suite 160
Colorado Springs, Colorado 80920
A division of Random House, Inc.

Scripture quotations are taken from the *New American Standard Bible*® (NASB).
© Copyright The Lockman Foundation 1960, 1962, 1963, 1968, 1971, 1972, 1973,
1975, 1977. Used by permission. (www.Lockman.org). Scripture quotations also
taken from the *King James Version.*

Reasonable care has been taken to trace original sources and copyright holders
for any quotations appearing in this book. Should any attribution be found to be
incorrect or incomplete, the publisher welcomes written documentation supporting
correction for subsequent printings.

ISBN 1-57856-548-0

Printed in the United States of America
2002—First Edition

10 9 8 7 6 5 4 3 2 1

This book is dedicated to the memory of
Steven "Doc" Jessup,
a native son and gentle soul
who served his country well,
dealt with adversities few have had to endure,
treated his fellow man with kindness and patience,
and loved his Lord.

Godspeed, old friend.

Of those who walked upon another world,
three are no longer with us:

Apollo 12 Commander Charles "Pete" Conrad,
the third man to set foot upon the surface of the moon,
whose endearing sense of humor will be missed.

Apollo 14 Commander Alan B. Shepard,
who in May 1961 gave his countrymen a reason to hope
and opened the gateway to the stars.

Apollo 15 Lunar Module Pilot James Irwin,
who on the lunar surface felt the presence of the Lord
and found there, perched gently atop a mound of soil
as if placed there just for him, a palm-sized, crystalline rock
that came to be called "Genesis."
It was the only pure white stone ever found on the moon.

Foreword

During the Apollo program, those of us who were scheduled to fly to the moon speculated about the possibility of ice, or any other evidence of water, existing there. I recall a number of discussions with my Apollo 16 commander, John Young, and our geology team about where would be the most likely spot to find such evidence. As I remember, we settled on the general area of the lunar poles. With this in mind, and knowing well the challenges involved in attaining a polar orbit, we informally floated the idea with some in management. We knew getting the go-ahead for such a mission would be a long shot, as the command/service module fuel budgets were rather tight for such a daring flight plan. Our idea was turned down, and Apollo 16 was assigned a landing site in the Descartes highlands, a region not too far southeast of the moon's center point as viewed from Earth.

Every phase of our training was rigorous and thorough. Each month, John and I would participate in a geology field trip. In December 1971, we were on what would be our final outing, since the launch was only three months away. This trip had taken us to the big island of Hawaii, where we were to study the lava flows on the flanks of Kilauea. The first day out, I caught the flu and was running a very high fever. That night, I had a vivid dream in which John and I were on the moon, and while reading *Ice*, the dream's haunting images came flooding back to me.

I dreamed we were in the lunar rover, traveling toward a place we had studied named North Ray Crater. As we crested a small ridge, we came across a faint set of tracks that had been made by some vehicle. Of course, we were very excited and requested permission to follow them. We turned right and at top speed followed the tracks. After a few miles we found a vehicle similar to our rover, in which two motionless spacesuited beings were seated, side by side. We stopped and went over to investigate. The two occupants apparently were dead. As I raised their sun visors, I was shocked to find John's face and my own staring back at me. Fortunately, the dream proved not to be a premonition of danger and death.

Nor did the dream cause me to begin thinking about God. I did not have a spiritual awakening on the moon—at the time, even though I believed in God and went to church, I did not think I needed Him in my life. I never really had given my life to Jesus as my Lord and Savior, nor trusted in Him. But as with Gary Lucas, the mission commander in *Ice,* I think each of us comes to a time in our lives when we are faced with the question: *Who is Jesus?* This point may come at a moment of danger or in a time of quiet reflection. For me, it came after a weekend Bible study in April 1978. In my car on a Sunday evening, I realized that in spite of all my success, I had no peace, and only by trusting my life to Jesus could I experience *true* peace.

We can't all walk on the moon, but we can all walk with Jesus. Like Gary Lucas and Charles Shepherd, I believe the world must hear the good news of God's love, revealed in Christ.

Charlie Duke
Lunar Module Pilot
Apollo 16

Publisher's Note

This is a work of fiction based on two imaginary missions to the moon. In order to set the stage, the author has interwoven the names of several well-known people—mostly astronauts and NASA personnel—and corporations into the plot, but all such people and corporations are used fictitiously, in a manner that is purely the production of the author's imagination. None of the events depicted surrounding the Apollo 19 and Apollo 20 missions ever happened, and any resemblance to actual events is entirely coincidental.

Abbreviations Used in This Book

These abbreviations and acronyms (among others) were coined by NASA and its contractors to streamline communications during training and in flight. Their use contributed to the highly characteristic sound of "NASAspeak," and in order to capture more fully the distinctiveness of manned spaceflight, I have incorporated them into the story:

ACA	attitude controller assembly
AEA	abort electronics assembly
AGS	abort guidance section (pronounced "aggs")
AOS	acquisition of signal
ARIA	Apollo range instrumentation aircraft
ATT	attitude translation
CapCom	capsule communicator
CDR	commander
CM	command module
CMC	command module computer
CMP	command module pilot (pronounced "simp")
COI	contingency orbit insertion
CSM	command/service modules
DECA	descent engine control assembly
ED	explosive devices
EDS	emergency detection system
EECOM	electrical, environmental, and communications officer (CSM) (pronounced "EE-com")
EVA	extravehicular activity
FAO	flight activities officer
FDAI	flight director attitude indicator
FIDO	flight dynamics officer (pronounced "FY-doe")
GNC	guidance, navigation, and control officer

HLRV	heavy lunar roving vehicle
INCO	instrumentation and communications officer
LM	lunar module (pronounced "lem")
LMP	lunar module pilot (pronounced "lemp")
LOR	lunar orbit rendezvous
LOS	loss of signal
MAX Q	region of maximum dynamic pressure
MESA	modular equipment stowage assembly (pronounced "MAY-suh")
MOCR	mission operations control room (pronounced "MOE-ker")
MSC	Manned Spacecraft Center, Houston, Texas
NASA	National Aeronautics and Space Administration
NSA	National Security Agency
OPS	oxygen purge system (pronounced "ops")
PLSS	portable life support system (pronounced "pliss")
PSI	pounds per square inch
RCS	reaction control subsystem
RT	radioisotopic thermogenerator
S-II	Saturn V second stage
S-IVB	Saturn V third stage
SEP	stage separation (pronounced "sehp")
SIM	scientific instrument module (pronounced "sim")
SM	service module
SPS	service propulsion system
TEI	trans-Earth injection
TELMU	electrical, environmental, and communications officer (LM) (pronounced "TELL-myoo")
TLI	trans-lunar injection
TPI	terminal phase initiation
VOX	voice-activated communications (pronounced "voks")

ICE

The LORD *said, "Behold, they are one people,*
and they all have the same language. And…now nothing which
they purpose to do will be impossible for them."

GENESIS 11:6

Prologue

Stars. So many stars.

He sat there on the cold, rough stone of a dusty boulder, leaning against the high stone crag of a house-sized rock that rose behind him and disappeared into the darkness above. The multiple layers of his suit did not allow him to feel the uneven texture of the stone beneath him, making his repose more comfortable than it might otherwise have been.

Peering upward through the transparent faceplate of his pressure helmet, the man's eyes danced from one sparkling pinpoint to the next as he marveled at the extreme brightness of the heavenly bodies' steady light. Never had they looked like this against the skies of home. Here, hidden away, many miles from the harsh glare of the sun, his eyes drank in all that the stars had to give. He sat in a place that had never known sunlight or warmth, a place so dark he could not see the ground around him or even the heavy garment he wore. Indeed, the only way he could determine the position of the smooth, mountainous horizon before him was by the sharp cessation of the stars themselves, where the velvet void in which they silently and eternally swam suddenly yielded to an unforgiving blackness. He had turned his suit light off—he wanted nothing to spoil the purity of the moment, the stillness, the peace. It was a tranquility beyond mere calm, an all-engulfing serenity.

But within that peace, held at bay but always there, waited a horrible, jealous violence. Mere inches from his fragile flesh, outside the pressure suit that enshrouded him, was an environment more cruel than any concept of Hell his mind ever had entertained. It was a cold beyond cold, so intense that every ounce of his flesh, once exposed, would freeze solid in moments. One would not even have time to feel pain, it had been said. He sat there on that rock, engulfed in death, mocking it with every continuing second of existence his suit provided. The suit *was* his life, for without it he had none.

The man, his ears filled only with the sound of his own breathing, thought back to the incredible, even impossible sequence of events that had led to his being in that place, at that time. It all had happened so fast, leaving not enough time to think, not enough time to devise a solution.

Not that there *was* a solution. In one brief moment, he had lost every option, every choice, leaving him without recourse. For all it mattered, he was dead already, marooned on a lifeless ball of rock, with no possibility of deliverance. The length of his life, once determined by disease or genetics or chance, was measured now by the meager amount of breathable air upon his back.

He knew that the last of his companions in life, stranded along with him, must already be dead. He now saw himself as little more than an unwelcome impurity on this barren orb, a tiny blight of living tissue marring the simplicity and sterile perfection of that pure, hard world.

So many regrets. He had lived his life as had so many others, taking moments for granted as if they would never cease coming, as if he would forever walk the world, coming and going and concerning himself too deeply with the trivial matters that dogged him each day. He had wasted so much precious time, disregarded so much opportunity.

And now his life had become all too finite. All that had gone before had wound toward this, spiraling in a mad rush toward a cold, lonely conclusion he never saw coming. Now, here upon the moon, he gladly would trade everything he ever had accomplished for just one fleeting moment back home. He longed to feel a gentle breeze playing in his hair and against his cheeks, the softness of his wife in his arms, and even the warm soil of home beneath his bare feet. The work of his hands meant nothing now. All the riches of the world meant less to him at that moment than a single hug from his child. They all were beyond reach now, the simple things that always had been his for the taking but too often he had ignored.

All those things were gone. All hope was gone.

He was—*alone*.

As he turned a small, flat rock over and over again in his gloved hand and thought of home, his eyes became wet. Dropping his gaze from the tear-blurred stars overhead, he came to look in quiet wonder at their reflection upon the wide, black lake that lay so still and glassy before him, its quiet shoreline mere inches from the toes of his boots. The stars alone betrayed the water's existence, millions of tiny, sparkling jewels glittering upon the liquid mirror of its surface. They beckoned from afar, creating through their reflections the impression of a bottomless abyss passing right through the rocky world, providing a starlit passage into which he might jump and somehow find home again.

With some effort, he swung his arm sidewise and flung the small rock out upon the surface of the water. Again and again it skipped, each slippery impact throwing rings of lazy, concentric ripples. He smiled as the reflected stars seemed to roll and dance over the disturbances and watched in wonder as the ripples slowly widened until they had covered almost the entire surface. The water seemed so thick, so gelatinous in the low gravity. He was still amazed at the very existence of the liquid, here where only hard, dense ice should exist, and he sat in awe of what had been achieved.

They had accomplished so much. They had been so proud. And that, ultimately, was what had killed them.

He looked upon the water differently then. Suddenly, it no longer was a miracle to him. *Water.* It was cruel and uncaring and brutal. It was devastation. It was desolation.

It was all that was left.

As he sat there in the icy, eternal silence, more alone than any man since Adam, he wept bitterly, crushed by the unfathomable magnitude of what he had lost. It all was gone. Everything.

Still weeping, he turned his suit light on then raised one gloved hand and held it up before his faceplate. Flexing his fingers a few times, he marveled at the simple complexity of the human hand. Such an elegant machine.

He knew he must wait no longer. It was time.

The man reached up and loosened the metal fitting at his wrist, something he had done countless times before in the safety and warmth of an atmospheric environment. He could not hear the distinctive click he knew must have sounded as the band rotated out of socket. Then, forcefully and irreversibly, the fitting flew apart, revealing bare flesh, as the sudden release of suit pressure propelled the glove away and into the voracious darkness around him. The life-giving air in his suit exploded from the open seam in a shower of tiny ice crystals, sparkling prismatically like shards of diamond in the beam of his light.

It was beautiful. It was the last thing he ever saw.

Just as instantly, the cold rushed in. They had been right—he never felt it. By the time his glove came to rest at the lake's edge a few seconds later, it was done. His frozen eyes stared sightlessly at his bare hand, still held up before him. His frozen heart lay still within his chest, its lifelong work finished.

There, in the dark, frigid stillness he sat, a quiescent monument to what once had been. Centuries would come, and centuries would go, and still he would remain there, just as he was at that moment, unchanging, forgotten, and alone.

So very, very alone.

I

"Yup…it's going to be a good day. I can feel it in my bones, Charlie."

Mission Commander Gary Lucas fastened his seat belt before pushing a contoured control handle forward, and with a sudden lurch they were underway. For the fifth time, he and his crewmate, Lunar Module Pilot Charles Shepherd, set out across the powdery plain, watching their vehicle's enormous wire-mesh wheels toss aside short-lived showers of gray lunar dust. The sun, though low on the horizon, was intensely bright, prompting both men to extend the white metal visor shades of their helmets.

"Fine day at the beach," Shepherd said with a smile. "All we're missing is an ocean."

"Just as well," Lucas replied, patting the heavily padded thigh of his pressure suit. "I forgot my trunks."

Their first four excursions had been conventional outings that took them up the base slope of a mountain adjoining the crater Cabeus and then eastward toward Malapert, where they had documented and collected rock samples. But today would bring them to the primary objective of their lunar flight, an expedition like none before, and the stakes had been raised—considerably so.

5

It was a mission of many firsts. The exacting rules on earlier flights had dictated that astronauts could traverse no farther than would allow them to return safely by walking, in the event of vehicle failure. This time, of necessity, they were relying heavily upon a transport which would have to carry them to their destination and back again, keeping them alive with its new, onboard life support system—for the target of their audacious journey lay almost forty miles from their landing site, far beyond the range of their backpacks, deep in the darkness of a vast, hidden basin.

The basin was a valley of shadow, a haunting realm that never had known the sun. Its exploration would crown one of the most spectacular scientific achievements in the history of man: the landing of Apollo 19 at the lunar south pole.

Their approach to the desolate orb had been like no other. The mission's two combined spacecraft, dubbed *Quest* and *Starlight* by Nineteen's crew, had swung low, slipping beneath the moon before attaining a polar orbit that carried them north-to-south on the near side at approximately fifteen degrees west longitude. The course permitted far fewer options should an emergency arise, such as that experienced almost five years earlier by the crew of Apollo 13. The men in the spacecraft and those on the ground now relied upon their abilities and their machines as never before—Apollo 19's was a nail-biter of a flight plan, but the possible rewards outweighed the danger.

The risky departure from the standard east-to-west equatorial orbit, which allowed for a free-return trajectory in the event of a crisis, had come as a result of a lunar photomapping probe launched eighteen months earlier, even as Apollo 18 was returning from its successful exploration of one of the most magnificent features on the moon, Schröter's Valley in the Ocean of Storms. That probe, dubbed *Aurora*, had taken the first photos of the moon's south pole, and its radar and photographic data had revealed something no one had expected to find.

Aurora had discovered an immense depression at the pole, concealed by the crater walls and mountain ranges that surrounded it. Nestled just beyond the limit of man's earthbound perception, it had escaped detection by even the most powerful telescopes. At its center rested what was believed to be the largest impact crater in the solar system, a deep scar that betrayed an ancient and violent collision, the worst the moon ever had suffered. Those who first laid eyes upon its transmitted radar image had named both the crater and its surrounding basin for the primary designer of the *Aurora* probe, the venerable Artemus Marlow, who had passed away just weeks before its launch.

Blasted deeper into the lunar bedrock than any other canyon, rille, or crater on the moon's surface, the 20-mile-deep, 180-mile-wide basin promised to yield more information about the interior of the Earth's companion than anyone before had dared hope. Geologists worldwide had pored over the data returned by the unmanned probe, knowing that the impact debris at the site, chunks of inner moon thrown out by the creation of Marlow, held answers to questions they would not have known to ask for decades to come.

At once, NASA had called for a launch delay and change of destination for the Apollo 19 lunar module, *Starlight*. The agency's final voyage to the lunar surface would be its most triumphant—or so many hoped.

The moonwalkers of Nineteen immediately had started a new training regimen, one focusing upon the harsh conditions expected at the pole. Their surface activity rehearsals intensified due to a multitude of new mission elements, among which were lights, heaters, and an ingenious set of signal-relay units necessary for maintaining radio contact from within the basin.

The centerpiece of the new hardware was a monster—the Heavy Lunar Roving Vehicle (HLRV), an intricate beast more truck than dune buggy, a colossus designed to expand considerably the scope of lunar-surface exploration. Its four independent-drive motors, one built into each wheel, were designed to give it sure footing over even the most inhospitable lunar terrain, and its intricate array of short-range radar units and gyroscopic guidance systems would provide its users with all the navigational data they might need. Its impressive umbrella antenna, almost seven feet in diameter, would allow the astronauts to remain in touch with Earth.

To stave off the intense cold the astronauts would encounter, a pair of small nuclear cores were housed in highly insulated wells at each end of the vehicle, within ingenious devices known as radioisotopic thermo-generators, or RT's. The cores, filled with plutonium-238, each radi-ated a constant heat of fourteen hundred degrees. When the time came, that heat would be distributed to all operational parts of the rover by conduits emanating from the RT's, providing warmth enough to compensate for the extreme cold of the basin, keeping the vehicle's essential systems within their operational temperature ranges.

Built three years earlier, the HLRV prototype and its only twin had rested unused and virtually forgotten in a Grumman hangar, waiting for their eventual donation to whatever science museums would have them, where they would serve both as curiosities and mute testimonies to man's unrealized exploratory potential. Upon the discovery of Mar-low, however, the imposing vehicle had been pressed into service, much to the delight of its creators.

The new rover was so large, in fact, that it had of necessity been launched a month earlier, alone atop its own Saturn IB booster, ferried to the lunar surface by an unmanned and modified lunar module descent stage dubbed the LM Truck. Welcoming the men to the lunar surface like an earthly ambassador, the waiting Truck had been a glit-tering, four-legged CARE package from home, the rover secured to its heavily reinforced shoulders where normally an ascent stage would rest. Its reaction control thrusters, which in a manned LM would have been attached to the upper section, instead were affixed to its four, outward-facing quadrants, between the landing gear fittings.

Before this mission had flown, the precision landing crown had belonged to Apollo 12's *Intrepid* and its crew, Pete Conrad and Alan Bean. Launched in November 1969, their target had been not merely a general lunar region but a previous landing site, that of the unmanned *Surveyor 3*, which had come down in a gently sloping crater in the Ocean of Storms. Part of their mission plan was to land near *Surveyor* and to retrieve parts of it for study back on Earth. *Intrepid* did well and came down only eight hundred yards from the targeted landing site, right at the western rim of the crater, only six hundred feet from *Surveyor*.

Lucas had kidded Conrad for weeks before *Starlight's* lift-off, boasting that the Apollo 12 record was about to fall. Conrad's laughing insistence that he had come down as close to a target as NASA would allow fell on deaf ears, as did his assurances that Lucas had no chance. A friendly contest flared to life—rivalry between the highly motivated pilots was nothing new, especially with Conrad, whose earthy wit and quick sense of humor were already the stuff of legend.

Initially, nothing more significant than a steak dinner had ridden on the outcome of *Starlight's* success or failure at setting a new record, but this latest challenge had swelled rapidly into a competition that swept like wildfire throughout the entire astronaut office. Without the knowledge of either Lucas or Conrad, the astronaut corps placed secret wagers on who would end up with the title. They created a pool and sold squares predicting just how near the LM Truck *Starlight* would land.

Things had gone well for those who had chosen Lucas.

◙　　◙　　◙

Gary Lucas and Charlie Shepherd drove on, moving ever closer to the rim of the waiting basin. During their extended foray, the pair would travel so deeply into the shadowed realm and so far from their lunar module that they would not return to their spacecraft for almost fifty hours. They would spend two nights on the rover, plugged into its environmental systems, living in their suits and eating liquid foods. These nutrients, contained in small, electrically warmed and heavily insulated "canteens," would be eaten through tubes inserted into the feed-port valves of the men's helmets.

As they drove, one astronaut pulled his air and cooling water from his backpack—his portable life support system, or PLSS—while the other's umbilicals were tied into the rover's environmental equipment. This way, in the event of a failure in any of the systems involved, one man would be protected and able to help the other. Lucas and Shepherd were alternating sources hourly, switching hose connectors, taking turns pulling from the rover's reserves and recharging their PLSS backpacks for later use away from the vehicle.

Anywhere else on the lunar surface, the merciless heat of the sun's direct glare alternated fortnights with the deep cold of darkness as the moon orbited the Earth and both revolved around the sun. The intense radiation and charged particles that bombarded most of the lunar surface had slowly changed it over the years, altering the story its rock and soil samples would tell to scientists in the laboratory. But there in crater Marlow and the basin surrounding it, the sun had never shone, leaving it a place of eternal darkness and unrelenting cold. It was a time capsule, unchanged, untouched, and irresistible.

Simply put, it was a treasure trove too tantalizing to pass up.

The rover moved along at an average of nine miles per hour over the rolling lunar terrain, and the LM so quickly had fallen behind that it now barely was visible amid the rocks and craters of the valley. All of the Apollo moonwalkers had discovered an interesting phenomenon during their outings on the surface: Since there were no visual signposts, such as trees or houses to provide a sense of scale, nor any atmospheric haze to obscure the horizon, the men could not tell, merely by looking, just how far they had traveled or how far they were from a given object. A rock or mountain in the distance could be one mile away or ten or one hundred for all the eye could tell. Fortunately, visual cues were not the only data available to the *Starlight* crew, and the HLRV's radar and odometer systems both told them that they had reached the rim of the southern depression.

"Okay, Houston," Lucas said, his eye drawn for a moment as the rover's forward-mounted television camera glittered gold in the sunlight. "We're on the crest of the basin, now. Another couple of hundred feet and we'll drop out of sight of the LM. Looks like a good place for the first relay unit."

"Copy that, Gary," Capsule Communicator Bruce Cortney replied from his console in the Mission Operations Control Room. "We've got a great picture."

Like all who manned the CapCom console, Cortney too was an astronaut, and during his shift he would serve as the only earthly voice to sound in the headsets of the Apollo 19 crew. All questions and comments, including even those of the flight director, were relayed through that single individual.

"We see you've come to a stop. Go ahead and set up, and we'll stand by for a transmission test."

It was time for new communications technology to come into play. Without it, once over the rim of the basin, the astronauts would lose radio line of sight with *Starlight*. Shepherd rose from his seat and walked to the back of the rover, where its heavily laden equipment bay waited. Sample-return containers, scoops, tongs, and all manner of rock-gathering tools were there in their places, awaiting use. Reaching into a tall bin, he withdrew one of two dozen long, telescoping devices, then retrieved a small battery pack designed to snap into place on its side. It was a communications relay unit developed specifically for the mission, well tested in the New Mexican desert. By placing a series of such relays along the path of their traverse, communication with the LM, and therefore Earth, could be maintained.

With Lucas' help, Shepherd extended the unit to its full twenty-foot height then unfolded its wide tripod and pressed it firmly into the soil of the basin's rim.

"Make sure it's stable," Lucas said. "If even one of these babies falls over, we break the chain and there goes Houston."

"Hey…no problem. Solid as Gibraltar."

The relay was indeed on steady ground. Shepherd flipped a switch to activate it and was rewarded with a green function light. A marker strobe on its upper tip began to flash once every couple of seconds. "That's one," he said. "Light's green. Good strobe."

"Roger," Cortney said. "We got a ping on this end. She's working."

The astronauts reboarded the rover and continued onward. Shepherd attached their Hasselblad still camera to a plate on his chest pack and shot a few test frames to make sure it was working. He had plenty of film magazines and was determined to give the guys back home all the footage they needed for their postflight mission studies. The compact 16-millimeter movie camera was mounted directly in front of him on a separate bracket.

Another couple of miles fell behind them, and after erecting another relay unit they pressed on. With each installation, Lucas used a small monocular to verify line of sight with the previous relay, ensuring no rocks or rises were in the way.

The line between light and shadow ahead was almost surreal in its harshness, and as they approached the zone of darkness, Shepherd felt trepidation growing within him.

"Floods on," Shepherd said, hitting a switch on the console. An array of intense quartz lights mounted on the front of the rover flared to life. Another smaller light unit that could be removed from its mount also lit up, attached to a flexible arm that could be aimed manually by Shepherd.

They erected more relays. More distance fell behind the rover.

"Radio check, Gary," CapCom requested.

"Loud and clear," he answered. "How me?"

"Read you. Break-break…radio check, Charlie."

"Five-by, Houston…reading you fine."

And then they passed into the intense shadow, prompting a period of adjustment as their eyes grew accustomed to the dark. Reaching up, both men reset the control boxes on their chests and activated the newly designed heaters in their suits. The heaters in their modified backpacks were designed to keep their pressure suits and everything therein, including the astronauts, functioning properly. Lucas switched on the rover's heat units, as was called for by the checklist. It grew darker and colder by the moment—even the light striking the surrounding mountaintops faded away as they drove deeper and deeper into the icy, black void. Only the tiny strobes flashing behind them betrayed the positions of the relays.

As they moved ever farther from the warming rays of the sun, Shepherd thought he felt the drop in temperature despite the many layers of his suit. The gauge on his left forearm read normal, however, and the sensation quickly passed, so he chalked it up to his own uneasiness.

As they pressed on, a new world unfolded before them, one where night ruled and the only light fell in white pools of their vehicle's own making. The stars overhead suddenly multiplied in number, taking on a clarity Shepherd never could have imagined. The soil, comprised largely of microscopic beads of volcanic glass, fairly glowed in the artificial glare of the rover's floodlights, reflecting the light back in the direction from which it had come. Shepherd and Lucas, in turn, raised their UV-protective, gold-tinted visors for maximum visibility and strained to see the nocturnal moon around them.

"A bit nippy outside, Bruce," Shepherd said, reading a gauge on his panel. "Minus 334 in the shade. A real winter wonderland."

"You guys holding up okay?" Cortney asked from the warm safety of Mission Control.

"Doing fine," Lucas said. "The heaters are performing as promised."

"And the rover?"

"You know, I wonder if she'll tow a bass boat," Shepherd kidded, patting the side of his passenger seat. "I could use one of these at home."

◙　　◙　　◙

Some in Mission Control were growing apprehensive. The two men were quite far from the LM now and getting farther all the time. The tension built not only among the flight controllers but among the visiting NASA brass as well—officials from all over the Manned Spacecraft Center had suddenly materialized in the room, some out of curiosity and some simply because they wanted to be there when history was made, and all crowded the controllers in the process. The room was always more crowded during the critical phases of each flight, a fact of which the flight directors were none too fond, but this occurrence seemed worse than most. Cortney looked upon the gathered suits with mild disdain, wishing that they would take their watching party into the separate, glassed-in viewing room that overlooked the MOCR.

"You've got an anxious crowd in this room, guys," he called up to the astronauts. "Lots of folks from all over. You have our undivided attention."

"I hope it'll be a good show," Shepherd's voice crackled.

◙　　◙　　◙

The moonwalkers erected more relays in the communications chain, keeping Houston's words flowing into the men's headsets. Shepherd and Lucas moved cautiously now through a darkness that seemed almost viscous. It surrounded them, pressing in upon them, and clinging to the rover as it made its way deeper into the night.

"Just think," Shepherd began, playing the manual flood lamp upon the ground along the right side of the rover. Its curly power cord dangled from the handle. "This is the first light this place has ever seen."

"It's sort of like nighttime in the Rio Grande Gorge, minus the scrub. Man...look at the stars...never knew there were so many."

Another voice broke in. "Gary, Houston. What is your current distance from the LM?"

Gary checked the digital odometer as the vehicle moved steadily forward. "Three-seven point oh-nine miles. We won't be going too much farther. Just erected the last relay. Chart shows that we're on the outer floor of Marlow Crater now. The angle of the surface is gradual...very gentle downward slope here on the outer flank. Scattered large boulders...a few smaller rocks. But the deep heart of the crater will have to wait for the next guys...looks like we've about reached the end of the line, communications wise. Could've used another ten relay units."

"Any sign of bedrock ejecta?" Cortney asked. Lucas imagined the mission geologists pausing in their labs, holding their collective breath as they monitored the conversation.

"Not sure...but we could stop and try sampling here. Soil appears pretty dark under the lights, darker than we've seen before...it's obvious that there are stark differences between this stuff and material that's been exposed to the sun." He paused. "Wait..."

Suddenly, breaking the thick gloom, something appeared ahead, beyond the apparent range of their fixed lights—tiny flecks of light, multiplying in number with each passing second, sparkling in the frigid void.

"See that, Charlie?"

"Yeah…what do you suppose it is?"

"You filming this?"

"As far as I know."

"Say again, Gary?" CapCom asked.

"Are you seeing this, Houston?"

"Apparently not," came the reply.

"Slow it down, Gary," Shepherd suggested. Whatever was out there, it was fascinating—it caught the light like dew in a spider's web or like the eyes of thousands of tiny creatures hiding in the darkness.

As Lucas and Shepherd studied the phenomenon with puzzled brows, the abounding points of light grew even more numerous. It looked as if angels had sprinkled flecks of stardust upon a wide, still sea of perfect black, mirroring the celestial expanse above them.

"What *is* that…?"

The floodlight beams fell more fully upon the ground ahead, and as Shepherd swung the manual spotlight forward, both men realized what they were seeing.

"Well, I'll be a son of a—"

"Charlie, Houston. What do you see?" There was concern in the CapCom's voice, just as when word first hit that something had crippled the Apollo 13 spacecraft some five years earlier. "Gary? *Somebody?*"

"Bruce, tell the geologists to gather round," Shepherd finally answered, excitedly. "We've got a surprise for 'em."

Lucas let out an ecstatic whoop. "Man, oh man…looks like *Christmas* came up here."

Littering the ground before them, lying in the ebony dust for as far as the light of the rover could shine, were jagged, irregular fragments of crystalline rock of varying sizes, ranging from marble to baseball to automobile sizes. They sparkled in the beams of the floodlights, showering the astronauts' eyes with a gift of brilliant color. The rocks lay scattered, obviously thrown from deep within the moon by the tremendous impact that had formed crater Marlow, the deep center of which was still many miles ahead. Chunks of what appeared to be pure anorthosites, obsidians, granites, and feldspars sat waiting to be collected. And were those gemstones among them? Sapphires, emeralds, rubies? Quartz, totally absent from any samples of lunar material previously brought back to Earth, shone before them in clear and rose and golden variations.

Incredible, Lucas thought. *You've got to have oxygen to get quartz—*

Color was everywhere—hundreds of thousands of tiny purple, orange, green, red, blue, and icy-clear facets caught the light of the floods, glistening like rare gems in a jeweler's case.

It was what they had come for—and more. So much more.

It had been a good day.

2

Wednesday, February 26, 3:17 P.M.

Clunk.

"Four out of five doctors recommend—"

Clunk.

"But, Marsha…you can't possibly leave Roger—"

Clunk.

"Only your hairdresser knows for sure—"

With a sigh, Diane Lucas turned the knob on her family's television from channel to channel, searching for any mention of the flight. Her husband had landed safely the day before—surely there was some coverage somewhere.

Nothing.

Soap operas. Commercials for dishwashing detergent, hair color, and used cars. Reruns of *Gilligan's Island* and *The Andy Griffith Show* and *Leave It to Beaver.*

All the important stuff.

"Hummph," she groaned, frustrated. Her husband was walking on the moon—on the moon!—and the world could not be bothered to pay attention. Gary and Charlie were supposed to be leaving the lunar module at any time, setting out on their third traverse, but to watch

18

television you would never even know anyone was up there, or that NASA existed at all.

Fine. Be that way.

She rose from the set, slapping the switch off. In a way, she was grateful that no reporters were camped out in her front yard. Any time a mission was up, they always trampled the crew's flowerbeds and flattened the grass with their equipment. But there should have been some interest, some respect for her husband's accomplishment.

You'd think at least a few of you would be ringing my doorbell, she thought, looking over the front yard of her Clear Lake home from the curtain of her dining-room window. She reached up and played with her dark brown hair for a moment, recalling the days of Gemini and early Apollo, when the astronauts and their wives were treated like royalty. Like heroes.

Now, it seemed, being the wife of an astronaut carried all the prestige of being the wife of a truck driver. She missed the attention a bit, she had to admit to herself, but mostly she felt bad for her husband. He had worked too hard, done too much, given too much of himself to wind up as little more than an asterisk in the history books.

Not many truck drivers on the moon, she mused.

While there was no television coverage, there was the "official" radio, casually referred to as a squawk box, in the kitchen. Apparently it was to be her only link to her husband for most of the flight. NASA had installed one of the small radio sets in each of the astronauts' homes, and during missions it received a direct and constant feed of all normal air-to-ground and ground-to-air communications, complete and uncensored. If she could not see what was going on, at least she could hear it.

And she really wanted to hear Gary's voice. She missed him. His time with the family had been precious and rare in the months leading up to the launch. It would be so nice to have him back again, after it was all over. They had much catching up to do.

Just as she reached for the radio's knob, the front door burst open and footsteps fell hard and furious against the tile of the entryway. She knew those footsteps.

"No running in the house, young man," she called out to her son, Jeffrey, who flew into the living room and tossed his schoolbooks onto the couch. The boy saw his mother standing at the kitchen counter and waved, smiling. His short, sandy brown hair was tossed, his clothes disheveled, his breathing heavy. Obviously, he had run all the way home. Obviously, he was only fourteen years old.

"Hi, Mom…sorry…I'm in a hurry…"

"Put those books where they belong. Do you have any homework?"

"Aw, Mom…"

"Do you?"

"Yes, but we're all going over to Ritchie's house to play ball. If I'm late, they'll start without me—"

"Put those books in your room and change out of those clothes. I want you back here in two hours to do your homework and eat supper. Understood?"

"Thanks, Mom!" he called, picking up his books and running down the hallway with them. "Is Dad on TV?"

"No," she called after him, shaking her head. "Maybe on the news tonight."

She reached for the radio and turned it on.

◙　　◙　　◙

Command Module Pilot Vic Kendall peered through the thick multi-paned glass of a small rectangular window, watching the lunar surface pass by only sixty miles beneath him. Other than visually, he sensed no motion at all—if not for the weightlessness, he might have been sitting in the simulator in Houston. The sight of the moon below still amazed him, but it had become too much just a part of the job for which he had trained. He was no tourist but was on duty, on watch, far from idle as he waited for his crewmates to return from the surface. Orbit after orbit, the panoramic camera in the belly of the service module was busy detail-mapping the features of the mysterious moon, gathering data for the cartographers back home. At that altitude, the pan camera's resolution could reveal objects as small as a man, detecting even the smallest of craters or other features that might have a bearing on NASA's selection of future landing sites.

Future landing sites, Kendall mused. *As if there will be any.*

On the way back to Earth, he would have to go outside and retrieve the film cartridges from the pan camera and a smaller mapping camera, along with the data tapes of a few other instruments, all mounted in the Scientific Instrument Module, or SIM, bay. He had practiced the spacewalk time and again in the huge water tank at the MSC, working with mock-ups of the equipment until he could perform the task in his sleep. In a way, the extravehicular activity (EVA) was his consolation prize for not being able to land on the surface along with his crewmates, and he was honored to carry it out—but the adventurer in him would gladly have traded that spacewalk for just one step onto the dusty solidity of the moon.

His mind drifted back to a lake in Indiana, one he enjoyed well and often in his youth. He could still feel the gentle rocking of the lapping waves against his tiny rowboat as he lay on his back and watched the autumn clouds pass by above. The wind in the trees was a lullaby, and he had slept away many afternoons on that lake, his unattended fishing pole flexing again and again as its line went taut, its bait taken, its motions unseen.

But there were no trees now, no gentle rocking to lull him to sleep. As *Quest* continued along in its orbit, Kendall had much to do to keep the vessel on an even keel. Gravitational anomalies in the moon's pull, called "mascons" for "mass concentrations," continually altered the spacecraft's orbital velocity, causing him to have to make minor course and velocity corrections. The polar orbit of the spacecraft carried it over considerably more anomalies than had been experienced by the equatorial flights of the earlier missions, presenting him with a challenge not faced by his predecessors. A particular concentration located beneath Mare Imbrium, the Sea of Rains, while subtle, was still heavier than any other he passed over, causing him to burn additional thruster fuel each time he overflew it. Fortunately, the pattern and intensity of the lunar mascons had been well mapped using the data from previous flights, and supplementary fuel had been added to *Quest* for just that purpose.

Kendall looked over at the two empty seats to his right. While the command module interior seemed roomy to him when occupied by three, with only one man aboard it felt downright huge. He had chosen to leave the other two couches in place rather than stow them, as a gentle, warming reminder that his companions soon would be back. He had dimmed the cabin lighting to improve viewing, and the only sounds were those of his own breathing and the constant, steady hiss of the air circulation system. The spacecraft was so serene, so calm, so quiet.

Too quiet.

After a week of keeping himself company, Kendall had grown tired of the isolation. True, during each orbit he had a brief interval of communication with the men on the surface, and while on the Earth's side of the moon he had the voice of CapCom in his earpiece. But that time was relatively brief as well, and he had been humbled again and again by the utter solitude of the far side.

The far side. To go there was to experience a total disunion only seven men had ever known, time spent cut off from every other human soul, beyond the eyes and ears of any living thing. If something happened, if the wondrously crafted machine failed, if fuel and oxidizer suddenly came together in an uncontrolled explosion of propellant and gases and metal, he would simply vanish from existence, and no man, despite conjectures, would ever surely know his fate. It was not a scenario Kendall dwelt upon, for such a catastrophic failure of the orbiting spacecraft would also mean death for the men on the surface below. He and *Quest* were their only ride home, their only refuge, their only hope, and without him their lives could be measured in hours.

Kendall knew NASA would already have branded Apollo 19 a success, at the top of the books in glory points scored for the agency. They had accomplished an extremely difficult polar landing, and their risky traverse into the frozen unknown of the pole had brought geological reward beyond measure. By now, everyone back in Houston surely was applauding their achievement and planning ways of using the success as a crowbar with which to pry more funding from the coffers of Congress.

It had been a long week. Finally, with all the lofty goals of the mission fully attained, the days of separation were almost over. Soon, Kendall thought with a smile, his crewmates would rejoin him in orbit, where he would dock *Quest* with the passive *Starlight*. The solitude had given him time to recall a few new jokes to tell on the ride home, and he looked forward to hearing Lucas' laugh and Shepherd's groan again.

He played with a space pen, spinning it in the zero-g, trying to float it toward and "dock" it with his small, gold-colored penlight. The crater Tycho passed below, its vast rays glowing like pearl in the harsh sunlight. The automatic cameras clicked, taking it all in, and Kendall, his face pressed to the window glass, allowed himself a moment of childlike wonder.

3

It was a small gathering, but one of shared concerns and common experience. The hour grew near, and at such a time the support of family was a blessing.

And family these women were, their kinship forged by the fire of long nights spent together, sharing their loneliness and their fears, wondering what training regimen their husbands were enduring at the moment in preparation for a dangerous mission each woman knew one day would come. A few of the long-suffering wives had seen their husbands taken from them along the way—Jean Bassett, Marilyn See, Betty Grissom—and others. Too many others. It was a cruel irony that none of the men had died in space, but in training or while flying between NASA centers. One by one, each woman had faced a spectre they all feared, a visitor they all dreaded. A spectre who haunted the wives of test pilots and astronauts alike.

The Angel of Death.

His visit struck terror into their hearts the moment they saw him. An official vehicle would arrive at their homes, and out would step a man who bore a message to be delivered personally, a blow that could not be softened, however gently the words were spoken.

The anguish of each new widow was shared by all, and each day every woman lived with the knowledge that her man could be the next to lose his life in the pursuit of the moon. It was a sobering sword to have hanging over one's head, but at the same time that blade had created a bond that had brought their individual lives together into a unified whole.

They were—*family.*

Diane Lucas sat on an avocado-colored sofa in Carol Shepherd's warmly lit living room, sipping hot tea as she waited for coverage of the lunar lift-off to begin. The night outside was cold, the sky clear, the stars brilliant. For most of the country it was just another Thursday night, but within this Clear Lake home it was a night of great import, a critical point in the flight plan of Apollo 19.

Katie Kendall sat next to Diane, her arms wrapped around her, her fingertips nervously kneading the pale green fabric of the sleeves of her dress. Her fingers trembled slightly as if cold. Her eyes were fixed upon the ornate console color television beyond the coffee table, its screen filled with the laughter of a Dean Martin roast of Jackie Gleason, yet she never reacted.

"Where's Jeff tonight?" Carol asked Diane, sipping from her own cup of hot tea with lemon. "Didn't he want to be here?"

"He's a *man,* now," she answered, in a tone that obviously mimicked one she had heard from her son. "Too old for these family vigils. He wanted to be here for his father's moonwalks...what they showed of them, anyway...but now that the exciting stuff is over, he's gone to Toledo Bend on a long weekend campout with some friends. They left right after school this afternoon. Gary had wanted him to go...Jeff's been looking forward to it for two months. Fishing, hiking, all that sort of thing. I don't think they even took a radio with them."

"Is he old enough to be going off like that?"

"Ritchie Parker's father and uncle went with them."

"Must be so hard to let go…"

"Why do they have to grow up, Carol?"

The chitchat went on, talk of family, friends, and a sharing of thoughts and ideas. Carol was the eldest of the three women, and Katie the youngest. This was the first time out for Katie, and throughout the flight she had been more nervous than on her wedding day. Her knees had turned to jelly as her husband's Saturn V had thundered from the pad, and as she stood and watched from the public viewing stand at Kennedy, she had fallen back onto the bleachers, overcome by the significance of the moment, her lack of sleep, and her fear.

With them in the house was a public relations official sent by the agency to answer any concerns the families might have as events unfolded. Noticeably absent was the press, which thrilled the quiet, reserved Carol to no end. She hated the commotion of reporters and the intrusion of microphones being thrust into her face, and felt she had nothing noteworthy to add to the reports of her husband's accomplishments, anyway.

She sat in a nearby chair, listening to the NASA radio on an end table next to her. Charlie's voice wafted from the speaker as he and his comrade made preparations for their departure, a voice of confidence and strength, the voice of a man she dearly missed. Everything in the room reminded her of him—the framed diplomas and certificates on the paneled walls, the trophies, the Air Force commendations, the autographed baseball on the mantle, and even the faint stain on the rug where he had spilled grape juice when news of the Apollo 1 fire first had reached them on that terrible January night in 1967. Three men had died when their capsule became an inferno during a launch-pad test—three good men who were among the best the country had to offer. That nightmarish event, known now within agency circles only as "the fire," had created an eighteen-month delay in the race to the moon and almost had spelled the end of the American space program altogether.

"It sounds like it's going well, Carol," Diane said, smiling reassuringly. "They'll be up in no time."

"Like falling off a log," Carol nodded, allowing herself a slight smile in return. "Charlie says it's no tougher than backing the station wagon out of the garage."

Katie's face was grim, her eyes filled with worry. "I just want them to come home."

"Don't worry, hon," Carol smiled, trying to lighten the moment. "They've got nowhere else to go. We're the only decent planet for miles."

◙　　◙　　◙

"We see your PSI at five-point-five, *Starlight*."

Pumping up the pressure within the LM cabin was not something Shepherd enjoyed. Hearing the craft's almost foil-thin aluminum hull pop and strain as the air filled the crew compartment was unnerving, and the sound reminded him of a beer can slowly being crushed. Afterward, however, it had been nice to be able to breathe for a while without his helmet, and even nicer to be able to scratch his nose.

The cabin was filled not only with oxygen, but with a pungent smell like that of burnt gunpowder. It was the lunar dust, tracked into the LM and still lingering within the crevices of their suits. They had used a vacuum hose attached to the forward hatch to get rid of much of it, but the pervasive, clinging powder was still in the air and still in the nooks and crannies of the cabin. Whether the sulfuric aroma was inherent in the soil or was a result of its mingling with oxygen they could not know, but its invasion of their nostrils was less than pleasant in either case.

Now they were back in their helmets, preparing for lift-off. As per procedure, they already had ejected all the dead weight they could find, tossing unneeded items from the LM's forward hatch before sealing it.

Among the castoff items were their lunar overboots, their visor assemblies, their EVA gloves, urine bags, waste bags, food wrappers, the still cameras they had used, and even their depleted backpacks. Shepherd's pack had come to rest on the ground after first impacting the LM's forward landing gear, but Lucas' still dangled from the forward corner of the aluminum porch just outside. Apparently, judging from what Shepherd could see from his window, the buckle hook of one of its nylon straps had caught in the joint at the bottom of the starboard porch railing. The pack's hanging there did not matter so long as it was well clear of the ascent stage above, and it was.

The rock boxes, filled to the brim with their crystalline treasure, were safely stowed, along with dozens of bags of pure, uncontaminated Marlow soil. Their eight days on the surface had yielded a rich collection of mineral samples, a gathering of more than 230 pounds Earth-weight, which would be studied and tested for decades to come. Their visit had been all they had hoped it would be.

"Coming up on four minutes," CapCom called. "You're go for lift-off at this time. Telemetry looks good."

Once more, Shepherd read from the checklist as everything was made ready. Every switch, every circuit breaker had to be in the right position for all to go smoothly, and the two tired astronauts wanted to make certain that everything did.

"ATT translation, four jets. Balance couple, on."

"Balance couple, on," Lucas repeated, flipping the toggle.

"Thrust controller to jets. Reset prop pushbutton. Abort Stage reset."

"Reset."

"Deadband to minimum."

"Minimum…roger."

Lucas took a final, lingering look out of the window. The valley of Cabeus was an incredible sight, and after more than a week it had become almost as familiar as home. He knew every rock, every little crater as well as he did his own hand. In the distance, the LM Truck, its Mylar blankets peeled back like the petals of a flower, stood stripped of the cargo it had carried from Earth. Lucas nodded a silent thanks to the craft, for it had made possible their successful foray into the Marlow basin. Some fifty yards away sat the rover, its remotely controlled television camera trained upon the LM, awaiting the lift-off. The vehicle had protected them from the cold, it had kept them alive, and it had returned them safely to their only ride back into orbit. It had been a faithful addition to the crew, and both men had developed something of a fondness for it.

"Wish we could take the rover home," Lucas sighed.

"Wouldn't that be great? Imagine the looks we'd get on the golf course."

"We're looking good at two minutes, Houston," Lucas said, smiling. "Master Arm, on. I've got two lights."

"Copy that," CapCom replied. "Two good ED lights. Still go." Those indicators told the men that the tiny explosive devices in the descent stage were primed and ready to sever the tie-downs and electrical connectors between the two stages, freeing the upper one to depart.

Something of a ceremony had taken place just prior to the astronauts' final climb back into the LM. With the television camera watching, Lucas had stripped a protective covering away from a stainless-steel plaque mounted to the front landing gear, between the rungs of the ladder. On it were diagrams of the two hemispheres of Earth, with a smaller image of the moon between them. Beneath these were engraved the astronauts' signatures and that of the president and these words:

HERE MEN FROM THE PLANET EARTH
COMPLETED THEIR FIRST EXPLORATIONS OF THE MOON
FEBRUARY 1975, A.D.
WE WILL RETURN IN PEACE FOR ALL MANKIND

Lucas had unveiled and read those words aloud as Shepherd looked on. Some in high places had fought the wording of that last line, demanding it be changed, thinking it committed the United States to a continued presence on the moon. The astronaut corps had insisted that NASA's duty was to leave such a challenge, such a legacy, and that a return to the moon was the very least the future of spaceflight should strive for.

The plaque stood as written.

Shepherd had reset his watch to the second, matching the event timer in the LM. It would be used as an alternative in case the ship's clock failed. Every system in the spacecraft had a backup, and even the backups had backups. That mode of design provided the astronauts with an ingenious safety net. All of the switches were wired in multiple configurations—rather than changing fuses or making repairs, the astronauts had merely to open different breakers or throw toggles in new combinations in order to make their systems work. Warning sensors would detect burnouts, and indicator lights would tell the astronauts of the problem, and a fix would be easy.

There was, however, one part of the LM that had no backup.

◙   ◙   ◙

"Say again, *Quest?*" Shepherd called through the static that had engulfed their communications. "Having trouble reading you, Vic."

"Suggest you try aft omni," Lousma cut in. "*Quest* will be over your position in six minutes."

"Roger…aft omni," Lucas confirmed, switching to a different antenna.

Vic's voice suddenly filled their earpieces. "…looking at the nominal elevation angle of two-six point five, with a delta height of…"

"We've got you now, *Quest*...say again."

They exchanged numbers and codes, all aimed at bringing about the earliest possible reunion of the two spacecraft. Lunar Orbit Rendezvous was a tricky beast, one held by a mathematical leash that could be counted upon to place both craft exactly where they needed to be for docking. Credit for the complex orbital mechanics used to bring about mission success was due in no small part to Gemini 12/Apollo 11 astronaut Edwin Aldrin, who almost single-handedly had revolutionized the way NASA thought about orbital flight.

"One minute coming up," Shepherd called. "I'm going to VOX." He switched his microphone to its voice-activated mode.

"Guidance looks good...verify circuit breakers in..."

◙   ◙   ◙

Flight Director Gene Kranz sipped from his bottled Coke, watching over the White Team like a platoon leader. Time and again, crises had arisen, and time and again these fine men had risen to the challenge, making the tough call, safeguarding those above whose very lives often depended upon the fast action of those on the ground. It was the toughest job on the planet, and his men were the best.

He expected nothing less of himself and of his team.

"We're standing by on the TV," CapCom Jack Lousma called up to the spacecraft.

A communications officer with his fingers on the camera controls nodded, for he would see to it that Earth got a good view of the lift-off and ascent. His name was Ed Fendel, and his practiced fingers had been on the television camera control switches for the lunar lift-offs of each rover-equipped mission, beginning with Apollo 15. Technical difficulties on Fifteen and Sixteen had prevented the camera from panning upward, which would have allowed the world to watch as the LM ascent stage on those flights had disappeared into space above. On Seventeen and Eighteen, however, all had gone flawlessly.

Lightly, Lousma followed up by quoting from a television series for which he knew Lucas held a fondness. "Don't adjust your set...we control the vertical."

"Roger that," Lucas' voice sounded, his smile evident in his tone.

Shepherd continued with the checklist. "Attitude Control set to Mode Control. Mode Control, both to auto."

"Auto, both."

"Radio check, *Quest*," Lucas called.

"Reading you five-by, Gary," came Kendall's voice. "I'm almost directly above you, now...ready and waiting."

"*Starlight*, Houston," Lousma cut in. "You're looking good to us. Thirty seconds."

⊠   ⊠   ⊠

Shepherd checked the abort guidance system—it would govern their ascent. "Guidance steering is set," he called, punching codes into the keypad of the navigational computer. "Stand by for the elevator ride of your life. Ten seconds. Abort Stage."

Lucas lifted a small, hinged, clear plastic cover that shielded a pair of pushbuttons on his main panel. "Abort Stage," he replied, pressing the squarish one on the right.

"Engine Arm to ascent..." Shepherd read off, and instantly Lucas had flipped the toggle. "Program 99..." He counted down. "3... 2...1..." Shepherd pressed the final button on the computer keypad. "Proceed...!"

A rapid succession of muffled pops sounded and a slight, sharp vibration struck beneath their feet as explosive bolts detonated, severing all electrical and physical connections between the upper and lower stages of *Starlight*. Unaware that he was doing so, Lucas held his breath and braced for the sudden, upward rush.

And waited.

Nothing.

"Manual!" Shepherd called, but Lucas' hand was already on the way. He jammed his thumb into the round red button before him, jammed it hard.

And again.

The hush was deafening. The stillness was brutal.

The ascent engine, the only part of the spacecraft with no possible backup system, was silent.

Outside, from beyond the glass of his window, a sparkle of motion caught Lucas' eye. His gaze shot to the rover, to the glittering, Mylar-covered television camera mounted there. Instantly, his heart sank.

Obeying a signal from Earth, one sent a few moments early to allow for the radio time lag, the camera was panning upward, into empty sky.

4

Carol Shepherd leaned closer to the NASA radio, listening intently now to the sudden exchange of data and procedures. The television set, still carrying its normal evening fare, glowed as it carried on across the room.

"I think…something's wrong," she said.

Diane rose from the couch. "What do you mean? Why do you say that?"

"Listen…" The astronauts and Mission Control were exchanging words that sounded too intense, too much to the point to mean good news.

"Aren't they up?" Katie asked, checking her delicate, gold-tone watch. "I thought they said lift-off was going to be at nine forty-two…that was four minutes ago. There hasn't been a news bulletin on the TV, has there? They haven't said anything's wrong…"

Carol turned up the volume so the radio could be heard more easily over the television. The voice of current CapCom and family friend Jack Lousma poured from the speaker, but his normally jovial voice now carried an underlying seriousness that worried her.

34

"Okay, Gary," he said, "we've got some numbers for you. At two-nine-one plus zero-three, we show RCS Alpha at 78 percent…Bravo is 73 percent…ascent ampere hours are four-six-two…that's four-six-two remaining…" There was a pause.

"Copy that," Lucas' voice replied. "Four-six-two."

"Verify Abort Stage and Engine Arm circuit breakers are in."

"Roger…" Another pause. "Abort Stage circuit breaker is in. Engine Arm circuit breaker is in."

"Verify Display/Engine Override Logic breaker is in…circuit breakers Stabilization/Control all closed on panel 11, except AEA and DECA power."

"Roger that," Lucas said, checking his breaker panel. "I'm showing 'white' on *all* those breakers…"

Diane, her face a portrait of concern, turned to look at NASA public relations man Henry Hurt, and found him on the kitchen phone. His back was to her, and though she could not make out his words, his tone was grave. As she watched him, she caught more of Lousma's litany to her husband—

"…and retry ascent at two-niner-three hours, seventeen minutes…"

"Retry?" she cried out. "He said 'retry'!"

"Something happened," Carol said, struggling to remain calm. "They didn't lift off. It sounds like they may have figured out how to fix the problem, though—"

"What *is* the problem?"

"I don't know. The engine didn't work. They're still on the moon."

Katie had remained silent to that point, not knowing what to say. Her husband was in orbit, not on the surface. His survival did not depend upon the LM's engine. *He* would be coming home.

Unless something else goes wrong—

She stood near the others, silently supporting them, offering what solace she could with her presence. Her eyes spoke to the others of shared pain. For their sake, she tried very hard not to cry.

All heads turned at the heavy sound of Henry returning the phone to its cradle. As the women watched, hope in their eyes, Henry walked slowly closer, stepping down into the sunken living room. He seemed reluctant to meet the women's eyes with his own.

"There *is* a problem," he began. "The ascent engine of the LM—"

He was cut off by an ominous, sudden voice booming from the television. A graphic that spoke of trouble filled the screen.

"This is an NBC News Special Report. From the NBC News Center in New York, here is John Chancellor."

A trusted face then filled the screen. The man had reported on wars and crimes and famines and natural disasters. Now he spoke as if to Diane and Carol alone.

"Good evening. NBC News has learned of what may be a disastrous development in the flight of Apollo 19. The planned lift-off from the moon, which was to have occurred at 10:42 P.M. Eastern Time tonight, did not take place due to a malfunction in the main engine of the lunar module, *Starlight*. That engine, the only means by which the two astronauts can leave the surface, did not fire when called upon to do so. Sources have told NBC News that manual attempts to ignite the engine also have failed. Astronauts Gary Lucas and Charles Shepherd are in no immediate danger and are working with NASA to solve the problem. If they cannot…if the engine does not work…there is no other possibility of rescue for the two men. We go now to Houston and our correspondent, Roy Neal…"

"No, no…" Diane said quietly to herself. Her hands covered her face. "This isn't happening…"

Henry went to her, placing a strong, reassuring hand upon her shoulder from behind the couch. "There are a lot of things they haven't tried yet, Diane. It's probably just a minor glitch. It's a very simple engine...I'm sure they'll get the problem corrected."

Carol's five-year-old son, Joey, walked into the room in his space-themed pajamas, carrying with him a plastic model of the LM his father had built for him a few months earlier. The boy accidentally had broken off a few of its more delicate parts but played with it still, pretending his father was aboard. Making a thrust sound with his lips, he flew the craft over to his mother, landed it on her lap, then paused when he looked up at her face and saw that her eyes were wet.

"What's wrong, Mommy?" he asked.

"Nothing, honey," she said, holding him close, stroking his short brown hair. "Your daddy's just going to be a little late getting home, that's all."

▨   ▨   ▨

Diane walked over to the window and pulled back the sheers veiling the winter night beyond. She saw only a reflection of the warm living room against the cold glass and leaned closer to block the room behind her from view. A chill splashed against her face, her breath throwing momentary pools of fog against the pane. Lifting her gaze, she looked toward the eastern horizon.

The moon was just rising, as full and brilliant as she ever had seen it.

He's there—

Something within her wanted to reach up, to free her Gary from the jealous orb that held him captive. He seemed so close. *He's right there—!*

As she watched, a cloud passed before the gleaming disk, a shroud of foreboding that drove it from sight.

Separating her from him anew.

🔲　　🔲　　🔲

Shepherd sat on the LM's wide, coffee can–shaped engine cover, munching on sugar cookie cubes. The only sound in his ears, other than that of his own chewing, was the drone of the air circulation system. He glanced around, making note of rivets, seams, and other details he had not bothered to examine before, knowing that somewhere behind those panels and bulkheads lurked the reason he and his crewmate were not safely on their way home.

A frustration he had fought earlier began to resurface, but again he turned it away.

Or perhaps the problem was in the engine itself, though he could not imagine how. It was small as rocket propulsion systems went, only eighteen inches high and a foot wide, and even with the added nozzle assembly it weighed only two hundred pounds. Its design was simplicity itself, comprising only four moving parts: mechanical valves for the inlet of pressurized fuel and oxidizer. There was no ignition system. Like the larger descent engine that had carried them to the surface a week earlier, the ascent motor burned two hypergolic chemicals that ignited upon contact with each other. No spark was needed for combustion. Unlike the descent engine, however, this one had no throttle—the engine was either on or off, burning at full power or not at all. The system, since it could have no backup, was designed to have as few intricacies and as few separate elements as possible. The fewer elements there were, the fewer elements there were to malfunction.

At least, that was the theory.

"Maybe there's a leak in one of the feed lines," Shepherd suggested, not really believing it himself. "Could be a rock kicked up on landing, or something."

"The telemetry Houston's getting would show that," Lucas answered, staring out the window. "Even if our gauges didn't."

"Yeah, I know." Nothing in the LM went unmonitored by telemetry. All the temperatures, pressures, voltages, quantities, and other states of being within the spacecraft constantly told their stories to those on the ground back home.

Shepherd considered the object upon which he sat. "What did it cost them to develop this engine? You remember?"

"Beats me," Lucas guessed. "I guess somebody should have spent a little more."

Shepherd sat a moment, pondering. "Whatever it was, it was a lot to pay for a darned uncomfortable seat."

"Yeah."

"Too bad they didn't give this thing a pull cord, like my lawn mower's got."

"Believe it or not, they thought about it. I read about that…a manual gizmo of some kind…"

"*Starlight,* Houston," a familiar voice sounded.

"Go, Houston."

"Gary, check your helium pressure on tank two."

He turned a knob in his main panel. "Reads three-zero-four-seven."

"Roger…that's what we show. There has been some fluctuation, though, in our numbers down here."

"How's it looking?" Shepherd asked. "It's been a couple of hours now…you guys getting close to a fix yet?"

"We're still looking at it, Charlie," Lousma said. "You'll be the first to know. I promise."

"Thanks, Jack," he smiled. "Nice to know we're at the top of the list."

Time passed slowly, too slowly, in the cramped LM. Neither man had showered in more than a week and a half, and neither said a word about the other's obvious need for one. After several moments of idle thought, Shepherd again contemplated the engine beneath him.

"We don't even have a screwdriver."

"What?" Lucas asked, turning from the window.

"We don't have a screwdriver or a socket set or anything. Seems they could have given us some decent tools...I mean, what if the engine just needs to be whacked with a hammer? We can't even get this cover off."

"Make a note of that for the next time we come up here."

Shepherd mimed writing in the air. "Bring...toolbox...from...trunk of car."

Finally, there was a crackle of static, and again a voice filled the air. "Okay, *Starlight,* we might have something for you."

Shepherd slid off the engine cover, and both men stood at their stations. "Go, Jack," Lucas said, giving his partner a thumbs up and a nod.

"The smart boys think you may be able to get ignition by depressurizing the spacecraft and trying the manual system again, after we give you a new routing configuration."

Lucas looked puzzled. "You want a cabin dump? What's vacuum got to do with it, Jack?"

"As nutty as it sounds, they might be right. They think now you've got a bad connection in a control line, caused by metal expansion. Your eight days on the moon is twice as long as Eighteen stayed, so you've had a full week of uninterrupted solar exposure to deal with."

"So how will depressurizing help?"

"The heat of the sun must have expanded the outer skin of the spacecraft. Combined with the expansion of the pressurized inner hull, there may be stress on a fitting somewhere, putting pressure on the wiring. Something may have moved just enough to short a connection or cause a stray ground."

Lucas and Shepherd looked at each other, weighing the words.

"Wouldn't your telemetry show something like that?" Shepherd asked.

"Yes, unless we're getting a false positive somewhere along the way. We show good pressure in both tanks and in the fuel lines. Assuming that data's valid, the problem has to lie in the electrical system. So, despite all appearances to the contrary, it seems the engine simply isn't getting a signal to fire. We think a zero-pressure start could fix it."

"How sure are you?" Lucas asked, doubtful of the procedure. "Not to knock the guys in the back room, but as theories go, that's a pretty big stretch. I mean, what we've got in here now...it's a lot of air to just *dump*. That's hours of breathing, there, Jack."

There was an uncomfortable pause. "I'll be honest with you, Gary...we're guessing here. We've been trying to pin down what might make your LM different from the others, and there isn't much. Our data down here says the same thing as your gauges...that there's absolutely *nothing* wrong with the spacecraft. According to everything we're getting from telemetry, that engine should have lit up the moon."

The commander looked at Shepherd, who shrugged then nodded. "I say we go for it," he offered. "If it doesn't work...what's a few hours?"

"Okay, Jack," Lucas said, nodding. "We'll give it a shot."

"Advise when you're ready. Your consumables are becoming a factor now, and we've passed the designated time for your second lift-off attempt. So we're not going to worry about a window... we'll just put you into a stable orbit for TPI and figure the numbers once you're up. We have loss of signal with *Quest* right now, but once he comes around from the far side we'll advise him of the plan. Houston out."

"Roger that." He switched off his transmitter.

Lucas reached for a trio of umbilical hoses and began to snap them into the connectors of his suit. "I don't know, Charlie…sounds like a reach."

"Well, when it's fourth and long and you're behind and time's running out, you gotta dig deep into the playbook."

"Yeah," Lucas said, "but I'm not so sure we've even got a ball to play with."

They suited up, checked each other's pressure seals, and pulled a handle to open the release valve in the forward hatch. The air hissed loudly as it drained away, giving the moon an infinitesimal increase in its almost nonexistent atmosphere.

Through their windows, they saw their precious oxygen glittering outside. Watching it transform into a useless cloud of ice crystals was torturous.

Listening to it bleed away was agony.

◙　　◙　　◙

Friday, February 28, 4:17 A.M.

Kranz sat white-knuckled at his console. That same, accursed image of the stationary LM still filled the main screen, a portrait of failure in living color. It was well after four in the morning now, almost seven hours after lift-off was to have occurred, yet no one had gone off shift. Quite the contrary, the men of all four teams had flocked to the MSC as soon as word of the engine malfunction had reached them. Those were their friends stuck up there, their family, and each controller and astronaut, to a man, was there to do whatever it took to reach up to the moon and pull Lucas and Shepherd to safety.

Kranz's eyes closed in prayer as the moment of the next attempt grew close. All around him, his men sat rigidly by, knowing there was little if anything any of them could now do. Every scenario they had ever experienced in combating an in-flight crisis had depended upon being able to make an intelligent analysis based upon solid information of some kind, whether that information took the form of telemetry from the spacecraft or data gleaned from simulator tests or something else.

Now, however, there was nothing to go on. They had no clue at all.

They had even put a duplicate engine, a one-to-one twin of *Starlight*'s, into a simulation chamber and had recreated all the conditions their telemetry said the real thing was experiencing on the moon.

The duplicate had fired.

They shorted every electrical lead connected to it.

Still it had fired.

They all but tore the guts out of it, trying to force it to fail.

As if in sheer defiance, it had fired.

Now they were forced to make guesses, forced to shoot blindly into the dark and hope something worked. They were trying to repair something that, as far as they could tell, was not broken.

Kranz hated guesswork, however educated it might be. In his experience, guesses *never* made things better and usually made matters worse. If only there were something—*anything*—they could pull from the telemetry, the slightest lead as to what to do, then perhaps the two good men up there might have a chance.

But there was nothing. According to every indicator they could wrest from the LM, it was a perfectly healthy machine. In reality, Kranz knew, it was not.

Starlight was a corpse—but they had to try something.

Kranz took a deep breath and set the hope-driven effort in motion, going around the room via headset. He could see from the faces around him that there was little confidence in the fix they had sent up—after all, they were grasping at straws and they all knew it. He spoke with confidence for the sake of the others.

"Okay, flight controllers, let's keep cool. We still have power, air, and water for a while, and time to sort things out if this particular fix doesn't work. Now…give me a final 'go-no go' for ascent. Retro?"

"We're go."

"FIDO?"

"Go, Flight."

"Guidance?"

"Go."

"Control?"

"Go."

"TELMU?

"Go."

"G and C?"

"Go."

"EECOM?"

"Go, Flight."

"Surgeon?"

"Go."

"INCO?"

"Go."

"Procedures?"

"We're go, Flight."

"FAO?"

"Go."

"Network?"

"Network is go."

Kranz nodded. "CapCom, pass the word on up. We are go for lift-off at CDR's discretion."

"*Starlight*, you're go," astronaut Bruce McCandless said into his headset microphone, his calm, almost soothing tone belying the gravity of the moment. Less than an hour earlier, he had been brought in as CapCom specifically because of his steady voice and reassuring demeanor, both of which had been evident during Apollo 11's historic first moonwalk. "Anytime you want to start, Gary. We're with you all the way."

"Thank you, Houston," came Lucas' reply from the speakers. The astronauts' microphones had been left open, and a few moments later, Shepherd read from the checklist once again.

"ATT translation, four jets. Balance couple, on."

"Balance couple, on," Lucas repeated, flipping the paddle switch as he had done before.

Kranz glanced over at Fendel, who was seated a couple of rows away and to his left. The dark-haired man nervously was drumming his copy of the flight plan with a pencil, sweat stains darkening the sides of his short-sleeved shirt. Before him on his console were the camera control switches, awaiting further use. Kranz could take the temperature of a room with a look, judging its morale immediately. He knew his men felt helpless as things were, and that meant their confidence could plummet to new lows if this lift-off attempt failed. He had to keep them together, keep them believing in themselves, their systems, and each other—and the one thing he did *not* want, if there was to be another moment of defeat, was anything emphasizing that defeat.

"Ed," Kranz privately called over the link, "stay off the controls this time around. Leave the TV camera where it is."

"Copy that, Gene," the answer came back. The man sounded relieved.

Shepherd's words continued to flow from the speakers. "Thrust controller set to jets."

"Jets."

"Reset prop pushbutton. Abort Stage reset."

"Reset."

The grainy image of the LM filled Kranz's eyes, its black-and-silver face fixed as if in a trance. Any second, the screen would contain an explosion of glittering Mylar confetti as the engine lit and the men finally headed back into orbit, leaving the valley of Cabeus forever behind them—

—*forever behind them*—

—*any second*—

—*please!*

"Guidance steering set to AGS," Shepherd called once more, clearly punching codes into the computer. "Ten seconds. Abort Stage."

"Abort Stage," Lucas confirmed as again he pressed the switch, hope audible in his voice.

"Engine Arm to ascent…"

Come on!

Kranz willed it to happen, his eyes boring holes into the screen.

Light, you son of a—!

"3…2…1…manual start!"

He thought he heard Lucas driving a gloved thumb hard into the button. And again.

Nothing.

Kranz stared in stunned silence at the image of the unmoving LM. A murmur of frustration filled the MOCR. Someone threw a procedures manual to the floor. Then, suddenly, there *was* motion on the screen, a whitish blur seen behind a window of the ill-fated craft.

A momentary burst of static filled the room's speakers. Lucas had slammed a fist into something.

Kranz felt the blow in his gut.

"Get that picture off the screen," the flight director ordered to whomever was listening. The big image immediately went black.

Kranz rose from his chair and started for the door.

"Room 210," he called out, determination in his voice. "And I mean everybody."

◙　　◙　　◙

4:27 A.M.

The press had begun its assault on the Shepherd home shortly after the first lift-off attempt, and more had gathered as the night went on. Carol, unwilling to deal with what to her were little more than vultures, had locked the door and drawn the drapes. Henry Hurt, public relations man that he was, had managed to give the throng just enough to keep them at bay.

Walter Cronkite was spreading the news to all America, his deep, fatherly voice offering no comfort to those holding vigil in the living room of Carol Shepherd. Young Joey, now in bed and asleep, did not hear his distressing words.

"…we now have received word that this latest attempt to fire the LM's ascent engine also has failed. This means that for the marooned astronauts, a lack of breathable air and battery power will quickly become a new problem. All we can do now is watch and hope and pray…"

Diane Lucas broke down, the tears flowing in a rush as she sobbed in the arms of Henry. Carol, seated in her chair, looked up at Katie Kendall, who had been pacing in obvious discomfort for more than an hour. Carol had spent some time watching her—what she saw in the young woman was not fear for her husband's safety, but something else. It was something the elder wife had seen before, something that threatened to isolate Katie just when she needed the others most, and they needed her.

Katie had not made eye contact with the other wives for quite some time, choosing instead to watch the television or the carpet or anything else. Finally, she glanced at Carol, who met her moist, reddened eyes but for a moment before Katie looked away.

"It's not your fault, dear," Carol began, her soothing tone carrying the wisdom of experience. "Don't feel guilty because your husband's coming home. The clock's been ticking toward this for nine years now, for Charlie...for me..." She looked away for a moment, toward something across the room, then back at the young woman. "It's not your Vic's time."

Katie allowed herself to look once more into the woman's eyes, deeply this time. She saw there a strength she did not understand—a strength she *could not* understand—one she knew she herself did not possess. She gazed deeply into those wet green eyes, finding there an enveloping comfort she had not known she needed, astounded that such a passion for the needs of another could dwell within one whose own husband now was almost certain to die in such a distant, cruel place as the moon.

"Maybe it's not Charlie's time, either...or Gary's..." Katie said with quivering lips, not believing her own words.

"Maybe not," Carol gently nodded, looking at her wedding ring. "But if it is...it is."

Katie, softly crying now, went to the woman, crouched beside her chair, and took her hand. "I don't understand, Carol...how can you be worried about *me*...about what *I'm* feeling...when it's *your* husband who's stranded up there?" She paused, afraid she had made matters worse. "I'm sorry...I didn't mean..."

"It's all right, honey."

"They're up there all alone, and yet—"

"They're not alone," Carol said, gently, her eyes glistening. "They never were."

◙ ◙ ◙

The phone rang. Henry left Diane's side and went into the kitchen to answer it, and after watching him for a moment Diane turned and silently took in the continuing news report on television. Men who did not know her Gary personally were discussing his situation with the cold detachment of a mortuary staff. And fittingly so, she thought— the unfeeling report had become little more than an obituary.

The conversation was short. Henry hung up the phone and calmly walked back into the living room. All eyes were upon him.

"They…want you to come down to the Center," he said. "They've sent a car. It'll be here shortly…you may want to get your things ready. They've also gone to find Jeff. I'll stay here with Joey, so don't worry about him. And don't worry about the reporters out there…the men we're sending over will shield you on the way out, and I'll give the press an appropriate statement when the time comes."

Katie nodded and gathered their long coats from the hall closet. As she handed them out, Diane took hers with some reluctance. The mere fact that they had been called to the MSC sent a chill down her spine—such was an exceedingly rare occurrence, and one that never meant good news.

Diane shuddered within. Carol closed her eyes. They knew.

They're letting us say good-bye.

5

5:45 A.M.

"So, let me get this straight…there was a *pool*…"

"Yup."

"And you bet on me, huh?"

Shepherd smiled, watching his crouching commander open the forward hatch of the LM. "Yeah…I had three squares, and good ones too."

"How good?"

"Almost any landing inside of a hundred and fifty yards, and I won at least something, so long as we didn't overshoot. John Young somehow wangled having the bull's-eye, though, so I'm glad we didn't come down within spitting range."

"How did I not hear about this?"

"Don't feel bad, Skipper. Conrad was in the dark too. The ol' boys in the office didn't want to add any more pressure by letting on…so's to keep it fair and square."

"Like it would have mattered," Lucas laughed. It felt good to have at least some of the stress bled away, stress that had built steadily since the first failed ignition. Both men slowly had become as used to the idea of being stranded as could be expected. There was no panic—they

50

were too well trained for that—only frustration and some level of occasional, momentary anger, more in Lucas than in his partner.

The mission commander dropped to his hands and knees, and with some difficulty began through the hatchway, head first.

"Okay, easy," Shepherd said, feeding Lucas' umbilicals safely through the open hatchway. "You should have just enough slack, here...okay...just a little farther..."

"Who bet on Conrad?" Lucas asked.

"Bean and Gordon...oh, and Kerwin," Shepherd replied. "That I know of."

"Lackeys," Lucas kidded. "It figures."

Almost completely out of the hatch now, Lucas extended a gloved hand as far as his bulky pressure suit would allow, reaching toward the base of the porch railing just outside, toward the dangling life support backpack he earlier had thrown overboard. Glancing down, he saw his next target for retrieval—on the lunar soil below the ladder rested the other PLSS, the one Shepherd had worn, its corner resting on the portside edge of the footpad.

"Almost..." he said, his fingertips just short of the nylon strap from which the pack hung. "How are my hoses?"

"That's about it," Shepherd said. "Maybe another few inches...not much more. Careful...don't drop it..."

Lucas leaned outward, twisting slightly sideways, and found the strap. "Got it. Pull me back...easy, though, I don't want to lose my grip."

Shepherd pulled on an attachment lug of Lucas' suit, gently bringing him a little farther into the cabin. Lucas braced his elbow and with some effort heaved the depleted PLSS up onto the porch.

"Okay, Charlie," he said triumphantly. "That got it. Guide me in."

In a few moments, both men stood side-by-side once again, with the recovered backpack resting upon the engine cover. The hatch was still open, the cabin still depressurized.

"Looks okay," Shepherd observed. "No worse for having hung out there."

Lucas reached down, pulled the PLSS recharge hoses from their stowage positions, and attached them to the backpack. He and Shepherd watched as gauges showed its oxygen and water supplies filling once again.

They had removed their annoying biomedical sensors and had shut off their telemetry and other transmitters to help save power, so the ground was unaware of their actions. They were still *receiving* signals, however, in case Houston needed to speak to them, but they had received no word from Earth for almost half an hour. Lucas liked having that small bit of privacy, in addition to the fact that for the first time in almost two weeks he had made a move without the whole world knowing.

Since they also had cut all electrical ties with the descent stage in their pre-lift-off sequence, the batteries down there, though still good, were now inaccessible. Even with rationing, their ascent batteries would last barely more than a day, and when the power went so would their air; without the environmental system working to pump it, any oxygen remaining in the tanks was useless to them.

As they watched the gauges, a crackle sounded in their headsets.

"*Starlight,* this is *Quest*...do you copy?"

Shepherd flipped a switch on his right-hand panel. The command module once more had risen above their horizon in its transit of the near side. "Hey, Vic...how's the view from up there?"

"Same as ever. Two things are missing, though."

"Yeah," Lucas said, "I wish we could help you there."

"What's the good word?"

"We've tried a dozen different ways of jump-starting this puppy so far...still no joy. The smart boys have nothing to go on."

Shepherd shook his head. "I think the well's dry at this point."

"You two have any ideas of your own?"

"Well, I recovered my PLSS," Lucas replied. "We're charging it back up, while we still have power to do it. Then, I'm going out after Charlie's."

"What for?"

"Even with the way we're conserving everything, the batteries are going to fail around 11:30 tomorrow morning. When we lose power, we lose life support…and when that happens, we're going for a drive. We might as well see just how far this rover will take us."

"Does Houston know about this plan yet?"

"No, and it doesn't matter. I refuse just to sit in a tin can and die."

"Look, guys," Kendall said, his voice as confident as he could make it. "No one's dying, period. I know you're coming up. No way I'm cutting out of here with you glory hounds down there getting all the attention."

Lucas smiled. "Yeah, well…we'll try to save you a seat on the float."

"I mean it," Kendall insisted. "This baby's built for three. *All* of us are getting out of here…you hear me? Kick the box…kluge something together out of twine and paper clips…do whatever you have to do to make that thing work, and as soon as you put her up into orbit, we'll blow this joint."

"Roger that," Shepherd said. "Appreciate your confidence, Chief."

"You guys hang tight…I'll see you on my next pass. Maybe by then, the guys back home will have…"

And then, the radio fell silent. *Quest* was gone again, headed once more for the far side. Shepherd shut off the transmitter.

"Well," Lucas said, "The sooner I go grab your pack, the sooner we can pump it back up in here and get out of these suits for a while."

Lucas slipped into his backpack and chest control unit, and Shepherd verified that its umbilical connectors were solid. The commander, feeling the new airflow within his helmet, dropped to his knees and began to back out of the hatch.

"Lucky thing my pack hung up on the porch," Lucas said. "I doubt I could've made it all the way to the bottom of the ladder on just the two minutes of air in my suit."

"Yeah," Shepherd smiled. "Lucky."

*   *   *

6:14 A.M.

Room 210 lay near the MOCR, a place of deep thought and mission planning where those in charge of each flight could gather to plot strategies. A huge, polished walnut conference table dominated its center, with data-scrawled blackboards and pull-down projection screens upon the walls, awaiting further use. A huge model of the Saturn V rocket stood in one corner, and next to it, atop a wide, waist-high shelving unit, were smaller display models of the Apollo spacecraft components. Posters and diagrams of various mission elements dotted the wall behind them. Kranz had taken a seat at the head of the table, next to MSC Director Robert Gilruth, a lean, balding man in his mid-sixties who had been with NASA from the beginning. In 1972, he had considered retirement but had chosen instead to remain in his position for the duration of the Apollo program. Both men were bent over large green-bar sheets of raw numbers that had been delivered by the Planning and Analysis Division, searching for the one tiny piece of information that could tip the scales in their favor.

For more than an hour and a half, the men of the MOCR had pored over their data. Those of the White Team crowded the room along with others who were working on the problem, all surrounding the impressive briefing table where Kranz and Gilruth sat. Those who could not find room to sit at the table stood around it, filling the room to the point that closing the door was difficult.

"All right," Kranz began, his face and upper body reflected in the highly polished tabletop. He held up some of the sheets of telemetry data spread before him. "The answer *has* to be in here. What can we do?"

"For starters," a voice sounded, "we keep Lousma off the CapCom console."

There was a mild round of nervous laughter as the tension momentarily eased. By coincidence, Lousma now had served as Cap-Com during *both* of the lunar program's most critical spaceborne emergencies—though the men of Apollo 13, with fall-back options upon which to rely, had managed to return safely to Earth.

A Grumman official spoke up. "Gene, we've been over every bit of telemetry again and again. Anything else we try to do at this point is more likely to create new problems than fix the existing one. The data says we have a good engine up there. It just won't fire...and for no reason whatsoever, as far as we can tell."

"There has to be a reason," Kranz stated flatly. "Is there any chance that we've got a hole in a propellant tank? That nitrogen tetroxide is corrosive, and it has a real talent for finding the tiniest leak and making it bigger...maybe we're losing oxidizer pressure and we're just not getting any readings saying so."

The Grumman man nodded. "That's possible...but since we show good tank pressure, a theory like that means we're totally throwing the telemetry out the window. And once we start doing that, *anything* could be wrong. Besides, if the problem *is* that kind of a leak, it's irreparable anyway...there's nothing Lucas and Shepherd can do to fix it."

Kranz shook his head. "I think we have to consider even the ridiculous at this point. Unlikely as it is, what if both tanks are filled with fuel? Or with oxidizer? Maybe the system's actually working, but there's no hypergolic mix."

"Impossible," the Grumman man said. "You couldn't do that if you tried. The inlet fittings are different sizes, and the filling systems are positioned to reach only the appropriate tanks. And again…that would be an irreparable problem."

"Besides," a controller added, "the fuel and oxidizer are of different densities and have different liquefied temperatures. We'd have known before launch that a tank had been misfilled."

"Okay, then," Kranz nodded. "Good. We're thinking it through. We've got two good men up there counting on us…and we're bringing them home, people." He scribbled something on a clipboard notepad. "There has to be something we can do to effect a repair."

Another controller shook his head. "Not that I really believe this, but maybe the problem's as simple as the fact that *Starlight* was the thirteenth LM to roll off the assembly line."

A groan went up in the room. "I was waiting for someone to toss that one out," Gilruth moaned.

"Well, it's happened before," the man went on. "Maybe LM-13 should just have been sent directly to a museum or something, and never flown."

"Actually, that might be as good a theory as any," a new voice rang out, sarcastic and heavy with frustration.

All heads turned to see the source of the voice, a tall, white-haired man who had just entered and was closing the double doors behind him. Kranz knew the voice at once—it belonged to George Stenner, the director of Grumman's Kennedy Space Center Operations. His white, short-sleeved shirt was rumpled as if slept in, and his tie hung loosely around his unbuttoned collar. It had been a long flight to Houston, one during which Stenner had tried with limited success to get some much-needed sleep.

"Come in, George," Gilruth invited. "You know this bird... What do we do?"

"According to the data, there's not a thing wrong with her," Stenner went on. "Everything up there is performing flawlessly."

"Obviously, there *is* something wrong," Gilruth said. "She's still on the moon."

"I said, 'according to the data.' Whatever *is* keeping that engine from burning isn't showing itself to us. We can't be getting the whole story from the LM, despite the numbers we're seeing."

"That doesn't make sense," Kranz said. "We're getting complete and consistent telemetry."

Stenner tried to explain, but had some difficulty. Too little sleep and too much coffee kept the words from coming as easily as they otherwise might have. "The best we've been able to determine is that something has changed the operational parameters up there. Either the data we're getting isn't really complete and some kind of weird cross-feed is filling the gaps, or it's complete but inaccurate."

"Inaccurate?" asked one of the other controllers. "How can it—?"

"Something is wrong, despite the rosy picture the data is giving us. That means the LM isn't sending us *real* data...and nothing we've been able to do has changed that. *Starlight* is, well..." He paused, searching for words.

"Is what?" Kranz asked. Stenner swallowed hard.

"It's as if she's telling us what she thinks we want to hear."

"Say what?" Gilruth asked, shaking his head. "The LM transmits raw telemetry. We've already verified our ground computers are working, so if you're right and the telemetry's junk then we're just getting bad data, plain and simple."

"No...it's not simple, Bob. If this were just a matter of faulty telemetry, the readings would be all over the map. You know that. We'd be getting haphazard garbage...good readings and bad ones. But what the LM's sending us *isn't* random…everything we're getting is telling us the spacecraft is in perfect shape."

Kranz rubbed his forehead. "Help me out, here, George…"

"A few hours ago, we put two separate engines into a test environment that exactly matched the conditions up there, and both fired. Again and again. The reason *Starlight's* won't function is known only to her…and she isn't sharing with us."

The guidance officer shook his head. " 'Sharing?' We don't have a 'HAL 9000' up there, pulling some kind of mutiny. All the LM has is a sixteen-bit guidance computer that has nothing to do with her telemetry."

Stenner nodded. "I know, I know. I didn't say the onboard computer is responsible. Like that fellow said before…maybe it all boils down to the fact that this is LM-13. Who knows? We've gone over this again and again at Kennedy, and the Grumman boys have been doing the same up in Bethpage. We've lived and breathed and slept this machine for thirteen years now, but what we're seeing out of it today…" He paused, looking like a father disappointed in his child. "I just don't know."

"*Thirteen* years," someone commented. "That's just great…"

"So, the LM's *haunted?*" Kranz uttered, frustrated by the ridiculous notion. "Or cursed? That's all we have to work with? All our numbers, all our hardware…they mean *nothing* right now? Do we drag a priest in here and perform some kind of ritual over the TELMU console, or what?"

"Might be worth a shot," someone muttered sarcastically.

A murmur of disquiet filled the room as the controllers began to realize how truly desperate the situation had become. Kranz gathered himself, then rose from his chair and held out his arms, motioning for silence.

"Quiet down, people," he said, looking at Stenner, who stood facing him at the opposite end of the table. The deliberation ceased, and the room fell silent.

"Talk to me, George," he gravely went on, back at square one. "What can we do?"

Stenner knew the LM, perhaps better than any other single man on the planet. He *had* to hold the key they needed to save two fading lives, and Kranz was determined to wrest it free. *There has to be something we've missed—!*

The silence in the room was oppressive. Stenner felt the weight of the men's eyes pressing in upon him, demanding an answer. *Needing* an answer. He was too weary for diplomacy, too tired even to ease the blow.

"Nothing," he said, defeated. "We can't do a thing."

◘   ◘   ◘

6:21 A.M.

It grew cold within the cabin. While the rear outer surfaces of the LM, those exposed to the sun, were far hotter than would be needed to grill a steak, the spacecraft's Mylar and standoff insulation kept any of that warmth from getting inside. The battery power was failing, and the stranded astronauts had shut down all systems not essential to their survival. That meant the heaters, the computers, the guidance system, and the transmitters had been put to sleep, awaiting a miracle from Houston.

Lucas stretched, pausing to rub a sore shoulder. Chilly as it was, it felt good to be out of his pressure suit once again. As he sat upon the engine cover, eating his dinner and waiting for news from the ground, he leaned back against the bulkhead shelves where the recharged backpacks were stowed. He had recovered the various discarded elements of their moon suits from the dusty soil outside, and those items now sat tucked into various nooks and crannies, awaiting use.

If it came to that.

"How are we fixed for PLSS batteries, Charlie?" he asked, his breath fogging before him.

"Six left…three for each of us. If we need 'em."

Three batteries—maybe twenty-one hours of backpack time total—

Shepherd had eaten already, having downed an entrée of chicken and dumplings. Lucas had chosen beef stew, which he ate from a resealable plastic pouch, dipping his spoon into the chunky mix in the reduced gravity as he paused to play with his food now and again.

"You know," Lucas observed, "this stuff's really pretty good after two days of nothing but soup."

His crewmate smiled. "Not 'soup'…'nutritionally enhanced semi-liquid extended-duration extravehicular rations.'"

"Like I said," Lucas smirked, also recalling their training lectures. "Soup."

Shepherd smiled, shaking his head. Dressed like his commander in only his cooling undergarment and in-flight coveralls, he sat on the floor, reading from the worn leather-bound Bible he had brought with him. It had seen better days—the gold gilding was all but worn from the edges of its fragile pages, most of which were filled with margin notes in his own hand. He had brought the book aboard the flight in his small personal-items bag, which also contained a little, white plastic figurine of an astronaut he had carried to the moon for his son, and a delicate silver locket on a chain, which he planned to give to Carol on their upcoming anniversary.

Lucas finished his meal and looked down from his perch, watching the man as he gently flipped through the book, noting the keen interest with which he drank in words Lucas himself never had taken the time to read. He had known Shepherd was a Christian, but it was something of an uncomfortable subject for Lucas, and he never had discussed the matter with him.

"That looks old, Charlie," he commented.

"Yup," Shepherd smiled. "My father gave me this on my tenth birthday. We were out in a boat, fishing for trout, back home. He and I, two poles, and a can of corn. That's all we needed. The sun was warm, but the breeze was cold. I can still feel it. He gave me this, out there on the lake…told me this book held the secrets of life and death, happiness and peace…and he was right. I've held on to it ever since."

"I miss my dad," Lucas said quietly, his eyes down. "Even now…it's been a long time, but I still miss him."

"I'm sorry, Gary."

There was a pause.

"So…why did you write all over the pages like that?" Lucas asked, returning to the previous subject. "I thought you weren't supposed to do that kind of thing. My grandmother had one, a big one. One of those 'family Bibles,' you know? She wouldn't even set anything on top of it, let alone write in it. She said it was disrespectful."

Shepherd grinned. "Well, I suppose that's one way of thinking. To me, though, this is a book to be used and understood." He thumbed through its pages. "I've made all kinds of notes to myself in here."

He set the book down on the floor of the LM's midsection then leaned his head back against the bulkhead. "Been a long time coming, getting here and all."

"Yeah."

"I mean, the whole history of man. We're on the moon, Gary."

"I know," Lucas chuckled. "That's the problem."

"No…I mean, *we're on the moon.*" Shepherd looked up at him, his eyes wide and filled with wonder. "Think of it…just think of it…"

"I'm trying not to, Charlie."

Lucas recalled the events of the previous days, pausing to reflect upon all they had accomplished. So many had worked so hard for so long to make their mission, their landing, a reality. And after all of the training, all of the planning, all of the blood and sweat and tears of hundreds of thousands, here they were.

Marooned.

He glared at one of the rock boxes they had brought back, a vacuum-sealed treasure chest filled with unearthly jewels of unequalled price.

And I'd trade it all for one good engine.

6

Shepherd stared blankly at the cluster of storage pouches arrayed opposite him. There, within the confines of the stubbornly quiescent *Starlight,* he allowed his mind to drift.

"You know, we were a good group, the class of '66," he began, breaking the silence as he recalled his selection as an astronaut. "When I got the call, Carol couldn't believe it. She acted like a kid in a candy store. But I knew down inside she was scared to death. Big unknown, space travel. She was happy because I was, but if she'd have had her way, I imagine they'd have taken someone else."

"I married Annie after I was already in training," Lucas said in reply. "Back in '65. Met her at a hangout of mine in Cocoa Beach, and it was love at first sight. I mean, you know how you look at someone, and lasers just shoot out of your eyes and lock in, and from that moment on…it was like that. We'd only known each other six months when we got married, but it was like I'd known her my whole life. Can't imagine being with anyone else. She really helped me get through training…without her being there, it would have been a lot tougher."

"Man, those first six months were brutal," Shepherd agreed. "Simulators, classrooms, field training...I went to Iceland. Talk about cold. Did they send you there?"

"No, I did most of my geology work in Hawaii."

"Hawaii? Lucky dog."

"Well, I had Alaska too, so it probably balanced out."

Shepherd laughed. "Things got even worse when I was assigned to my first flight. Backup pilot on Eighteen, right behind Dick Gordon. You know how it was...sixteen-hour days. If I wasn't asleep, I was training. Spent as much time in the air as on the ground. Barely saw home at all. I was lucky to see Carol's face once a week. Frank Borman told me once that back when he was training for Gemini 7, he could find any knob or switch or piece of equipment in that spacecraft blindfolded, but when he went home, he couldn't find a water glass in his own kitchen."

Lucas laughed. "I believe it."

Shepherd picked up his Bible again. Flipping to a spot in the book of Psalms, he read one passage aloud. " 'My soul thirsts for Thee, my flesh yearns for Thee, in a dry and weary land where there is no water.' "

" 'Where never lark or even eagle flew,' " Lucas added, a momentary, faraway look in his eye. Both men allowed a moment of reflective silence to hang within the cabin.

"You're right about one thing," the commander went on. "This place is as dry and weary as it gets. Nothing up here any God would be interested in, that's for sure."

Shepherd softly shook his head, flipping pages. "No, no...He's here."

"You really believe that?"

He looked up from his Bible. "Sure, Gary."

"Still? I mean...even if He is, don't you feel like He's let you down?

For the love of Mike…you're stranded on the moon. You want a God like that?"

"He's got a reason for what's happening. I don't know what it is, but I know there *is* one."

Lucas was amazed. "How can you not be angry? How can you love a God who would do this to you?"

"I *was* angry," Shepherd admitted. "At first."

"You? I couldn't tell it."

"I didn't say anything. And I wish I hadn't been. It passed after a while…with a lot of prayer and remembering. I've learned after a lot of years of experience that nothing happens without crossing God's desk first. Even when things seem rotten, there's a reason for it we just can't see. For instance: I was turned down for the group of '63 after doing really well on the exams, or so I thought. I barely met the age requirement, but I met every other qualification, passed every physical test, and thought I was a shoo-in. I wanted to go to the moon more than anything…it was like it called to me at night, you know? I felt like I was destined to come up here.

"Well, despite all that, someone else got my seat. I ran everything I had said or done through my head over and over, trying to figure out where I'd slipped up. I even wondered if maybe they'd turned me down just because they already *had* a 'Shepard.' I'll tell you…I was so disappointed I couldn't eat, couldn't sleep, the whole bit. I lost weight. I got an ulcer. I let it get to me."

"Doesn't sound much like faith…for a Christian, I mean."

"Well, I *was* a Christian, but I wasn't all that close to the Lord at the time. I let everyday stuff weigh me down…let it keep me too preoccupied." He paused in thought. "Anyway, the next year, I took a teaching position at Lowry. That's where I met Carol. And now, every night when I go to bed, I thank the Lord for her and for our son and for keeping me out of the group of '63…because if He hadn't, I never would have met her. And, if I *had* gone into NASA back then, I might even have wound up on the Apollo 1 crew. Who knows."

Shepherd looked up at his friend and commander and saw his mind turning things over. "What about you, Gary? Where are you, as far as God goes?"

"Well…I haven't really made up my mind about that."

"Ah," he nodded. "Sitting on the proverbial fence."

"I guess so."

Shepherd smiled. "Well, you're not alone. Pretty crowded up there."

"I suppose."

"Remind me to tell you sometime why there really *is* no fence."

A heavy silence hung in the close cabin for a few moments as Lucas wondered about Shepherd's words. A voice cut into his thoughts. "*Starlight,* Houston."

Lucas activated their transmitter and hit his talk switch. "*Starlight.*"

"Gary, we've got someone here who would like to say hello."

There was a pause, and Diane's voice filled their earpieces.

"Hi, Gary."

Shepherd pulled out his earpiece and set it on his shoulder, giving Lucas as much privacy as he could.

"Hi, hon," Lucas smiled, happy to hear her voice. "How're the home fires?"

"Everything's fine," she said. "They tell me your night hasn't been so good."

"Yeah," he smiled slightly, "we've had better."

◎   ◎   ◎

Diane dropped her head, trying very hard not to break down. She sat at the CapCom console, rows of colored lights flashing on the panel before her. *Keep it light,* she had been told. But he was her husband, and these might be the last words they ever would share.

"I miss you so much," she said, clutching the headset cord, wrapping it around her fingers. Her hands were cold.

"I miss you too, babe," Lucas said. "I'd give anything to be able to hold you right now."

"What are they saying, Gary?" she asked. "Can they fix it?"

There was a silence. "I don't know, Annie. It doesn't look so good."

"But...there has to be something they can do..."

"Listen," he went on, "remember that time in Cocoa Beach when you first fixed me your chicken-and-mushroom casserole? It was a surprise dinner, and you were so proud because you had never cooked for me before, and you had worked on it all day..."

She thought back. That day was chiseled into her mind, as clearly as if it had been yesterday. It was the one-month anniversary of their first date, and she had tried so hard to make everything perfect. The lights were low, and tapered candles burned softly on the table. Their song, Elvis Presley's "Loving You," was playing on her console phonograph as Gary walked in. As the music played, he held her, and from that moment each knew they would be spending the rest of their lives together.

"Yes," she smiled, the tension broken. "I remember, Gary."

"And I told you how much I loved it, and since then you've fixed it for me for every anniversary..."

"Yes," she nodded. "You mean you really *didn't* like it?"

"No, it was great...but I've always been allergic to mushrooms, Annie..."

She laughed and cried at the same time, eyes wet, hands trembling slightly. Her mind momentarily drifted away from the sights and sounds of the console before her and the room around her, filled instead with a sweet collage of images of his face, his smile, his sparkling eyes.

"Oh, Gary…"

So that explains the hives, she realized, remembering that he had always blamed them on some new aftershave or laundry detergent or whatever. She had never put two and two together, linking the meal with the skin rash he soon developed—

"You could have told me," she smiled through moist eyes.

"What? And miss seeing that beautiful face of yours light up?"

She looked down, trying not to cry.

"I love you."

"I love you too," Lucas said, his voice breaking but slightly. "Whatever happens here with Charlie and me…you hang tough, okay? You and Carol, uh…help each other…things will work out…"

Tears began to flow down the woman's cheeks. "Oh, Gary… don't…"

"You'll be taken care of…I've seen to that. The house, everything. It's covered. If anyone gives you a hard time, you call Bruce Cortney. He'll be there for you. He and I have discussed this. Just call him if you need anything."

There was a silence as neither spoke but simply shared their final moments together, separated by more than two hundred thousand miles.

"I'm sorry, Annie," he began. "I'm sorry we never had more kids…"

"That isn't your fault," she answered, tears running in black-mascara streams. "It wasn't anyone's fault. It just…wasn't to be."

"I wish it had been, though…I wish you had a whole gaggle of 'em there to help you through all this. A whole house full."

"Well, we got it right the first time."

He laughed. "How *is* Jeff? Is he with you?"

"You know him," she said, sniffling and wiping her cheeks with tissues. "Mr. Adventure. He's out camping at Toledo Bend…but they sent someone to pick him up. He'll be here soon."

"Oh, yeah…this was the big weekend."

"I don't even know if he's heard yet. I do know he misses you terribly, just like I do…"

"He's a good boy. I'm so proud of him I could burst."

"Me too."

"You tell him I love him. Tell him every day."

"I will…but he knows. He loves you too…and he's so proud of you…we both are…"

She wanted to go on, but the words would not come quickly enough. Dead air filled her ears as tears filled her eyes.

◉   ◉   ◉

Lucas could hear his wife crying softly on the other end. He felt his own resolve weakening. His jaw tensed. His throat ached. He gripped the yellow handhold bar before him, clutching it tightly as if to draw strength from it. He did not want to break his last tie to her, but knew he must.

"I better go," he finally said, struggling to contain his own emotions. "We have to conserve power…and Charlie's gotta talk to Carol still, I'm sure…"

"I love you, Gary," Diane repeated. "Always."

"I love you too," Lucas said, envisioning her face. "Always."

◉   ◉   ◉

There was a little crackle in her ear as Lucas turned off his transmitter.

Diane took off the lightweight headset, messing up her carefully arranged hairstyle as she did so, and set it onto the console before her. Putting a hand to her hair, she stared at the set, as if at any moment Gary would somehow emerge from it and take her in his arms again. It had been her final link to him.

She looked over at Cortney, who had just come on duty as Cap-Com and had led her to the console from the viewing room outside. Placing one hand upon the headset, she looked up into his eyes, a question written upon her tear-stained face. He understood and nodded.

Diane gathered herself, wiping her eyes with the tissue again, then picked up the headset and pulled its plug from the socket in the console before her. Gently, she wound its cord around its headband, picked up her purse and rose from the chair, clutching the headset to her chest.

She left, taking it with her.

7

Vic Kendall stared at the switch. His hatred for it had grown during the lonely hours. From between its gray, protective guard bars it mocked him, calling his name, screaming of the failure that had doomed two good men to a lonely end on a barren world devoid even of the gentlest stirrings of air.

For the thousandth time, he read the words printed just above it—

SPS THRUST DIRECT ON

Throwing that switch would ignite the engine of the huge service propulsion system, hurling *Quest* out of lunar orbit and into a trajectory for home. Kendall's very survival depended upon that burn. Without it, he, like the others, would be a prisoner of the silent moon, doomed never to see home again, orbiting as a corpse until mass concentrations and other factors caused his orbit to decay, smashing *Quest* into the lunar surface, months or even years hence.

When the time for the burn came, most likely, the guidance computer and not Kendall would be in control, timing it to the millisecond—and, to his relief, he would never have to use the dreaded manual switch before him.

Where he himself was concerned, the burn meant life.

Yet that one solitary toggle switch, identical to so many others arrayed before him, now cried out of other things—the looming shadows of abandonment, of solitude, and of death.

He looked away, tearing his weary eyes from the control panel and back to the window. He had just crossed the northern terminator and was over the near side once more, soon to approach the place where his companions waited. Already he had dropped twenty miles lower into a stable forty-mile orbit, which would be within easier reach for a LM with limited power. Perhaps they had made it—perhaps they already were approaching a rendezvous orbit, and soon they all would be headed home together. *Perhaps*—

"*Quest,* Houston," a voice called. "Do you read?"

Kendall allowed himself a spark of hope. He hit his talk switch.

"Go, Houston."

"Hey, Vic," Cortney said, trying to be upbeat. "Get any sleep on that last orbit?"

"No," he quietly replied, shaking his head. "Too much to think about, I guess."

"Well, that's certainly understandable…"

"I take it they're still not up."

There was an uncomfortable pause. "No…not as far as we know. We lost comm with them about twenty minutes ago…we assume that's due to a loss of transmitting power on their end. You may be low enough to talk to them on your next pass, though."

Kendall recalled Lucas' words from the day before. *The batteries are going to fail around eleven-thirty tomorrow morning.* He glanced down at his watch, set to Houston time as was the norm.

It was almost seventeen minutes past eleven.

"Listen, Vic…your consumables are going to become a factor before too long. As of now, you've been in orbit almost a day and a half longer than the flight plan called for, and by the time you break orbit we may be looking at well over two. We've taken your new orbit into account and have gone over the numbers, and right now we're looking at a trans-Earth injection burn at 349:17:42 ground elapsed time…"

"Isn't it a little early to be planning that?" Kendall snapped. "They're still alive down there."

"Vic, if we go past that time and hold the burn for a later orbit, assuming *Starlight* can even get off the surface, there won't be enough in the way of consumables to keep three of you alive until splashdown. That makes their rescue a moot point, and we lose three men instead of two."

Vic was unswayed. "So, we'll go into low-tide mode, cut the partial pressure, and sleep all the way home…but I'm staying."

"Look, Vic…we really feel that—"

"I'm not leaving here until there's a less-than-zero chance of their coming up. You hear me?"

There was only silence from the radio.

"Did you read that?" Kendall insisted. "*Quest* waits. Period."

Still, silence.

"Roger, *Quest*," Cortney finally replied, knowing that the final call truly fell into the hands of the man in orbit. "We're…watching it closely. We'll keep you apprised…Houston out."

Without thinking, Kendall slammed a fist against the wall of the cabin, hurling himself up off of his couch in the process. Grabbing the support strut above him, he halted his drift, cursed his carelessness, and maneuvered himself back into his seat. The frustration of his own incapacity to save his friends had been steadily tearing at him, but he bit his lower lip, took a deep breath, and tried to maintain discipline. Despite the circumstances, still he held out hope.

Surely, something had made itself apparent at the last moment, an eleventh-hour miracle that, even now, was propelling *Starlight* from the surface. *If they're up and fully conserving their power for flight, they might not have contacted Houston yet—*

He glanced at his docking window, at the laminated crosshair target within it. *I'll have to handle the docking completely alone—they'll make orbit, but they likely won't have the power to make final docking maneuvers. That's okay—if they can just get into the ballpark, I can still reach them—*

He flexed his hand, eyeing the thrust controller handle. He had trained for that off-chance. Even a dead LM was within his grasp if it had managed to limp into space and make orbit, however low. Only fifteen miles up or ten or even five—still, he could reach them.

There was a faint crackle in his headset.

"…is *Starlight*…come in, *Quest*…" The words were drowning in static.

Kendall hit the switch. *Please, Gary—tell me you're up—!*

"Read you," Kendall said, his heart pounding, his fingers crossed. "What's the word, guys?"

"I have to make this quick," Lucas' voice faintly said. "The batteries have about had it. The environmental system just gave out…"

Shepherd's voice cut in. "You did all you could, Vic. Staying up there now won't help us. You've got someone waiting for you at home…don't let her down."

Kendall refused to concede defeat. "Look, I've done some math of my own. I figure I'm okay to stay up here another couple of days and still get us all home." He fought the swell of emotion that wrenched his throat. "Three came up here, and three are—"

"Get your butt home," Lucas insisted, the signal weakening with each passing moment. "That's an order."

Kendall stared hard at the two empty couches beside him.

"Charlie and I are suited up," Lucas went on. "We're abandoning the LM, Vic. There won't be any more attempts at lift-off. We're heading over to the rover as soon as we finish talking to you…we're going to go and see what we can see."

Kendall was stunned. Though its shadow had been looming for days, cruel reality suddenly came crashing down. Slowly, he spoke, coming to grips with harsh and agonizing truth. "I'll…I'll pass that along to Houston, then…"

"No need, buddy," Shepherd replied. "We'll holler at them as soon as we hit the dusty road…the rover should have plenty of power for that."

There was nothing left to say. Kendall struggled for words. They lodged in his throat like barbed things, bitter and hard.

"Gary…Charlie…I couldn't have asked…for two finer…" The words would not come. He paused. "It's…it's been an honor, gentlemen…I don't know how I'll ever…" He let the thought trail off. "You guys…you, uh…you take care, now…"

"You too, Vic," Lucas said, the signal breaking up into radio hiss. "Kiss my wife for me…but no funny stuff. And take Jeff to a ball game, will you?"

Kendall smiled, despite watery eyes and the ache in his heart, for there was a special NASA brand of graveyard humor, particular to the astronaut corps. There had to be—the job would be intolerable otherwise.

"Same here," Shepherd's voice filtered in. "Tell Carol I love her."

"I will. I promise."

Lucas' weary voice, drifting in and out, was barely audible above the static. "Just about…according to the gauges…better sign off… careful going home…"

And then silence.

"Gary…?" No answer.

Kendall shut off the radio and sat within the smothering stillness of the cabin, his mind numb, his thoughts shadowed and indistinct. All hope was gone now. The faces of his compatriots hung in a diminishing vapor before him, faces he would never see alive again. To the core, his very being fought to do something, *anything*, yet there was nothing to be done. His hands shook slightly, seeking an action, awaiting a command from his brain that was not forthcoming. An insane impulse flashed into his mind, a momentary compulsion to join his friends and dive the CSM into the lunar surface, where the craft would crash and explode and hurl debris for miles as it splattered itself across the frozen desolation of Marlow—but the notion was gone as quickly as it had come.

He was passing over them now. If they looked up, they would see him as a star in the heavens, sailing steadily past, arcing from horizon to horizon. As his spacecraft soared on, out of reach a mere forty miles above them, he sat there in the quiet confines of the command module, his mind striving to cope, his will struggling to refocus upon the new priorities that had been forced upon him.

He had trained for the lone-return contingency—every CM pilot had.

But none had ever had to do it before.

Against his will, his weary eyes again sought out one dread control switch nestled among the hundreds spread before him.

SPS THRUST DIRECT ON

The words taunted him anew and more fiercely now, piercing his heart, a spectre of failure. They cried out of a reality of abandonment, of a sureness of solitude, and of a certainty of death.

He did not call Houston, did not tell them what he had heard from the surface. As his craft again slipped around the far side, Kendall simply closed his eyes hard, shutting out the pain. His welling tears, squeezed from their place, clung to his lashes in quivering droplets before shaking free, to hang in the air before him like tiny beads of crystal.

◎　　◎　　◎

11:40 A.M.

Kranz heard them as he walked up the corridor, a clipboard with a large, blue-lined notepad in hand. The muffled voices echoed down the pristine halls and grew louder as he approached. Already, within the past thirty-six hours, NASA had held nearly a dozen such press conferences, and of those Kranz had participated in more than his share. Now it had begun again, a cross-examination as menacing and perilous as any courtroom's, a barrage of questions, rumors, and accusations that only the sharpest retort could deflect.

Tired as he was, he did not feel all that sharp at the moment, and he certainly was not in a frame of mind for the hot seat. His face reflected the weariness behind it, lines and puffiness surrounding the mild redness of his dry, fatigued eyes. His shift in the MOCR had ended only minutes before, and his mind was still elsewhere, a place two hundred forty thousand miles away.

He took a deep breath and opened the door of the auditorium to the voice of NASA Director of Flight Operations Christopher Kraft. Heads turned at once upon Kranz's entrance, and he saw dozens of those in the seating area leafing anew through their lists of questions as he stepped onto the platform and took his seat at the briefing table. Already in place were Kraft and astronauts Jim Lovell, Bruce Cortney, and Deke Slayton. Cutaway models of the Apollo command, service, and lunar modules sat before them, ready to serve as visual aids if needed.

"...and as a result," Kraft was explaining, the NASA logo hanging large and bold before a shimmering blue curtain behind him, "additional quantities of all consumables are provided aboard *both* spacecraft. Those safety margins are finite, however."

"Jack Parker, *Dallas Times Herald*," a reporter stated, rising from his front-row seat. "Mr. Kraft...does all this mean that the men are already dead? There's a rumor that—"

Kraft winced, cutting him off. "No. We have *no* indication of that at this time. Our last communication with *Starlight* indicated that there remained more than two hours of breathable air aboard the LM, and that was less than half an hour ago. They also have emergency air in their backpacks."

"Why has there been no communication in the past hour?"

"Limited battery power," Kraft answered, running a hand through his thinning hair. "It's preventing them from communicating with us by voice, but once the command module emerges from the far side again, pilot Vic Kendall and the men on the surface should have short-range contact. The content of that interchange will be relayed to us. Lucas and Shepherd also have the capability of contacting us via Morse code, using their computer, should the need arise."

"Have they done so?"

"Not at this time."

"What is happening in the Mission Control Room?" a female reporter asked.

Kraft looked to Kranz, silently pleading with him to field the question. Kranz shifted slightly in his chair, poured a cup of ice water from a pitcher before him and took a sip.

"The...uh," he began uncomfortably. "The flight controllers...are still working hard to come up with a fix. As long as there remains any chance at all of bringing those men home, we'll keep trying."

"No," the reporter said. "I mean the mood. What are the men in there saying? What are they feeling?"

Kranz looked away for a second. "Well, the mood's understandably solemn. We've never been in a position like this before." He nodded in the direction of Lovell. "Even on Apollo 13, there was data to go on, information we could use to plan a working strategy. With this mission, that hasn't been the case."

Another newsman jumped in. "Are you saying that there's been a fault in the telemetry you're receiving?"

"The telemetry has been less than helpful," Slayton fielded. "But we've gotten responses from all the critical sensor points. This is a very simple engine we're talking about here. It hasn't changed since the program began. Either it burns or it doesn't, and thus far, it hasn't. That in itself is something of a two-edged sword...since it *is* such a simple machine, there are only a limited number of things one can do to effect a repair, and we've already tried them all."

"I think it's important to remember that," Cortney chimed in. "The engine in *Starlight* is identical to those that were in *Eagle* and *Intrepid* and all the other LMs before her. Those fired. For some reason, this engine has not. There's no single person or entity to blame here...nothing was done differently on this flight, as far as the ascent engine itself goes. The same contractors who built this spacecraft and its component parts built all the others, and they were successful."

"That's pretty much what we were told after Apollo 13 exploded," a man called out.

Lovell held up a finger. "There *is* a difference here. The oxygen tank that failed on *our* spacecraft failed because of damage incurred during a faulty postfactory ground test, when too high a voltage was hooked up to it. It was perfect when it rolled off the assembly line but was damaged later, before final installation. That engine up there on the moon was submitted to no such secondary testing, and there's no similar chain of events that we can point to as a possible cause."

"How long do the men have?" a voice asked. "An hour? A day?"

"Something like that," Kraft answered.

"I mean, precisely?"

"Something like that."

"Is Kendall in any danger?" another woman asked. "He's been in orbit almost two days longer than planned, as it is. Can he come home alone?"

"That is an eventuality he's trained for," Kraft nodded. "It isn't something we like to talk about, but hard reality demands we take it into account. To answer your questions, yes, he can and will come home alone, if necessary. And no, he is in no immediate danger. As I explained before, the command module always carries additional supplies of air, power, and water that we hope we won't have to use, but on every mission they're there if needed. And, in this case, we may be looking at keeping just *one* man alive on the ride home, not three."

The cold words stung Kranz and the others at the table.

"When will Kendall be leaving the moon?" asked a reporter in a blue suit.

"That may take place sometime during the next several orbits," Slayton said. "It depends on the numbers. We want to make sure we put him down in the Pacific and in daylight. And there are a lot of other variables."

"So the astronauts on the surface will be dead by tonight," an older, gruff, news-weathered man in a gray hat said, almost accusingly. "What do you plan to do with the bodies…just leave them up there?"

"We're not prepared to discuss any specifics on that at this time," Kraft replied, his patience obviously wearing thin. A murmur swept the assembled press.

Lovell stepped in. "It isn't a contingency we've ever pursued. Generally, when we're talking about the rescue of a *live* crew, there's simply none possible because of the distances involved and the complexities of planning a launch window. That's why there are so many redundant systems in the Apollo…it *has* to work. But in this particular case," he looked at Kraft, "well, it just isn't something we've considered."

"Any other questions?" Kraft asked.

"Have Lucas or Shepherd offered any last words?" a faceless voice called out.

Kraft shook his head. "No, nothing like that."

"You have to understand, people," Kranz cut in, "we're still working the problem. No one has given up here. I wish I had a nickel for every successful, last minute fix I've been a part of, both in training and during actual mission flight. If those men up there at some point were to decide to throw in the towel, which isn't likely, it would probably happen after they'd lost all ability to talk to us." He paused for a moment, something still plainly on his mind. "I *would* like to ask you all for prayer on their behalf. I think that would be appropriate at this time."

"I know those men up there," Cortney said. "We in the astronaut corps signed up knowing that this is a dangerous line of work, despite our precautions. We *all* believe that the program's well worth the loss of a few lives. There have been and there will be losses along the way as we eventually push farther out into space. Personally, if it were me up there, I'd want the program to go on…and I'm sure Gary and Charlie would tell you exactly the same thing."

"All right, then," came a follow-up, "have they said good-bye to their wives at least?"

"They have spoken to them," Slayton answered. "As to the content of those conversations, they were personal, unrecorded, and unmonitored. You'd have to ask the wives what was said"—his tone became stern—"but I'd prefer you not do that."

A NASA public affairs officer abruptly appeared and stepped onto the platform. "That's it, ladies and gentlemen," he said, much to the relief of the men at the table. "There will be a prepared statement issued at nine o'clock this evening, in this room and by Telex."

Kranz and the others rose without a word and headed for the door. They were tired and frustrated and ready to get away from the eyes and ears of the press. Kranz had been the last to arrive and now was the last to leave, pausing for a moment to watch as the reporters quickly gathered their film cameras and yellow pads and made for the doors at the rear of the room. They were anxious to reach the telephones of the newsrooms and report to their respective organizations, leaving the orange-upholstered seats of the auditorium empty for a precious few hours.

Kranz sighed, his jaw clenched, air hissing between his teeth. From past experience, he knew what the NASA public relations official had meant by "prepared statement"—it would be a brief, carefully crafted missive the like of which Kranz had not seen since the night of the fire and had hoped never to see again: "Apollo 19 astronauts Gary Lucas and Charles Shepherd died tonight when the life support systems in their stranded lunar module failed…"

He left as he had entered, pausing near the door long enough to glance at his notepad before flinging it and the clipboard into a large metal wastebasket. Only the top sheet of the clean, new pad had been written upon, and even then Kranz had scrawled only four words, words that meant nothing now, a message to himself—

Bring them all home.

He stepped into the suddenly empty corridor and headed back to Mission Control. He would not yet go home to his wife and a hot supper, not while there was still a man up there who was not yet out of the woods. Once the burn occurred and Kendall was safely in his trans-Earth coast, then perhaps. But not before.

One man was coming home.

Two were not.

And for Kranz, their ghosts would never die.

8

Bathed in frigid shadow, Lucas stepped from the LM footpad for the last time. He had not expected to feel lunar soil beneath his feet again, but as he looked upon the tiny hemispheric maps inscribed on the stainless-steel plaque mounted before him, he knew that it was not the surface of the moon he was doomed never again to know.

It was Earth's.

He looked up at the face of the craft that had betrayed him. It had condemned both him and his friend to death, a sentence that would surely be rendered before the day was out. As the LM stared down upon him, its blue-coated, triangular windows suddenly became unfeeling, mocking eyes, its hatch a laughing mouth forever open in cruel derision.

No, he realized, *not mocking—weeping. Not laughing—wailing.*

Before Lucas' watching eyes, a transformation washed over the cold, metal face. Its appearance had changed in an ethereal manner that would not have been evident to anyone else. He now saw guilt there upon the silver and black of that aluminum and Inconel countenance, a sadness forged in the unforgiving pyre of failure. Guilt. Regret. Remorse.

"It's okay," he said inaudibly, his soundless lips tracing the words as his gloved hand gently stroked the bottom rung of the ladder one last time. "You did all you could." She was no mere spacecraft, no mere machine—she was *crew*.

He turned from the LM and headed out across the valley, toward the rover waiting some fifty yards away. There Shepherd already stood, patting the passenger's seat as if in approval. He had already done what little physical preparation was necessary to ready the huge vehicle for further use, and now he waited as his commander approached, watching as a brief shower of dust kicked up with each lilting step.

Lucas knew he had seen his last full day of life. To dwell upon that fact was torture, so he shoved aside his imminent mortality and replaced it with an everyday manner some might have found unfathomable.

It was not denial. It was—living.

"Mirabelle."

"What?" Lucas asked, his boots pressing step after step into the warm lunar soil as he grew closer. "'Mere' what?"

"My father's bomber in the war," Shepherd continued, his radio-filtered voice carrying an air of fondness. "She was a B-17, a real beauty. He was the copilot…twenty-five successful missions into Germany. And later it was the name of my first car. Paid fifty bucks for her…man, what a steal…"

"You lost me," Lucas smiled, unsure of what had sparked the topic. He now stood alongside the left-hand flank of the rover, opposite Shepherd, facing him, and as he brushed a bit of dust from his seat with a gloved hand, his crewmate went on. "What are we talking about?"

"Great little car. Forty-nine Packard. Boy, if that baby could talk…"

Lucas laughed. "Where are you going with this, Charlie?"

"I think we should name the rover."

"Name it?"

"Well, sure."

"Name it what?"

"I told you. *Mirabelle*."

"Why?" he asked teasingly.

"It's been as much a part of the crew as you and me, and it's really held up its end, unlike…well, unlike a certain engine I could mention."

"Mirabelle?"

"It's a good, solid, 'rover' sort of name, with a proud Shepherd history behind it."

"What's wrong with…'Rover'?"

Shepherd rolled his eyes and shook his head, as if Lucas' question was preposterous.

"What?" Lucas asked. "What's wrong with that?"

"It isn't a *dog,* Gary."

"Well, it isn't a girl, either. Or a bomber. Or a Packard."

There was a silence as both men resisted the tugging temptation to laugh out loud. Finally, after a few moments, Shepherd raised his gold-mirrored visor, glared at his commander from within the crystal clarity of his helmet, and spoke in a serious tone.

"Don't make me come over there."

Lucas broke out in hard laughter, followed instantly by his companion. It felt good, a solid laugh after too long without. Their eyes now watering, both men used their handgrips and climbed aboard the vehicle, settled into their seats, and fastened their seat belts. As they ran quickly through the power-up checklist, their console gauges flared to life once more. Oxygen quantity readouts flickered and stabilized as the environmental unit came online.

"Man…the oh-two level's pretty low," Lucas noted. "Enough for maybe another couple of PLSS recharges for each of us, but not much more. We may as well just stay on our backpacks and refill them as we need to."

"Batteries look good, though," Shepherd smiled, reading the needles. "I'd say she's got a good sixty miles left in her. Maybe more."

"You bring the buddy hoses?"

"Yup...figured we might need them."

"Then I say we hit the road."

Lucas pressed the control handle forward, and once again the motors in each of the rover's independently powered wheels came to life. With a slight surge forward the vehicle set out once more, following tracks it had made days before, headed back toward the depths of Marlow. Lucas watched the LM Truck to his left as they passed it and took a final farewell glance at *Starlight*.

"She was a good ship," he commented. Shepherd understood his tone. The craft had been his first command.

"Yeah...yeah, she was."

Lucas hit the comm switch and glanced up at the huge, glittering umbrella antenna splayed wide above him. It faced behind them, toward the blue planet hugging the horizon. Lucas smiled, took a glance at Shepherd, then spoke, an impish grin on his face.

"Houston...this is *Mirabelle*. Do you read?"

Shepherd laughed out loud, his joyous sound once again filling the ears of Lucas' headset.

"This is *Mirabelle*," Lucas repeated. "Come in, guys. Who's asleep at the switch down there? Bruce? Jack?"

"Say again?" came a puzzled voice from a Mission Control Room quietly waiting out a period of loss of signal with the orbiting command module. *"Quest?"*

"Close," the commander replied. "It's Butch and Sundance, back on the air. The rumors of our demise have been greatly exaggerated."

"For the moment, anyway," Shepherd chimed in.

"Hey, guys, it's great to hear from you!" CapCom Cortney said. The MOCR suddenly came to life as the flight controllers jumped back to their consoles, put their headsets on, and excitedly turned their attentions to a voice they thought never to hear again. "What's the story?"

"We're back on the rover, Bruce," Lucas smiled. "Charlie named her *Mirabelle,* after the 'famous' World War II bomber of the same name. I'd like to ask that any further communications be addressed to us as such." He smiled even more widely and reached over to give his friend a slap on the thigh.

"Roger, *Mirabelle,*" Cortney came back. "Whatever you say."

"We're headed back into Marlow…we decided to take the rover as far as she'll go and see what we can find. No sense just sitting around, you know?"

"Sounds good to me," CapCom said. "We concur."

"Where's Vic right about now?"

"On the far side. He's coming up on TEI…just minutes away now."

Trans-Earth injection. *Quest* was headed home.

"Look, Bruce," Lucas said. "You do whatever it takes to make him understand that this wasn't his fault. He has to believe that, and you have to help. Katie's going to have to work to keep him on an even keel for a while, and he's going to need to talk to someone who's been there, someone who's flown."

"I imagine you're right," Cortney agreed. "It tears a man up inside to have to, well…" He paused, letting the words drop away. "Even to save his own life. And the press, and the world…who knows what they'll dump onto his shoulders."

"It's going to be worse for him than for Charlie and me, Bruce. And I know him…he'll blame himself for the rest of his life. It'll overshadow everything else he ever does. I wouldn't wish that kind of future on anybody."

"I'll do all I can, Gary…I promise you that."

Shepherd stared straight ahead, contemplating the exchange. It was true—he and Lucas would die relatively quickly, their lives ended without prolonged suffering. But not so for Kendall—he might well be bound by lingering anguish and marked by the world forever, remembered only as the man who left his friends behind to die on a lifeless ball of rock.

"We'd appreciate it, Bruce," he added. "Consider it our last request."

There was a momentary silence. "Roger," came the reply.

The edge of Marlow grew near. Both men knew that once they dropped over the edge and out of direct line of sight with Earth, they would lose communications, for the string of relay antennas they had erected were useless without a powered LM to send their radio signals on to Earth.

"We're getting close to the edge, Bruce," Lucas said. "Looks like it's about time for us to sign off."

"Good luck, guys," Cortney said, his voice heavy. "You take care…you hear me?"

"You know it," Shepherd replied. "Who knows…maybe we'll get lucky and find us a Stuckey's along the way. They're everywhere."

"If you do," Cortney said, his grief only barely concealed by jest, "pick me up a pecan log, will you?"

"Will do," Shepherd smiled.

The dark rim spread wide before them. Time for words was running out. Lucas pulled on the control handle and brought the rover to a stop.

"Look…thanks for all you've done, Bruce," he said. "You and everybody else. We couldn't have asked for better support than you've given us. I guess it just wasn't to be, this time out."

Shepherd chimed in. "And keep pushing, guys…we have to stay in space. Mars is just waiting for us. Don't let 'em kill the program. Don't let 'em turn it over to the robots."

"You have my word, Charlie."

"Okay…we're heading down into the basin now," Lucas said.

"This is *Mirabelle,* signing off. Take care, Bruce. Over…and out." He pushed the handle forward once again, and with a gentle lurch the rover pressed on.

As they dropped over the edge and started down the outer slopes of Marlow, static filled their ears. Shepherd reached out with the blue silicone tip of a gloved finger and, with a flip of a switch, shut off their radio.

They would not need it again.

◙   ◙   ◙

12:27 P.M.

At the CapCom station, Cortney pulled off his headset and let it drop onto the console before him. It clattered to the edge and fell, stopping inches short of the floor, swinging as if from a gallows on its taut black cord. Leaning on his elbows with his head in his hands, Cortney closed his eyes and inhaled deeply, letting the air fill him until his lungs hurt. His sandy hair stood like rows of new wheat between his fingers, his clammy palms against his forehead. He sighed loudly, trying not to let it all sink in, but he could not stop it. His throat felt tight. His mouth went dry. After a few minutes, he glanced up at the clock above the big screen before him.

Only a matter of hours now, and then—

He felt a hand on his shoulder.

"Go on home, Bruce," Kranz said. "Grab some lunch and get some shuteye. Nothing else you can do here. Gold Team's coming on in ten minutes, anyway…and Kendall won't come out of LOS before then."

"Okay," he said, nodding slightly, his mind numbing. "Okay, Gene. Thanks."

Slowly, the man rose from the chair and headed toward the door.

◙   ◙   ◙

Kranz watched him go then looked down at the dangling headset. He pulled it up by its cord and tapped it against the console a few times as unfocused thoughts and images danced within his mind. He saw faces encased in glass, their hopeless eyes reflecting the harsh glare of a barren land.

Their ghosts would never die—

He dropped the headset onto the station top and went back to his own flight director's console. He had sent Cortney home, yet he himself would not leave. Not with the shift change, not with the fall of night, and not with the dawn of the next day.

◙   ◙   ◙

A red Corvette convertible passed a guardhouse outside the Manned Spacecraft Center and pulled onto NASA Road 1. Dark, heavy clouds obscured the midday sun. As Cortney pushed hard on the accelerator, headed toward Clear Lake and home, the chilled winter wind rushed through his hair and roared in his ears—but not so loudly that it could drown out the distant voices that still rang there.

◙   ◙   ◙

At that same moment, on another world, another vehicle retraced the dusty tracks its own wheels had made a few days earlier, driving ever deeper into a place where nothing breathed, nothing stirred, nothing lived. Hard shadows closed in, clutching like greedy, gnarled hands at everything within their reach. The rover's headlights snapped on as it was swallowed up into the vast jealous sea of black, never again to know the light of the sun.

9

Diane Lucas sat at her kitchen table, lightly scratching at its glossy surface with a polished thumbnail. An empty coffee cup rested near her hand. Clad in a pink floral bathrobe, she stared blankly at the reflection of her nail in the deep shine of the blond wood, her thoughts a world away. She was not crying, not at the moment—she had done much of that the night before, and she was weary. The sharp, cold wind whistled outside, seeking a way into the warm, still house.

Oh, Gary—

Carol walked into the room, leaned down and hugged her friend, their friendship now forged in the fiercest of emotional fires. Their eyes still betrayed traces of red from a long and painful night, a night of denial and regrets and loss. Determined to hold back a new flood of tears, Carol gently rose, rested her hand upon Diane's shoulder for a moment, then made her way over to a nearly empty coffeepot resting on the stovetop.

"How long has this been here?" she asked, trying her best to remain strong. "When did you put it on?" When no answer came, she turned to see Diane slowly and silently nodding a disjointed yes, her eyes still fixed upon the table before her.

"Diane, honey…?" she repeated.

"Oh…a few hours, I guess," the woman replied. "This morning…sometime."

Carol dumped the coffee into the sink, ran some hot water, and filled the pot anew. Placing it back onto the burner with fresh grounds, she took a seat next to her friend. "It'll just be a bit."

"Thanks for coming over last night," Diane said, her voice low and weary. She was exhausted, and it showed. "I knew I wouldn't sleep a wink."

Carol reached out and silently held her hand for a few moments. "Right now, we all need each other, dear. You and Katie and I."

"How is she?"

"I left her last night around midnight, before I headed over here. She was holding up okay…but for her, things are a bit different. She's afraid of what all this is going to do to Vic…the pain he's going to go through and how it might change him."

"What did you tell Joey?" Diane asked. "Has he asked about his father?"

"He's at my sister's house. Spent the night there. I haven't had to face that particular problem yet. I don't know what to tell him, not exactly. What about Jeff?"

"I'm dreading hearing from him," Diane said, her voice low. "Surely he's heard by now, and I don't know where to begin or what to say. Any minute, that phone will ring and—"

"And you'll hear a voice you need to hear right now," Carol cut in. "He's a good boy, and strong, Diane. The two of you will have to lean on each other." She looked down at her hands, pausing. "I wish you two weren't so alone in this."

Diane, knowing Carol well, looked up at her friend. "You mean Jesus, don't you?"

The woman nodded, her wet eyes looking away, deep in thought. "I can't imagine trying to face something like this without Him, not now."

Diane began to cry but fought hard to keep it inside. "Why, Carol? Why Gary? Why was he taken away from me…from Jeff…?" She shook, covering her face.

Carol paused for a moment. "Heaven knows…I need Him. I'm not strong enough to handle something like this, on my own. I used to just crumble at every crisis."

"You?" Diane asked, wiping her eyes. "You're like a rock…the way you coped when your sister passed away was just…inspirational. And look at you now."

"Well, I can't take any of the credit. Back before I even knew Charlie, my father died…his heart…"

"I remember," Diane said. "You told me about it."

"I took it very badly…I shut out the world, stayed in the house all the time, brooding and letting the empty days slip away. I didn't let my mother or sisters console me at all. I was so angry at God. I barely ate a thing for weeks…" The woman managed to smile slightly, hoping to lighten the moment for her friend. "…which is a great way to lose weight, although I wouldn't recommend it."

Diane allowed herself a little smile, as well. She looked out the window, at the bare branches of the young, delicate trees in her backyard. They moved in the biting wind as if clutching at it, trying to take hold of a life-giving springtime warmth that was not yet there.

Gary planted those trees—

"Then later," Carol continued, "I met Charlie, who went to a little church up in Colorado, near Lowry, where he was stationed. He had been raised a churchgoer, but it had always been more of a social thing for him. His faith wasn't really grounded yet, even then.

"The people of that church showed me the Christ they knew.

Together, Charlie and I came to know Him too. It's the only thing that gets me through life…and I know that, up there on that moon, Charlie is drawing upon that same strength."

Diane spun her wedding band slightly, feeling the warmth there, recalling the moment the faceted gold circlet first had been slipped onto her finger. She still felt a link to Gary, a bond that spanned all distance, all time.

"They're still alive, Carol."

"I know."

"I mean it…I can feel it."

The women's gaze turned to the wide kitchen window, beyond which lay a darkened winter day that clawed at the fragile panes. In Diane's eyes it had become a compassionless world, chilled by a permeating, seemingly inescapable despair.

"Gary and I…we've never believed. I wish I could find a strength like yours…a faith like that in a God like that."

"I could introduce you," Carol said, her voice gentle.

"I'm…I'm just not ready, Carol…" Her unsteady voice fell away, into a silence that spoke deeply of the pain within her. Her eyes turned aside to fix upon a face before her, a face that was not there.

"I know," Carol softly nodded. "It would be like losing him twice…and once is more than anyone should have to bear." Her words were met with silence. "Who knows, honey…with Charlie up there with him, thumping that old Bible of his…" She smiled. Her reddened eyes glistened in the ashen light of the window.

Diane's glance returned to the warmth of the woman next to her. Their eyes met, and held, and a soothing something flowed between them, making Diane feel as she had as a small girl, nestled in the sheltering, comforting embrace of her mother.

The phone rang.

❖   ❖   ❖

5:10 P.M.

A king's ransom in gemstones and precious minerals glittered all around the two men, catching the lights of the rover as it continued toward a destination unknown.

"Well," Shepherd said with resignation, "at least we were able to *tell* the guys about these rocks."

"Man," Lucas agreed, "what those geologists would have given to get their hands on these beauties." He smiled, thinking of the man who had taught the Apollo moonwalkers everything they knew about investigative geology. "Professor Silver's probably as upset about losing *them* as he is about us."

Charlie grinned at the joke, a sly sparkle in his eye. "Real shame. We did such a good job of packing all those samples too…and there they sit, in a sealed box in a busted LM. I guess we just should have mailed them home."

Lucas smiled. "Imagine the postage."

"Imagine the purple conniption ol' Silver would have had when the post office lost them."

Both men laughed, their raucous sounds magnified within their helmets. As the laughter died away, Lucas casually looked down at his suit's oxygen gauge, just as he had done a dozen times since abandoning the landing site.

"A watched pot never boils, and a watched phone never rings," Shepherd offered, taking note of Lucas' concern, one he certainly shared. "Maybe a watched PLSS never runs dry."

"Sure would be nice, wouldn't it?"

The distinctive tire tracks from their previous expedition into

Marlow, cut clearly into the deep, black dust, now swerved beneath and past them as they drove along. They had followed the tracks all the way, and with each now-useless communications relay they passed Lucas remembered the promise of that day. It seemed so distant now, a lifetime away.

The tracks ran out. Once again, the rover crossed onto virgin ground.

"Here we go," Lucas said. "We just passed over the rainbow."

"New land. Want to stop and stake a claim?"

Five, ten, fifteen more miles fell behind them. They drove on, deeper into the depths of Marlow, deep into the viscid darkness. The world ended at the limit of their floodlight beams, dropping away into nothingness only several dozen feet ahead. The unmerciful cold, kept in check only by the heaters in their rover and their backpacks, clung with avaricious fingers to the Teflon-coated Beta cloth of their suits, waiting for its chance to seep into them.

The cold was not the only thing pressing upon Lucas.

"So, tell me, Charlie," he began, breaking the ponderous silence, "if there's a God, why do people suffer and lie dying in hospitals and go down in plane crashes and get stranded on the godforsaken moon? Good people…people who deserve better. What kind of God lets stuff like that happen?"

Shepherd paused before answering. "Popular question," he replied, "with an unpopular answer. We live in a world *we* made…a universe we made. It didn't start out like this. Right out of the hand of God, it was perfect…no pain, no suffering, no death. Those things didn't become a part of Creation until we chose to walk away from Him."

"So He's just getting even?"

"No, no," Shepherd said. "Nothing like that. When we turned away from His perfection, we were stuck with all that was left to us… *imperfection.* You can't blame God for that, Gary."

Lucas, determined to throw Shepherd a curve he could not handle, tried again.

"Well, if He's as loving as you say He is, why doesn't He just step in and put things right? If He's God, He can do anything. Why doesn't He end the suffering…why doesn't He save everybody?"

"That's the wrong question," Shepherd said.

"Okay, then…what's the *right* question?"

"The right question is, 'why does He save *anybody?*' We walked away from *Him.* He gave us everything we could ever need or want, and all He got in return was the back of our hand. He doesn't owe us a thing."

"Maybe not," Lucas conceded.

"And despite all that, since we couldn't save ourselves, He satisfied His own perfect justice by stepping in and taking the penalty *we* should have paid. *Amazing grace,* Gary."

In silence, Lucas pondered the words. They tore at something deep within him, something that stubbornly fought to keep them at bay.

Hours passed. Farther into the hidden places the men drove, exposing secrets held for ages by the intractable Marlow. Larger and more portentous boulders now surrounded them, towering massifs jutting up from the ebony soil, their scope betrayed only by the stars they eclipsed as they rose from the darkness. In addition to these, Lucas found himself having to steer abruptly from side to side in order to clear an increasing number of smaller jagged rocks that forced him to move the rover as if through a maze. The going was slow and treacherous.

"It's like driving downtown," Shepherd commented, noting the colossal stone facades on either side. "Ejecta's getting more dense. We must be getting pretty close to ground zero."

"No more sparkly rocks, either," Lucas noted. "None of the colorful stuff. Whole different geology through here…must have come from a lot deeper down. I bet there's a lot of iron out there."

"And other metals. Grade-A ore," Shepherd agreed. "I wouldn't doubt it at all. Quite a mining outfit you could run up here…"

Both men gazed up at one huge edifice as it passed ominously close along the left side of the rover, the nearly vertical face of an immense chunk of rock that towered a hundred feet upward and was canted somewhat over them, blocking out half the sky. Lucas could have reached out and touched it. Shepherd swung his portable light up and onto the sheer wall, watching in fascination as the beam played upon the craggy surface.

"Solid iron…has to be," he said. "Imagine the force that launched that baby…what an impact that must have been."

After a few moments, the rock wall fell away and receded into the darkness behind them. Before Shepherd could swing his light back into its forward position, the steady downward incline that for so long had been beneath the rover sharply gave way to level ground. The ride became smoother—*much* smoother—and the feel of the rover's wheels against the surface changed, as if their reinforced piano wire mesh no longer found the soft traction offered by the deep, powdery lunar soil. Lucas, noticing the odd variation at once, turned his full attention to the ground ahead of them.

The tiny radar screen on his console was vacant for the first time since entering Marlow. The inclinometer read zero. The floodlights suddenly found no stones in their path, no sheer walls, no obsidian soil. It was as if the vehicle had been swallowed alive by a vast expanse of nothingness that could not be pierced by quartz beams or short-range radar emissions.

"Gary…"

"Yeah…I don't like it, either…"

"Something's wrong…"

A memory flashed into Lucas' mind that seldom came to the fore. Standing behind his house on a starry April night, his backyard telescope at the ready, a young Gary Lucas had strained to locate a faint, newly discovered comet that had been mentioned in the newspaper. Unfortunately, he had made the mistake of walking outside directly from the brightly lit kitchen where he had been eating supper and reading of the find, and bedtime had come before his eyes could fully adapt to the darkness.

That night he had learned that sometimes one must first lose the light if truly he wishes to see.

He leaned forward and shut off the rover's forward floods.

"Why'd you…?"

"Kill your light, Charlie…"

Shepherd switched off the portable lamp, and the darkness fully engulfed them. Lucas could not see his hands before his face. He listened to the sound of his own breathing as it resonated within his helmet, his eyes straining to find something, anything, in the blackness ahead. He slowed the rover to a bare crawl.

"What, Gary? There's nothing…"

Then their eyes began to adjust.

"Look at that…"

There *was* something out there, in front of them and all around, scattered pinpricks of light that covered the ground—but whatever it was that now surrounded the rover, it was different from the glittering minerals they had seen before. These tiny lights were constant and crystal clear, unchanged by the motion of the vehicle, framed above by the incomprehensible blackness of the unlit and mountainous horizon and by the expanse of—

Realization began to set in. Lucas struggled with the evidence of his own dilated eyes. *No—it couldn't be—!*

Shepherd looked to his right, toward the ground just beside the vehicle. Thousands, millions of brilliant points of light surrounded them, unmoving and somehow much more distant than they should have been. Leaning over the side of the rover, he pulled the hand lamp from its mounting arm, switched it on, and looked down.

"Gary…!" he said, astonishment in his voice.

Lucas reflexively pulled back on the control handle. The rover came to an abrupt stop.

Shepherd's next words came breathlessly. "I don't believe it…!"

He stared in silent wonder at the stunning spectacle that stretched beneath him, beneath the rover. His face was bathed in the warm light of his hand lamp, which, though pointed downward, nonetheless also shone upward from below.

Rather, its reflection did, with crystal clarity.

The glittering display all around them, the impossible lights shining beneath them, mirrored from above, were *stars*.

10

Lucas reached down and opened the rover's tool compartment, the glow of his suit light gently bathing the rear of the vehicle.

"What do you think it is?" Shepherd asked, still playing his portable flood against the glass-smooth ground next to the vehicle. "Some weird lava flow?"

"Beats me," Lucas said, reaching in for a long-handled rock hammer. "Something this smooth and this extensive...I don't know. A sheet of obsidian, maybe?"

"Whatever it is, it flowed like crazy and leveled out before it cooled. It must be a mile across, I'd bet...maybe more, since the radar isn't seeing anything."

"Reminds me of a skating pond," Lucas commented. "Annie's parents had one out behind their house, up in Michigan. But even that wasn't as mirror-perfect as this stuff."

"Whatever it is, it's good and solid. The weight of the rover isn't affecting it at all."

Lucas walked around to Shepherd's side of the vehicle, gripped a handrail, and braced himself against it. Leaning down as best he could in the bulky pressure suit, he swung the steel claw of the hammer into the hard, level surface beneath them. Then again and again. The sharp contact barely made a mark.

"Man…tough stuff."

"Are you breaking the surface at all?" Shepherd asked, noticing that the suit light attached to his commander's chest box was aimed too high and not at the ground. He adjusted the hand lamp to throw more light onto the target of Lucas' hammer.

"Thanks, Charlie…that helps." He swung again, much harder this time. "Well, I *think* I'm getting somewhere…made a few stress marks. If I can hit the same spot a few times, maybe I can get it to…" Again the hammer impacted the glossy mystery beneath his feet, and again. "If I can hit it just right…"

Another swing, and a small chip came free. Lucas paused, his labored breathing sounding heavily within his helmet. "There…got it."

"Way to go, Skipper," Shepherd smiled.

Lucas bent over and with blue rubber fingertips picked up the half-dollar-sized piece of material. Bringing it over into the light of Shepherd's lamp, the two men examined it closely.

"Beats me," Lucas said. "Awfully clear for natural glass."

He handed the sample to Shepherd, who turned the half-inch thick sample from side to side and watched as the lamplight passed cleanly through it. "Sure looks like ice, doesn't it?"

"Yeah, but it can't be…not in a vacuum, not like this," Lucas said. "It's impossible. Out here, liquid water couldn't last long enough to form such a smooth surface. It would boil away and turn to vapor…or rather, snow."

"I know, but look at it."

"Has to be glass…or quartz, maybe. Must have flowed up out of the mantle during the heat of the Marlow impact."

"Something this perfect?" Shepherd held it up before his faceplate, looking through it at the lens of the lamp. "Glass?"

"Most of the soil up here is glass, Charlie. You know that."

"Yeah, but look…there isn't an impurity in this anywhere."

"Maybe cooling in one-sixth gravity made a difference somehow. I don't know...sure would be nice if Silver were here."

"I've got an idea," Shepherd smiled, unfastening his seat belt. Stepping down from the rover, he took the piece of mystery material and moved toward the front of the vehicle.

"What are you up to?" Lucas smiled.

"How hot is this casing, do you think?" he asked, indicating the insulated metal cover of the forward heater core.

Lucas walked over and looked down at the miniature nuclear furnace. "Pretty hot. Even with the insulation in there, and with this cold...I'd guess it's around two hundred degrees up top. Maybe three."

"That's about what I'd figure."

Shepherd extended his hand and set the chunk of material directly onto the metal cover. At once, the sample began to *melt* from beneath, boiling violently away into the vacuum around them before instantly refreezing as fine snow.

"Will you look at that..." Shepherd said, astonished.

"Well, I'll be..."

In seconds, the sample was gone, having become a wintry dusting that encircled the core housing and whitened the framework at its base.

"Frozen hydrogen? Or methane?" Lucas wondered, astonished.

"Not cold enough for that. Even out here."

There was a heavy silence as Lucas accepted the evidence of his eyes, however incredible.

"*Water,*" Lucas conceded, looking out at the mirrored stars of the great ice sheet around them. "Somehow, it's water. Millions of gallons of it"—he turned to look at Shepherd, a wry stubbornness entering his voice—"which doesn't change the fact that this is clearly impossible."

"Water on the moon," Shepherd whispered in wonder. "Think of it..."

"Must be miles across. Who knows how long it's been here? Had to have come in with whatever impacted to make this basin…a comet, maybe."

"This much water? Wouldn't it have vaporized in the heat of impact? And why isn't there any soil or dust mixed in with it?"

Lucas smiled. "Well, let's hear *your* theory, Dr. Sagan."

"I don't have one," Shepherd admitted. "Not yet. Too early to call."

As the men moved back toward the sides of the rover, Lucas noted with new astonishment each step he took upon the glassy surface. He paused to toss the hammer back into its bin.

"This is big, Charlie," he said, closing the compartment lid. "This is important…if only we could tell Houston. They should know about this…it could make the difference in whether they decide to appropriate the funds for a moon base or not."

"They'll find it eventually," Shepherd commented, climbing into his seat. "When they find *us*…a hundred years from now."

"Thanks a lot," Lucas said, mounting the rover. "I'd kind of forgotten about that."

He reactivated the rover's floodlights and pushed the drive handle forward. With a slight jerk they began again, moving deeper into the ominous void of Marlow, neither man speaking, their lives ebbing away with each breath they took. Lucas, knowing that anything of any interest would likely lie at or beyond the edge of the glacial sheet beneath them, turned to the right and hugged the shoreline as he drove along.

"Wow," Shepherd said, shaking his head. "Who'd have thought…this ice alone justifies every penny ever spent on the program. And then some."

"What I wouldn't give for enough battery power and oh-two to get us back out of this basin and into radio range," Lucas said. "Just ten seconds of good, solid communication…that would do it."

"Might as well ask for a highway from here to Houston."

"Yeah, I know."

"Speaking of oh-two," Shepherd commented, checking the oxygen gauge on the console, "that last PLSS refill about did it. Not enough left for another. We also used the last of the carbon-dioxide filters."

"C-oh-two should be the last of our worries."

They let the thought fade into prolonged silence.

"Man, look at this place," Shepherd finally said, changing the subject. "My granddaddy and I did a bit of ice fishing when I was just a knee-high astronaut…and if I'd known that you and I were gonna find a lake up here, I'd have brought a pole."

A twinkle shone in Lucas' eye.

"Okay…this guy's sitting on the ice, with a bucket, a saw, and a pole," he began, chiming in with a joke. "He cuts a hole into the ice, sits on the bucket, and puts his line in. After a short while, this booming voice says, *'There's no fish there.'* The guy looks up and doesn't see anyone talking anywhere, so he keeps on fishing. Doesn't get a single nibble. After a few minutes, the same voice, from out of nowhere: *'There's no fish there.'* So the guy moves to a different spot, a ways off, and cuts a new hole. A little time passes, and he still doesn't get a bite. The same voice sounds again, only more insistently, *'There's no fish there.'* Finally, the guy looks up and asks nervously, 'Is this God?' And the voice says, *'No…it's the rink manager.'*"

Shepherd broke into hard laughter. His guffaws were music in Lucas' headset. Tears filled the man's weary eyes as the stress bled away, if only a little.

"It wasn't *that* funny," Lucas smiled.

"Yeah, but I'm tired," Shepherd replied, trying to catch his breath. "And I never heard that one."

"I got it from Conrad," he grinned. "Had to clean it up, though."

"I bet you did…"

Both men roared anew, taking extreme joy in the moment. Neither had slept in almost twenty-four hours, and the laughter fed upon their fatigue.

Suddenly, Lucas realized Shepherd wasn't laughing anymore. He looked to his right and found an expression of deadly concern within the faceplate of his friend's helmet. The man was looking down at the readouts atop his chest box, his brow furrowed, his eyes darting.

"What, Charlie? What is it?"

"I just got a tone, Gary…"

"What's wrong? What do your indicators read?"

Shepherd had heard an electronic warning in his headset, the voice of his pressure suit speaking to him. The tone could mean three things—either his oxygen flow was too high, his suit fan was malfunctioning, or—

"I'm losing pressure," he said, reading a gauge on his right wrist. "PSI's down to two-point-nine and falling. Oh-two gauge is dropping too."

"How fast?"

"Fast enough."

Shepherd began to reach for a metal lever mounted to the side of his chest unit, the activating switch for the emergency oxygen supply mounted atop his backpack. Called the Oxygen Purge System, it was a sealed unit consisting of two small, highly pressurized spherical tanks that operated independently of the backpack's systems. Acting alone, it could supply a man with enough air to keep even a leaking suit pressurized for up to thirty minutes.

"Hold it, Charlie," Lucas said sharply, stopping him. "Are you snowing anywhere?"

Shepherd looked down at his legs and torso, then at each arm, watching for a telltale spray of ice crystals. "Doesn't look like it…but I can't see every place."

Lucas stopped the rover abruptly and jumped out of his seat. Moving quickly to Shepherd's side, he leaned down and looked closely at the seams of his companion's suit, checking for some evidence of a pressure leak.

"Put your light down here."

Shepherd pulled the portable lamp from its mount and held it low. Lucas took it from him, stretching its curled power cord to the limit as he held it close to the soiled, once-pearly white fabric of the man's suit.

"I don't see anything, either. Not in your suit, anyway…"

Lucas considered the buddy hoses they had brought, a pair of umbilicals that, if absolutely necessary, could allow one man to live off of the air in another man's suit. But before he resorted to that, shortening both their already limited lives, there was one other option.

Handing the light back to Shepherd, the commander reached down and picked up the loose ends of the umbilical hoses at the man's feet, hoses connected to the rover's life support system. He then climbed up onto the floorboard and stood over his imperiled crewmate.

"Let's hope it's the backpack, and not the suit itself," Lucas said, reaching out to disconnect its supply hose from a fitting just below Shepherd's chest unit. Tossing the useless umbilical away, he rammed the curved metal end of the rover's feed hose into the now-vacant, blue aluminum coupling and clicked the seal shut. After also replacing the suit's outflow hose, he reached over and pressed a button on the forward console.

"Keep your fingers crossed," Lucas said, watching the readouts as the rover's much-used environmental system came to life once again.

Shepherd heard a new flow of air within his helmet and felt a cool breeze against his sweat-beaded face. With hopeful eyes he peered at his wrist gauge. Slowly, the tiny needle began to rise. It came to a stop a few moments later.

"That's got it, Gary!" he said triumphantly, intently watching the gauge. "Back up to three-point-seven…just like the doctor ordered."

Lucas leaned down and connected the backpack's dangling air feed umbilical to the rover's fill valve. Activating a purge pump, he began to drain the damaged unit's remaining oxygen into one of the vehicle's tanks.

"I hope we haven't lost too much," he said as the precious gas flowed into the rover. Air's kind of hard to come by up here." After several minutes, the oxygen quantity readout for Shepherd's backpack read zero and Lucas removed the now-useless hose from the rover.

"That was a close one," Shepherd said, relief in his voice.

"And so you don't cook and/or freeze in that suit…" He switched out another hose, connecting Shepherd to the system's water-feed line.

"Scoot forward a little, " Lucas said, moving behind him. "I want to check the plumbing." Leaning in over the side of the rover, he adjusted his suit light and examined the damaged backpack closely, pulling back its padded cloth cover in order to expose some of its inner components.

"See anything?" Shepherd asked. There was a pause before the answer came.

"Yup…there's a buildup of ice back here. Looks like one of the feed lines picked up a stress leak somewhere along the way."

"Probably happened when we threw it out the hatch."

"I bet you're right," Lucas nodded. "Judging from the way it was lying, it probably caught the rim of the footpad. Maybe a weld cracked, and after a while the leak got big enough to cause real trouble."

"Glad I didn't have to tap the OPS just yet…but I'm sure to need it in a few hours, anyway."

"We both will."

"How long do you think the rover's air will last?"

"Well, with what we just put back in…longer than it would have." He paused, standing beside his friend and crewmate. "You okay?"

"Yeah," Shepherd smiled. "Thanks, Gary."

Lucas smiled as he returned to his own seat. "Wait till you get my bill...*then* see if you want to thank me."

They sat quietly for a moment. Shepherd looked up into the starry void and said a silent prayer, thanking his Lord for his continued life.

Lucas also gazed into the heavens above them, pondering the astonishing vastness and magnificence of the universe, his mind darkened.

Is Charlie right? he wondered skeptically. *Are You really up there?*

He gazed at a single star of incomparable brilliance.

If You are—why did You leave us here to die? What kind of God—?

He expected no answer and heard none.

They stared into the expanse above, their suited forms side by side, their hearts a million miles apart. It was a timeless moment, one shared by two men who walked the same perilous road, yet on two different paths.

Lucas pushed the handle forward, and they were under way once more.

◫   ◫   ◫

Sunday, March 2, 2:56 A.M.

The room was quiet, even for the middle of the night. No one joked, no one moved, no one spoke. One reporter, flicking the edge of his press pass with a thumbnail as he sat in the darkened viewing room, would write the next day that the place carried the feel of a funeral chapel, not a spaceflight nerve center. A tangible fog of defeat hung in the air, weighing heavily upon all within, wringing any sense of accomplishment from the mission. So they had landed at the lunar south pole. So they had made incredible discoveries there. So what.

There was no consolation prize when good men died.

Cortney walked into the MOCR, carrying a cup of hours-old coffee in one hand and a revised flight plan in the other. He climbed the steps to the second tier of control stations and made his way along, studying the faces of those around him. No one looked up as he took his place in the CapCom's seat, nor reacted when he caught the tangled headset cord and spilled his coffee on the console.

Mopping up the lukewarm brown puddle, he looked up at the clock. In four minutes, he along with the rest of the world would know if the third member of the Apollo 19 crew was headed safely home.

"CapCom's go, Flight," Cortney called into his headset as he finally settled in. "Bright-eyed and bushy-tailed."

"Okay, Bruce," the flight director replied. "I hope you got some rest."

"Enough."

If all had gone as planned, Kendall's CSM should have burned its engine during the backside of its current and final orbit of the moon, sending it out of orbit and earthward. The burn would have lasted only minutes, bringing *Quest* around the edge of the moon and back into radio contact at a precisely calculated moment.

"Coming up on acquisition of signal," the public relations officer, seated in the upper row, called into his microphone. "One minute, thirty seconds. Standing by for AOS."

Every controller in the room watched his console screen, waiting for the telemetry that would fill their readouts with scrolling numbers, each declaring the condition of some part of the spacecraft. As was common during times of stress, some held fast with both hands to their stations' so-called security handles, the grips by which the rack-mounted television monitors at each could be removed for servicing.

"One minute," the flight director called over the link. "On your toes, people."

Cortney glanced to his left. There, Dr. Charles Berry, the flight surgeon, was readying himself for the biosensor data that would, at any moment, flood the screen before him. Cortney noted the three sets of indicators labeled there, bearing the names of three brave men, flat lines that with peaks and valleys earlier had signified the heartbeats and other vital signs of the Apollo 19 crew.

Everywhere there were reminders. Everywhere.

"Standing by," the public relations man repeated.

At once, and right on time, every screen in the room was filled with illuminated digits that jumped like frightened things, flickering for an instant before aligning themselves into readable information.

"We have good data," the communications officer called over the link. "Telemetry is go."

"Welcome back, *Quest*," Cortney called into his microphone. "This is Houston. We see you're on your way home."

"Roger that," came the curt reply.

"We'd like the residual numbers on that burn, Vic, as soon as you've got them."

There was no response. It was an unusual quiet, one that hung uncomfortably within the MOCR.

"*Quest*, Houston," Cortney tried again.

"Uh, look," Kendall's voice finally began, breaking slightly. "I need a few minutes up here…um…" There was a long pause, too long. Just as a concerned Cortney moved to hit his comm switch again, other static-laced words sounded on the speakers. "Just give me a minute."

"Houston, standing by," Cortney replied. He looked down, then glanced again toward the flight surgeon's console. Sure enough, data on

Kendall's physical status was filling the screen under the watchful eye of Dr. Berry.

◙   ◙   ◙

Berry's eyes jumped from the heartbeat and respiratory readouts to the pulse rate and endocrine displays. He scrutinized the screen for a moment then sadly nodded, knowing what story the data told. He had seen such readings many times during his years of service, at hospital bedsides, in training, and at war. He dropped his head then flipped off his monitor and looked away as if to allow a distant patient a moment's privacy.

They were the readings of a weeping man—one who was grieving, cruelly haunted by two empty flight couches.

II

Sunday, March 2, 3:12 A.M.

Lucas felt the change. Beneath him, even through the multiple layers of his pressure suit, he felt it.

The rover was dying.

Finally, after so many hours of faithful service, *Mirabelle* had done all she could. Lucas and Shepherd had followed the shore for many miles, watching the black dust beach and the ground just beyond for any sign of the extraordinary, any glimpse of the peculiar—rather, any *further* peculiarity. But now the rover's lights had dimmed perceptibly, its forward speed had dropped slightly, and its steering was more sluggish. Its batteries were nearing the point of depletion, and when they failed, they would fail quickly.

Shepherd soon would lose the life support the hardy transport had to offer, and his lifespan would be numbered in minutes. Lucas looked over at his sleeping friend, knowing their time was drawing to a close, and momentarily considered letting the man sleep peacefully through the end of his life. Wouldn't that be more humane, after all? Wouldn't that be what any man would ask for?

Your average man, perhaps, Lucas knew. *But not someone like*

Charlie—a man trained to push the envelope, to live life to its fullest and face its most dire challenges head-on—

Lucas pulled back on the control handle, stopping the rover abruptly. The vehicle rested some twenty feet from the shoreline, still upon the glassy surface of the impossible lunar glacier.

"What is it?" a waking Shepherd asked. "Where are we?"

"End of the line, Charlie," Lucas said, shutting off the rover's lights. A fluid darkness surrounded them, stifling in its totality. "Not much left in the batteries, and we need what there is to keep your pumps going…for as long as they can, anyway."

"What does the power gauge read?"

Lucas reactivated his suit light. "Just about zero," he read. "But maybe there's a bit left in the tank, anyway."

"Maybe she's like my granddaddy's old pickup truck," Shepherd smiled, retrieving his suit light from a small storage bay next to his seat. "That thing still had a hundred miles in her after the needle hit empty."

"I hope you're right about that."

"How far did we get?"

"Check it out," Lucas smiled, checking the odometer. "A little over eighty-seven miles. This baby was built to last, that's for sure."

Lucas rose from his seat. "I'm going to head down the shoreline a bit, on foot. I think I saw the glint of something up ahead…caught our headlights sort of funny. Just for an instant, though. I'm not sure."

"How far have we traveled on the ice, do you think? Just how big is this thing?"

"Well, according to the navigation system we've been moving in a fairly gentle curve, following the shoreline for the last thirty miles or so. Either it's just long and narrow, or it's *really* big."

"Well, I'm impressed in either case."

"I'll be right back…you sit tight."

"Wish I could come with you," Shepherd said, looking down at the umbilicals that connected his suit to the rover. He finished attaching his light to the bracket on his suit, and turned it on. "But I'm kind of tied up at the moment."

Lucas looked into the eyes of his friend. "Promise me that before you tap your reserve oh-two you'll take every possible second of air out of the rover's tanks."

"You got it, Skipper," Shepherd smiled. "That's an easy one."

"Good man."

"Keep in touch."

"You'll be so sick of my voice you'll be tempted to shut off the radio." Lucas headed for shore. "I'll be back in a few, as soon as I check this out."

"I'll be here," Shepherd waved.

◙　　◙　　◙

Lucas walked on, his feet sinking slightly into the dark soil ashore. In a few short minutes, the man was some distance away and all Shepherd could see was the small white pool thrown by his suit light.

"Nothing yet," Lucas' voice sounded. "I'm almost sure I saw something up here, though…"

"What kind of thing…was it?" a yawning Shepherd asked.

"Beats me…just an odd reflection. Probably a mineral outcropping of some kind."

The beam of Lucas' suit light grew smaller as he started around a bend in the shoreline. Shepherd watched the distant, dancing pool of white as it moved upon the ground and against some stone bluffs, which rose beside the ice in the distance. His commander was barely discernible now, and he had trouble making out the man's movements.

"I wish I had a pair of binoculars," he said. "Not that I could use them with this helmet on…"

"Wish me a sandwich while you're at it," Lucas kidded. "I'm starving."

Shepherd gazed up at the constant stars, ever amazed at their beauty. "Look at all the stars," he began. "That's the galactic core, right there…beautiful. Beautiful." He yawned again and his tired eyes grew wet, blurring the dazzling points of light into dancing, flowing streaks.

"Sure could use a Motel 6 right now," he called. "Or an Air Force cot, for that matter."

A glint from within the open storage compartment next to Shepherd caught his eye. Smiling, he reached into it and withdrew a plastic Ziplock bag containing his Bible, his son's astronaut figurine, and the locket for Carol. The book's worn, gilded pages caught the beam of his suit light. He again thought of the day his father had given it to him, out in a boat and on a lake, one not so different from the one that sprawled beneath him at the moment. He smiled at the comparison.

Of course, the lake back home had not been frozen, and this lunar miracle was not likely to have been stocked with trout. But Shepherd nonetheless felt a warm and welcome connection with that day, with his father and with the Lord whose Word he now held in his hand.

He still was very tired. Even normally, every movement within the pressure suit was an effort, and just wearing the cumbersome thing was work. A full day of doing so took its toll on the human body. He laid his head back against the padded helmet liner, his eyes closing of their own volition, his body demanding rest once more.

"Hey, Gary," he called, half-asleep, "remember in the LM…how I told you there was no fence…?"

He paused, waiting for a reply. None came.

In a moment, he was sound asleep.

◙   ◙   ◙

Lucas made his way along the shoreline, his light revealing the soil ahead only a few yards at a time. The dark was so thick, so stubborn.

"Keep an eye on the gauges," he called, reminding his crewmate. "Hit that OPS the second you have to."

He had walked a few hundred yards without seeing anything noteworthy and was about to turn back when something ahead caught his light in the same odd way he had noticed from the rover. He hastened forward, bouncing along in the low gravity as quickly as the uneven, rock-strewn surface would allow, finally nearing a most extraordinary—*something*.

His light fell upon it more fully. Lucas paused, his mind not accepting what was before him. Cautiously, he stepped closer.

"Charlie...I don't believe it."

It rose from the dusty soil, its sizable base resting mere inches from the edge of the ice sheet. Gleaming metal with an odd, pearlescent sheen glittered in the meager beam of his suit light, metal fashioned into an enormous structure of astounding complexity. Its surface bore an intricate array of geometric shapes, all flowing from one to the next with an organic fluidity that defied any manufacturing process Lucas could envision. It rose beyond the range of his light, disappearing into darkness some forty feet above.

"I found something, Charlie...!"

He walked around the object, studying it, seeking anything that might indicate a doorway or other entrance. Whatever it was, it was certainly big enough to be occupied—Lucas estimated the size of its base at twenty feet square. He circled it twice, three times, four times, yet could find no obvious point of entry.

Gleaming metal pipes over two feet in diameter protruded from the base of the structure on the glacial side and followed the downslope of the shore, eventually disappearing into the ice. There were six such conduits, equally spaced, extending from the building like the tines of a fork. A few other, larger pipes rose from the soil and connected to the metallic enigma at various points along its height.

"What are you?" Lucas whispered, moving closer. He leaned in, running a hand along the outer surface of the object, and encountered a deep rectangular depression, perhaps two feet tall and three feet wide, between two of the large, ascending conduits. Lucas detached his suit light and held it higher in order to get a look into the squarish hole, which was only a couple of feet deep.

The light fell upon an intricate, circular arrangement of hundreds of crystalline facets, all interlaced in a polished silver framework. Its myriad colors—reds and blues, yellows and greens—were all of the purest value, surrounding a glossy central disk of perfect black that shone oddly in the light.

Bracing himself with one hand against the edge of the opening, he leaned in and held his suit light closer to the dark, dinner plate–sized conundrum, trying to discern its purpose.

After a few moments, he felt a vibration through the layers of his glove. Lucas yanked his hand away from the structure, startled by the sudden activity. Inside the rectangular bay, the array of crystal facets began to glow, dimly at first, but growing ever brighter.

He pressed the visor of his helmet against the metallic shell of the structure and *heard* it—a powerful whine, rapidly magnifying in intensity, the hungry roar of an enraged beast rising from hibernation after a long sleep.

The once-black disk at the center of the crystalline array now glowed a blinding white, surrounded by a hypnotic display of brilliant, pulsing color. Backing away, Lucas almost tripped over another, smaller conduit line, largely buried in the lunar soil, that led away from the base of the structure and continued farther along the shoreline than the others. He followed its length with his eyes and saw it disappear into blackness beyond the range of his suit light.

A tone sounded in his headset, startling him.

Lucas looked down at his oh-two quantity gauge. It read zero-zero. His PLSS was empty.

He reached to the side of his chest-mounted control box and flipped the lever that so patiently had awaited activation. The emergency oxygen supply atop his backpack awoke, flooding his suit with its limited reprieve.

His life had just become horrifyingly finite. He had thirty minutes left.

"Charlie…I had to activate my OPS…how are things on your end?"

No reply.

"Do you read me, Charlie?"

Silence.

He held up his black Omega watch, strapped by a long band around the left wrist of his pressure suit. He had been gone from the rover for fifteen minutes already.

He did not know why he was getting no answer from Shepherd, but he did know that it would take fifteen minutes to go find out, if he headed back. That would be half his air, half his remaining time, and the exertion would not allow him to reduce his airflow in order to prolong his life any further. If for some reason Shepherd were already dead, and Lucas then attempted to return and follow the buried conduit, he could not get any farther than he was right now before his air ran out.

But if Charlie was still alive, the only chance they *both* had to survive—if it existed at all—must still lie ahead of them.

Setting the timer ring on his watch for half an hour, Lucas made a hard decision.

He turned and began to follow the conduit as it led him farther around the bend, away from everything he knew and toward whatever awaited him.

Away from the rover and Shepherd.

◙   ◙   ◙

Lucas did not witness the full awakening of the colossal machine. As he left it behind, the entire structure began to glow with a faint bluish light that overlaid its gleaming metal skin, revealing the entirety of its towering form.

Nor did he see the sight that unfolded at its foundation, a sight that could not be, yet was.

Ripples began to move there as the ice responded to the rekindled energies of the mechanism, creating gentle waves that reflected its unworldly light as they radiated outward, lapping gently against the divergent metal conduits that had given them birth.

And water flowed upon the moon once more.

◙   ◙   ◙

"Charlie…"

Shepherd awoke with a start. "Read you," he instinctively uttered in reply, his mind still clouded. A headache pounded fiercely within his skull, forcing him to wince as he tried to open his eyes.

"Hello…?" he spoke again, his thoughts unfocused.

He knew he had heard a voice. He had heard his name spoken.

Did I dream it?

His hands rose to grasp his throbbing head but were stopped short by the barrier of his helmet. "Oh, yeah," he mumbled, sitting up as straight as he could in the rover's seat. He struggled to awaken but swam in half-sleep.

The pulsing headache assaulted him anew, pressing against his eyes, his temples. He fought to think, to get a grip on where he was.

The rover—the moon—air!

He looked down at the gauges on the rover's console, laboring through haze-curtained eyes to read their telltale figures. He clumsily moved his suit light to shine more fully upon them.

Oh-two, zero-zero. Power, zero.

The rover had died.

Shepherd felt his consciousness slipping away.

NO—! There's something I have to do—something—!

Years of astronaut training kicked in at the last possible moment, shoving his confusion aside, and he managed to activate the lever on his chest box. Instantly, new life rushed into his suit, into his helmet, flooding his lungs with oxygen. He breathed the cool air deeply and greedily, sweat stinging his eyes. It began to bathe his brain, bringing him back from the edge, returning him to full awareness.

"Thank you," he whispered as he gathered his wits. "Thank you, sweet Jesus."

He reached down and freed himself of the now-obsolete hoses that bound him to the carcass of the rover, then stood up, his calves cramping with the effort. His arms and legs ached. His head pounded with each motion, a symptom of oxygen starvation and carbon-dioxide poisoning that now would subside.

Shepherd reconnected the water-feed line of his backpack and turned on its temperature control system. It worked, and at once he could feel the water as it circulated through the fine, interlaced tubing of his undergarment. He picked up the bag containing his Bible and the other personal items, said a fervent prayer of thanks, and slipped the bag securely into a deep utility pocket on the left thigh of his pressure suit. Steadying himself against a yellow handhold bar, he paused to make sure his balance was restored before stepping down onto the ice.

"Good-bye, *Mirabelle*," he smiled, patting the rover's floorboard as he stood next to it. "You were one fine lady."

Shepherd knew that relaxed, passive breathing might gain him well more than half an hour of OPS time, but walking over uncertain terrain in a pressure suit was anything but passive. He set the timer ring on his watch for the standard thirty minutes, then turned and headed out across the ice, taking careful steps. "Gary?" he called into his microphone, but no answer came back. "Gary, this is Charlie…do you read me?"

He looked in the direction Lucas had gone but saw nothing. Only darkness, the stars above, and their reflections in the frozen mass.

Something had changed, however.

The reflections in the distance were *moving*. The mirrored points of light that had been so rock-steady now were wavering, and whatever was causing the odd motion appeared to be spreading, growing rapidly closer.

Shepherd moved more quickly toward the shoreline, wary of a slip on the glassy ice yet even more fearful of whatever it was that was bearing down on him. When he was ten feet from shore, he looked again and saw the phenomenon only a few yards away to his left, almost upon him.

And then it was.

He suddenly fell as if through the ice, coming to a jarring stop as his boots met solid ground two feet below. He almost fell in the low gravity but took a panicked step forward and managed to keep his balance.

"What the…" he began, looking down to find the last thing he thought he would ever see on the moon.

He was standing knee-deep in water.

Shepherd reached down and scooped up some of the liquid in his gloved hand, but the instant he pulled the water clear of the lake's surface it boiled into vacuum and fell from his fingers as snow. Slowly he waded forward, carefully keeping his balance, rising higher out of the water with each step as he neared the shore. As he rose, the exposed wetness on the legs of his suit also boiled into vapor, surrounding his limbs with a fine white haze as it instantly froze, as it must.

At least, as it *should.*

He stepped up onto the bank, fully out of the water now and dry as a bone. Looking back, he shone his suit light onto the lake and watched the seemingly gelatinous surface as it undulated slowly in the low gravity, gentle ripples catching the starlight as would any lake at night back home.

"That's impossible," he uttered in disbelief, knowing the temperature of the basin around him to be an unmerciful 340 degrees below zero.

He brought the light up, shining it farther out, where the rover had been. The faithful vehicle now was submerged in some eight feet of water, almost entirely vanished from sight. Only the coppery, fabric mesh umbrella of its high-gain communications antenna still was visible above the surface.

Knowing his time was short, Shepherd turned and set out along Lucas' path down the ebon beach.

Twenty-seven minutes.

12

"Nineteen, Houston," Cortney called. "How are you doing, Vic?"

"It's *Quest*," Kendall insisted, his tone sharp. "Not *Nineteen*."

There was a pause as Cortney, his face contorted in a grimace of self-chastisement, looked over at Kranz. *How could I have slipped up like that?* The flight director nodded, motioning for the man to relax and keep his focus.

Both men understood the difference. As a flight progressed, the designation for the spacecraft changed depending upon the phase of the mission taking place. On the way from the Earth to the moon, the combined craft was addressed by its mission number. However, once separation of the modules had taken place, two call signs were used— one for the CSM and one for the LM. Only after the two craft had redocked and the astronauts were reunited was the spacecraft again addressed by its unifying number.

Quest and *Starlight* had not redocked. The men had not been reunited. Kendall was not going to let that fact be minimized, not in any fashion, however trivial.

"Roger, *Quest*," Cortney nodded. "We fully and apologetically concur."

He paused a few moments, listening to the silence in his headset, dreading having to bring up the next subject. Only moments earlier, a planned spacewalk had been cancelled, one during which Kendall was to have retrieved the film he had shot of the lunar surface, orbital views taken by cameras mounted into the side of the spacecraft's service module. It was not an exercise to be undertaken by a single man, without the backup of a crewmate who normally stood by in the open hatch, just in case.

"Vic," he reluctantly went on, "they've decided to forego your EVA and forget about the SIM bay. We can't afford a full cabin depress and, uh...since you're...uh..."

"Since I'm alone they don't want me going outside," Kendall said for him. "Right?"

Cortney, his head down, did not want to answer.

"Roger that," he finally confirmed. "Just...take it easy and try to get some sleep."

◙   ◙   ◙

Seventeen minutes.

Shepherd checked his watch again, following the bootprints left by Lucas during his earlier foray into the dark. He rounded bend after bend, weaving between huge rock outcroppings, making his way steadily forward.

"Gary?" he tried again. There had been no answer, and Shepherd had grown fearful of his crewmate's fate.

Then he saw something resting on the beach at the water's edge.

Softly glowing, it stretched upward almost sixty feet, an immense silvery monolith rooted to the soil by huge fingers of polished metal. A half-dozen of them extended into the lake, which lapped thickly and gently against the shore. Another partially buried conduit led into the distance, down the beach and out of sight.

The impressive machine did not look like anything a human mind would have conceived or like anything human hands could have constructed.

What in the world—?

He paused for a moment, reached out warily to touch it, and felt a gentle vibration through the fingertips of his glove.

No time—!

He realized Lucas must already have given the object a reasonably thorough examination, for his tracks completely encircled the thing several times before continuing on, into the black unknown. Reluctantly, Shepherd moved on, following the pipeline and the treaded bootprints as they led away.

His stomach growled fiercely. His muscles protested with each step, each movement. Every part of his physical being was nagging of neglect, begging for attention. He drove himself onward through the thick lunar dust, following the beach, the reduced gravity causing him to move almost gracefully despite his exhaustion.

The conduit soon vanished into the soil, but the succession of footprints continued, following the water line. Another five minutes passed, slipping inexorably away as Shepherd pressed forward, fearing what he might find at the end of the trail. Apprehension built within him, fed by the eerie silence of his radio.

"Gary?"

A vague and whitish form appeared ahead, the beam of his lamp barely reaching it. It was ghostly—and familiar.

"Gary...?"

Shepherd approached, fear filling him. Still a dozen yards away and only dimly caught by the light, the shape was much too still, shrouded in menacing darkness. It rested quite near the water's edge.

"Gary...answer me..."

The heavily clad figure was sitting on a huge rock and leaning against a rough stone wall, the side of a colossal boulder. It wore a white pressure suit. Its arm was raised, its hand held in an awkward position before the visor of its helmet, as if looking at it. Its pose was as if carved of stone.

Shepherd saw something on the ground, at its feet.

A glove—!

NO!

The raised hand was naked, bare skin against unforgiving vacuum, its fingers rigid, clutching at nothing.

Shepherd momentarily stopped short and looked away, horror-stricken. His heart pounded, climbing into his throat. His breathing staggered and became erratic and shallow. After a moment, gathering his resolve, he forced his feet to move again.

His light fell upon the body fully as he grew close, only a dozen feet away. He saw the figure distinctly now and in terrifying detail, but the clarified image only tore at his mind with new talons. Breaking from one whirling torrent of confusion only to be engulfed by another, Shepherd stared in disbelief.

Whoever the dead man was, he was not Lucas.

Filled by a tremendous wash of relief, Shepherd drew alongside the man. The white pressure garment that clothed the corpse was quite similar to an Apollo moonsuit but was different in many critical ways. His visor shielded a horror of a face, one frozen into an eternal expression of sorrow, with frost-coated eyes that stared ahead, unseeing and devoid of color. His hair was short and stark white. His exposed hand, like the rest of his body, was apparently human but on a much greater scale—Shepherd estimated the man would have stood at a height of some eight feet.

"Who were you…?" the stunned moonwalker wondered aloud. "Where in the world did you come from…?"

"I don't think he's gonna answer you," a voice sounded in his headset.

Startled, Shepherd swung first one direction then the next, seeking the man he knew must be there. His light finally fell upon Lucas, who had appeared from behind the angular, house-sized boulder against which the mysterious body had been leaning.

"Gary! Oh, man…!" Shepherd rushed to his friend, and an imminent bear hug was stopped only by the constraints of his pressure suit. "I thought this poor guy was you…at first, anyway…oh, man, am I glad to see you!"

"Likewise, Charlie," Lucas smiled.

"What happened? Where were you?"

"Long story. The radio wouldn't work, and I couldn't get through to you…"

"Same with me. Has to be all the iron out here…got between us maybe."

"Probably. Anyway, right after I found *him*"—Lucas indicated the unearthly corpse—"well, my suit light gave out and I was stuck in the dark. Couldn't see a thing. Not until you came along, and I spotted the spill of your light against those rocks over there."

"Who do you think he was?" Shepherd asked, looking with pity upon the dead man. "Looks like he killed himself."

"Who knows…but I'd guess he's been dead a while. Could be he was a part of a failed Russian mission, one they covered up."

"Russian? Look at the guy…he's huge."

"Maybe they're growing them big for the space program. Maybe they shaved a gorilla. I don't know, Charlie…in any case, it doesn't matter now."

He pointed toward the ground. "Whoever he was, he left footprints. They have to lead back to wherever he came from…maybe back to a lander. I was about to follow them when my light conked out."

Shepherd nodded his approval, checking his watch. "I'm down to eleven minutes, here…whatever we're going to do, let's do it."

They continued on, Shepherd in the lead, his light on the trail of bootprints. Minutes passed, precious minutes. The trail led on, winding along, tracing the beach and cutting through boulder fields.

"I don't see anything yet," Shepherd said. "Just more prints."

"Charlie…"

He stopped to look back at Lucas, who was struggling to stay on his feet.

"What's wrong, Gary?"

"So…tired…"

Lucas began to drop to his knees. Shepherd caught him then looked down at the man's oh-two gauge. It read zero.

"Gary…your OPS…!" Shepherd reached for the lever, but found it had been thrown already.

"Used…that…before…"

"Come on!" Shepherd cried out. "Stay with me here!"

"Headache…can't see too good…"

Lucas was passing out and Shepherd was struggling to support his weight, causing him to use his own dwindling oxygen supply even faster. He checked his watch again.

He was one minute past his time.

I'm still getting air—

Shepherd practically dragged Lucas for a short distance before finally letting him drop to the soft lunar soil. Leaving him for a moment, he walked a few steps forward, past and around an outcropping of angular boulders.

Looking down in desperation, he found a jumble of new footprints pressed into the soil, hundreds of them, atop and beside each other, all leading toward and away from something just ahead. Walking another fifteen feet, he brought his light up and discovered salvation.

It was a door.

Cut into the jagged stone of a cliff face, it stood open, ten feet wide and fifteen high. Beyond it was a darkened, circular chamber, one that had to be—

An airlock!

"Gary!" he shouted, turning from the discovery, rushing back to his friend. In moments, he reached Lucas, who lay terribly still.

As he bent to lift his fallen crewmate, his own airflow abruptly ceased. The hiss in his helmet died away.

The residual oxygen in his suit would last only a couple of minutes.

"Gary! We found it!" He grabbed Lucas' right arm and pulled, half lifting the man and half dragging him, face down. Though Lucas' spacesuited form weighed only fifty pounds in the one-sixth gravity of the moon, Shepherd struggled. The exertion was too much. The air inside his helmet grew hot and moist and stagnant.

"Help me, Lord," he prayed, his breaths hard and ragged. "Please help me…"

Dragging his motionless friend across the dark soil, he backed toward the door, his head pounding, his breathing shallow and rapid. A whine filled his ears.

He pulled Lucas through the open door and into the chamber, dropping the man's limp arm once they had reached the center of the smooth, dust-coated floor. He labored to reach the wall next to the doorway, frantically seeking a way to close it.

He fell hard against the unyielding metal and unclipped his suit light with uncertain fingers. Holding it before him, he prayed for its beam to show him a switch or lever.

There was none.

There was, however, a glossy disk of perfect black that shone oddly in the light.

Shepherd's knees began to fail. His head swam, and he leaned heavily against the wall, his awareness fading. He dropped his suit light, which skittered and came to rest a few feet away, shining across the floor.

He looked back and up through the doorway. The stars outside, increasingly, were blocked from view by something—something *moving*. The black disk on the wall now glowed white.

A door was dropping, eclipsing the portal through which they had just passed. Still leaning, Shepherd felt a solid impact reverberate through the wall as the door hit bottom and locked into place, sealing the chamber.

He slid to his knees then fell limply onto his side. He thought he heard a roar, a thundering rush that echoed beyond the shell of his helmet.

Something caught his eye, moving in the beam of the fallen light. Beyond the haze of his rapidly fogging faceplate, he saw the dust they had tracked in swirling in tight circles, mounting up from the floor—

—and into the *air*.

In a desperate gamble, Shepherd reached over with shaky fingers and released the pressure seal of his left glove. Pulling with all of his remaining strength, the glove came free and air rushed through the breach.

Into his suit, not out.

He felt the sweet icy flow move into his helmet, and drew of it deeply. His lungs filled readily, bathed in pressures they had not known since before the launch.

Frost appeared but for a moment on the walls and ceiling, a white rust that left a glistening film of moisture as it warmed and vanished. Something had begun to heat the chamber. The thickening atmosphere grew more comfortable.

Gary—!

Shepherd crawled over and tore loose the padded visor assembly covering the man's pressure helmet. Releasing a catch on the red metal attachment ring that held the fogged bubble secure, he twisted the helmet counterclockwise, pulled it free, and tossed it away.

"Gary!" he cried out, lightly slapping the unconscious man's face again and again with his bare hand. "Come on, Skipper…don't leave me here alone…"

Shepherd reached up and removed his own visor assembly and helmet, hurriedly casting them aside before removing his other glove and turning back to Lucas. The man was not breathing.

"Gary! Wake up! Stay with me!" He pulled the insensate man's headset cap away and began mouth-to-mouth resuscitation, and after a few desperate efforts was rewarded as Lucas, eyes still closed, convulsed and drew a sharp breath.

"Yeah!" Shepherd smiled. "That's the way…"

The man began breathing on his own. Shepherd, himself exhausted, fell to one side and came to rest, his head against the cool, polished floor.

After a few minutes, the weary LM pilot gathered enough strength to strip himself of his spent backpack, and its dead weight fell aside with a thud. After removing his own headset cap, he pulled himself over to a wall and leaned against it, sitting up, watching his commander as the man continued to regain consciousness. Finally, Lucas' eyes fluttered open and he struggled to one elbow, obviously confused.

"Take it easy, Gary," Shepherd said in a reassuring tone. "Lie still. Let your brain come up to speed."

"What…" the man began, his gaze unfocused. "Charlie?"

"Yeah, Skipper. It's me."

"What happened?"

"Close call…another minute and we'd both have been goners. But we're okay now. You just relax."

Shepherd looked at the circular chamber surrounding him. Its walls and ceiling were of a bronzelike metal. Ornate, lustrous silver support braces ran up the walls and arched inward above, meeting at a central ring overhead. Faceted light strips stretched from floor to ceiling, casting a warm, gentle light within the room.

Another door, still sealed, loomed opposite the one they had entered. Life would lie there, if at all, he knew, beyond its mysterious, steely face.

He looked down at the pressure gauge on his wrist. It was pegged at the high end, telling him what he already knew: The air pressure in the chamber was much higher than that in his suit had been, possibly higher than that at Earth's sea level. Breathing came easily, and the increased oxygen was soaking into his tissues, healing his addled mind, his overburdened muscles. He put his head back, shut his weary eyes, and waited for much-needed sleep to overtake him.

"Charlie…?" Lucas began, his awareness still coming back.

"Yeah?"

"Where are we?"

"Long story."

"We were on the moon…"

"We still are."

"My air was gone…"

"So was mine."

"Where's the rover?"

"At the bottom of the lake."

"The *lake?*"

Shepherd smiled. " 'No fish there…' "

"How did I get *here?* Where is this?"

"I dragged you."

"Dragged me where?" Lucas almost pleaded. "Come on, Charlie, where are we?"

"Stuckey's," Shepherd grinned, his eyes still closed. "They're *everywhere.*"

13

Sunday, March 2, 7:30 P.M.

Gene Kranz sat alone in his office, awaiting the moment he had been dreading for hours. Cold, harsh night filled the world beyond the windows, the wind whistling sharply through the young, bare trees outside. A green-shaded lamp to one side threw an island of tinted light across the top of the desk; the rest of the room swam in shadow. The walls, covered with commemorative plaques, framed photos, and crowded shelves of flight plans, textbooks, and technical reports, stood silently by as the overworked man remained unmoving, staring at nothing, an untouched cup of coffee growing cold before him.

He thought back to that first day upon the Cabean plain, when the moon still seemed to welcome their trespasses, when with overflowing hearts two men had gazed with new eyes upon the surrounding, rolling lunar hills—just as Moses long before must have embraced the sight of the land of milk and honey promised to his people.

So much pride, they all had felt. So much pride.

As his drifting eyes moved across the well-used room, they eventually came to rest upon one prized, circular item of burnished metal that shone in the dim light—a ten-inch-wide, mounted stainless-steel replica of the Apollo 13 mission emblem. Upon its gleaming surface

134

were engraved heartfelt words of deep appreciation, words written long before by once-endangered men whose lives had been spared:

TO GENE KRANZ
"WHITE FLIGHT"
THE BEST THERE EVER WAS
FROM THE GRATEFUL CREW OF APOLLO 13
JIM LOVELL   FRED HAISE   JACK SWIGERT

White Flight. It was a nickname Kranz treasured, one the stalwart leader of White Team had gained following the Apollo 13 mission. He had led his men in the almost impossible task of bringing the badly crippled spacecraft home when the odds had said it could not be done.

White Flight had said otherwise.

Cherished images filled his mind, images of triumph and flag-waving and applause in Mission Control as three brilliantly colored parachutes opened, filling the main screen with glory where none had appeared for days.

Of course, finally, there had been cause to celebrate. The legendary power of "the vest" was not to be denied.

For each mission since the Gemini days, his wife had made for him a new vest, always white and sewn with silver thread, and each vest had become a symbol of mission success for the men of the White Team. Even after the flight of Apollo 13, it was said—with tongue planted firmly in cheek—that "the vest" had seen to it that the crippled vessel had returned home safely. For Kranz, wearing the garment was not so much superstition as tradition, symbol more than sortilege, as was the fact that he began the morning of each launch day by coming into the office before any of the controllers arrived, in order to stand alone at attention and listen to a rousing version of "The Star Spangled Banner," followed by the occasional Sousa march.

That was the system, and it always had worked.

But now, victory had vanished, and lethally so.

Only two weeks earlier, Kranz had watched Lucas take his first step from the forward footpad of *Starlight* at the base of her ladder. It had been a proud moment, but one ultimately unlike any other in the American space program, and its significance had not been lost on those who watched from their consoles at the Manned Spacecraft Center.

There should have been a eulogy.

Seven times before they had beheld a similar image, and seven times before they had waited in amused interest to hear the words each mission's commander would utter as he planted his first footprint into the powdery lunar soil.

Those first words—each moonwalker's soul speaking to the ages. From the sublime to the silly, the words had come, from Neil Armstrong's immortal, "That's one small step for man, one giant leap for mankind," to the diminutive Pete Conrad's, "That may have been a small one for Neil, but it's a long one for me," to Fred Haise's classic, "Better late than never," on Apollo 18. Each time, Kranz and the others had watched the almost surreal scene in silent anticipation, careful not to be involved in conversation or otherwise distracted when the words came.

Then came Gary Lucas' turn. Before their eyes the man's grainy image stood, his pressure suit marked by a commander's red stripes on his helmet, arms, and legs, his right hand upon a rung of the ladder. When he stepped from the footpad, his boot well below the limited view of the television camera, his voice poured from the speakers.

"These are our last steps on the moon, for now," he said, the words filtered by the slight crackle of distance, "but with vision, they will also be our first steps through the gateway to the stars."

Leave it to Lucas to throw down a gauntlet. The statement would make a fitting epitaph for the Apollo program, and Kranz was certain it would be remembered as just that. They had witnessed a swan song.

Nineteen was the end of the line.

A little over two months earlier—one week before Christmas—unexpected budget cuts had canceled the flight of Apollo 20 despite the fact that its hardware already had been built and was standing in a full stack, awaiting disposition, within the Vehicle Assembly Building at Kennedy. NASA now had no funding for ground support for the once-planned mission to the crater Copernicus, and without the men in Mission Control, the men of the communications network, and those on the recovery carrier, the bird would not fly. Kranz, for one, was so proud to be a part of the American space program that, if asked, he would have worked the mission for free.

But then, he *always* would have.

Here it is, less than six years after the triumph of the first landing, and it's all over but the shouting. He found that he simply could not bring himself to think of the Apollo program in the past tense. Not yet.

The original plan had called for a small moon base to be in place by 1976. Then the date had been pushed back to 1978, then 1980, then who knew when. Kranz knew that turning their backs on the moon in such a manner was tantamount to forsaking their children's future in space—*we've walked upon another world, and now we're just going to leave it? We should have a base up there. We should keep a presence up there.* The ball had been dropped and, to his astonishment, everyone seemed content just to let it lie there, kicked aside and forgotten.

Have we learned nothing?

NASA launched Skylab in 1973, and it still drifted safely in Earth orbit, awaiting the crews who on occasion would arrive to keep it company. The station would remain up there for at least another five years, meaning at least another five manned launches, and for that reason Pad 39A was to remain Saturn-friendly and would not be modified for use by the upcoming space shuttle program. Some on Capitol Hill had wanted NASA's Saturn launch capability scrapped altogether in favor of total commitment to the shuttle, eliminating the nation's heavy-lift booster capability, but fortunately wiser heads had prevailed and the great rockets—the technological wonder of their day—would stay.

Let 'em have 39B, Kranz thought, staring at a framed photo of the Apollo 10 launch, *but leave my Saturns alone.*

The reverie broke. He looked down at his watch.

It was time.

With a familiar click, he switched on a small desktop radio, its gold-tone dial shining in the meager light. Always tuned to a local news station, he often listened to it during the workday as his nonflight duties allowed.

The still air filled with a deep, resonant voice, one permeated with hard-earned authority.

"...must interrupt our regularly scheduled programming to bring you this special address by the president of the United States. We take you now to the White House."

Kranz gazed blankly upon the warm, polished woodgrain of the radio's casing, unblinking, dreading the words that would pour from its fabric-covered speaker. Another voice sounded, one that in recent days had become all too familiar.

"My fellow Americans, I speak to you tonight from the Oval Office. The unfortunate events of the past few days, following so closely and so cruelly on the heels of what appeared to be such a triumph for our nation and for the human spirit, have certainly diminished us all. Two of the three brave souls who departed our warm planet aboard Apollo 19, who on behalf of us all ventured so far from home in their noble quest for knowledge, will not be returning to us. Fate has ordained that these men, who went to the moon to explore in peace, will stay on the moon to rest in peace.

"These brave men, Gary Lucas and Charles Shepherd, know that there is no hope for their recovery. But they also know that there is hope for mankind through their sacrifice. These two men are laying down their lives in mankind's most noble goal—the search for truth and understanding."

The words pierced Kranz like daggers, striking deeply.

"They will be mourned by their families and friends; they will be mourned by their nation; they will be mourned by the people of the world; they will be mourned by a Mother Earth that dared send two of her sons into the unknown.

"In their exploration, they stirred the people of the world to feel as one; in their sacrifice, they bind more tightly the brotherhood of man.

"In ancient days, men looked at the stars and saw their heroes in the constellations. In modern times, we do much the same, but our heroes are epic men of flesh and blood.

"Others will follow and surely find their way home. Man's search will not be denied. As we continue our quest for the stars, men will die out there among them. But these men were the first, and they will remain foremost in our hearts—for every human being who looks up at the moon in the nights to come will know that there is some corner of another world that is forever mankind."

The voice and its torturous words fell silent. Kranz turned off the radio, drew a few deep, arduous breaths, and let welcome silence dominate the room once more. His eyes drifted to the treasured steel plaque, and he momentarily clung to that warm spring day when tragedy had turned to jubilation.

But that was long ago, and such miracles were no longer forthcoming.

Not this time, he forced himself to acknowledge, a ponderous and oppressive sorrow filling him, making it difficult to breathe. *Not these men.*

Wiping a tear from his eye, he rose from his desk, turned off the lamp, and headed for the door. There was work yet to be done. Two hundred thousand miles out in the emptiness of cislunar space, and growing closer each second, was one man who still had a chance to reach home.

One man.

14

Monday, March 3, 9:43 A.M.

"Charlie…did you pack the car?"

Shepherd stood near the hallway in his living room. He turned his head to find Carol standing to one side, at the entrance to their kitchen. She wore a summer dress, the pink one Charlie had given her for her birthday, and held in her arms a small, shaggy blond dog that panted loudly.

"Charlie?"

"Uh…yeah," he tried to recall. "I think I did, hon."

Footsteps suddenly sounded behind him, and a shoulder banged into his own. Moving slightly to one side, Shepherd saw Kendall walk by smiling at him as he moved fluidly past. The man wore a helmet-less pressure suit of an older design, the silvery apparel of the Mercury flights. Kendall continued onward, into the foyer and out the open front door.

Another man passed Shepherd, dressed for a moonwalk. The man nodded, and Shepherd reached out to pat him on the shoulder.

"Hey, Ed," Shepherd said with a smile. "You coming too?"

"Sure, Charlie," Ed White nodded. "Wouldn't miss it."

Shepherd looked toward Carol, who stood petting the black,

panting longhaired dog. It was then that he noticed the line of men coming down his hallway, emerging from the den and headed toward the front door, following Kendall and White.

"I guess I missed the party," Shepherd said.

"Not really," Jim Lovell replied, closing a small, leather-bound book he carried. "You're just in time."

One by one they passed. Aldrin, Borman, Schweickart, Grissom, a dozen others. All dressed for flight, all headed for the door. Finally, Lucas walked past, bringing up the rear.

"We don't have all day, Charlie," he said, headed outside.

Shepherd ran over to Carol and kissed her on the cheek. He could smell her perfume. "I won't be long, Carol."

"I know."

He patted the head of the dachshund she held and turned for the door, suddenly realizing that, like the men ahead of him, he was wearing a pressure suit. He emerged into bright sunlight and headed for the driveway, where his maroon station wagon waited. Up on blocks, its tires were gone. Several of the astronauts were already aboard. Others stood chatting with neighbors who had walked over to say good-bye.

Shepherd slid into the driver's seat, plugged his umbilical into the dashboard; the doors suddenly sealed with the loud, decisive clank of locking latches. He was alone. The hiss of air sounded within his helmet. He reached out to close the glove compartment, careful not to lean into the wedding cake on the passenger seat.

With a roar, the engine fired. Shepherd's gut sank as the car propelled itself upward. He loved the sensation. He always had. In the rearview mirror, he could see that he was alone except for the excited, panting St. Bernard in back.

"Easy boy," Shepherd smiled. "We'll be there soon."

He pulled back on the flight stick. Upward they arced, and the Earth fell away. The sun shone brilliantly upon the hood of the car, forcing Shepherd to lower his gold visor to cut the glare. It became dark within his helmet, so dark he could not see.

The hiss faded away. He opened his eyes.

Suddenly, he was not where he had been. Suddenly, he was no longer in the car but in a room, an odd room, in a place he did not know—not until a moment had passed, and with it the disorientation of sleep.

Shepherd rubbed his eyes, rolled over, and sat up. He was on a hard, polished floor, one dusted with dark gray soil. As the seconds passed, he began to remember.

Lucas stood at the mystery door, examining its edges, studying its seals. As Shepherd began to move, the commander turned to see him stirring.

"Good morning, sleepyhead," Lucas smiled.

"Morning," Shepherd winced, squinting as his eyes adjusted to the light. "What a dream…"

"What happened?"

"I can't remember…it's gone now. I think I was flying a dog." He noticed that his commander had stripped down to his white cooling garment, which in appearance was not too dissimilar from the long underwear Shepherd's grandfather once had worn.

"Sounds exciting," Lucas smiled.

"How long was I out?"

The man checked his watch. "Almost fourteen hours. I just got up myself, maybe twenty minutes ago."

"I must have been beat. I never sleep that long."

"Oxygen deprivation'll do that to you."

Shepherd reached up to scratch the beard that had blossomed upon his face over the past few days. "I wish I had a razor."

"You and me both."

"Man, am I thirsty. And starving."

"Can't help you with the food," Lucas began, pointing at their spent backpacks. "But do what I did...get some cooling water from those. Tastes sort of metallic, but any old port in a storm."

Shepherd opened a drain valve, cupping the freed water in his hands, and drank. Momentarily satisfied, he glanced around the room, familiarizing himself with its odd lines.

"Did you say something about a *lake* earlier?" Lucas asked.

"Oh...yeah. Well..."

"You mean the ice, right?"

"Sort of..."

"What, Charlie? What did you see?"

"Something happened. The ice melted...there's water out there now."

"That's impossible."

"So what else is new?"

"That big machine," Lucas thought aloud. "I must have activated it somehow. All I did was look at it, and things started to light up...I never touched anything, though."

"That would fit."

"*Liquid* water? You're serious?"

"Yup. The rover's air ran out. I'd just left her and was heading out to find you. Suddenly, the ice got all weird and melted right out from under me. The rover sank right to the bottom. I had to wade to shore."

Lucas considered the story. "I'd never have believed it...but after finding this place, whatever it is..."

"What do you think?" Charlie asked. "Russian base?"

"I don't know who else could have gotten up here...but come to think of it, I hope not. If it *is* theirs, they're *way* ahead of us."

"I remember seeing a lot of footprints outside. You reckon there's anyone else here?"

Lucas looked around the room. "Not likely. If there was, you'd think they'd have rescued the guy we saw out there, or at least have buried him. And it looks like no one's taken any notice of us."

Shepherd considered his own hand, recalling the horror of the frozen and forgotten man. "What do you think happened to him? Suicide…or murder?"

"No way to know. A better question is how long ago did it happen? How could the Russians be so advanced that they could have gotten up here and built this base while we were still figuring out basic orbital flight? Putting up a place like this must have taken years."

"At least."

"And if they beat us here, why didn't they say so? They're sure not the type to win a race and keep quiet about it."

"China, maybe?" Shepherd guessed, not really believing the suggestion. "But we never detected any launches…"

"Hmmm," Lucas began.

"What?"

"You don't suppose…"

"*What?*"

"Aliens," he said dramatically, "from outer space."

Shepherd shook his head at the suggestion. "I'm not ready to go there yet."

"It kinda makes sense, Charlie. At least more sense than the Russians or Chinese. We've been watching them pretty closely. And how do you explain that lake out there?"

"I can't…but I'm not buying the Martian theory."

A slight smile crossed Lucas' lips then was gone. "You don't believe in flying saucers, Charlie? Or life on other planets?"

"Nope."

"But what about the probabilities? With all those stars out there, you don't think there's intelligent life tooling around?"

"I haven't seen any."

"Neither have I," Lucas conceded. "But the math says they're there, and I'm just wondering how long it'll be before we meet up with them."

"Well," Shepherd said, "first I'll wonder which country back home was advanced enough to build this place."

"You really think someone from Earth did this?"

"They must have, Gary."

"Why?"

"For one thing," Shepherd began, holding up the Beta cloth bag containing his Bible, "doesn't seem to be much room in this book for space folks."

"I knew it," Lucas smiled. "You old preacher man...you should have tried for the pulpit."

Shepherd smiled softly. "Naw. I'm not the type. Too much of an itch in my britches. I always had to keep moving...keep flying higher and faster."

A few silent moments passed.

"So, why isn't there a fence?" Lucas suddenly asked.

"What?"

"What you said before, about me sitting on the fence..."

"Oh," Shepherd nodded. "Long time ago, I felt pretty much the same way about things as you do now. But then I figured out that just like you're either physically alive or you're not, you're either *spiritually* alive or you're not. Took me a long time to see that."

"I don't think it really matters what you believe, as long as you believe it."

"Lots of folks feel that way. But there's a deep logic to Christianity that I just couldn't get around."

"Logic?" Lucas asked, his brow knotted. "I thought it was just a faith thing. Feelings and all that."

"No, no," Shepherd replied. "It goes a lot deeper than that. This is an orderly universe…not perfect anymore, but orderly. That's why orbital mechanics and the other laws of physics are so fixed. There's a basic logic underlying everything. Ours is a God of both compassion and order." He held up his Bible bag again. "Same goes for the book He gave us. It has to be for real."

"I don't know," Lucas said. "I don't see how a lot of the stuff in there *can* be real."

"Well, I know what I know, and if you're meant to see things differently, Gary…you will."

Shepherd managed to stand then stretched. Stiffness filled his limbs. His joints ached, but not badly. After removing his pressure suit, he adjusted the lay of his cooling garment and joined Lucas, who had gone back to scrutinizing the walls and door.

"Must be ten feet high," Shepherd observed, his neck craned toward the top of the doorway.

"Our friend outside was a big fella, remember?"

"Any idea how to open it?"

"None," Lucas admitted. "No sign of a handle or lever or switch anywhere. Just that black disk on the wall… I hoped it was a touchplate, but when I pressed it nothing happened. Must be a concealed camera or something. How did you get the other door open?"

"It was open when I found it."

"Okay, then…how did you close it?"

Shepherd looked back at the outer door. "I don't know…it just closed. And then the air pumped in."

"You must have done *something*."

"Well," he recalled, "I looked for a switch, but I never found one. I'm fuzzy on that…I was about out of air. And it was dark in here then…I remember using my suit light."

"The light," Lucas mused, as something clicked. "You know, now that I think about it, that thing out by the lake reacted when I shined my light against it…" He indicated the dark round object next to the door. "Maybe you *did* find the switch, Charlie."

Lucas turned and crossed to their discarded and scattered equipment. Finding Shepherd's darkened suit light, he picked it up and found the toggle already in the on position. In a futile effort, he clicked the switch.

"Dead," he said. "Like mine. Now what?"

"Well, if these doors really are light-activated, then whatever turns them on must be around here someplace…right?"

"Better be," Lucas said, "or we spend the rest of our short lives in here."

The men scanned the room. One panel, protruding slightly at a point high on the wall, stood out.

"Looks like it might open," Shepherd observed. "It's way up there, though."

Lucas walked over and stretched as high as he could, but his fingertips fell well short. "My kingdom for a stepladder."

Shepherd dragged their empty backpacks over to the wall and stacked one atop the other. "Try this, Skipper," he suggested. "Might be just enough."

Lucas climbed atop the packs as Shepherd steadied him, and tried again. His fingers barely reached the bottom of the panel. He slapped at it, his angle awkward.

The panel popped open slightly. Lucas slipped the tips of his fingers beneath the metal plate and swung it open farther still, revealing a shallow storage compartment. Small devices of gleaming metal and polished crystal hung on racks within it, waiting for use.

"Jackpot!" Shepherd smiled. "You think?"

"Looks like," Lucas agreed. "But I'll need another foot or so in order to reach 'em."

"Coming up," Shepherd said. Leaning against the wall next to his commander, he cupped his hands to form a step up. Lucas lifted one leg and placed a foot into his crewmate's hands.

"Ready?"

"You only weigh thirty pounds here, remember?" Shepherd replied, bracing himself. "I could probably do this one-handed. Go."

Lucas pushed upward, lifting himself also with one hand as he grabbed the lower sill of the storage compartment. He reached up into the racks and grabbed two of the hanging devices with his free hand, accidentally knocking a third loose to fall onto Shepherd's head.

"OW!"

"Sorry, buddy," Lucas laughed. "Got 'em…you can let me down now."

"With pleasure."

Back on solid ground, Lucas handed one of the units to Shepherd and began to examine the other. The object had a flattened, rectangular handle of iridescent silver metal, inscribed with an intricate and artistic pattern of curved lines and geometric shapes. At the tip of the device was a faceted, teardrop-shaped head of clear crystal, which glistened and seemed to capture the light of the room.

"No switch," Shepherd observed, scrutinizing the device in his hand. "How do you turn it on?"

"Beats me. But assuming this isn't a ray gun and just works the doors, it must use the same wavelength as our suit lights."

"Don't point it at me, just in case."

Lucas shook the device, squeezed its handle, tried to twist its head, tapped it against the wall and did everything he could think of to activate it. Nothing worked. "I dunno. Maybe the batteries are dead…no telling how long these have been hanging here."

"I'm gonna try it anyway…" Shepherd walked over to the untried door and raised the device. Before it grew too near the black disk, he paused.

"Gary? What if this thing works…and we find out the hard way that *this* door opens to the outside too?"

"Then," Lucas said, "we die today instead of a week from now. We're on borrowed time anyway."

"Right," Shepherd nodded. He raised the unit and held it close to the black disk, watching its glittering reflection there.

The proximity ignited a glow within the crystal, an ember that rapidly swelled to become a brilliant, blinding white as the device came fully to life. In response, the black disk began to radiate as well, matching the brilliance of the crystal with an ethereal light of its own.

There was a rumble as a slumber of ages came to an end. Lifting from the floor, the door began to open, a rising curtain revealing a chance for life.

Shepherd took several steps back, pausing next to Lucas. His heart pounding, he watched as the door continued to rise. There was only darkness beyond, and his eyes fought to adjust. Finally, the portal was fully open before them and the reverberation ceased. A deep silence filled the air.

"After you," Shepherd said, dark humor lacing his words. "Rank has its privileges."

"Thanks."

Lucas stepped forward, his eyes searching the void ahead. As he reached the threshold, lights flared to life before him.

They revealed a straight corridor that sloped gently downward, stretching a dozen yards beyond the doorframe. Vertical lightstrips, spaced equally along its length, bathed the passage with warm, inviting light. Its walls and ceiling, cut with grooved, linear facets that ran their length, were made of the same bronze-tone metal as those of the airlock chamber. Its floor, also like that of the airlock, was polished smooth.

Shepherd paused to retrieve his personal-items bag from the leg pocket of his pressure suit then followed as Lucas stepped cautiously into the corridor.

There was another door facing them, directly ahead. Unlike those the men had seen already, there was a symbol upon its steely face. Like the others, it was sealed shut.

Sealed—and waiting for a key.

15

Monday, March 3, 10:02 A.M.

It was such a beautiful craft.

Bruce Cortney gazed upon the contractor's model on his desk, a scale replica of an Apollo lunar module. Her builders had presented the vehicle to NASA and to America after many designs had been drawn up and rejected, after many mock-ups had been built and rebuilt. She had wound up a ship designed purely around function, with little consideration given to aesthetics and with every possible pound of weight trimmed from her already lean frame. Yet, despite this, she was gorgeous, the first true spacecraft, a creature built for a vacuum that could not function in a planetary atmosphere.

They had come to embrace her, the astronauts of the Apollo program. She had carried them to the moon, had given the world the fulfillment of a dream it had desired for as long as mankind had walked the Earth. She was a lovely maiden of glittering gold and sparkling silver, a precision-built treasure unlike any other. She was a miracle, a testament to the inventiveness and determination of man.

But now, like an executioner's blade, she had struck down two good men.

He was tempted to hurl the model across the room, but buried the impulse. Doing so could not help matters, of course, and the last thing anyone in the building needed right now was to yield to the sorrow and frustration and anger that had descended upon them all.

Stay focused—there's still a spacecraft out there.

His discipline did not, however, save the pencil he held in both hands, which yielded to his pent-up grief and splintered with a sharp snap.

As if in response to the sound came a knock at his open door. He looked up to see Diane Lucas standing in the doorway, her face devoid of its usual lively expression. She wore a dark blue, almost black knee-length dress with a broad white collar. In her delicate hands she held something squarish nestled loosely within a brown paper bag.

"Oh, Diane," Cortney said, standing. "Please, come in."

He quickly circled his desk to arrange a chair for her, grabbing a small stack of telemetry reports from its seat and dropping them aside. The woman took a few steps into the room, glancing around as she approached.

"I've never been in your office before," she said. "I think I've seen more of this building in the last two days than I saw in the ten years before that."

"Oh?"

"I've been making the rounds all morning…thanking you all for your efforts."

"Sit down," Cortney said gently, motioning toward the chair. "What can I do for you? Name it."

Diane took a seat in the plush chair, clutching the package to her chest. "I want to thank you for last Friday…for your kindness." Tears welled up in her eyes, but she bravely held them back. Cortney found himself fighting the same battle.

"It was the least I could do, Diane," he said, remembering the headset. "The very least."

"Bruce," she said, looking down at the wrapped something in her arms, "I have something for you. Gary always said he wanted you to have it if…" Her voice died away.

"Oh…I couldn't, Diane…"

"No…he wanted it." She reached out and set the object onto his desk, atop the paperwork that lay there.

Cortney leaned forward and picked it up. Her eyes met his, a deep reassurance within them. He slowly pulled away the heavy brown paper.

It was a framed photo, a black-and-white eight-by-ten of Lucas and him standing next to their T-38 trainer jets on the flight line at Ellis Air Force Base. In the picture, Cortney was looking directly into the camera, his expression one of quiet, military dignity. Lucas, standing next to him, seemed equally somber—until one noticed that his raised hand was behind Cortney's head, his first and second fingers visible above the man's hair, poking up like antennas.

A laugh broke through, and Cortney shook his head. "I *always* hated this picture."

"It's been hanging in our den for years," Diane said.

"I know," Cortney said with mock derision.

"Your friendship meant a lot to Gary," Diane said. "I wanted you to know that."

Cortney looked at the years-old image, seeing it with new eyes. "I do know, Diane. And he meant more to me than I can put into words. He was a good friend…no one on Earth I'd rather have on my wing, watching out for me. Knowing him was a privilege."

She smiled. "He used those same words about you just a few weeks ago."

There was a pause, a painful silence.

"You doing okay?" Cortney asked.

"No," she admitted. "With time, maybe. Right now, I feel like I want to die. It's been really hard on Jeff, too…and that worries me.

He's shut me out the last couple of days, ever since he got home from the trip…stays alone in his room."

"We all grieve in our own ways," Cortney said. "Try not to take it personally…it's the pain that's driving him right now."

"I know that. But I need him…we need each other."

"Just be there for him. That's all you can do."

She rose and stepped around to the side of the desk, near the door. Cortney met her and held her for a few moments, letting her draw strength from him. He could feel the pain inside her.

"Anything you need, Diane," he said quietly. "I mean that. We all feel that way. You call any of us, any time of the day or night. We'll be there."

"Thank you, Bruce," she smiled, a wet mascara smudge beneath one eye. Cortney pulled a handkerchief from his pocket and wiped it away.

"Better," he smiled.

She moved to leave, pausing at the doorway to look back at him.

"Anything," he repeated. She managed a smile and was gone.

He turned back to his desk and picked up the photo again. He gazed upon that frozen moment, captured forever in silver oxide, memories flooding his mind.

Good flight, buddy—Godspeed.

With a bittersweet smile, he crossed to the wall of his office and pulled a framed certificate of merit from its long-held place of honor. Tossing the award onto the small, piled-down sofa beneath, he gently hung the photo upon the empty nail.

"Better," he said.

◙   ◙   ◙

"Please tell me this is a restaurant," Shepherd said. "I'm famished."

The two stood before the wide door, pausing to consider the cryptic emblem etched into its cold, hardened surface. It was a deep blue insignia over two feet in height, an inverted triangle interlaced with unevenly broken lines and what appeared to be a language neither man had ever seen.

"Or a bathroom," Lucas added. "With a shower."

"Yeah, a bathroom. Definitely a bathroom."

"What does this sign say to you?" Lucas asked, indicating the door.

"It says, 'Welcome to Stuckey's...we're always open.'"

"Works for me," Lucas agreed, placing his lightkey against the black disk. The light there rose as did the door, accompanied by the familiar rumble. There was no hiss of rushing air as the seal broke.

"Well," a relieved Shepherd said as the crack beneath the door widened, "this one doesn't lead outside, either."

The sound of the rising barrier ceased, and the door stood fully open. Again, a thick blackness waited beyond. Lucas and Shepherd both stepped forward, pausing at the threshold of the beckoning chamber. Lights within the room ignited in response, welcoming them, filling their eyes with aesthetic lines and vibrant hues and a magnitude of science beyond their ken.

Like lost children, they entered. With his first steps across the threshold, Shepherd realized that they had left the one-sixth g of the moon behind them and were feeling full Earth gravity again, an impossibility as far as he knew. His body felt heavy and sluggish—it would take a while to readjust.

Their stockinged feet made no sound as the explorers moved warily across the polished granite floor and into a massive, circular chamber easily three times the size of Mission Control back in Houston. Silent in stunned amazement, Shepherd's eyes drank in the marvel around them, dancing from one glistening object to the next, unable to fix in understanding upon any one of them.

"Holy cow..." he managed under his breath, which fogged white in the hard, chilled air. Lucas was too astonished to speak.

The room was a symphony of flowing organic design. What to both men appeared to be immense display screens, dark and silent, arched high above and around the overwhelmed astronauts, surrounding them, catching the light with a pearlescence that lived within their curving faces. Below, stretching wide beneath each screen, jutted smooth, featureless consoles of the same pearly black. Between each screen and console pair rose ponderous wall supports of gleaming silver, anchored by deeply rooted bases into the floor. Supporting a vast, domed ceiling, they stretched like huge, overhanging tree trunks and converged high above, forming a wide, inverted central cone that was shallow in depth and hollow at its center. Plush, flowing chairs of great size, spaced evenly along the consoles and upholstered in a pebbled leather of deep oxblood, floated on protruding arms of metal. Recessed lights, hidden by a flowing, sculpted soffit that encompassed the ceiling, threw jeweled pools upon the consoles, seats, and floor. The few expanses of wall that otherwise were barren harbored deep, shadowy alcoves where, it occurred to Shepherd, unpleasant surprises might easily lie in wait.

Something was nestled within the central nexus above. Directly over the heart of the cathedral-like chamber, both majestic and inert, hung an enormous orb of what appeared to be pure diamond. Scores of thick, crystalline protrusions, flawless and covered with thousands of precision-cut facets, emanated from a common, central point and reached outward in all directions. At least twenty feet in diameter, it threw subtle, myriad reflections as it caught the gentle light. Directly beneath the orb was a deep, wide circular pit lined by a knee-high wall and an unusually tall handrail barrier, within which was a somewhat larger but otherwise identical counterpart for the sphere above.

"Would you look at that," Lucas said in an awed whisper, finally finding a voice. "It's back-to-school time, Charlie…we don't know a thing."

"I'm inclined to agree."

"This isn't Earth science," Lucas said. "Can't be."

"We'll see."

"My, but those Martians are a clever lot."

They walked deeper into the room, watching their reflections as they played against the sleeping screens high above them. Shepherd heard an odd echo, the sound of their breathing coming back upon them as if cleansed, magnified, and returned.

"What do you suppose this is?" Lucas wondered aloud, his eyes scanning the chamber.

"A war room?" Shepherd guessed. "You know...like in that movie *Doctor Strangelove.* Remember?"

"Yeah, I remember." The commander walked nearer one of the chairs, then reached out to touch it. "The leather's dry...hard like an old saddle. May have been here for a while. Imagine...while we were working ourselves ragged trying to get our first guy into orbit, this place was already here and probably already abandoned."

"So no one's home, you think?"

"I sure hope not," Lucas pondered. "A *war* room...something tells me we couldn't begin to take these guys."

Shepherd nodded. "Not until we get a few good meals and a week's rest under our belts, at any rate."

"No," Lucas said. "I mean *Earth.*"

"Oh."

Shepherd cupped his cold, aching hands against his mouth and exhaled forcefully, trying to warm them. "Man...it is *freezing* in here."

"Stands to reason. No sense wasting power if no one's there to appreciate it."

"Look for a thermostat."

"Weird," Lucas noted. "There's no dust on anything."

Shepherd's eyes scanned the consoles around them, as if searching. "You suppose there's a radio here someplace?"

"Sure would be nice, wouldn't it? But I wouldn't even know what one looked like around here, let alone how to work it."

"Maybe we'll get lucky."

After several minutes of cautious examination, Lucas gestured toward another door that stood on the opposite side of the room. "Speaking of luck…I'm going to check in there. Who knows…might be a cafeteria."

"Careful, Skipper."

"I'll be right back…give a shout if you see anything."

As Lucas crossed to the sealed doorway, Shepherd approached a nearby console. Closer inspection revealed nothing to him, no clue concerning its function or origin. He reached out to touch its smooth black surface, watching the mirror-perfect reflection of his hand as it steadily rose to meet his touch, but contact never seemed to come. His fingertips could not feel the panel, despite the fact that his fingers sensed the pressure of doing so.

"Wow…" he whispered, sliding his fingers along the frictionless surface. Scientifically fascinated, he leaned closer and detected an infinitesimal space beneath his fingertips, a gap visible only because they did not fully meet their reflections. Shepherd smiled widely, finding delight in the phenomenon, and pressed his palm fully against the panel to see if increased pressure made any difference.

It did—but not the difference he had tried for.

Brilliantly lit symbols suddenly ignited within the panel, complex geometric shapes and configurations combined with more writing in the strange language of the chamber's door. A deep hum immediately began behind him, startling him, a noise that jumped an octave as he spun around, his heart in his throat.

The orbs had begun to rotate, throwing light like mirrorballs against the walls of their housings, turning slowly in opposite directions as the resonance grew louder. Another octave. The orbs spun faster.

Shepherd's hair stood on end, rising on his head, his arms, his chest. A dry crackle danced upon his flesh as the static charge intensified.

And life returned to a slumbering giant.

A tremendous, blinding bolt of white arced from orb to orb, twisting insanely as it closed the circuit between each one, casting a wash of pure, cold light throughout the room. The upper sphere descended, still rotating as it inched downward, and with each inch the arc grew brighter and louder, vaporizing the air.

"Gary..." Shepherd uttered weakly, his voice hushed with astonishment.

His eyes remained locked upon the unearthly display as he ducked behind the console's chair. Now almost touching its lower companion, the upper orb finally halted its descent and the two moved as a dedicated entity, counterspinning, connected by a cascading river of energy. Then, as Shepherd watched, transfixed, the single bolt broke into dozens of white-hot rivulets that flowed hypnotically upon and between the glassy, protruding spines.

From behind, a new swirl of light, color, and motion caught the corner of his eye. He spun back toward the console and quickly lifted his gaze in disbelief.

The empty display screen directly above him now had become a living thing, a scene of depth and substance upon which planets moved, stars danced, and the sun blazed.

A star map, within which a solar system dwelled.

Trying to take it all in, Shepherd backed away from the incredible image and right into Lucas, who had returned. Both men's unbelieving eyes were fixed upon the display, and as they watched in mute fascination, fully and realistically rendered worlds followed their accustomed transit paths around the yellow star at the system's core. Colorful lines of red, blue, and orange traced courses between some of the planets and their moons, accompanied by momentary flashes of writing as if identifying their purposes. Geometric figures appeared and disappeared, first in one place and then another, again and again.

It looked like a window onto space.

"What did you do?" Lucas asked, his eyes still locked upon the display.

"I touched the panel. That was all...I just touched it."

"Can't leave you alone for a minute."

"Is that...*our* solar system?" Shepherd wondered aloud.

"At first glance, it would seem like it, but..." Lucas pointed to the map's outer planets. "All four of the outer gas giants are ringed. And that planet there, where Earth would be..." He indicated the ugly, disfigured world. "It's just a mottled gray, like a dead moon."

"Maybe it's some kind of cloud cover."

Lucas shook his head. "If it is, I guarantee nothing lives there."

Shepherd nodded, scanning the map. "Those first two planets look a lot like Mercury and Venus, but the fourth...it has oceans. Big ones. Can't be Mars."

"You're right about that."

"Nine planets altogether," Shepherd counted. "But no Pluto. And there's an extra one right there, between the fourth planet and the first gas giant."

That first gas giant slowly rotated before them, finally revealing a ruddy, elliptical feature in its southern hemisphere similar to one both men knew all too well.

"Does that look like the Great Red Spot to you, Charlie?"

"Well, yeah...but if that's Jupiter, what's with the mystery planet? And why do Mars and Earth look all wrong? Where's Pluto? And why all the rings on the other giants?"

"I don't know," Lucas said, throwing his arms up. "I'm in the dark, same as you."

"One thing's for sure," Shepherd said. "Whoever these guys were, they got around. Look at all the lines connecting those worlds. I've seen proposed flight paths in textbooks that look just like that. They've got to be somebody's travel plots, and a lot of them are centered around the third planet and its moon—"

"Busy place for a dead world."

"—and there must be a dozen routes directly connecting it with the fourth. I guess it was a popular spot too."

"Two moons, no waiting."

Shepherd pointed. "And the fifth planet—"

"Which our system doesn't have," Lucas added.

"—it wouldn't have been an easy place to find a parking space, either."

"So you're conceding the 'alien' thing?"

"Nope," Shepherd said stubbornly. "Not till I shake hands with one."

"Face it, Charlie. This place was built by beings from another star system, and that's it, up there on the screen. Sure would explain a lot. Who knows what part of the galaxy that's in…might be a million light-years away."

They stood in silence for a few moments, watching the map as the star system upon and within it lived before them. Lucas tore his eyes away to consider the light show at the center of the room. As he drank in the reality of the vast technology apparent all around them, fear filled him.

All of his years of training were useless now. He was at the mercy of his surroundings, wholly without control over his situation, knowing that for the first time in his adult life he knew—*nothing.*

He was terrified.

"I'm right, Charlie," he said, his voice hanging heavily in the still, frigid space between them. "But I wish I weren't."

"About what?"

"This place has never known the hands of man."

16

Monday, March 3, 10:56 A.M.

Carol Shepherd sat in her living room, watching the television announcer as he spoke of the pending memorial service. Dull, gray morning light struggled through the chilled, curtained windows. Surrounding her, resting atop tables and countertops, were dozens of covered dishes, partially eaten foods brought by sympathetic friends and relatives, foods that were not likely to be finished off. The informal wake had started early and had lasted for just over two hours, after which the visitors had vanished as quickly as they had come. Such a funereal gathering had occurred every time a test pilot or astronaut had died, and Carol recalled her own presence at one such event—that at the home of Martha Chaffee, shortly after the fire had taken the lives of her husband, Roger, and the rest of the Apollo 1 crew.

And after each wake, it seemed each widow disappeared from the face of the Earth, torn from the sorority of astronaut wives by the relentless NASA public relations machine. Membership in the closely knit "wives club" was reserved for those married to living, breathing astronauts, those whose husbands still trained and flew and cheated death on a daily basis. The agency did not embrace defeat in any phase of the program; it could not afford to. Too much was at stake. So every failure was quickly swept aside, to be lost forever in the glare of each new success, each new triumph.

And the widow of an astronaut was failure personified.

Diane had come early and had left early, needing to take care of personal matters at the Manned Spacecraft Center. Marilyn Lovell, Susan Borman, and many others had been there as well—so many friends, so many hugs, so many shared tears. Katie Kendall, who had brought her famous broccoli-and-rice casserole, visibly struggled to remain composed during the entire event. Guilt was consuming her, little by little—misplaced guilt over the fact that her husband was coming home when two other husbands were not.

Several of the ladies had offered to stay afterward, but Carol had declined. There was much to think about, much to pray about, much to remember.

Such an odd custom, bringing food, she thought. *Starvation isn't the problem; losing my husband is. But I suppose they feel they must do something.*

The spacecraft was now approaching Earth, the announcer said. Kendall's smiling face flashed upon the screen, a photo taken during training for the mission. Carol could see her Charlie's shoulder encroaching upon the left-hand side of the screen—the original photo had been a shot of all three men.

To just cut them out that way—!

She turned off the television, her eyes reddened, weary, and dry. She had spent the overnight hours in prayer for the most part and had slept little. Twice during the night the stress had brought on sudden nausea, forcing her to rush to the bathroom. A spectre of anger had risen within her time and again, anger toward God for taking her Charlie from her. But each time it happened, her faith rose just as quickly, assuring her that all was under control, that no event takes place in life that surprises her sovereign Lord. She trusted her Father and the Savior He had sent into the world, and she knew that all things happen for a reason, that all events are a part of a great design that has been unfolding since before the dawn of time.

Still, the pain was real. Very real.

Joey was in school, and his teachers were doing well in shielding him from the press. Carol knew it was important to surround him with as much normalcy as possible, to shelter him from an onslaught of hard reality he was not yet equipped to handle. The five-year-old would not be able to deal with the tragedy that had befallen his family, could not grasp the harsh fact that his father would never come home again. The narrow innocence within him held no concept of death.

His mother found part of herself envying him.

◙　　◙　　◙

"If my stomach gets any emptier, I'll implode," Shepherd said.

The men entered the corridor Lucas had discovered a short time earlier, behind the door in the far wall of the "war room," as Shepherd had dubbed it. The corridor lights had come on with Lucas' first step across the threshold and had remained on after he had left to investigate the clamorous light show his crewmate had accidentally initiated.

"It isn't as cold as it was," Lucas observed, trying not to think about food. "Heaters must have kicked on."

"Another fifty degrees," Shepherd said, "and I'll be happy."

"Charlie," Lucas teased, "you are *so* high maintenance. There's just no pleasing you. 'I need warmth…I need food…I need water…I need oxygen.' It's always something."

"Well, excuse me for being a carbon-based life form," Shepherd grinned.

They continued on. Accents of glass and gleaming metals, set into the walls and ceiling, caught the light. Cautiously, they moved past the polished bronze wall segments of the expansive corridor, which featured doors spaced along its length. Twelve of the sealed portals had the familiar steely sheen but the last, centered in the far wall, was solid white.

Lucas paused to try his lightkey at the first and second doors. Both rose to reveal new corridors beyond that stretched into darkness and distance.

"We should have brought a bag of bread crumbs, Charlie," Lucas said with all seriousness. "This place is a maze."

"Looks that way."

They opened door after door. Every new portal revealed a new corridor, and every passageway looked the same. Each was branded with cryptic symbols and letters similar to those they had discovered earlier.

"We need an Earth-Mars dictionary," Lucas said.

"Maybe."

"You are one stubborn man."

"Yup."

Lucas chuckled. "Well, at any rate, we might be at the hub of this place...the corridors seem to converge here."

They reached the white door, which towered opposite the now-distant doorway of the war room. The red insignia emblazoned upon it differed from the others they had seen, suggesting both uniqueness and importance.

"What have we here?" Lucas wondered aloud. He held his lightkey to the black disk. The door rose. The men stepped forward and lights ignited to reveal a familiar circular chamber.

"Another airlock," Shepherd realized. "Only bigger...and this one has *those*."

He pointed to the racks of enormous spacesuits that lined the walls. They stood row upon row, silent sentinels waiting to serve, obviously designed to be worn by beings much larger than Lucas and Shepherd.

"Well," Lucas said, "at least we know our friend outside wouldn't have stood out in a crowd."

"Looks like 'the NBA goes to outer space.'"

"Man…these guys were *huge,*" Lucas said, examining one of the suits more closely. "Look at that helmet…big as a bushel basket."

The suits were brilliantly conceived and executed and looked unused. While covered in white fabric like conventional NASA suits, they bore no insignia at all, no flags or other markings. And they were simpler in design, built without the hose fittings and other hardware that cluttered the outer surfaces of the suits Apollo moonwalkers wore.

"Must have internal backpack connectors," Shepherd noted. "Internal hoses. Nothing to get hung on things. Nice."

A look of concern crossed Lucas' face. "Charlie…?"

"Yeah, Skipper?"

"There's only one empty rack here…has to be the suit we saw on our friend outside."

"Stands to reason…"

"No other suits are missing."

A heavy silence stretched between them.

"Yeah," Shepherd nodded, understanding. "Why do I suddenly feel like Goldilocks, and the bears are at home?"

Newly wary of their plight, the men walked the circumference of the room, examining the exotic, oversized equipment that hung neatly and undisturbed within its varied alcoves. Some of the items seemed vaguely familiar; others gave no clue as to their functions.

"Big bears," Lucas commented.

Shepherd's eyes soon fell upon the chamber's other door. He suspected it would lead outside, onto the lunar surface. "I say we don't open that one."

"I'm right there with you," Lucas agreed. "Come on. Let's find something to eat."

The men left the airlock and closed its door behind them, then stood at the indoor crossroads now facing them. "All right," Lucas said, "which way, Goldie? Take your pick."

"There," Shepherd said, pointing back at one of the open doors. "That one."

"Any particular reason?"

"Nope."

"Works for me."

They entered the new corridor and made their way along, their footsteps silent against the hard, cool floor. Doors lined its walls on either side, each sealed tightly. The first one opened to reveal a small chamber, as did the second, and the third. All were empty, their walls and floors barren save for a single, wall-mounted protrusion that might have been a seat.

"What do you suppose went on in here?" Lucas wondered.

"No idea," Shepherd shrugged.

Every room, every corridor they explored featured a small, crystalline array housed in a clear dome, usually mounted to the ceiling. Lucas surmised these were part of a base-wide security camera system.

"Smile, Charlie," he said, indicating one of the units. "We're on *Candid Camera*."

They moved farther along the corridor. In a moment, they found themselves before yet another door.

"My turn," Shepherd said, raising his lightkey to the portal's black disk. With a quiet rumble, the door rose to reveal darkness beyond. Once again, lights flared to life as the men stepped into the room.

After but one step, they stopped abruptly. Startled, their minds fought to accept the gruesome sight suddenly laid bare before them. A scene of savagery on a massive scale filled the cavernous chamber from wall to wall. Clearly, the now-silent room once had been the site of a vicious man-to-man battle.

And those who had fought there apparently had died there.

Huge, uniformed corpses lay strewn where they had fallen, their torn and mutilated flesh now mummified, their bodies contorted in horrifying, agonized poses. They appeared human, except for their great size. Several of them had been dismembered, and judging from the abundance of bloodshed it had happened while they were still alive. The dark remains of dried blood and splattered tissue, reduced to a hard, caked powder, covered much of the walls, the floor, the ceiling. What must once have been furniture lay toppled and broken, hurled in combat or crushed beneath bodies. The deep, violent char of what may have been concussion charges scarred the walls of the room, which once had been lined with heavy shelves. Most of the shelving had been pulled from its mounts and toppled, damaging its contents as they had fallen. Unrecognizable equipment lay everywhere, smashed and useless. Sparkling fragments of glass, ceramic, and metal shone in the light. The oppressive quiet was wildly discordant with the sheer devastation of the scene, and only added to its unreality.

Lucas and Shepherd walked cautiously into the room, careful not to step on the bits of jagged debris. They felt true fear, their minds flooded with wild imaginings of the combat that had taken place.

"There must be a dozen of them," Lucas managed, his eyes still wide, his pulse racing.

"At least," Shepherd agreed, scanning the room. Cold sweat broke out on his forehead. "Hard to tell."

"What in the world could have happened?"

"And *when?*"

With reluctance they walked through the room, surveying the carnage, looking for any clue as to the identity of the giant race. They found none. One thing, however, was obvious—the battle had been fed by exceeding hatred.

"What do you think?" Lucas asked, fighting a wave of nausea. "Insanity? Mutiny?"

"Whatever it was," Shepherd said, "it happened a long time ago." He pressed the tip of his lightkey against the outstretched forearm of one of the fallen combatants. The flesh crumbled into dust under its touch. "A very long time."

"Shake hands with the Martians," Lucas said. "If this happened that long ago, *we* didn't build this place."

"You may be right," Shepherd conceded. "But these guys look almost human."

The astronauts moved carefully between the bodies, still searching for any sign of their origin. Tattered uniforms—each one black, maroon, or dark green—hung loosely now upon the desiccated forms.

"The fabric looks almost new, except for the damage and bloodstains," Shepherd observed. "No sign of decomposition…it still glistens. Like Beta cloth."

"Glass fiber," Lucas agreed. "Wouldn't break down. Makes sense."

He looked down at one form, a body that lay broken and twisted over the shattered remains of what must have been a table. Its face was pointing upward, empty sockets staring at him, the flesh around them ripped away to reveal bone beneath.

Lucas turned away with a groan of revulsion. "This one had his eyes torn out."

"And this one," Shepherd indicated from halfway across the room, "or what's left of her…was a woman."

Lucas shook his head in pity. "No one deserves to die like this."

He had noticed several odd, elongated devices scattered among the bodies, discolored at one end as if by heat. Some were broken in a manner suggesting they had been used as clubs, some still clutched tightly by lifeless fingers. "Those things look like weapons. Who *were* these people?"

"I don't know," Lucas said. "But I'm glad I never met one."

"The night is still young," Shepherd replied with an ominous tone.

17

They moved back into the passageway, leaving the gruesome scene behind them. Lucas extended his lightkey, took a deep, cleansing breath, and sealed the portal shut.

"Man," Shepherd said, "opening doors around here just got about a thousand times creepier."

"I *never* want to go back in there," Lucas said.

"Amen," Shepherd agreed.

They inched their way along the corridors, more slowly now. Their imaginations, fed by hunger, fatigue, and uncertainty, ran wild—every little sound now brought visions of attacking corpses to mind, making them jumpy, impeding their progress. Fighting their full Earth weight added to their languor as their bodies continued to adjust.

The science they encountered was beyond their understanding. Colossal machines hummed and glowed, filling entire rooms, carrying out their programmed functions—whatever they might be—just as they had since their creation. Apparently self-maintaining and immune to the ravages of age, they seemed to have been waiting patiently for new visitors to call upon their services. Occasionally, one would react to the men's presence, increasing its activity as they grew near or going quiet as if in hiding. The marooned astronauts spent hours walking the mammoth base. For every corridor they walked, two others seemed to appear. They opened door after door, if only reluctantly. Fortunately, they discovered nothing more menacing or nightmarish than convoluted mechanical equipment and storage rooms—with no more mangled bodies anywhere in sight.

Unfortunately, neither was any form of sustenance.

"You know," Lucas pointed out, "even if we find food, it's bound to be dust by now."

"Keep a good thought," Shepherd said. "We didn't come this far just to starve to death."

"Water's more likely…if they can keep a lake on the moon, they can run pipe."

"Gonna find a water cooler any minute now."

" 'Everything happens for a reason'…that's what you said, right?"

"Everything."

"I'm holding you to that, Charlie."

They rounded a corner and entered a new corridor, one unlike the others they had seen. There were more doors here than in other areas of the base, dozens of them, spaced evenly and closer together. Lettering and a distinctive colored graphic marked each door. The intimidating, almost gothic passageway stretched far into the distance, threatening to unleash countless unpleasant surprises upon them. Carved wooden accents and veined stone supports arched massively overhead, mixing with the bronze and gray metals of the walls and ceiling, with gargoyles and other statuary nestled into the many ornamented alcoves. Limited pools of orange light spilled from overhead, filling the corridor with menacing shadows.

"Terrific," Lucas said. "Interiors by Dracula."

"This would be creepy even by Transylvania standards," Shepherd observed. "*Beyond* creepy."

"Why is this area so different from the rest of the place?"

"Must be someone's idea of 'homey.'"

Realization dawned. "All these doors. You know what this looks like…"

"Yeah. It does."

The first door of the wing beckoned them. Lucas paused, took a deep breath, then held his lightkey up to the black disk. The rumble sounded. The door rose.

A chill gripped his spine as he stepped forward, the motion igniting recessed, orange-yellow room lights. In an instant, he and Shepherd both knew it was as they had thought. As they had feared.

They had found living quarters. *Occupied* living quarters.

A lifeless figure lay sprawled across a table where it was seated. Naked save for a small waistcloth, one of its arms dangled limply over the side. Dried blood covered much of the tabletop, which when fresh had dripped onto the polished stone floor, forming a wide puddle that had flowed almost all the way to the door.

Perhaps twenty feet square, the room was as astounding as any within the base. Earth tones dominated. The design of the room swept organically from side to side and from top to bottom, the walls, the door frames, the furniture. Sparkling, intricate crystalline sculptures embedded in the walls like rivers of colored fire flowed from wall to wall and from wall to ceiling. Small statues and other apparently personal items rested within varied and asymmetrical lighted alcoves.

A wide, trapezoidal bed dominated the chamber, dressed with blankets woven from blue glass fiber, judging from the way they caught the light. A thick, built-in table of dark, veined wood stood to one side, emerging from the wall and floor as if it had grown there. What little showed of its upper surface was polished mirror smooth.

Moving inside, Lucas saw a bladed weapon on the floor beneath the dead man's pendent, mummified hand, apparently still lying where it had been dropped.

"Suicide," Shepherd realized.

"No doubt."

"I don't see a note."

Lucas walked closer then stooped to pick up the knife. It was the size of a machete and heavier than he expected. Its straight, tarnished blade, though stained with old blood, still bore an intricate engraving. Its darkened ivory handle, displaying several stylized female figures intertwined with other, more bizarre forms, was a wonder of craftsmanship, a work of art that must once have been a proud possession.

Two other doors in the room stood open. A cursory glance told Lucas that one led into a closet of sorts and the other to sanitary facilities, but he did not feel it appropriate to explore them further, not with the occupant still there. For that, they would wait for vacant quarters.

If there were any.

As Lucas examined the knife more closely, Shepherd looked upon the body, upon the expression of anguish still carved into the dead man's face. A long, deep wound cut cruelly into his neck.

"Poor guy," he said. "What could have driven these people to… to *this?*"

"We may never know," Lucas said, testing the balance of the knife. "Not unless we learn to read their language. Has to be a written record here someplace."

"You're not suggesting we rifle through this guy's stuff looking for a diary, are you?"

"No…I was thinking more along the lines of a commander's log. Probably be accessible from the war room."

They examined the artifacts in the room more closely, hoping to determine the identity of the base's inhabitants. The objects of painted and sculpted artwork that spotted the walls and stood within the alcoves all depicted the same basic theme and were as unpleasant in their subject matter as they were elegant in their execution.

"Torture," Lucas noted. "On a nightmare level. It was an art form to these people."

"They could have taught the Nazis a thing or two," Shepherd said, lingering on one particularly grisly painting. "What these guys must have done to their enemies…"

Something else, resting across the chamber, caught Lucas' eye. He walked over and picked up a flat, oddly shaped piece of clear material an inch thick, which had been standing in an alcove beside the bed. Within the crystal hung a likeness, a fully dimensional, full-color photo image of a stunning woman. She was dressed in a most revealing manner, with jewelry and a hairstyle that did not suggest any culture Lucas was aware of. Her hair was dark, but her eyes, glistening like rare gems, were piercing and unlike any he had seen.

"Three-D," he said. "I mean, I've seen holograms before, but nothing like this…looks like she's actually standing there."

He brought the portrait to Shepherd, who took it and studied its imprisoned image for a few moments before handing it back.

"Must have been his wife," he suggested. "You think?"

"Maybe he owned her… I'm not so sure these people knew what love was."

"I wonder what her name was," Shepherd said.

Lucas contemplated the woman's face again, momentarily taken by the fact that she, like the man at the table, must be long dead and forgotten.

After he returned the photocrystal to its place, the men departed the room without hesitation. Lucas brought the knife with him, earning a questioning glance from his crewmate.

"You never know what you might run across," Lucas said, as they stepped back into the corridor. "Or whom."

"That's for sure," Shepherd agreed, sealing the portal behind them. They moved to another door.

18

"Hey…!"

The word drove deep, burrowing into a heavy, grudging sleep.

"Charlie…!"

Shepherd opened his eyes. Seeking the source of the voice with slumber-dulled senses, he found Lucas standing in the open threshold of his room, leaning against the doorframe.

"You gonna sleep all day?" Lucas smiled. "I'm starving…aren't you?"

"Yeah," Shepherd moaned, sitting up in bed. "I'm up…I'm up."

"Get a move on…early bird catches the worm. I want to find the cafeteria before the line gets long."

"Early worm gets eaten," Shepherd said, rubbing his eyes. "Give me a minute."

He looked back toward the door, only to find it empty. Lucas had moved down the hallway, impatiently starting the search for edibles without him. They were into their second full day without food now, yet the hunger pains had lessened from the day before. Still weak, Shepherd knew from his survival training that ketosis had set in, that his body had given up on his stomach as a fuel source and was now burning its own stored fat.

He swung his legs to the side, and his gaze fell fully upon the room in which he had slept. It was much like the first quarters Lucas and he had found, which had been one of many "occupied" rooms they had seen. All had been suicides. Finally locating a pair of vacant side-by-side rooms, Lucas and he had decided to settle in for the night and resume their search for food in the morning.

The room was devoid of personal items and had apparently never been assigned a resident. The bed beneath him was comfortable despite its age, and it adjusted to his body contours as he moved, as if it were filled with a thick gel padding. The blue glass-fiber blanket, though lightweight, had been warm.

Shepherd stood and stretched. Momentary lightheadedness swirled within him then faded as he lowered his arms and shuffled toward one of the room's other doors. Passing the closet, he walked into the sanitary facility, which was not too unlike an earthly bathroom.

The light ignited as he entered. Before him stood a large mirror, inset into the wall and rising to a height of nine feet. Everything in the room was designed for a user much larger than he. The basin, a polished metal unit that flowed gracefully from the wall and floor, rose almost to chest height. Nearby, what was obviously a toilet sat ready for use. It had no hinged lid or seat, but its bowl featured a sliding cover that retracted silently into the wall before use. The room also featured a large, circular shower, which he knew he would have to use, and soon. But not now, for Lucas was waiting.

Shepherd felt like a child as he stood at the oversized basin. As he reached out, the motion of his hands activated the spigot and water poured forth freely. He had found the night before that he also could vary its temperature by raising and lowering his hands. He reached up and in, cupping the water and drinking his fill before splashing his face.

Gazing into the mirror, he reached up and scratched at the substantial facial hair that had blossomed upon his jaw. He, like Lucas, had not shaved for quite some time. It was not quite a full beard he now sported, but it was scraggly and bothersome—he had always been clean shaven, as the military had dictated, and preferred smooth skin to this itchy growth.

"Man, I hate beards," he muttered, scratching still.

Glancing upward and to his right, he spotted a cabinet in the wall. It opened easily, revealing what appeared to be a large, ornate straight razor and several small porcelain containers.

"Standard issue, I guess," he said to himself, reaching upward. "For somebody, anyway."

Opening the razor, he found its blade exhibited the same odd quality he had found in the war room, at the console there—as he ran a finger up and down along the flat of its decoratively engraved side, he could not feel it.

"Hmmmm," he wondered, lifting the blade to his jawline.

With a small test pull, he carefully drew it along and could barely sense the contact with his skin. He saw, however, that hair was vanishing in its wake, falling away to rain upon the edge of the basin, without shaving cream, without a lubricant of any kind. Delighted by the discovery, he proceeded to give himself the closest and most comfortable shave he'd ever had. Caught up in the experience, he momentarily forgot the time and enjoyed the feeling of becoming himself again.

"Much better," he smiled, splashing his face as he looked into the mirror. "There you are, Charlie ol' boy...I missed you."

Remembering Lucas, he silently chastised himself for having taken so long. Leaving the personal-items bag and his Bible safely on the bed, he grabbed his lightkey and headed for the corridor, closing the door of his adopted quarters behind him.

"You know," he began loudly, "I've been thinking...if these guys came from that system we saw on the big screen..." He paused, sensing an unusual quiet. "Gary?"

Unsure which way his friend had gone, he called out again. His voice echoed unnervingly along the macabre passage, but no other response came.

He tried Lucas' door—perhaps the man had decided to wait in his quarters. The knock brought no response, and upon entering he found the room vacant. His calls toward the open bathroom door went unanswered.

Shepherd turned and proceeded down the hallway, headed toward unexplored territory, now the most likely place to find his friend. The corridor soon twisted sharply to the right, then to the left again. The sound of gently running water whispered from up ahead, and Shepherd quickened his pace. After a short distance the passage widened into a spacious, open atrium, a circular area some forty feet across. Its domed ceiling stretched high overhead, upon which was painted a bizarre mural depicting graceful birds and ravishing women, combined discordantly with victims of unspeakable atrocities, hundreds of them, their bodies intertwined with their tormentors'.

At the center of the atrium stood a glittering fountain, masterfully sculpted from what appeared to be lunar anorthosite. From its midst rose the towering figure of a woman hewn from the same white stone. Her expression was intense, her features utterly exquisite. Her flowing gown swept outward as if caught by wind, and beneath her feet were chiseled the bones of what Shepherd sensed had been conquered enemies, protruding from the rippling surface of the water. In her hand was a knife much like the one Lucas had found.

Wherever he was.

"Gary!" Shepherd called, but still no answer came.

Four doors, spaced evenly, circled the atrium. Two stood open.

Darkness lay beyond both doorways, save a subtle blue glow coming from the nearest one. Shepherd moved cautiously toward it, and a sound swelled in his ears as he grew closer, the low, persistent drone of operating machinery.

"Gary…you in here?" he called from just outside, ears pricked, listening for any sign of Lucas. Even though he received no reply, he entered.

Like so many others, the room was filled with unfathomable machines. A cylindrical something dominated the center of the room, a massive obelisk fifteen feet high and ten wide that glinted a dark silver in the light. It was surrounded by smaller support units that were still quite large in their own right, all of which were joined to the primary by curved, glowing rods of shaped crystal. Blue light coursed through the clear conduits, arteries feeding intense energies into the central mechanism. Throughout the room, tiny multicolored display lights twinkled like stars, dancing within glossy black panels that also housed scores of colorful though indecipherable graphic readouts.

It was beautiful, technologically speaking.

Shepherd peered upward. High upon the cylinder was a wide wraparound strip of more crystal, also glowing blue, encircling its upper body a couple of feet from the top. More plumbing was visible behind the transparent cerulean band, metal tubes that gleamed silver, gold, and copper.

"Water heater?" he joked aloud, awed by the level of science attained by the mysterious race. "Or a life-support system," he more seriously wondered. "I'd bet dollars to donuts. Just imagine what we could learn if we could haul this baby back home."

He walked around to the side of the great machine, only to find an impassable jungle of connecting hoses, pipes, and luminous tubes. Certainly, Lucas had not gone through there.

"Skipper?" he called out, over the deep, throbbing hum of the machinery.

He returned to the atrium, puzzled and a bit annoyed.

Well, just run off, why don't you!

Shepherd walked to the other open doorway, certain now that his commander had gone that way. He began to call out, a hint of irritation in his voice. "I'm gonna tie a bell around your neck if you're gonna—"

As he entered the room, lights rose. His voice abruptly died away.

In front of him, the floor fell away to reveal a vast, sunken rotunda, a place that must once have been the religious heart of the base. Stone arches soared high overhead, supporting a ceiling of gold and a central dome of shimmering blue. Row upon row of long, sculpted stone benches stretched before him, sharply tiered to give a better view of the focal point of the room—an elaborate altar, erected at the feet of a towering statue, upon which lay the remains of a final, ghastly sacrifice.

The place was an abomination, an archaic chamber of horror and of death. A deep, unpleasant chill settled into Shepherd's spine.

He walked deeper into the cathedral, descending the steep aisle steps, struggling to believe his eyes. The majestic statue was covered in solid gold and stood almost forty feet high. Its head was like that of a cobra, its threatening hood stretched wide, its mouth closed. Its body was like that of a Herculean man, and in its broad hands it held a pair of polished stone spheres that struck Shepherd as representing two worlds. Its legs were those of a bull, powerful and muscular and firmly planted. Between its feet was a pit filled with ash-covered coals, long cold. The huge altar before the imposing visage was crafted of reddish, veined stone that sparkled subtly in the warm orange light of the room.

Atop the altar, its face contorted in agony, was the decomposed body of a woman. Once clad in the standard glass cloth uniform, the upper part of her now-tattered clothing had been torn away as if hurriedly so. Something shiny and metallic protruded from her chest.

As Shepherd slowly grew closer, he could see a heavy coating of dried blood covering the top of the altar, blood that also had collected in a trough that ran around its outer edge. The object jutting from the body was a huge serrated knife, inlaid with gold and silver, and had fully opened the victim's chest.

Beside the altar and flush with the floor was a great, circular pit, the bottom of which almost vanished into depth and darkness. Peering into it, Shepherd saw the shadowed forms of tangled skeletons and dried remains—dozens of violated creatures piled where they must have been hurled.

Sacrificial animals!

Fortunately, much to Shepherd's relief, a fallen, fatally injured Lucas was not among them.

He backed away from the pit and looked again to the woman's corpse. *If they sacrificed animals, why is one of their own people lying dead on the altar?*

Shepherd shook his head in disgust and repulsion, overwhelmed by it all. He gazed up into the eyes of the pagan sculpture, eyes that shone like ruby. Stepping closer, he reached out with some hesitation and put a hand to the cold, smooth stone of the altar and felt there the icy wretchedness of its builders.

"Father in heaven," he began, "what kind of people..." He breathed deeply and gathered himself, then called out again.

"Gary! Where are you?" No response. "Gary!"

Turning aside, he spotted an open archway, the entrance to an antechamber obscured by deep, eerie shadow. Unsure and wary, he stepped into the large room and found two rows of great caged enclosures, fully recessed into the floor and running along either side of a wide, central walkway. There was no safety rail. Cautiously, he peered down into cell after cell as he slowly walked the length of the room. All were paved in black stone and carpeted with the scattered remnants of what once had been beds of hay. Within them all also lay the desiccated carcasses of animals, surely intended for sacrifice but left to starve. All were oversized, and among them Shepherd recognized the remains of goats, pigs, and some kind of deer. There were a few other creatures he could not identify, things with thick tails and leathery hides.

Reaching the end of the walkway, he turned and hurried back into the main room. Truly concerned now for the well-being of his friend, he determined to search the entire base, even those areas they had already seen. In his earlier days, Lucas had been adventurous, even reckless at times. But this—it made no sense.

How could he have vanished so fast? No pilot goes anywhere without his wingman—unless he has no choice—

Shepherd, heading toward the exit, ascended the steps and paused at the top to take a final look back over his shoulder.

"Gary! Are you in here? Answer me!"

There was no reply, save the suffocative quiet of the altar and the primal horror that lay atop it.

What kind of people—?

He left, sealing the door behind him.

19

Tuesday, March 4, 2:49 P.M.

"*Quest,* Houston…we show entry interface in one minute."

Cortney, speaking from the CapCom console, looked up at the big screen. It now displayed a television picture of the flight deck of the carrier *John F. Kennedy,* which was navigating the southern Pacific en route to its assigned rendezvous. Sailors hurried to and fro within the frame, preparing to receive the spacecraft that they would soon haul aboard.

"Roger, Houston," Kendall's voice sounded.

Kranz sat in his flight director's seat, also watching the screen. In just a few short minutes, its rectangular frame would be filled by a glorious splash of red and white as the capsule's main chutes opened, bringing *Quest* safely home. Every controller in the room had his attention trained upon the last-minute telemetry streaming from the spacecraft, and every telltale number looked very, very good. She was now only moments away from a fiery reentry, her unstoppable plunge bringing her back to Earth.

"We've got your signal coming through ARIA, Vic," Cortney called. "Loud and clear."

"Roger," came Kendall's voice from the speakers. "Entry attitude one-five-three degrees. FDAI scale five-by-five."

"Good data," Cortney confirmed. "Everything's right where it's supposed to be."

Distant words filled the room again, the voice of a busy man. "Looking good at twenty-eight volts…spacecraft control to CMC… and point-oh-five-gee roll."

"Bull's-eye, *Quest*…you're coming right down the middle. Ten seconds from blackout…we'll see you on the other side."

"I'm getting a glow out there…would you look at *that*…"

High over the Pacific, the capsule plunged into the atmosphere at more than thirty-five thousand feet per second. It was quickly surrounded by a lengthening envelope of ionized material hotter than the surface of the sun, an incandescent trail of scorched air and ablative resin stripped from *Quest*'s heat shield by the atmosphere. No radio signal could penetrate that burning, vaporized sheath.

"Loss of signal," the public affairs officer announced to the world from his console on the back row.

The minutes ticked by. Everyone in the room waited as they were accustomed to doing, their data screens blank. Cortney looked over his shoulder and saw Katie Kendall standing behind the expansive glass of the press gallery. The anxiety she felt was evident on her face—it was her first reentry, and the last hurdle to bringing her husband safely back to her.

At that moment, the striking young woman turned her head from the main screen and saw Cortney watching her. Their eyes met, and she almost looked away, but did not. Smiling warmly, he gave her a reassuring thumbs-up. She smiled back, seemed to relax a bit, and took a seat in one of the red upholstered gallery chairs.

Her eyes went to the clock on the gallery wall. Those who knew such things had told her the blackout would last only three minutes.

"Coming up on acquisition of signal," Cortney called. "Standing by."

Kranz tapped his console with a pencil, waiting calmly, his eyes darting from man to man within the room.

Good men—no military commander ever had better.

The countdown clock above the main display reached zero then reset for the next event to come. Splashdown.

"And, that's AOS," the public affairs officer said into his microphone. "Waiting now for word from the spacecraft."

The men in the room took a deep, collective breath, their eyes locked upon their individual screens, anticipating the data stream that now would flicker back to life.

"*Quest,* Houston," Cortney called. "Standing by."

Katie held her purse tightly, wringing its leather strap in her white-knuckled hands.

"Houston, *Quest,*" came Kendall's voice over the speaker, music sweeter than any she had ever heard. "What a ride."

Katie squealed with delight. She jumped up and down a couple of times, releasing the death grip on her purse. It fell to the floor, but she did not notice.

"Copy, Vic," Cortney answered, a wide smile on his face. "We've got you on this side of the big blue."

The camera on the aircraft carrier panned the skies, searching for some sign of the returning command module.

"Drogue chutes are out," Kendall said. "They look good."

The smaller parachutes trailed behind the spacecraft, slowing and stabilizing it for the main chutes to follow. A few moments passed. All was going perfectly.

"I'm at eleven thousand feet…and there go the mains," came the voice again. "One…two…two chutes…the third seems to be having trouble…"

There was a long pause. Katie, her hands intertwined before her face, peered over them, her eyes fixed upon the main screen.

"No...there it went!" Kendall cried out. "I've got three good mains."

"We copy, *Quest*," Cortney replied.

Kranz watched the dancing television image. Whoever was operating the camera on the deck of that ship obviously did not do it for a living. He looked down at his console, at the bright green status lights there that told him all was well, that the mission was as good as over, that this man was as good as home.

One man—!

Finally, the capsule broke the clouds and the television camera quickly found it. Small as it was upon the screen, it was a wonderful sight.

"We've got you on the TV," Cortney said. "Smile, Vic."

The picture switched to an angle taken from one of the recovery helicopters, a much closer view. The three red-and-white chutes billowed full and wide, conveying their precious cargo safely homeward.

"Recovery One, calling *Quest*," sounded a new voice, that of the helicopter pilot. "I have a visual. We're right on your wing. Standing by."

"Roger, Recovery," Kendall answered. "Glad to have you out there."

The spacecraft hit the water with a white splash. The flight controllers rose in subdued celebration, patting each other on the back and shaking hands. For the first time ever, though, the splashdown triggered no flag-waving, no cigar lighting, no triumphant graphic on one of the room's huge rear-projection screens, declaring another successful mission.

This time had been different.

Katie cried tears of happiness, overcome by the joy of the moment.

That joy was not felt by all.

Bring them all home—!

Kranz sat motionless, arms folded against his console, fixated upon the main screen as the events there took place exactly as they had twelve times before. The Earth-fallen *Quest* bobbed up and down in the blue, gently whitecapped water, finally at rest. Seared by the violent heat of reentry, her mirrored silver Mylar finish was tarnished a burnt gold in those places where it had not been peeled away entirely. Three spherical gold-and-white safety bags quickly inflated atop the capsule, helping to ensure it would not flip over in the choppy seas.

"I'm at Stable One," Kendall said, reporting the capsule's upright orientation. "Ready and waiting."

Navy frogmen leaped from the recovery helicopters and dropped into the water, bringing with them an orange, specialized flotation collar to be attached to the spacecraft, as well as a red rubber life raft. One diver climbed upon the raft after securing it to the side of the capsule, then reached up and used a special tool to open the hatch. He half disappeared into the dark opening for a few minutes, obviously conversing with Kendall, then pulled back and left the open hatchway clear.

As had happened twelve times before, the first man emerged from the spacecraft. Gripping the adjoining handholds, he pulled clear of the squarish opening and slid into the waiting raft, nestled into one corner, and peered up at the rescue helicopter circling overhead.

Kranz stood, his unblinking eyes still fixed upon the image.

Then, as had *never* before happened in the history of Apollo, the recovery diver closed the hatch and locked it—with only one man in the raft.

One man.

For Kranz, the world came crashing down.

Bring them all home—!

He turned away, the blow driven hard into his gut as the finality suddenly and horrifyingly became real.

They had *failed* two daring men—men who had trusted others to bring them home safely, men who had lost their lives as a result of that trust.

Men who had trusted *him*.

Kranz wrenched his eyes shut, the agony filling him, his eyes awash. Reaching up, he clutched at his white vest, rending it open, forcefully tearing the buttons from their places. They clattered upon the console and the floor. Teeth clenched, he ripped the sundered vestment from his body and threw it to the ground.

The stunned room went silent. They had seen.

The power of the vest had been denied.

20

Dizziness flared then passed. There was a piercing white light. It too faded.

Lucas' senses returned to him. Stunned for a moment, he stared ahead, trying to grasp his new and impossible surroundings. His peripheral vision was blurry but slowly clearing. A distant roar filled his ears. He could not recall where he had been only a moment earlier, but he knew it had not been *here*.

He peered blankly through the graduated, triangular window before him, clad once more in his pressure suit and helmet.

His gloved hands rested lightly upon *Starlight*'s flight controls.

As if in a dream, the stark, golden-brown lunar terrain, now a desert of confusion, passed before his eyes as it moved steadily upward within the frame of his view port. The sight was hypnotic; for an instant or two, despite his astonishment, he allowed himself to be owned by the moment.

A voice sounded in his headset, startling him.

"Looking good, here, *Starlight*," the CapCom said. "We show a good burn."

"Roger that," Shepherd's voice replied, filled with anticipation. "Everything is right where it should be."

No, a bewildered Lucas knew. *It isn't—!*

He felt a steady vibration and his weight upon his soles as he stood on the Velcro-lined floor of the cabin. That meant the engine was burning, its throttle wide open. The LM was decelerating, the moon rushing up to meet them.

We're landing—

His vision cleared, bringing everything into sharp focus. He turned to see his crewmate standing at his right elbow, the man's eyes dancing from one illuminated panel readout to another.

"Charlie," Lucas began with disciplined alarm, *"how did we get here?"*

"No kidding…been a long road. Hard to believe it's finally happening."

"No, no…I mean…"

He glanced at his watch, set as always for Houston time.

Five-thirteen in the morning, he read. *The twentieth of February—but that was almost two weeks ago!*

Part of his mind frantically cried out that something was wrong, that he was badly out of phase with reality as he knew it. A larger part, however, did not.

A dream, he knew, creates its *own* reality, its own past, its own rules.

But this is no dream—!

The bulky suit he wore, the hiss of air in his helmet, the solidity of the cabin around him—it all spoke only of focused, lucid truth, overflowing his senses with hard and undeniable evidence.

—is it?

He found himself accepting the incredible, unfolding situation. His mind would have it no other way.

I've gone back—!

His eyes went back to the window. All his life he had looked upon those same mountains, those same plains, but from a much more distant vantage point. In childhood he had used a parade of small telescopes to gaze upon the surface of the beckoning orb, thrilling at the hard definition of the uplands and craters of a chaste world no man had ever touched.

Now those same features called to him afresh with the allure of new snow, drifting past only fifty thousand feet below him, a distance that over the minutes to follow would dwindle to nothing.

It was a moment he had trained for. It was a moment he had longed for.

It was a moment that *had happened already.*

His eyes rose to the digital event timer on the panel before him, a phantom counting down, the seconds passing in luminous green.

No—something's wrong—!

His mind now was flooded by a prolonged sense of déjà vu that overrode his every thought, his very being.

What—?

Everything he did, every move he made, every glance at the flashing panels around him screamed of repetition, of recent memory.

Lucas shook his head, trying to clear away the haunting fog that weighed so heavily within him. He struggled to grab hold of the reality around him, but like smoke between his fingers it slipped away.

No—can't land—the engine—something wrong with the engine—!

Shepherd, glancing to his left, read the obvious turmoil on his commander's face, watching as the man's eyes darted from side to side as if searching.

"What's wrong, Gary?"

"Nothing...I'm okay..."

Is it because of the simulator? Am I remembering the sims?

"You don't look so okay."

What was it—what was I just thinking about—?

Lucas *knew* there was something he needed to remember, something important about the spacecraft—but the harder he tried to regain a handle on the thought, the faster it faded away. Then it was gone altogether.

With little choice, Lucas accepted the situation around him and turned his thoughts toward the landing. The intrusive sensation within his mind subsided, freeing his concentration.

He had a landing to make.

As they slowed, allowing the grayish orb a tighter grip upon them, they descended along a planned arc unforgivingly dictated by Isaac Newton, Pythagoras, and the flight dynamics analysts in Houston. At the right moment, the LM rolled onto its back, facing upward and away from the moon. At once, its aft-mounted landing radar acquired the surface, bringing new and valuable altitude and range data into the mix.

"*Starlight*...we show radar lock."

"Roger," Lucas confirmed. "Forty-three thousand feet and we have radar."

Shepherd punched another code into the computer, telling it to begin using the new flow of information in its computations. The Earth shone bright and blue, now high within the forward windows, a precious gem afloat in a sea of blackness.

"No place like home," Lucas smiled.

"I can see my house from here," Shepherd winked, leaning forward and craning his neck upward.

"Velocity light..." Lucas reported, as a warning indicator momentarily flickered on then went dark again. "No...it's out, now. Radar looking good. Altitude looks very good."

"Pitch over," he called out as the LM assumed an upright attitude, allowing the astronauts their first view of the landing site ahead. Lucas was astounded, and for a few moments the words would not come. His wide eyes drank in the sight of their destination. "Man...Cabeus is right there, right where it's supposed to be..."

"Just like the simulator," Shepherd smiled. "Except for *that...*"

It was incredible. Ahead, beyond the rolling, brightly sunlit valley floor spread below and before them, was a sea of darkness as deep as space itself. It looked for all the world like a hole cut in the moon, as if the ground itself just fell away into nothingness, leaving a hungry, empty void where dragons lurked, waiting to devour anyone so foolish as to intrude upon their domain.

"Why do I get the feeling we'll land, and there'll be Rod Serling standing off to one side in a spacesuit and tie?" Shepherd quipped. "Man...that is one dark zone out there."

"Say again, *Starlight?*" Cortney asked.

"Not much light at Marlow. We're at sixty-eight hundred feet," Shepherd responded, "and four miles out. Coming in nicely...sixty-seven hundred...right down the pike."

Courtney came back, his voice breaking up slightly. "You are go for landing, *Starlight*. Repeat...you are go for landing."

"Roger...we're go. Six thousand feet," Shepherd advised his commander. "Coming in at seventy-five feet per second."

Lucas took manual control of the throttle and steering jets. He alone would land the LM now as his crewmate called out the crucial data that the radar and computer gave him. He told himself it was just like flying the simulators.

Like, perhaps. But not the same thing.

The dusty surface loomed closer. Despite his confidence, doubts flared and faded in the darkened corners of his mind. The image of the lunar surface filling their windows was not merely a plaster-of-Paris model, and an error in judgment at any crucial moment would not mean a simple recycling of data tapes so he could begin again.

There were no wings slicing through air, as with every other craft he had ever landed. It had no wheels, no runway to land on, no ejection seat to fall back on should something go wrong at the last second. He was riding an engine mounted within a fragile box-kite construct of aluminum and explosive liquids and glittering Mylar, all precariously balanced atop a central, fervent plume of thrust as if on a lofty, teetering, hundred-foot pole.

And Lucas, like the seven mission commanders before him, was rapidly approaching solid ground having never actually landed a LM before.

Such was nothing new to his breed. He had been an Air Force test pilot before entering NASA's astronaut program, and flying craft that never had been flown was what he did. It was who he was.

And he loved it.

"Altitude fifty-five hundred, coming in at seventy. Looking good."

The forty-mile-wide crater Cabeus loomed to their right as they grew ever closer to the ominous expanse of darkness ahead. Lucas strained, looking for the LM Truck that waited there, somewhere among the pockmarks and shadows.

"Twenty-two hundred," Shepherd continued. "Forty feet, thirty feet per second down. Looking good. Two thousand, twenty-five down. Twenty down. Thirty-five forward."

It has to be there somewhere—

"Fifteen hundred feet, seventeen down…"

Lucas abandoned his visual search for the Truck and focused instead on finding a nice, flat place to land. They would locate the waiting craft by foot if necessary, and since Houston was still getting telemetry from it, it had to be there somewhere. Looking beyond a trio of small craters nestled at the base of Cabeus, he came to focus on a nice, smooth plain ahead, one devoid of shadows indicating pits or boulders.

"There," he said, thinking aloud. "Right there…that looks good…"

"Passing one thousand feet," Shepherd called out. "Thirty forward, ten down. Coming in nicely."

Suddenly, Lucas became aware of a large shadow and several tiny ones lurking within his landing site. Unlike every past mission, he did not have his LM's shadow out before him as an added visual gauge of his altitude—the sun was to *Starlight*'s left rather than behind her—so Lucas had to use his pilot's instincts as no Apollo commander before him had been forced to do.

"Looking good from over here," Shepherd said. "Five hundred feet, coming in at fifteen. Eight down. Fuel looks good…10 percent remaining."

"Well, I'll be a…" Lucas began, staring intently out the window. "There…right there…"

Shepherd's eyes remained locked upon the computer and his gauges. This close to the surface, he had no time for sightseeing. "Fuel at 8 percent. Two hundred fifty feet, coming in at twelve forward. Seven down. Five down."

Lucas did not speak, focusing all of his attentions upon the landing. The LM was more responsive than the simulators ever had been, it seemed. *Starlight* was alive, sharing a heartbeat with him, responding to his every touch and thought with instant precision.

"One hundred fifty feet, ten forward. Five down…6 percent."

Here we go—good girl—that's it—almost home now—

"Seventy-five feet, five forward. Four down…"

"One minute," came a warning from Houston. Fuel was getting low. In sixty seconds, *Starlight* would be on the surface, one way or the other—they were too low now for an abort.

"Fifty feet…three forward…"

Lucas watched the smooth spot just ahead of and below them, and silently began to scold himself. *Get it down—get it down—!*

"Quantity light," Shepherd called out, knowing it was their last fuel warning. "Anywhere's good, Gary…"

The final seconds seemed an eternity. Each man held his breath. Lunar dust, stirred by the brutal winds of their engine thrust, flew in hard, straight streams up into their field of view, cutting their visibility almost to zero.

Any second now—

"Contact light!" Shepherd cried as the little disk on his panel lit blue. The long, delicate probes reaching downward from *Starlight's* three rear-most landing pads finally had touched solid ground.

"Engine stop!" Lucas called out, hitting the kill switch. Both men gripped their respective handhold bars as the craft gently free-fell the final few feet of its quarter million mile journey, settling with a slight shudder upon the surface as the engine vibration ceased.

Shepherd, following procedure to the letter, immediately began to read the first items from the postlanding checklist. "Descent engine command override off...engine arm off..."

A flurry of motion, his gloved fingers finding the right switches with practiced precision.

"Program four-thirteen is in," he added, punching in the code that told the computer they were on the surface.

And then, with brilliant moonlight streaming through the window before him, bathing his lowered face in its chaste, white radiance, Shepherd said a silent prayer of thanks.

"Charlie," Lucas began, smiling at his friend and copilot, "check it out." He nodded in the direction of his window.

The dust outside had cleared the instant the engine had been turned off. For the first time, Shepherd looked outside—and broke into laughter.

Lucas pressed his push-to-talk switch and made it official. "Houston," he said, his voice triumphant, "*Starlight* has come ashore."

"Copy that, *Starlight*," Cortney replied. "We knew it all along. Stand by for stay/no stay."

Less than a hundred yards away, waiting patiently and safely upright as they knew it had to be, stood the glittering form of the LM Truck.

"Tell Conrad," Lucas smiled, "there's a new champ in town."

"We copy," the CapCom's voice came back. "He's a couple of seats down from me…just how close did you get?"

Lucas laughed anew. "If we'd have had another coat of paint on this baby, we'd have hit it. Tell Pete to have Gorski's fire up the grill, and I want all the trimmings. And when *Quest* comes around from the far side, tell Vic he owes me a Coke."

Shepherd was still laughing, his eyes drinking in the sight of their foil-wrapped companion. Beyond the Truck and at the horizon all around them, a low haze settled quickly and was gone, the last remnants of the dust storm spawned by their descent engine thrust.

After a few moments, he flipped a switch to his right, momentarily cutting off their headset mikes.

"It gets better," he said, punching Lucas playfully on the arm.

"How's that?"

"I just won a hundred bucks."

Lucas laughed. The fact that he understood his friend's comment when he should not have escaped his attention. Casually, he turned to check the circuit-breaker panel to his left, to verify that all was as it should be.

Then, suddenly, the dizziness swept him once again, accompanied by its swirling white light. He staggered to one side before catching himself, and as his focus settled he quickly realized that he was no longer within the cabin of a spacecraft.

Fully suited for a moonwalk, he was out on the surface, near the landed LM Truck. The sense of déjà vu overcame him once more.

He swung around to see *Starlight* resting peacefully upon the surface, his footprints and those of Shepherd leading back in her direction.

Near her, its colors dramatically catching the light, stood an American flag—one he and his crewmate obviously had erected.

Why can't I remember coming outside?

"Charlie..." he began, awash in confusion. "Something's wrong..."

Shepherd stood upon a sloping ladder affixed to the side of the Truck's descent stage, removing the multisectional shroud of padded Mylar insulation that had protected the rover during the landing phase. He paused and looked down at Lucas.

"How do you mean, Skipper?"

Lucas, standing near one of the craft's landing struts, shook his head, his memory fighting a losing battle. "I...I don't know..."

"Is your suit pressure okay?"

Lucas instinctively glanced at a gauge on his wrist but quickly looked away again. "Yeah...it's fine. I didn't mean that..."

"What then?"

"Nothing," the addled man said, shaking his head. Lucas felt the sea of uncertainty slipping away as his mind began to adjust. "Forget it. I just thought..."

Did I black out? Should I say anything?

Deciding to remain silent, Lucas joined in the deployment of the rover, peeling away a glittering Mylar flap in its side in order to withdraw a series of flat nylon lanyards. Each was connected to one of a series of spring levers, pulleys, and lock releases—it was a clever mechanism, one through which, in the one-sixth gravity of the moon, two men could do the work of a dozen without breaking a sweat. They went to work, deliberately and methodically, following their wrist-mounted checklists step-by-step.

First, they released a set of lock-down clamps and freed the rover. Then, together, they pulled a pair of ramps from the shallow platform atop the Truck, telescoping them slowly outward and downward until they reached the lunar surface. As a series of counterweights kept its inertia down, Shepherd and Lucas used the lanyards to carefully and gently guide the vehicle down the ramps. Still in its folded configuration, it rolled on a set of small belly wheels that would be removed once the men deployed the main wheels.

"There she comes," Shepherd said as the rover neared the soil. "I'll hold her there, Gary, while you unstow the drive wheels." Lucas leaned over the folded chassis and pulled on a series of torsion bars. The forward body folded outward and locked into position, followed in turn by the vehicle's large, forward wheels of reinforced piano-wire mesh.

"Man, but this baby's big," Lucas commented. "Seems even bigger up here than it did back home. It's got to be the size of a tow truck."

The rover came farther down the ramp as Shepherd fed out the lanyards. Finally, the vehicle's forward wheels made their first mark on the ashen lunar surface. Lucas reached up and repeated the procedure at the rover's aft end, releasing the rear chassis, which automatically locked into its extended position.

"Looking really good," Shepherd said. "Perfect."

"That's it, Charlie," Lucas said, waving the rover forward. "Keep her coming...there goes..." The rear of the rover reached the base of the ramp, and its back wheels in turn found solid ground. Shepherd felt the lanyards go slack.

"That's got it! Hot dog!" Shepherd called. "Now all we gotta do is kick the tires and take her once around the block."

As Lucas began to speak again, the words were lost—as was he.

Dizziness. Light.

When it subsided, he found himself still on the surface, now near the landed *Starlight.* Glancing to his left, he saw the LM Truck in the distance, its wrappings still intact, the rover still loaded atop it.

What the—?

Shepherd now stood only a few feet in front of him, having just driven the lower segment of a two-piece flagstaff into the surface with the side of a rock hammer. In his left hand was its matching upper half.

"Here you go," Shepherd said, extending a hand toward his commander as if asking for something. Lucas looked down and realized he had been holding an American flag in his right hand, one wrapped loosely around an extended, telescoping support. As if in a dream, he put out his hand, gave the flag to his friend, and watched with an odd detachment as the man began to raise the banner.

I'm losing my mind!

Unrolling the three-by-five-foot nylon flag, Shepherd attached its horizontal support bar to the upper section of the staff with practiced ease, and in turn fastened the pole segment into place atop its lower counterpart. The flag now hung loosely, its upper edge sleeved around its outstretched support, its embroidered stars glowing brightly in the morning sunlight. He affixed it to the upright staff by a small, white Velcro strap sewn to the flag's lower corner, which held the banner taut so that it appeared to fly in the airless void.

"Pretty as a picture," Shepherd smiled.

"Looks beautiful from here," came the voice of CapCom. "Well done, guys."

As he stood there, his mental foundations tenuous at best, Lucas knew there was something very wrong in what was happening, in the very fact that it *had* happened, but he could not imagine what that something was. Buying again into the reality of the moment, he gazed upon the flag, drinking in its beauty, its brilliant hues an oasis of color on an otherwise colorless world. Pride and patriotism swelled within him, forcing all doubt aside, and as he moved back a few steps he gloried in the sight.

He knew the flag's fabric would not last long on the harsh moon, but then it was not meant to. All that mattered was that it fly proudly for the duration of the mission itself, in sight of the television camera.

Afterward, when it stood abandoned and unseen, its nylon fibers would fade quickly under the constant and merciless barrage of the unfiltered sun. Already, he was certain, the flags planted on earlier missions had gone white, their color bleached away by ultraviolet rays, and it was only a short matter of time before their very fabric turned to dust and fell from the staffs on which they hung.

But they had done their jobs well and magnificently.

Both astronauts paused and faced the flag, bathed in the importance of the moment.

"I just want to say how honored Charlie and I are to be here today," Lucas spoke, reciting a speech he had written and memorized. "I dedicate this moment not only to our great nation, but to all of you who made this flight possible. The three of us up here are but the barest tip of the iceberg, the most visible part of a force of hundreds of thousands of dedicated individuals whose untiring efforts put men on the moon."

"May God bless America," Shepherd added, and both men saluted the proud banner.

As Lucas gazed upon the stars and stripes, the vertigo returned. His eyes filled only by the white light, he began to fall, his balance suddenly gone. Instinctively, his gloved hand flew from its salutary position, reached out and caught something solid. The hold barely steadied him as he clung there, desperately and without understanding, his heart pounding, sheer terror claiming him. When his vision cleared and he glanced down at his grasping hand, fighting to free his rattled mind, he found only a deeper mire of confusion. The overwhelming wave of déjà vu returned.

His hand held fast to a rung of *Starlight*'s ladder.

Shepherd was gone. The flag they had erected was nowhere in sight.

Lucas found himself standing on the craft's forward footpad, ready to set foot upon the pristine soil beneath him.

For the first time.

His mind was torn violently from its moorings.

Lost, he leaned back and looked up at the shadowed window where Shepherd stood looking down. Clearly, the man had not yet begun his initial moonwalk. His familiar, jovial face, framed within the red-rimmed triangular port, betrayed no sense of alarm, no thought of concern.

"Charlie...I..." he struggled. "I don't..."

"Make it a good one, Skipper."

What's happening?

He closed his eyes and sought some measure of sanity, picturing his wife, his son, their home. The tumult eased, reluctantly allowing reason to return. He swung to look again at the powdery surface beside him, then glanced up and over at the LM Truck, which safely stood upon the Cabean valley floor a short distance away.

Atop it waited the heavy rover, still untouched and secure beneath its protective golden blankets.

Lucas furrowed his brow, his eyes fixed upon the stowed vehicle. Fading wisps of memory rose up and danced within him, like smoke on the wind.

"Mirabelle..."

"What, Gary?" Shepherd asked, surprise in his tone.

Lucas fought hard, but it was slipping away. "Bottom...of the lake..."

"Say again?"

He shook his head, his eyes closed tight. After a few moments, the sensation of life in replay dwindled and was gone. Centered once more, he breathed deeply and tried to recall the words he had planned for that long-awaited moment, his monumental first step onto the moon. Finding them, he stepped outward with his left boot, leaning his full weight into the endeavor.

"These are our last steps—"

Abruptly, the vertigo and light again swept reality from under and around him. When once more he found stability, everything had changed. His limbs trembled. He fought not to cry out, to collapse, to yield to the chaos.

His foot, suddenly clad only in a white sock, had found not frigid lunar soil but a soft cushion of deep, warm grass. The ladder, the space-craft were gone. He stood now within the edge of a lush forest, his right hand pressed against the rough bark of a towering tree. His pressure suit had vanished, leaving him clad once more in his liquid cooling garment. The huge knife he had been carrying was wedged behind the cluster of coolant tubing at his waist. Breeze stirred his hair. Smoke hanging in the dense air stung his eyes and filled his lungs.

It was night, with blackness ruling above. A warm, dancing light from up ahead spilled upon the woods around him, firelight as if from a raging pyre. From nearby came an ocean of chaotic voices. Every-where, horrifying screams echoed and died, cries answered by blood-curdling peals of demoniacal laughter.

Everywhere.

21

Lucas pressed himself hard against the jagged bark, clinging to the solidity of the standing timber. He had become a sailor lost at sea, tossed overboard by the crashing waves of a great storm and left at their mercy, with nothing but icy, hungry sea and merciless, crushing pressure waiting beneath his feet. The tree was a life preserver, its rooted substance against his drifting flesh, and he clung to it as if to life itself. The biting harshness of the bark dug into his cheek, the pain now a welcome bit of hard reality.

He breathed slowly, deeply, trying to make sense of all that had swept him away from his friend and into this new and terrifying place. Slowly, he began to think, but reason would not fully come to him.

Okay, Gary, he began, *think it through—*

He struggled, his overwhelmed mind unfocused. His breaths came deep and slow. Taking some measure of control, he began to calm himself, averting the panic that, unchecked, could prove fatal.

The air is dense, he realized, forcing that much logic to the forefront. *I'm feeling my real weight—there's at least a full gravity here—*

The screams he had heard sounded again, louder, closer. His concentration broke as if fighting to keep its distance.

No—think! Figure it out—this isn't the moon—can't be!

He reluctantly pushed away from the tree he had been embracing and sought the shadow of another, one closer to the source of the fire-light. Only a few dozen feet away, the forest ended and yielded to a clearing, and as he peered into that clearing he saw monstrous beings, their eyes reflecting the golden wash of the flames around them, even at a distance. Terrifying beings. Familiar beings.

Already, even as the sight filled his smoke-stung eyes, he strove to formulate a rational explanation, a fixed anchor. He stared in horrified fascination as the behemoths fought each other in the glow of the inferno, gigantic men whose slightest blows would fell the best Earth had to offer. They battled, wielding bizarre weapons in the streets of a dying town, one that must once have been impressive but now was gutted and ruined as if by war. Huge yellow-bathed gargoyles overlooked the chaos from high perches. Buildings everywhere burned, their timbers collapsing mere feet from the combatants, their windows shattering in the heat, their exposed steel framework glinting in the searing light. Despite the devastation and the thick haze, Lucas knew the structures once had been extremely elaborate in style—a hideous style that both was garish in its approach and grotesque in its execution.

It was a style he had seen before.

"Transylvania and then some," he whispered aloud.

I'm on their home world! How the—?

He pressed himself deeper into the cool shadow of the tree, out of the streaming heat and light of the fires, closing his eyes as he scrambled for a more palatable answer. None emerged from the knotted tangle of confusion and disbelief, pinning his reason, threatening his sanity.

Charlie, he remembered. *Is he here too?*

Slowly, he peered around the tree, toward the noise and light. As he watched the chaos unfolding before him, he could not believe that these same combative, murderous men had traveled into space, leaving their mark as they went and taking what they wished, conquering whole worlds, perhaps—

How could these guys build a house together, let alone a spacecraft? Or that moon base?

Yet they had, he was certain.

As the battle went on, men pursued and caught screaming women amid the rubble, savaging them like animals. Some of the victims managed to elude their attackers momentarily but inevitably fell prey.

I've got to get out of here—

Lucas had no desire to move into the fray. He knelt within a dark thicket of dense brush, wishing himself invisible, knowing that his best bet was to gain some sense of direction and, without losing it, move deeper into the forest. The last thing he needed was to be further lost.

He looked up into the night sky, hoping for a guiding star to fix upon, but the heavy smoke blocked his view. He considered a trick he had learned as a Boy Scout that entailed using the trees as fixed points for determining straight-line movement through the woods. He admittedly possessed few options, and none that offered immediate deliverance, so he stood and took a step out of the foliage.

Just as he had cleared it, he heard a new sound. Something else was moving through the woods.

Lucas froze, his ears pricked, his heart racing.

"Charlie?" he called quietly and with uncertainty. No reply came. The sound echoed again, the distinctive crunch of fallen branches beneath approaching feet.

Very loud, very large feet.

He did not move, hoping that whatever the thing was would pass without noticing his presence. But the steps grew closer, the crunching even louder. In the inky darkness of the forest, he could not see their source.

Lucas held his breath, fearful that whatever it was might hear his pounding heart. Then, suddenly, the footsteps stopped. He strained to hear any sign of the thing, knowing it was near.

Then he knew. *It was listening too.*

In the terrifying silence, he became aware of breathing, a deep, wet, raspy sound of air passing in and out of lungs, a sound much too loud to have come from a man.

Any man.

Slowly he began to crane his neck upward, trying to zero in on the source of the breathing. Higher his gaze rose and higher still.

Too high for anything *close* to human.

The footsteps sounded again, angling toward him now. He felt the ground beneath him shake as dry, colossal branches yielded to a moving, massive weight, their splintering betrayed by loud, repeated cracks that swept across the forest floor toward him.

It's almost on top of me—!

Lucas considered his knife but instead spun and bolted for the clearing. The footsteps sounded directly behind him, louder, faster. At a dead run he passed the final few trees and broke into the open, cutting a path to the left and toward the nearest structure, the nearest refuge. Diving into black shadow, he rolled behind and against a partial wall and went still, his own breathing coming in deep gulps, his heart screaming in his ears. Hugging the low stone parapet, trying to meld into it, he fought to listen. Minutes passed.

The footsteps had ceased. He crawled forward, cautiously peering around the broken edge of the wall, back in the direction from which he had come. Casting his weary, smoke-stung gaze into the forest, he watched for an eternity but saw no sign of the thing that had pursued him.

It had gone.

He lay still, flat on his back, staring blankly into the darkness above. Billows of black smoke, boiling in the rising heat of the fires, spread wide as far as he could see, catching the orange light and moving as if alive. Lucas allowed himself simply to breathe deeply, his eyes closed against the stinging air. His hands shook, partly from fear and partly due to his blood-sugar levels being perilously low.

The screams continued in the distance, as did the sharp clamor of breaking glass and the heavy rumble of collapsing walls. After several minutes, Lucas sat up, knowing he was not yet safe, aware that his survival hinged upon finding a secure hiding place.

Rising to his aching feet, he leaned hard into the structure beside him. Its stonework was cool against his sweat-dampened flesh, and he felt the edifice change from stone to metal to glass as he moved along, seeking an opening. Finally finding a heavy door of polished timber, he warily pushed it open, peered around its edge and into a darkened room. Just enough firelight spilled in from the windows of the opposite side to allow him to see that the room was unoccupied, so he took a deep breath and worked up his courage.

Here we go—!

Lucas moved quietly through the open doorway and into what seemed to be a living room. The place was an odd mix of ancient and advanced technology, with archaic items of stone and wood living in harmony with intricate devices beyond his understanding. He felt dwarfed both culturally and physically. A trio of heavy leather chairs in a triangular arrangement faced each other near the center of the room, one of them toppled onto its side. They were huge, each with a ponderous wooden frame that looked as if it might weigh a ton. The leather was knobby and mottled in vivid, almost unnatural colors, unlike any he had seen.

What appeared to be a display screen arched up one wall and onto the ceiling, its inert surface capturing the meager light like black pearl. Tiny lights of red and blue shone steadily at one edge, lights that could be seen only from a particular angle. Directly over his head hung a shallow, transparent dome some five feet across. He could not guess its function, but it was much like those he had seen within the moon base, only larger. Other apparently advanced devices rested in various places around the room, and Lucas hoped none was part of an intruder detection system. An enormous, freestanding fireplace of stone and steel stood against one wall, filled with the cold ashes of past fires. An odd, trenchlike pit ran from its hearth to the seating area, catching Lucas' foot as he moved and throwing him momentarily off balance. He slipped and fell to the hard floor, but not quietly.

The fall toppled a small ornamental metal sculpture, the crash filling the house and stopping his heart.

He froze, terror filling him. Any second, he knew, an angry colossus of a man would storm into the room and tear him to pieces. He turned, every muscle tensed to bolt from the place, but held up just long enough to realize that the only response to his hunger-induced clumsiness was silence. No one was coming. No one was home.

Terrific, he chided himself. *Why not use a bullhorn—*

Moving more carefully, Lucas made his way through the smoke-tinged room and toward a wide, rounded doorway that looked as if it might lead to a kitchen. His heart leaped as his gaze fell upon a table and a large rough-hewn wooden bowl that rested there, filled with large pieces of fruit. He seized a couple of the edibles and held them before his eyes.

If they can eat it, I can, he reasoned, dismissing any concerns that the luscious find might be toxic. Starvation was his only other option, and it held little promise.

Pulling one piece after another from the bowl, he ate greedily, sweet juice covering his lips and chin. Something like huge grapes, then something else that was small but resembled a melon, one after another he wolfed them down. Nearby, on a rough cutting board, rested half of an overlarge loaf of bread. He tore chunks from it until his hunger had been satisfied.

Water—

Lucas scanned the darkened room, searching for a source. There was a basin over which hung a spigot similar to those Shepherd and he had found in their adopted quarters on the moon. Moving carefully toward it, he reached out a hand and activated the stream with its proximity, then cupped the cool, wet wonder in his hands and drank until his thirst fell away.

Wiping his chin and pausing to gather himself, he turned and watched the turmoil beyond the barred, glassless window. Malevolence hung in the air, mingled with the smoke. Half a block away, hideous men some fifteen feet tall battled among themselves, giants among giants, the wide, curved blades of their weapons sparking with white heat as they collided again and again. The blades nearly always found their mark, dismembering some and decapitating others in a sickening nightmare of warfare without rules. Blood ran freely in the streets.

The buildings rising into the night, though largely ruined, nonetheless were amazing. Elements of glass, steel, and stone, fused as one, flowed seamlessly into one another and created multistoried works of decadent art that almost seemed to have grown that way. As he watched, a twelve-foot gargoyle with outstretched arms, widespread wings, and glowing red eyes toppled forward from its perch and fell to the street below, crushing a pair of bloodied combatants who never saw it coming.

Not all of the women he saw were victims. Many were giving themselves aggressively to men who were more than happy to oblige, laughing as they reveled in their flesh. Others, swinging bladed weapons with learned efficiency, were felling other women and men near their own size, some of whom already were seriously injured. No sooner had the fatally wounded fallen than their female attackers set upon them, stripping the still warm bodies of anything of value before disappearing in the fiery confusion.

What kind of planet is this—?

With his bodily needs met and with no immediate physical threat descending upon him, and as the leaping flames and cruel struggles outside filled his sight, Lucas' mind began to reason again.

What happened? I was in the base—I woke up Charlie, and he said "give me a minute," and then I turned around—

His memory failed him. *And suddenly, I was in the LM, and we were landing—!*

He recalled the huge star map Shepherd had discovered.

This must be one of the planets in that system—

He realized that perhaps an entire galaxy now separated him from his wife, his son.

"Annie…" he whispered in despair, seeing her face before him.

A thunderous sound came from the main room. Something large had fallen heavily upon the floor in a clatter of metals and wood. A sudden laugh followed, a deep bellow that shook the darkness.

Lucas, his heart pounding, leaped behind the table and dropped to the floor. Holding his breath, he peered beyond the table's central pedestal and back through the doorway. He knew he was barely hidden, but to attempt a move anywhere else would surely give him away.

A rumbling voice spoke, the odd words carrying no meaning.

"Sestu trianna gleedu," they sounded, in a subdued and awkward tone that seemed self-satisfied. Though he did not know the words, Lucas detected a distinct slur in the delivery, one he had heard time and again in bars and taverns around the world.

He's drunk—

More laughter followed, more words.

And talking to himself—

Lucas crouched lower as an immense man stumbled into the kitchen, mere feet away. He was clad in heavy robes of blue and green, robes that were torn as if in a struggle, and upon his huge feet he wore laceless, soft leather boots. As the colossus grew closer, he lost his footing and fell against the table, knocking both it and the unseen Lucas backward before catching himself and managing to make his way across the room. Muttering to himself as he opened a storage cabinet, the man reached up and withdrew a large deep-blue bottle and lifted it to his lips.

He didn't see me—

The astronaut watched as the drunken giant scratched his hirsute chest, pulling his outer robes looser as he made himself more comfortable. A glint of metal revealed a bladed weapon at his belt—fresh blood was upon it—and Lucas' hand instinctively went to the great knife he still carried. He held his breath anew as the man shuffled back across the kitchen floor, his legs unsure, and headed back into the living area.

Left alone in the kitchen, Lucas began to breathe easier.

A sudden racket filled the living area, that of breaking glass and toppling furniture, one crash atop another. Then a heavy silence. Lucas froze, listening for any further sign of movement, any indication that it was not safe to move. The silence continued.

He rose from his shadowy hiding place and moved toward the kitchen door, his unshod feet silent against the polished stone. Hands trembling, he leaned into the wall separating the two rooms and peered around the edge of the doorway. He began to breathe a bit easier as his eyes scanned the near darkness.

The giant had dropped into one of the massive chairs Lucas had seen earlier and passed out. The bottle he had carried lay broken on the floor beside him, blue shards catching the dim light.

Lucas warily stepped closer, making his way toward the outside door. His eyes on the sleeping man, he almost tripped over a great bulging sack of cloth, one brimming with what he realized must be looted goods. Items of gold and silver, jeweled treasures and wondrous technology, had spilled from its open top and onto the floor. Small, strange instruments glittered invitingly, but Lucas' curiosity fell second to his desire for self-preservation, and he headed without delay toward the waiting door.

Once outside, he again paused in the shadow of the house. The screams were louder now—and closer.

Okay—now what? The woods aren't safe, the town's not safe—

Lucas cut continuous glances from side to side, seeking inspiration for a course of action. The dancing flames threw moving shadows everywhere, creating phantom attackers that lurked at the limits of his peripheral vision. The house still blocked his being seen by those on the street, but it also limited his view of the town. If there was refuge, it would have to lie there—*something* lurked in the forest, something that might wish to make a meal of him, something he did not want to encounter again.

Inching his way to the edge of the house, he chose to make a break for another building that stood some two hundred feet away. It was one of the few in that part of town that was not engulfed in flame, a three-story structure of flowing red stone that seemed unoccupied and had an inviting, open door. Seeing no other apparent target, he took a few deep breaths and studied the terrain he would cross in reaching it. Fortunately, the way ahead was not completely in the open—a few larger clusters of dense underbrush and debris would provide cover along the way, and Lucas considered them as he decided upon his exact route. Noting the craggy rubble and metal shards scattered widely before him, he wiggled his stockinged toes, wishing they still rested within his heavy-soled moon boots.

Stealing quick looks around the corner, he chose his moment and broke into a dead run, his movement slowed by the weakness in his limbs. With his eyes fixed upon the first man-sized clump of growth and twisted metal, he covered some forty yards of open ground and then fell behind the thicket, ending up on hands and knees. After a few fearful moments, he raised his head toward the ongoing chaos and found that he had not been seen. Those who battled nearby were too occupied with their own situation to notice a running stranger. From his new angle, Lucas noticed an open alleyway lying closer than the building he had chosen as his target, and for a moment he considered it as an alternate destination—but then he saw the shadows of multiple struggling giants sliding along its walls and ruled it out entirely.

Lucas gathered himself for a few moments then sprang to his feet and began again. Mindful of the jagged hazards still lurking in the dense grass, he zigzagged in order to follow the smoothest path but found it impossible to completely avoid stepping on the smaller fragments of stone and ceramic that suddenly lay everywhere. He slowed, knowing that a foot injury could prove fatal if it hobbled him in this place, where potential attackers loomed everywhere and speed was his greatest defense.

He reached the overgrown remains of a low stone wall and dropped to his knees behind it. Casting a sideward glance, he judged himself still a good hundred feet from the open door. Keeping his head down, he listened as the nearby fighting continued. The agonized screams and unintelligible shouts were louder than before.

Are they getting closer?

After resting for as long as he dared, Lucas pulled himself to his feet and again began to run. Twenty yards farther along, a shriek to his immediate left startled him and he turned to see a terrified woman in a tattered blue robe being attacked at the entry to the alleyway. Her assailant towered over her, his deranged eyes wide as he repeatedly pulled her long dark hair, yanking her head cruelly from side to side before shoving her to the ground. As the brute laughed at his chosen victim, pinning her now with a heavy foot, he tossed his bladed weapon and his outer robes aside, his intention clear.

Lucas slowed, captured by the unfolding horror, transfixed by something he did not yet realize, something some deep part of his mind had already seen.

The woman screamed again, pushing helplessly against the massive limb that held her immobile. In desperation she looked to the side, her eyes seeking help from someone, anyone. Her pleading gaze fell upon Lucas, who immediately found his eyes locked with hers. He stopped dead, lost in her supplicating gaze. In the intense firelight, in that instant, he saw her dark, wet eyes, her high cheekbones, her raven hair—

And he knew that face, those eyes.

Annie!

Lucas' body moved instinctively, breaking into a frantic run toward the woman, in a curved path he hoped would prevent his being seen by the beast atop her. His hand went to the knife at his waist, and in a second he had pulled the huge blade free and was raising it into the air.

I'm coming!

Lucas had one shot at saving the woman from the nine-foot colossus assailing her, and one only, he knew.

He doesn't see me—

Surprise was his only advantage. He had one chance to save his Diane, and if he failed they *both* would die, horribly and painfully.

The almost-naked giant had dropped to his knees and was straddling the woman. Roaring with laughter, he laid heavily upon her, pressing her hard into the clovered soil. The woman screamed again, beating her ineffective fists against the vicious brute.

The giant did not hear the running man bearing down upon him from behind. He did not see the angry, resolute eyes of the displaced astronaut, nor sense the flashing blade held high, poised to strike.

With the woman's frantic screams filling his ears, Lucas leaped into the air, bringing his full weight and as much inertia as possible to bear against his foe. With all the strength the astronaut could muster and with both hands white-knuckled around his knife handle, he slammed the blade downward.

There was a sickening sound as it struck just below the shoulder blade, slicing between ribs as it drove deep into the man's back. Carried by his momentum, Lucas landed upon the giant, forcing the knife deeper, then shoved with all his strength until only the hilt remained exposed. The wicked man cried out, his eyes tightly shut in pain, and knocked Lucas away as he fought to raise himself to his knees.

The blow had not been fatal.

Lucas rolled free and took hold of the injured man's own dropped weapon, struggling to lift it from the ground. It was enormous and cumbersome, its polished, already bloody blade awkward in his hands. He swung around and managed to raise it into the air before immediately bringing it down again, the weapon's own weight burying it in the manbeast's upper chest, its steel finding his heart. The giant cried out, defiantly lunging at Lucas and knocking him to the ground before falling upon him in the same motion. Then, suddenly, the immense ogre went still.

The woman managed to wriggle free and rose to her feet, but Lucas was pinned awkwardly by the dead weight of the Goliath he had slain. One huge, viselike arm was locked around his left leg, and his right, bent beneath him at an awkward angle, flooded him with pain. His heart still pounding, his limbs shaking with adrenaline, he looked up into the woman's face as she bent down and pushed against the dead hulk, trying to free her savior. For the first time Lucas realized her great stature, saw her lovely face clearly. She was easily six and a half feet tall, though still graceful and exquisitely feminine.

You—you aren't Annie—!

With strong hands, the woman took hold of Lucas' arm and tried to pull him free, but she was interrupted by rapidly approaching voices.

Others were coming down the alley, huge figures in dark flowing robes, their faces hidden behind grotesque masks. A half-dozen men, maybe more. Lucas saw them and his blood ran cold.

"Go!" he said, pointing away, pleading with her. "Get out of here!"

They locked upon each other's faces for a moment, their eyes speaking universal pleas. She obviously wanted to help him but knew there was no time. He still saw the image of Diane in the woman's beautiful, passionate face and wanted her safely away.

She looks so much like—!

"Go...now!"

"Dorali...carojella!" the woman said softly, her tone serious, her voice like music. Releasing Lucas' arm, she looked again at the approaching group and finally, with obvious reluctance, turned and ran. Lucas watched her as she headed swiftly and directly toward the forest.

"No!" he tried to call out, warning her. "There's something out there...!"

He glanced back and found the towering, hooded figures almost upon him, then looked again in the direction of the forest. But the darkness had consumed all sign of the woman.

Powerful hands descended upon him. As he was pulled free of the massive body atop him, Lucas looked into the faces of his captors and saw eyes glinting wetly from behind the eyeholes of their hideous masks, death's heads forged of blackened metal. Something icy pressed hard against his forehead. The world fell away.

⬚　　⬚　　⬚

From within the relative safety of the forest, the woman watched as firelight revealed the stranger's unconscious form shackled by the black-robed men. Tears flowed as she watched, angry at herself for her inability to help him. She knew who the dark figures were, knew the grisly fate that awaited the brave little man who had risked his life to save hers. She had thought never to see his like again.

They carried him away, into the alley and out of sight. The woman turned at once and fled into the woods, tracing a familiar path through the dense growth, headed toward the one island of safety in the demoniacal world she knew.

That haven stood waiting—but it would not wait for long.

22

It had been two days since Lucas' disappearance, and Shepherd had run out of ideas. Panic repeatedly tried to surface but was beaten back by years of survival training and exercises in reason. After enduring life-or-death struggles amid jungle growth and desert sands, in the air and on the water, and on land and in space, it was not easy for an astronaut to be rattled, especially not one of NASA's finest.

Not easy—but not impossible.

For forty-eight hours, locating his friend had been foremost in Shepherd's mind, but his repeated searches had been fruitless. Since there was no way out of the base, he knew that the man had to be there *somewhere,* meaning that for some reason he was unable to respond to Shepherd's persistent calls. Surely Lucas was unconscious or badly injured or perhaps even—

No. He's alive—I just have to find him.

But now, Shepherd knew, he had to pause to ensure his own survival, or both might perish. His body, denied sustenance for almost a week, was growing weaker by the hour, and if Lucas was indeed hurt, a compromised rescuer would do him no good.

Shepherd stood staring at the monolithic mechanism before him.

Like so much of the technology of its builders, it was almost a work of art, a fluid jumble of steel and glass some twelve feet high, covered above with the same colorful, indecipherable graphics he had seen throughout the base.

Only now, he was certain, those markings meant *food.*

He glanced around the room again. A dozen wide, oblong, irregular pits had been dug into its floor, all neatly covered with the same polished, stony material that made up the floor. All were of the same depth, about four feet, with gently scalloped edges and descending steps cut into each end. Rising within each pit, supported by a flowing central pedestal of polished crystal, was a translucent tabletop shaped to follow the outline of the hollow it occupied. Each table shone like colored pearl, each with a half-dozen shallow and roughly rectangular surface depressions cut into its surface. Apparently, those who dined there were meant to sit in the contoured hollows of the pits' edges as they enjoyed their food.

This has to be a dining hall—

On one of the tables, in one of its depressions, rested a large, ovoid metal tray covered with the darkened remains of what must once have been an unfinished meal, left uneaten who knew how many years before.

He looked again at the machine, towering silently against the wall as if challenging him to solve the mystery of its function. It was the only thing standing in the room—it *had* to be a food dispenser of some kind. Toward its bottom was what might have been a dispensing door, a rectangular depression three feet wide that looked as if it might open.

If only I can figure it out—

Remembering the devices in the bathroom of his adopted quarters, he reached out and waved his hands before the thing, moving them through the air as if conducting an orchestra. Nearer, farther, side to side.

Nothing.

He moved closer, placing his palms against the cool contours of the machine, pressing lightly, pressing harder, trying first one odd protrusion then another like a man groping for a light switch in a dark room.

Nothing.

Shepherd paused, his stomach growling commands to proceed. The enigma just stood there, defiantly keeping its secrets.

Okay, Charlie, think.

He turned back toward the seating pits, hoping some clue might make itself apparent.

Man, those tables are big!

Whirling back toward the device, he craned his neck upward.

Of course—so were these people! I've been whapping this thing on the knees—!

Stretching to his full height, Shepherd jumped and began to slap at the obelisk, his hand striking the colored graphics scattered high on its face. Once, twice, three times. When there was no response, he gripped its edge and pulled himself just high enough to allow a more prolonged contact between his palm and one of the symbols. He managed to hold the awkward position for only a moment or two before falling back to the floor, but not without a reward.

A sound.

He paused. Something inside the machine had stirred. Waiting a moment, he heard nothing else.

"Come on, baby," he wished aloud. "Charlie needs a sandwich..."

He reached up and tried again. Again, the sound. He pressed against more of the graphics. And again and again. Each time, the machine made the odd little noise, a subdued squeal not unlike that of a gopher caught in a burlap sack. Sometimes the sound varied slightly, having a lower pitch than usual. Again and again, between attempts, he looked down at the assumed dispenser door but found it sealed as tightly as ever.

"Well, what are you doing?" Shepherd asked in frustration. He banged on the heavy, knee-high metal door, but it would not budge. "What's the problem…are you empty?"

It appeared to be a standoff, man versus monolith, and something had to give.

"All right," he said, rolling up his sleeves. "No more kid gloves."

He jumped up and struck first one part of the machine's face then another. Half a dozen times he set upon the arcane mechanism, and each time he heard the little sound.

The apparent door at the bottom stayed shut.

"Well, dang it!" he moaned, breathing heavily. "A Coke…anything!" More weary from his assault than might otherwise have been usual for him, he paused for a moment to catch his breath and think.

"Okay…what else is there? What am I missing?" He scanned the front of the machine. "A coin slot? A magic word? What?" He stepped back. "I gotta sit down…"

He stooped to pick up his lightkey then spun toward the tables again—and his eyes went wide.

They were covered in food, all of them. Tray after tray, one for each blow he had delivered, for each order he successfully and unknowingly had placed.

Like a kid on Christmas morning, he moved closer in disbelief, drinking in the sight of the banquet spread before him. There were more than a dozen full meals there: steaks, breads, vegetables, fruits. Some he recognized, many more he did not.

"Yes!" he cried out, almost leaping into one of the pits. For an instant, however, he paused, his training speaking to him.

What if it's poisoned? What if Earth folks can't eat this stuff?

"I'll die anyway," he whispered in answer to his own question.

There were utensils upon each tray as well, unusual ones, but he bypassed them at first in favor of his trusty fingers. Taking deep, greedy bites, he found the breads delicious and moist, the fruits succulent, the meats hot and tender and juicy.

"Man, but Stuckey's knows how to cook!" he rejoiced, mouth full, laughing loudly.

The enormous steak before him was a good two-pounder at least, cooked medium rare. It seemed like beef, but Shepherd would not have staked his life on that, given its unearthly origin. Managing the odd tongs and serrated knife provided, he took bite after bite and was carried back to every backyard barbecue he had ever given. No fat had been trimmed, which only added to its wondrous flavor. Nearby, on other trays, rested what looked like roast chicken but on a much larger scale, thinly sliced ham, a light-colored meat that looked like turkey, and a much darker reddish one he could not identify.

The vegetables resting next to his steak, apparently beans and sliced tubers of some type, were brightly colored in vivid greens and yellows. They too had been cooked, but still retained a curious crispness that made them unusually pleasant to eat. The fruits seemed more conventional except for their great size—grapes, cherries, and apples spread before him, glistening in the light, cool and as sweet as any he had ever tasted. The breads were far richer and more filling than those he knew, seemingly baked with coarse-ground whole grains and honeyed spices. Shepherd felt he could quite happily have eaten nothing else for the rest of his life, each loaf was so delicious.

In addition to their generous portions, each oval tray also held a glass and metal goblet. Some were filled with cold water while others brimmed with different types of fruit juices, and Shepherd drank of them all between bites so as to help the food go down better. It was a virtual banquet, one laid out just for him, and as his hunger fell away, the generous repast became one of the finest meals he had ever enjoyed.

Thank you, Lord, he remembered. *You always provide—always.*

His shrunken stomach filled quickly. His hunger almost satisfied, his mind began to analyze both the huge machine and the food it magically had produced. Continuing to eat at a more casual pace, he gazed at the device in wonder, considering how it might have performed its culinary miracle. *Who knows how many years that thing's been sitting here, with nothing in there gone rotten, nothing gone to dust—and this stuff just appeared out of nowhere!* He thought back to a science-fiction television show he once had seen, where whole meals instantly emerged from a slot in the wall when a button was pushed. *Could it be? Food created from raw matter? Spoil-proof proteins and whatever else, formed by these machines into any shape or type of food desired?*

"Hey, Mr. Spock," he said with a smile, "chicken or fish?"

A few more minutes passed, and he grew full. As he took a few final sips from his cup, he looked upon the uneaten food all around him, hating to waste even a bite of it.

I'm gonna need a doggy bag—

Calmer now, he stood, leaned back against the side of the dining pit and began to worry once more about Lucas. Part of him wanted to assume the blame for the man's disappearance, an ember of guilt threatening to become a flame.

If only I hadn't taken so long. If only I hadn't paused to shave. If only I'd turned right instead of left when I walked out of my quarters—

If only the engine had fired.

Shepherd fought back the theoreticals, knowing they could accomplish nothing. Allowing his thoughts to drift, he peered through the open doorway at the great fountain beyond, the sound of flowing water filling his ears.

Water! He still was amazed. *Not just water, but plumbing—on the moon!*

Beyond that, across the atrium and exactly opposite the dining-hall door, stood the life-support room, its door still open. He could see the great machine carrying out its designed function, just as it must have done for hundreds if not thousands of years. The gleaming device was humming away, its icy blue strip still glowing, its many pipes and conduits still dutifully doing whatever it was they were doing.

An adjacent door was not open. Shepherd had sealed the one leading to the sacrificial temple chamber after his initial visit there and had not reopened it. The chill Shepherd had experienced there had taken several hours to leave him, and he had no desire to revisit the sensation.

Despite having gone through the rest of the base three times in search of Lucas, Shepherd had found no sign of him. Shepherd had even gone back into the airlock through which they had first entered the base, wondering if somehow his friend had managed to find an oxygen supply, suit up, and leave. As outlandish as the idea was, he had to take a look if only for his own peace of mind. He had found both pressure suits right where they had left them, their backpacks spent, their sooty components scattered upon the floor.

Where are you, Gary?

Shepherd picked up his lightkey and began toward the door. The food machine again caught his eye, as did the mysterious panel at its base, and he paused as a thought occurred to him. Glancing back at the dining tables, curiosity flared.

"Hmmmm…"

Retrieving one of the food trays, he carried it over to the hulking, silent machine and leaned over to place it near the apparent door. At once, the panel snapped upward and out of sight, revealing a small, enclosed compartment into which he pushed the tray. Then, as quickly as it had opened, the door closed again.

"Handy," he said, smiling again.

He collected the other trays and their trash, and one by one returned them also to the machine from which they had come. Each time the panel opened there was no remaining trace of the previous tray, but where exactly it and its garbage had gone he could not guess.

As Shepherd left the dining room, its lights went out behind him. Pausing to wash his hands in the fountain, he casually peered through the last doorway on the atrium and into the darkened fourth chamber.

This must have been a gymnasium, he had concluded upon its discovery a couple of days earlier. *At least, someone's idea of one.*

He had found the sports facility the day Lucas had vanished. Now, walking slowly up to the open door of the ghostly room, he paused just within the entrance. Warm lighting acknowledged his presence.

The room was circular, and tiered seating climbed high upon its walls, surrounding an enormous area twice the size of a basketball court. At its exact center stood a heavy, two-foot-wide donut of polished metal mounted atop a ten-foot pole of the same material. The entire floor of the arena was paved in polished white stone, what there was of it—deep, circular, bowl-shaped pits more than eight feet in diameter covered it completely, spaced so closely together that there was little floor left between them. Fearful that Lucas might have fallen into one of the pits, Shepherd already had checked them one by one, walking as if on a tightrope as he made his way along. Even now, he could not begin to guess at the rules of the game that must have been played there, but whatever it was, he knew it had been violent—copious amounts of dried, powdery blood still stained the floor, the central pole, and even parts of the seating area.

"Gary?" he called as he had a hundred times, but as usual the only response was a cavernous echo. He took one final lingering look before turning away and starting his search anew.

Craterball, he mused. *What better place.*

23

Black. A sea of black.

Diane looked upon the familiar faces of those gathered for the memorial service, all of whom were dressed in their darkest, most solemn attire. The entire NASA astronaut corps was present, along with their wives, most of whom privately had expressed their condolences during the week following the loss of the two men. Administrators, flight directors, mission controllers, simulation operators—all were there, all still carrying the weight of a belief that they must have missed that one crucial clue that would have brought the lost men home.

Also in attendance were cherished family, treasured friends, a few local politicians and law-enforcement officials, and dozens of uniformed military men with whom Diane's and Carol's husbands had served, many of whom neither woman readily knew.

Diane's gaze rose to the lofty, ornate wall at the front of the room, which stood nearby and to her right. Her eyes fixed upon the magnificent, burnished cross that dominated it and towered above the pulpit beneath. For a moment she allowed her mind to drift away from the pain that clawed at her, trying to break through her defenses.

Look at that—the way the light from the windows plays against the gold.

It was exquisite, an impressive creation in aureate metal that spoke of devotion and perhaps even passion in whoever had crafted it. For Diane, however, it spoke of nothing more.

It's lovely—

A gentle squeeze of her left arm interrupted her unfocused contemplation. Beside her sat Carol, also dressed in flowing black, her winsome though weary features obscured by the veil she wore. The two women clung to each other, merging their strength, drawing from something beyond themselves that they might survive the moments to come.

It would not be easy.

The service was being held in the church the Shepherds had attended since moving to Houston many years ago. Carol knew the building well, having attended the Sunday service each week, having once taught Sunday school there, and having served as part of numerous charity functions that had provided everything from meals to much-needed clothing for many in want. At Carol's request, Diane had helped out once or twice but had never felt a need to take things any further than that, spiritually speaking. Having discussed many possible locations for the memorial, the two women had agreed that this house of worship was the most fitting site for it, given Shepherd's love of the place and Lucas' oft-stated indifference toward such formalities.

The two, along with Carol's son, Joey, sat to one side at the front of the room, a special place generally reserved for those awaiting baptism or some other sacrament. Their otherwise vacant pew was an island of emptiness within the crowded sanctuary, and from their seats both women could watch the darkly attired assemblage around them. There were few empty seats, but more visitors came through the door each minute. Diane looked toward the entry, awaiting the arrival of her son, who had paused in the vestibule to speak with a few close friends.

She knew the president was somewhere near. He was to speak during the service, and Carol had said she overheard someone mentioning his arrival. Most likely, the man was waiting in one of the anterooms, ready to emerge when the service was nearer at hand. Knowing his presence might serve as a distraction from the two men who were the day's true focus, he had expressed that concern to both Diane and Carol by telephone the day before, assuring them that the event would not be politicized in any way.

Her eyes skirted the crowd, bypassing them all as she continued to look for Jeff. Not finding him, she spent a few moments scanning the hundreds of faces that filled the chamber. Some of them, she had not seen for years.

So wonderful that they came—my Gary was so special to so many. And Charlie, too, of course—

Diane's eyes fell upon Vic and Katie Kendall, who at his insistence had taken a seat across the sanctuary, far from the widows he believed he had created. For a moment, her eyes caught his—but the troubled man quickly turned away, his gaze dropping aside, his expression one of great pain. Katie held her husband's arm tightly, as if doing so would prevent his ever being lost to her.

Vic—I understand, Diane wanted to cry out. *You did what you had to do.* Days earlier, she had tried to reassure him, to convince him that she did not hold him responsible for the loss of her husband, but the attempt was in vain. For a moment she considered going to him once more, there and then, to reiterate that all had been beyond his control and that he had no reason to feel responsible. She feared that again he would not hear her words, that the burden of misplaced guilt he refused to relinquish would not allow it.

Time—it will take time.

Little Joey sat at the end of the pew on the other side of his mother, his legs swinging restlessly as he peered around at the surrounding forest of people, all of whom seemed quite upset.

"Why are they mad?" he asked.

"What, honey?"

"All these people…they look mad."

Carol stroked his hair. "No, no…it isn't that."

"Where's Daddy?" he asked quite innocently.

"I told you, sweetheart," his mother said, caressing the side of his face with a cool hand. Her voice broke slightly. "He went to be with Jesus. We won't be seeing him for a while."

She reached into her purse, pulled out a roll of Certs and handed one to the boy, hoping it might help keep him occupied.

"How long?" he asked, popping the mint into his mouth.

"How long what?"

"How long until we see Daddy?"

She swallowed hard and looked down into his innocent eyes. "I don't know, Joey."

"I hope it isn't long," the boy said, fidgeting with the hem of his jacket as the kicking finally ceased. "It was long last time."

Diane overheard. Lengthy periods when training or other NASA business kept the astronauts from their families were the norm. Some intervals were longer than others, but none unbearably so.

She closed her eyes. If she tried, she could almost lie to herself—*he's away in training again, that's all—just like he always was before.*

She felt the presence of someone taking a seat next to her and found Jeff suddenly to her right.

"You snuck up on me," Diane quietly said, patting his hand.

"Roger's mom said she'd be happy to run whatever errands we

might need," her son responded. "I told her I couldn't think of any but thanked her anyway."

"That was very sweet of her," Diane said, peering around in a further attempt to keep her mind distracted from the purpose of the gathering. Her eyes found a lone television camera, which was being set up in an out-of-the-way location to one side of the room, its glass eye emerging from a curtained alcove usually reserved for the storage of metal overflow chairs. The press had been allowed minimal access, the camera and the sanctum's existing sound system providing a single feed of image and sound to be shared by all.

Think of all the people who will be watching. The whole country— the whole world—

Bitterness crept in.

A world that couldn't be bothered to watch him land on the moon.

"I'm so sorry," a familiar feminine voice cut in. Diane spun to find Marilyn Lovell and her husband, Jim, standing at the end of the pew. The woman leaned down to hug first Carol then Diane, her own eyes reddened. "You know we're here for you, both of you, any time day or night."

"Thank you," Carol nodded. "That means so much."

Diane smiled bravely. "Thank you, Marilyn."

Lovell knelt beside Joey. "Such a fine young man. How are you doing, champ?"

"Well," the boy began, shyness in his voice, "I wanted to bring my 'pollo, but Mommy said no."

"The little model Charlie built for him," Carol clarified.

Lovell smiled at the young man. "Well, your mommy's a pretty smart lady. I'm sure she had a good reason." He patted the boy twice on the knee then stood and nodded a silent reassurance to both Carol and Diane.

"Hello, Jeff," the seasoned astronaut added, looking beyond the two women as they continued their subdued conversation with Marilyn. "Your father spoke of you often. He was very proud of you."

"Thank you, sir," the young man said.

Lovell placed a hand on his wife's shoulder, indicating that the service was about to begin. Marilyn reached out and took the two women's hands one final time then went with her husband to find their seats.

"They're wonderful," Carol said with a slight smile. "Charlie and I never met two finer people...present company excepted." She took Diane's hand and they held the embrace as music they had selected began to play, a gentle, sweeping passage of strings and woodwinds.

As she listened, Diane became aware that Jeff had stood. Turning, she found the impressive figure of the president growing near, compassion evident on his burden-lined face. In his left hand was the worn, leather-bound Bible that had provided him time and again with the wisdom he needed in the performance of his elected duty. Two black-suited Secret Service men accompanied him at close quarters, their ever-watchful eyes scanning the room from behind their dark glasses.

The president extended a hand and Jeff took it, but the gesture quickly became a heartfelt embrace.

"I'm so very sorry about your father," the man said softly, pulling back to arm's length. Diane saw a tear in his eye. "He served his country well, Jeff, and taught us all the true meaning of patriotism...and that is a fine legacy for any man."

"Thank you, sir," Jeff said, trying to maintain his composure.

The president approached Diane and Carol and stood before and between them, leaning down to take their hands, each in turn.

"Gary will be missed, Diane," he said, looking into her eyes. "We are diminished, all of us, for having lost him."

Diane held his hand in both of hers for a moment, drawing from his strength. As she gazed into the chief executive's eyes, no words came to her, but she did manage a nod of appreciation for his.

To Carol, he quietly spoke as one Christian to another. "You know Charlie's in our Lord's presence now, Carol…such a wondrous place that must be." The woman smiled through welling tears and nodded.

"Thank you," she whispered.

"I look forward to the day when I meet him again."

The president took a seat next to Jeff as his agents stood nearby. When the music ended, the minister approached and thanked the president for coming before turning to Carol and taking her hand. The gentle white-haired man was her pastor, her steersman, and a longtime friend of her family.

"Be comforted, Carol," he said. "He's only away, not gone."

"Thank you, Andrew…it means so much that you're here."

He smiled assuredly then turned and took his place behind the elevated pulpit at the front of the room. The chamber went utterly silent.

"My friends," the robed man began, his deep, rich voice echoing slightly, "we have come together today to remember our friends Gary Lucas and Charles Shepherd. Those of us who personally knew them were truly blessed, and those who knew them most closely, who had the honor of calling them 'friend' or 'husband' or 'father,' now feel a sense of loss that no words can adequately express.

"These brave men boldly left the sparkling blue world our Lord made for us, setting out from this grand oasis toward an unknown and desolate land, seeking to bring their fellow men a greater knowledge of the vast creation around us. Yet, though they traveled a quarter of a million miles into the harshness of space, never did they leave the presence of our Father, who was with them throughout their journey. As is written in Psalm 139, beginning at the eighth verse:

"If I ascend to heaven, Thou art there;
If I make my bed in Sheol, behold, Thou art there.
If I take the wings of the dawn,
If I dwell in the remotest part of the sea,
Even there Thy hand will lead me,
And Thy right hand will lay hold of me.
If I say, "Surely the darkness will overwhelm me,
And the light around me will be night,"
Even the darkness is not dark to Thee,
And the night is as bright as the day,
Darkness and light are alike to Thee."

After a pause, he went on. "On our behalf, Gary and Charlie walked into a great darkness, a valley of shadow where no man before them had been. It takes a special brand of courage to venture so far into the unknown, to leave behind everyone and everything one knows for the sake of a noble quest."

Vic Kendall cringed at the word.

"However," the man went on, "doing such as this was nothing new to these men, both of whom had risked their very lives again and again that their country might be a more secure place.

"Such courage is hard to put into words, but the very essence of such noble men *has* been expressed, penned by a pilot named John Gillespie Magee Jr., and these words live in the heart of every pilot, every astronaut, and in everyone who labored so diligently to send our courageous explorers into space."

The minister made a subtle gesture toward the crowd. Apollo 15 astronaut James Irwin rose from the front row and mounted the dais, stepping behind a smaller wooden lectern to one side of the pulpit. Taking his place behind the microphone, he found upon the lectern a small, tattered, once-folded sheet of yellowed paper, which he had readied earlier. After pausing for a moment to compose himself, he began to read:

"Oh, I have slipped the surly bonds of earth
and danced the skies on laughter-silvered wings;
Sunward I've climbed, and joined the tumbling mirth
of sun-split clouds—and done a hundred things
you have not dreamed of—wheeled and soared and swung
high in the sunlit silence. Hov'ring there,
I've chased the shouting wind along, and flung
my eager craft through footless halls of air.
Up, up the long, delirious burning blue,
I've topped the windswept heights with easy grace
where never lark, or even eagle flew,
and, while with silent, lifting mind I've trod
the high, untrespassed sanctity of space,
put out my hand—and touched the face of God."

Diane trembled, fighting to remain composed, her downturned face in her hands, her son's arms now around her. The poem, entitled "High Flight," had been her husband's favorite, so much so that he always had carried the very copy from which Irwin had read, clipped from a newspaper, in his wallet. When she had asked that it be read at the service, she thought she would be able to hear its words without hearing Gary's voice speaking them, but she was wrong.

She lost her battle and wept deeply.

24

Wednesday, March 12, 9:29 A.M.

He had known better days.

Dr. Thomas Paine sat in his Washington D.C. office watching the quiescent whiteness outside. Large, wet flakes were falling, as they had been all night and all morning. The trees stood as silent white sentinels in the stillness, their pleading branches now almost invisible against the pale gray sky. It had been a heavy late-season snow, and the purity of the thick frozen blanket seemed almost to disguise the deathly pall that had descended over the NASA Headquarters building.

Almost.

Maybe I should have gone ahead and retired from the agency. GE wanted me back, and their offer was good—perhaps that would have been better—

Paine thought back to his days as a World War II submarine officer and his early career as an engineer with General Electric. Throughout all he had experienced, throughout all the tours he had served, throughout his entire stint as NASA Administrator, *never* had he sensed the oppressive dread that now hovered over the space agency, the tangible air of finality that threatened its very existence. He could feel it in every breath he drew, every word he spoke, every move he made. It was as a living thing, a gelid demon that now lurked in every hallway and every office, making every thought, every intent, every plan seem worthless before its first utterance.

Such a fragile thing—

Word had come down that those with the power to do so were about to end the space program entirely. By pulling its funding, Congress could then funnel those dollars into the earthbound causes so many of its members deemed to be of greater value. A closed Senate subcommittee hearing was to be held that very afternoon, at which those supporting NASA's continuation would offer their best rationale, hopefully to fall upon ears not yet deaf to it.

On top of the matter of NASA's survival there was now another issue at hand, one that hinged upon the first and had been introduced only days earlier. It would be a tough sell, no doubt, a proposal not likely to please the gathered skeptics but one that could not wait for more favorable circumstances.

Paine took a long, slow breath as he watched the placid snowfall, losing himself in its encompassing gentleness. He had experienced few moments of true serenity during his tenure, and for a few precious minutes he allowed his mind to ride untethered upon the calm sea of white before him. His mind drifted back, sailing the years in an almost kaleidoscopic fashion, skimming from flight to flight, year to year, moment to moment, glory to glory.

So much has changed, so fast—where are the cheers we heard in July of 1969, when Neil took that first small step? Where are the dreams that so many dropped at our doorstep, praying that we would make them a reality?

At any moment the ax could fall, he knew, ending the careers of hundreds of thousands and, at the same time, virtually ending the foreseeable future of man in space. A sad, hollow shell of an agency might be left standing, a few useless offices in a few useless buildings, a monument to the pushing of meaningless paper. Houston, Huntsville,

Kennedy, and the other facilities either would be turned over to the military or become museums filled with sad relics of a day when mankind dared to slip its surly bonds and reach beyond the world of its birth.

The National Aeronautics and Space Administration, at least as the world had known it, would be no more.

Paine recalled the day President Johnson had appointed him deputy administrator of the agency, during the struggle that followed in the wake of the fire. Even then, though three men had died, all eyes remained forward, set upon the luminous target that hung in the starry night sky, beckoning to all of mankind. The problems were solved, the course recharted, and Apollo flew on wings that carried her closer to her goal with each mission. Then, after his swearing in as administrator—only months before the triumphant lunar landing of Apollo 11— Paine had been allowed to bask fully in the warm glow of a collective dream fulfilled. He and his men had been heroes before the free world.

But now, it was different. The deaths of Lucas and Shepherd had caused too many to reassess, too emotionally and too quickly, the need for spaceflight.

The race had been won, they said. There was no further reason for space exploration, they said.

No one else should die in space, they said.

Maybe Von Braun was right. Would it have made a difference if we had done it his way, and had taken it slower? Should we have built his orbital station, then gone to the moon, then built a moon base, then gone on to Mars? We could have developed a permanent presence up there, spread ourselves more widely throughout space. So what if it would have taken longer to reach the moon than the end of the decade? The Russians couldn't have beaten us anyway—they can't build a big enough booster. Their level of technology simply can't reach the moon—

He slowly shook his head, staring blankly out the window.

If only we had known that fifteen years ago—

The intercom buzzed. Paine spun slowly in his chair and reached out to press a button.

"Yes?" he asked.

His secretary's voice sounded, as pleasant as it was direct. "Dr. Paine...Dr. Gilruth is here."

"Thank you, Marci...please send him in."

He stood as his office door opened, held wide by his attractive, dark-haired secretary, and in walked Bob Gilruth. The woman departed, quietly pulling the door closed behind her.

Both men wore doleful faces, knowing the gravity of the hour. Gilruth approached the desk, fearing further bad news.

"Thanks for coming, Bob," Paine said, rising to shake the man's hand. "How's Houston these days?"

"Cold and quiet," Gilruth answered, his tone somber.

The men took their seats, Paine behind his desk and his visitor in a large, padded leather chair before it. Gilruth glanced around the room, knowing it well. So often, within these walls, they had discussed their strategies for reaching the moon, speaking of achieved technological wonders that in some cases had been impossible only months before.

"Wernher couldn't join us," Paine said. "He had pressing business at Marshall this morning, but he'll arrive this afternoon for the hearing. We did discuss the matters at hand a bit, and he expressed his thoughts...rather eloquently, in fact."

"They're not wasting any time, are they?" Gilruth frowned, angry over the governmental assault. "These guys can't order lunch without deliberating for a month or two, and here it's been what, a *week* since Kendall returned? Why the rush to judgment?"

"Better to place blame in a hurry than to risk taking it, I suppose."

"Have there been any changes?"

Paine shook his head. "Not as of an hour ago. Things are still split pretty much down the middle, and no one on the Hill seems inclined to budge. The hearing's been moved from one o'clock to two, though, so we have a little extra time to figure out what to tell them." He paused. "It doesn't look good, Bob. We may lose everything...might even have to abandon Skylab."

"Well," Gilruth offered, a full measure of frustration in his voice, "whether NASA as a whole lives or dies is probably something we won't have much say in. If it lives, we make the push for Mars. If it dies, well, I guess I'll be spending a lot more time on my boat. Sounds like we just keep flying until they shoot us down, and hope the parachutes work."

Paine nodded in silence. "That's about the size of it."

"As for the other issue," Gilruth went on, "you know my stand. We have the means, and the hardware's already in place. That may not be true a month from now, but today it is, and today I say we go."

Paine nodded a silent affirmation, seconding the thought.

"We can't just leave them up there, Tom," Gilruth went on. "You and I both knew Charlie and Gary. At the very least, we owe it to their families to bring them home. If we do nothing, never again will anyone be able to look up at the moon without seeing it as a place where two Americans lay dead, and no one wants that. Public opinion's leaning toward going back up, at least according to the mail we've been getting."

"Bob, you'll get no argument from me," Paine said. "You know that. But there are a lot of folks who think another flight, even for something like this, is a needless risk of human lives and a case of throwing good money after bad." He paused, glancing down at the tangle of papers on his desk. "And this talk of shutting down NASA altogether makes it that much harder to lobby for a recovery mission."

"Almost to a man, everyone in the agency thinks we should go.

And many in Congress. The Apollo 20 stack is gathering dust in the Vehicle Assembly Building, ready for roll out."

"It would have to be a two-vehicle flight, just like Nineteen."

"I spoke with Lee not an hour ago," Gilruth said, recalling his conversation with the recently appointed Director of the Kennedy Space Center, Lee Scherer. "By the time the next launch window opens, they can have another LM Truck ready to go, and another heavy rover...the prototype's sitting twiddling its thumbs at Grumman. The Saturn IB we were preparing for next month's Skylab flight could be modified to carry it, using the same shroud configuration we used on Nineteen. We just plug in the same navigational computer program we used before, and the bird will follow the same trajectory and put down at the same landing site."

"You make it sound simple," Paine almost smiled.

"The hardware is there, and my men are ready, too. They hate a quiet MOCR. All we need is a go."

"I know it *can* be done," Paine nodded, momentarily playing devil's advocate. "Question is, are the naysayers right? Should we risk another mission for the sake of two men who have perished?"

"Suppose it was 1943, and they'd gone down in a sub in the North Atlantic," Gilruth said, recalling Paine's past history. "If you had the means to recover them and bring them back to American shores, wouldn't you? Those men up there have a right to the sanctity of a proper burial, if nothing else. Their families need closure...the whole country does. We'll never be able to put this behind us if we just leave them up there...every time the moon comes up at night, we'll have to look at each other and ask ourselves if we did the right thing."

Paine smiled, appreciating the man's passion. "Those were Werner's words, almost exactly. He's told me on several occasions that this country is a marvel to him, that its freedoms are a rare and precious thing…and I guess after what he went through with the Nazis at Peen-emünde, he'd feel that more keenly. Like so many of us, he put his life into getting us to the moon before the hammer and sickle could be planted up there…and now, he wants the boys brought home."

"Everything's in place," Gilruth said. "The men and the machines. All we need now is a miracle."

Paine spun slowly in his chair and looked upon the continuing snowfall.

"Unfortunately, Bob," he said, "those seem to be in short supply."

25

This place is way too big and way too quiet.

Shepherd sat at a console in the war room, legs pulled up, warmly nestled into its huge, hardened leather seat as a boy might sit in his father's favorite chair. The deep, morguelike silence of the enormous room fell upon him oddly, seeming quite wrong to him—surely this was a place meant for noise and light and activity. It was, he knew, a sleeping titan, a genie in a lamp, waiting to be awakened and summoned for duty.

As if not to disturb it, he found himself remaining very, very quiet.

Having recovered a space pen from the pocket of his discarded spacesuit, Shepherd had begun to make journal entries on the note pages of his already cluttered Bible.

It's been eight days since I lost Gary. I've turned this place upside down, and he just isn't here—how is that possible? I've checked every room, every corner, every cranny again and again, but there's no sign of him. I've even looked for secret panels, trapdoors, you name it. Nothing.

He flipped a few pages along, turning to a crude, two-page map he had sketched, room by room, of the base's interior layout. Each room had been marked with a tiny X and a time of day each time he had searched it, allowing him to keep track of where he had been, and when.

There were a *lot* of X's.

But he has to be here—

He was far from certain of that. There was nowhere left to look.

—doesn't he?

"Where are you, Skipper?" he called aloud. "Did you catch a flight home or what?"

As best he could, he also had drawn a copy of the star map display that still hung above him, hoping one day someone might use it to figure out where in space the depicted system was. More detailed diagrams of its major planets filled a page of their own, along with the travel paths that encompassed them.

Life on other planets—could it really be? Maybe Gary was right—

He had seen an incredible array of support machinery during his search, things of chrome and steel and glass fashioned into working art forms by methods unknown to modern man, with so many flowing conduits and living light displays that he could not count them all. Each complex device performed a function he could only guess at— the mechanic within him was fascinated, longing for a thousand-piece toolbox and a few years to disassemble and study them all.

The rest of him was terrified, dreading the very real probability that he would *get* those years.

His head dropped back, his mind drifting back to Earth, to Houston, to his young son, to his wife. He knew the terrible anguish she must be feeling, believing her husband dead. As if to call out across the void, he closed his eyes and leaned back, centering Earth in the cross hairs of his mind's eye.

Oh, Carol—if only I could tell you I was up here. If only you knew I was still breathing and thinking of you with every breath and seeing your sweet face—

His heart cried out to her.

I'm alive—don't give up on me, honey, I'm alive!

Frustrated, his eyes popped open and searched the room as they had so many times, longing for the sight of something—*anything*—that could be used to send a signal home. As always, nothing made itself apparent.

If only I could hold you one more time—

He looked up at the incredible visual display that swept above and over him, drawing him in. Watching as the worlds living there cut steady paths through black, eternal space, he began to consider something he earlier had decided against.

"Okay," he said, accepting the apparent facts and making a decision. "Gary's gone. I don't know where or how, but he's gone. So...I can sit up here for the rest of my life and grow old and gray and probably go insane from loneliness, while everybody I know thinks I'm dead...or I can *do* something and see if I can't figure out a way to phone Houston before I go nuts and start talking to myself."

He slid from the chair and dropped to the hard floor, leaving the pen and Bible in the seat as he moved slowly along the console, toward the next operator's station.

"Big guy," he said with both humor and gravity, "this is your wake-up call."

After pausing for a moment, he extended a hand, fingers wide, and lowered his palm to the smooth ebony surface of the panel.

"Be nice, now...no funny stuff."

Shepherd pressed his hand against the enigmatic surface. As before, he could feel pressure but nothing else against his flesh. At once, it came to life with a dazzling array of brightly colored shapes, some of which seemed to slide across the panel, moving like sharks on the hunt just beneath its surface. The vast screen above him blazed to life at the same instant, filling to its limits with an intricate, detailed map of the entire base.

"Terrific," Shepherd groaned, looking up at the brilliant, multi-hued three-dimensional display. "*Now* you show up."

He studied the vivid blue lines that delineated the interior layout of the installation, his gaze jumping from room to room as each familiar location cried out to him.

There's the war room and that main corridor hub—and there are the airlocks and the atrium and the dining hall—

He frowned as he saw a few of the less pleasant sites he had discovered in his explorations.

And that sacrificial temple and the supply room battleground and the living quarters where some of these poor souls committed suicide—

It was all there, and he had explored every room on the map.

Except one.

What's that?

At the end of the corridor hub, just beyond the spacesuit storage bay Lucas and he had discovered, stood an immense circular area three times the size of the war room. It had no other door, not that he could see, and seemed made for—

"A hangar!" he realized. "Sure…they would have needed one! How else would they get in and out of here?"

It was the only place he had not searched, but it held little promise, he knew. The map indicated the hangar might be exposed to space and to the lethal cold outside. If true, Lucas could only have gone in there had he been wearing his pressure suit.

And I know you didn't try to wear one of those "big and tall" specials we found in the other airlock, because I checked for that already and all the ones we saw are still there. Not that we could wear those if we wanted to—

"Wait a minute…" he began, his eyes dissecting the diagram.

What is that right there? Is that a pressure door? Is the hangar sealed off and pressurized? And what if there's a ship sitting out there—one that can reach home—?

"Please…let there be…" he prayed aloud, already in motion.

He ran to the spacesuit bay, his socks slipping on the smooth stone as he rounded each corner. Upon arrival, he found the room just as he had last seen it—as before, only one gigantic suit was missing from its rack, presumably that worn by the frozen corpse outside, and nothing else had been disturbed. There was no sign that his commander had been there without him.

He took a long, steady breath and considered his options. First, he closed the door through which he had entered. Then, after a few moments spent examining the choices available to him within the spacesuit bay, he pulled a braided synthetic utility rope as thick as his little finger from its hook and looped one end through an elongated lightening hole in a steel wall support. Wrapping the cordage several times around his body, he tied it off, securing himself solidly in place.

If there's vacuum on the other side of that door, and I can't get it closed again fast enough—

He would quickly become as the forgotten man outside had been—frozen and very, very dead.

But surely, any race as advanced as this one would build in a safety mechanism to prevent a door from opening between two areas of different atmospheric pressure—

Wouldn't they?

Dear Lord, help me—

"Here goes nothing," Shepherd said gravely, doubt and fear filling him as he raised the lightkey to the panel. He took a deep breath and held it, praying all the while that he had guessed right.

A rumble sounded, resonating menacingly through the walls and floor. At the place where reinforced door and polished floor merged, a space appeared and steadily widened. Shepherd braced himself, knuckles wrapped white around the steel of the wall support. But there was no mad rush of air, no furious tornadic wind trying to sweep him to his doom.

"Yes!" he cried out in triumph, his heart still pounding.

The door lifted slowly, dramatically, revealing a deep blackness beyond. A wall of stale, frigid air swept in, instantly dropping the airlock temperature below zero. As the steel barrier reached its fully open position and went silent, Shepherd untied himself and approached the wide, gaping maw cautiously, his eyes straining to find something, anything, in the darkness.

"Gary...?" he called into the void, his breath fogging white. His voice echoed, coming back to him in a creepy, haunted castle fashion. "You out there?" He paused to listen, hope swelling within him. Then, more quietly, "Please...?"

Stepping forward, he crossed the threshold. Gentle light splashed upon him, warmer and more reddish than usual. He had expected the lights of the hangar even as they ignited, but he had not fully been prepared for what they revealed. Nor was he prepared to find himself slightly airborne with that step forward—crossing without warning into one-sixth lunar gravity, he lost his balance and fell gently to the hard, frigid hangar floor. Then, with care, he found his feet once more and stood in stunned awe, drinking in the sight before him.

"Wow," he whispered, his face and hands losing feeling, his eyes watering in the extreme cold.

Before him was a cavernous chamber. Wall segments of polished blue metal separated by massive, rising braces of shining steel, formed a perfect dome. Comprised of irregular plates interlocked in a quiltlike fashion, the walls caught the light, each plate differently, lending a subtle multihued effect. High along the dome, dozens of heating units glowed orange, throwing their light and heat into the chamber. Six-sided and interlocked in a wide band that encircled the hangar, they spoke to Shepherd of a metal-lined, biomechanically enhanced beehive.

The center of the ceiling was dominated by a round door of gleaming metal nearly half the size of a city block. That the circular portal was made up of five smaller, pie-slice sections was only subtly betrayed by the direction of grain in the metal of which they were made. The floor, polished as if still new and perfectly level throughout, stretched far before him, as wide as two football fields.

Complex multileveled structures of steel and glass rose within the cavern, one to each side. They bore piping and support equipment and were much like some of the launch pad structures used at Cape Kennedy. However, as with everything on the base, they carried in their flowing design an inherent style, an artistic flair that distinguished them from their earthly, more utilitarian counterparts and made them not merely functional but pleasing to the eye.

Despite the bitter cold, Shepherd stepped deeper into the chamber and noted that two large, shallow white circles had been set into the floor, crossed by painted green and yellow lines that ran straight before ending at the hangar walls. The intersecting stripes were labeled here and there with writing as if different segments were designated by different numerals, and overall they gave the impression of runway markings, perhaps suggesting vehicle maintenance and storage areas as well as launch positions.

Shepherd noticed that the place looked new, almost unused. No oil spots or fuel stains marred the floor, neither were there tools or any other kind of loose equipment scattered about. Well familiar with aircraft maintenance, he thought this fact odd before realizing that, based upon all he had seen, such crude elements as liquid fuels, petroleum lubricants, and pneumatic tools were likely well below the technological level of the facility's builders.

"It's the Astrodome all over again," he said in astonishment, his teeth chattering, his stockinged feet dancing slightly, his voice still echoing even as he spoke quietly. "And then some." He could not imagine the machinery used to maintain an atmosphere within such a place, especially when surely it would have needed to be evacuated and repressurized again and again.

A grievous sense of disappointment settled in as his initial amazement faded. The hangar was empty. No gleaming ships on launching cradles, no magnificent alien saucers, no fiery chariots waiting to carry him back to Earth.

No Lucas.

That's it—!

His frustration swelled into anger and determination. He turned and left the hangar, closing its door behind him. Like a man on a mission, he forcefully strode back into the war room, his face stern, his brow furrowed. Warming his hands as he moved, he burst into the room and called out loudly.

"All right, no more Mr. Nice Guy…!"

He moved quickly from panel to panel, slapping his palm against them all, bringing the room to amazing, brilliant life. As he moved through the control center, waking each station, the light and sound rose.

"Come on, baby," he commanded loudly, "give me a radio!"

He proceeded from station to station, panel to panel, but to his dismay, as they came to life, none had a clear function. Dazzling white light spilled upon him as the magnificent crystalline orbs in the center of the chamber intensified their flow, the demand for power increasing exponentially with each slap of Shepherd's hand.

One panel remained dark, however, despite his touch. He scowled and chalked it up to a systems malfunction, then moved on to the next station, encircling the entire room before ending up once more before the map display.

His eyes scanned the now-active room. Dozens of incredible light displays in swirling motion surrounded him, doubling as they reflected in the glassy floor. One screen held what looked like a vast schematic of complex, interconnected systems; one a high-altitude image of the moon, centered on the Marlow basin; and all of them featured intricate, dancing graphics that now proudly declared their streams of mysterious data to eyes that could not understand them.

If there was a communications system somewhere before him, he could not recognize it.

Well, I don't guess I could have expected a phone booth—

Disappointed, Shepherd again turned to the moon base map and took a moment to scrutinize the lay of the land, searching for clues to an undefined puzzle. For the first time he truly appreciated the vastness of the installation and the amazing array of connected, different-sized lakes that surrounded it. He counted them and found they numbered twelve. The base proper rested near the largest of these and was linked by snaking conduits to what must have been a hundred large, blocky objects, six to eight of which rested at the shoreline of each body of water.

So, that's it—I had my suspicions, but now I'm sure—

"Those big machines out there keep the lakes from freezing somehow…"

And the liquid water is carried into the base by underground piping—

"It flows from the lake, into the base, and back again, recycling over and over…a sealed system…"

Shepherd studied the network of machines outside, marveling anew at how they did what they obviously did.

I still don't get it—what keeps it liquid with no atmospheric pressure and such intense cold? Why doesn't it just boil away into snow?

"Was the ice already here," he wondered, "or did you bring it with you?"

All that water out there—it almost could be Minnesota—!

"Visit the deep, dark basin of ten thousand lakes...and stay for a while..."

Like, for the rest of your life!

Fighting despair, Shepherd dropped to his knees and closed his eyes, seeking a calm, a power beyond himself.

"Father in heaven," he quietly began. "Where is he?"

Gary!

"Please...help me understand...there has to be a reason..."

◙   ◙   ◙

As he prayed, he was heard.

As he spoke, he was watched.

As he rose to his feet, he no longer was alone within the base.

After countless years of patient slumber, eyes had opened and ears now listened. The lonely astronaut was being studied and considered by an intellect beyond any on Earth, a colossal mind that realized it was no longer alone, that its centuries of seclusion finally had ended. It was a survivor, one that held the answers to the greatest riddles of ancient history and knew secrets far beyond the mere imaginings of man.

It did not, however, know the identity of the diminutive, oddly dressed man in the control room. Its powerful and ancient energies splashed unnoticed against Shepherd's body, permeating flesh and bone and sinew, searching for answers. In moments, the stranger's genetic self had been laid bare to the penetrating eyes that scrutinized him—and he had not been recognized as creator nor as ally nor even as human.

Fearing it had fallen into enemy hands, the entity cried out for help.

It was heard.

26

Firelight spilled into the room, casting shadows of iron bars upon the rough, stone ceiling.

It was night once more. Lucas huddled in a dark corner, willing himself to remain as unobtrusive as possible. After waking on a straw-covered stone floor with a pounding headache, rotting hay upon his lips, Lucas had spent his first hours in the cell trying to figure out where he was and what had happened to him. He remembered the beautiful woman he had seen in the clearing and his attack on her assailant, but nothing else before the darkness clouding his battered mind had lifted to reveal the chamber around him.

He looked at his hands, as he had done so many times since his capture.

I killed a man—

He had acted to save another, yes, but never before had he taken a life. Even now he could feel the knife in his hands as he buried it deep in the attacker's back. Even now he could hear the sound it made as it was driven into a living being, splitting bone and sinew as it—*killed someone.*

These hands—!

Yet another wave of nausea struck him. He fought hard to keep the sickness back, and for the moment he succeeded. Trying to keep his mind from dwelling on the deed, he surveyed his dismal surroundings.

Some forty feet wide, the roughly circular room was crowded with dozens who, like him, apparently had found themselves there without warning, without choice, without hope. Its walls were lined with hollows and alcoves that served no clear purpose, its floors multileveled and roughly hewn from cold, unforgiving stone. Mounted at the center of its cracked, smoke-darkened, plaster-shelled ceiling was another of the strange domed arrays he had seen earlier in the house where he'd found food.

The ground-level dungeon was filled with men whose lives were rushing toward a terrifying end. None of the incarcerated were among the largest of their world—though they were much bigger than Lucas, all were significantly smaller than the hulking guards who had imprisoned him.

He had watched the others as they fought over the meager portions of food that the guards tossed to them now and then, scant morsels meant not to provide sustenance but to incite violence. Beneath him, stretching from wall to wall, the damp and uncomfortable bed of putrefied hay and decaying bone filled the air with its pungent scent. A polished stone trough of water, perhaps five feet long, was affixed low on one wall, its contents continually renewed by a means Lucas could not determine. He would not die of thirst.

He would not have the time.

His thoughts fell upon someone else, someone over whom he now worried, someone for whose well-being he, as mission commander, was still responsible.

Someone who was no mere crewmate, but a friend.

Charlie—are you here somewhere, on this world? Are you safe? If only—!

He bowed his head, hating that control over his life had been so thoroughly wrested from him.

If only that engine had fired—

An explosion of sound reverberated against the dank, stone walls. The cell's heavy, reinforced wooden door had flown open as it had time and again, perhaps three times an hour throughout his week in the oppressive chamber. Sometimes new prisoners were thrown through the door and into the room, but just as often someone whose time had come was taken away. Lucas shrank into shadow, looking away as a trio of massive robed and well-armed men stormed inside.

Please, not me!

Shoving dozens of frightened captives to the floor as they made their way through the room, the robed men, their faces hidden behind ornate death's-head masks, crossed it in its entirety before homing in on one poor soul and dragging him, screaming, from the cell. Other guards, armed as always, stood in the doorway, preventing any of the unfortunates inside from escaping. There seemed to be no rhyme or reason to the men's choice of victim—prisoners who had been con-fined but for hours were as likely to be taken as those trapped for days. Just as it always had, following each abduction, the thunderous slam of the door faded away and an uneasy quiet settled in, a quiet that filled the chamber like a dense fog.

A quiet of dread. A quiet of foreboding.

In moments the unthinkable would happen. Again.

Lucas drew a deep breath, temporary relief soaking him. He trembled, the stress having taken a heavy toll. His hands over his face, he struggled to steady his nerves, feeling his hot breath against his palms. The smoke from outside had soaked into his hair, his skin. It stung his reddened, irritated eyes.

A cheer rose beyond the solitary oval window. The prisoners rushed it, crowding the sill for a view of the horror beyond.

Lucas had already seen it. During his first few hours in the dismal cell, he had remained silent, staying away from the food, taking water only when it was clearly safe to do so, not wanting to do anything that might lead to his being set upon. Finally, however, driven both by fear and intense curiosity, Lucas had joined the others at the window. He had regretted it immediately.

Now he tried to shut out the nightmarish sounds that poured into the cell. A rhythmic chanting began, occultic voices filling the room. Then, as the chanting continued, he heard the abhorrent screams and thunks and dull thuds he had heard so many times now, followed by the invariable acclamation rising from the gathered crowd outside. Nausea rose within him again, and he curled tightly into the corner, pressing his face against the clammy stone.

He was haunted by the abomination he had beheld days before, an unspeakable horror that, since his arrival, had taken place hundreds of times.

Beyond the heavily barred, glassless aperture in the cell wall was a wide courtyard surrounded by flaming ruins. A monstrosity of an idol more than four stories tall, a menacing statue of polished marble and golden inlays, stood gleaming in the orange light at the center of the courtyard. It was a cruel amalgam of man, beast, and demon, a thing that spoke of cruelty on a barbarous level. Before it, a massive structure overlaid with the tawny glint of polished human bone stood some twenty feet high, the empty sockets of thousands of tightly packed, grinning skulls peering out at the throng of drunken, sometimes naked, always violent men and women surrounding them.

Their pitiless faces bathed in firelight, the revelers cheered as a prisoner was carried kicking and screaming up a flight of stairs and secured to an altar at the summit of the platform. A masked priest stepped forward and overshadowed him, his flowing robes a deep red, his almost-concealed eyes wide and bloodshot, a long-fanned ember of insanity burning within them. He began the cadenced mantra, leading the gathered crowd in its frightening, hypnotic rhythm. Then, in seconds, with practiced precision and a flash of blood-soaked blades, he completed the sacrifice.

There was a flash of green light, and as the cheers of the throng swelled anew, another grinning, polished trophy was placed within the gruesome structure of the sacrificial platform.

And the crowd goes wild—

The remainder of the body, no more now than offal, was shoved from the edge of the altar to fall limply and heavily into a deep pit.

It was over. For now.

Always distancing himself from the huge men trapped with him, Lucas had kept his eyes discreetly upon them, fearing attack. The room often erupted into violence, sometimes as one man beat another to death over a scrap of bread, sometimes for no reason that Lucas could determine. As the prisoners fought, they argued viciously in their bizarre language. These small giants were but beasts, driven solely by anger and self-interest, intelligent animals devoid of any thought for their fellow men. Had they not been stripped of their weapons upon their capture, Lucas believed none would still stand.

Oddly enough, one of the giants reminded Lucas of his son. Perhaps it was in the way he carried himself, the cadence with which he spoke, or the manner in which he moved. Lucas was grateful that Jeff was not in this hideous place, that he was safe at home with his mother.

I love you, son. Always.

Weak from fatigue, he nodded off for moments at a time, his body too long without food and adequate rest. Digging his nails into his palms, hoping the pain would help him to remain awake, his attention occasionally fell upon a fellow prisoner sitting against a nearby wall, a large, lean man who also appeared to be trying to stay out of harm's way. He had been tossed into the cell the day before, and as far as Lucas knew had taken neither food nor drink since. In an attempt to keep his mind occupied, the astronaut had studied him repeatedly, memorizing the man. His features were distinct and memorable, his hair dark, his eyes piercing and blue, his nose sharply formed. There was a sadness in his wet eyes, cohabiting oddly with a fierce cruelty that lived there as well, the same savagery that blazed within the eyes of almost all who lived on this brutal world.

The minutes flew away. A man engaged in a short-lived struggle with another brute suddenly crashed to the hard floor just a few feet from where Lucas lay and went still, his neck broken. The marooned astronaut stared into the man's wide, angry, sightless eyes.

The cell door burst open.

27

Wednesday, March 12, 4:49 P.M.

The day had gone from bad to worse.

Dr. Paine shook his head, frustrated by the barrage of narrow-minded, slanted questions that bombarded the four men called to answer them. For hours they had felt their backs against brick, the firing squad before them armed with rhetoric.

They could at least have offered us blindfolds—

Paine stared at the reflection of his microphone in the table's polished walnut surface, hating every moment of the ordeal. To his left sat Gilruth; to his right, Von Braun, and all showed signs of battle fatigue. He had gone through similar proceedings, it seemed, at every turn during the disastrous launch failures of the early years, the pioneering attempts of the Explorer years, the triumph of the Mercury years. Now, without John Kennedy championing their cause in the White House, it was happening again, this time without constraint, small minds behind big mouths trying to make their mark on the world, whether for good or ill.

There are none so blind—

He glanced around, thankful for the absence of press coverage. If he and his agency had to get shot down, at least it would be done without firsthand coverage on the evening news. NASA's image had taken a beating in the media following the loss of the two astronauts, and while he doubted they could stop the bleeding, he was grateful to see it slowed at least by the sealed door behind him.

The administrator returned his gaze to the gathered panel, a dozen men seated side-by-side behind a high, expansive dais at the front of the room. The polished walnut concavity of its broad face reached to the limits of his peripheral vision.

"So, Dr. Von Braun," Congressman Parker went on, his rough voice heavy with sarcasm, his burly hands strangling the base of his microphone. "What you're telling me is that man is doomed if NASA doesn't continue?"

"At some point," the scientist said, his accent thick, his patience thin, "this earth will no longer be able to support mankind. Whether this comes as a result of overpopulation, nuclear war, pollution, or asteroid bombardment, I cannot say. But the only way to ensure the survival of man is to take ourselves to other worlds."

"I think what my esteemed colleague is saying is that it is wise not to have all of our eggs in one basket," Gilruth added.

"It's a big basket, Doctor," Parker insisted. "And what are we talking about here…a hundred years? A thousand? A million?"

"Or," Paine said soberly, "it could be next week."

"Or," Parker responded, "never."

The congressman looked down at the papers before him, satisfaction etched upon his face. He had succeeded in kicking the legs out from under most every point the men had made during his few minutes of query time, he believed, and already was thinking of ways to spend a slice of NASA's former funding on projects affecting his own constituency. "I yield the remainder of my time, Mr. Chairman."

A slight, balding man seated at the center of the panel nodded, turning toward another man three seats down and to his left. "Thank you, Mr. Parker…I believe we'll now hear from the Democratic gentleman from New York…Mr. Gormann."

"Thank you, Mr. Chairman," Gormann began, his hard, steely eyes a sharp contrast to the short blond curls upon his head. His scrawny frame hung loosely within the expensive blue suit he wore. "Dr. Paine, for several hours we've discussed the merits of space flight as a whole. But now"—his tone became one of incredulity—"is it my understanding that you have also come here today to discuss sending another mission to the moon…and *next month?*"

"Yes, sir," Paine replied, his voice stern. "That is correct."

"The Apollo 20 mission was canceled some time back, was it not?"

"Yes, but not before the hardware had been built and readied for flight."

"What is the point, Dr. Paine?" the man asked bluntly. "The men are dead."

"But not forgotten. They should be brought home."

"Why?"

"Merely from a practical standpoint, it would be injurious to our country just to leave Gary Lucas and Charlie Shepherd up there. National morale demands that those who serve be brought home to American soil if at all possible."

"This is the moon we're talking about," Gormann said, "not Normandy or Saigon."

"All the more reason," Gilruth jumped in. "How do we leave our children and grandchildren a moon they can't look at without a spectre of American failure looming over their heads? It would be an eternal, nightly billboard for a nation that sent two good men to die on a beach a quarter of a million miles away from home, then turned its back and left them there. It would be a symbol of death in the sky… forever."

Paine sat more erect in his seat. "We've been getting thousands upon thousands of telegrams and letters from the American public. By better than a twenty-to-one margin they want the astronauts brought home, and I think we should listen. We are, after all, here to serve the people, those who elected each one of you and trust you to make the right call."

"The 'right call,' Dr. Paine," an indignant Gormann replied, "is whichever one we decide best serves those who elected us. There are a lot of folks out there who go to bed each night hungry, or without medical care, or without a roof over their heads, and the funds necessary to fly yet another pointless rocket to the moon could go a long way toward helping a lot of those people. Americans want their own taken care of."

"That's exactly the point we're trying to make," Gilruth stated.

Gormann stared silently, his eyes boring holes through the man.

"The Americans you speak of spent *far* more on cigarettes and alcohol over the last fifteen years than our government spent on the space program," Paine said. "A hundred times as much. But find me one person who instead would have given the money they spent on those indulgences to shelter a family or vaccinate a needy child. Most would say that helping the poor is fine, sir, as long as someone else is doing it."

"And *we* are someone else," Gormann replied.

"The spin-off benefits from NASA to the average American are staggering," Gilruth added. "Medical procedures have advanced by leaps and bounds as a result of space-related research. Kidney dialysis machines and pacemakers are saving more and more lives each day. We have ways of preserving food now that we didn't before. Computers are smaller and faster, improving banking and commerce. I wouldn't be surprised if, just a few years from now, there were a computer in every home."

Gormann was amused. "What for, Dr. Gilruth? Nobody needs a computer in the house, not unless you're a scientist out of a science fiction movie."

"Nevertheless," Von Braun said, "the spin-offs are real and benefit us all in thousands of ways that we do not yet realize, and may not realize for years to come."

"The spacecraft is pretty much in place, sir," Paine said, trying to get back to the subject. "A recovery mission can be flown without undue expense, and without the added cost of hardware-related delays..."

The polished wooden door of the room suddenly burst open, startling a page who stood sentry just within. A man in a dark blue suit rushed in, his eyes wide, his face etched with purpose. After pausing to flash his government identification to the page, the man hastened down the aisle, went immediately to Paine's side, handed him a folded data printout and began to whisper in his ear. The director's face filled with astonishment, which soon spread like wildfire to the faces of Gilruth and the others as they saw the data the oversized sheet contained.

"Order," the chairman insisted, banging a gavel. "These proceedings are not to be interrupted in such fashion—"

"Mr. Chairman," Paine began, cutting him off, his voice laced with excitement. "I've just received news that has a *strong* bearing on these proceedings."

"The subcommittee will hear this information, Mr. Paine," the chairman said, obviously dubious. "But do not waste our time."

Paine looked to Von Braun, exchanged a few guarded whispers, then addressed the panel. "Sir," he began, glancing at the classified paper, "I have just been informed that a strong signal of undefined origin has been detected by our radio telescopes in Australia and at Goldstone. It's thousands of times more powerful than any signal generated in our spaceflight communications and lies within a frequency range much lower than any used by the Manned Space Flight Network. The signal is a carrier wave bearing a repeating, encoded sequence...which, according to our best guess, is trying to trigger a response."

"Coming from *space?*" the chairman asked.

"Not just space, sir," Paine replied. "It's coming from the *moon*."

A loud murmur filled the room, prompting the chairman to bring his gavel down once more.

"Order," he insisted. "Mr. Paine, are you telling me that the men up there are *alive?*"

"I don't know, sir," he answered, passing the paper to his colleagues. "Their consumables should have been depleted over a week ago…but I don't know."

"It doesn't seem likely, then," Gormann said. "The signal must be coming from some other source…a Russian spacecraft, perhaps."

"We know and monitor the frequency bands used by the USSR, sir. This signal is not one we've heard before. Nor have we detected a launch at Baikonur within the past year, or from any other location within their borders. It cannot be the Russians."

"Oh, but it *can* be a message from two dead men," Gormann said, irritation evident in his voice. "This is ridiculous."

The man who had brought the information to Paine again whispered something to him.

"We've intercepted a few messages from Moscow," Paine said. "They're as mystified as we are, though they're now assuming we still have an active mission up there."

"Why would they think that?" Gormann snipped. "Don't they watch the news?"

"Triangulation places the source of the signal near the lunar south pole," Gilruth added, studying the sheet. "That *is* the area where Apollo 19 landed."

Voices rose anew among the gathered onlookers. Several on the panel looked at each other, their questioning faces seeking a simple explanation.

"So," the chairman said, "all we know is that we *don't* know who's transmitting this signal."

"There's only one way to find out," Gilruth said, trying hard to hide the smile fighting its way to surface. "Sir."

"What kind of theatrics are these?" Gormann said, raising his voice in an accusatory tone. "Mr. Chairman, I must object…"

The doors flew open and another hurried man entered, this time hastening toward the subcommittee chairman. A presidential aide, he apparently bore a message from the White House. As he and the chairman spoke in hushed tones, Paine watched intently, realizing from their body language that the skeptical leader of the gathered panel was receiving confirmation of the incredible occurrence, if not a directive from the president.

"This hearing will stand in recess until tomorrow morning at eight o'clock," the chairman said, raising his voice as soon as the private conversation ended. "This new information must be considered before any further discussion can take place."

28

"Gary!"

The cry was loud and bitter and rang of desperation.

More than that, it was a final, official declaration of surrender.

Shepherd stood in the atrium, defeated, having turned up no sign of his missing crewmate. There was simply no place left to look—in fact, there had been no place left for quite some time. His was now a very finite world, and he had seen every square inch of it. Again and again.

It had grown late. He headed into the corridor and toward his adopted quarters, where his bed waited. Without purpose to fill his days, he now felt little reason to rise in the mornings at all, save the needs to eat, drink, and use the sanitary facilities. Yet rise he did, as he had been trained to do.

His had become a simple existence, one he would not wish upon anyone.

Each step along the hallway was a burden to him. Futility seemed now to own every facet of his life.

I know there has to be a purpose for all this, Lord, but I don't have a clue what it might be—

So many times since becoming stranded within the base he had

268

thought of the Psalms, of the sudden and uncanny relevance of words he had heard all his Christian life, words that only now had become utterly real for him—

Even though I walk through the valley of the shadow of death, I fear no evil; for Thou art with me.

If ever there was a valley of shadow, it was Marlow. If ever there was a looming death, it lay in the airless cold that waited just outside his new and ancient prison.

Shuffling into his room with little energy and even less enthusiasm, he stripped out of his cooling garment and draped it over the back of a chair, deciding he was too tired to launder it. Cleaning the outfit and his socks, in essence the entirety of his wardrobe, had become a part of the scheduled routine he had established for himself since Lucas' disappearance; every night, he would wash the garments in the bathroom basin, then hang them over the chair to dry. Despite his lack of an alarm clock, he awoke each morning at about the same hour. His meals came at the same times: breakfast, lunch, and dinner. His searches of the base had been systematic and thorough, always following the same route, always yielding the same result.

He plopped onto his back on the comfortable, spacious bed, recounted his efforts and retraced his steps, just as he had at the close of each day.

There has to be something I've missed—some room I've overlooked—

His mind labored but the puzzle remained unanswered. Reluctantly yielding to defeat, he stared at the smooth gray ceiling. Tomorrow, he would resume his routine, but the searching would stop.

I'm here, Gary. Right here.

"Oh, Carol," he began, whispering to her as if she were lying next to him, "I'm still here, honey…but I might as well not be, for all the difference it makes." Other fears rose. "Don't give up on me…I'm still here…"

It had become more and more difficult to suppress the fear that constantly rose within him, fear that he would live out his life alone and forgotten, just like his only companions, the people who now lay dead throughout the place. More than once he had pictured a lunar expedition, a thousand years hence, finding his mummified remains alongside those of the base's builders—what would they conclude? Would they wonder why this one man was so much smaller than his companions? Worse yet, would they succeed where he had failed and find Lucas' dusty corpse as well?

"Well," he uttered, considering the surreal chain of events he had experienced since abandoning the crippled spacecraft, "I guess it beats suffocating in a cramped LM." He rubbed his eyes. "But not by much."

Reaching up to a bedside shelf, he retrieved the small trinket of white, formed plastic that had become priceless to him. He recalled the morning a few days before the launch when his son had brought the little spaceman into the living room, offered it to him, and asked him to carry it with him "for luck." He had hugged Joey tightly at that, telling his precious son that he would be honored to escort such a special toy to the moon.

He studied the tiny figurine, noting its fairly accurate moonsuit with some amusement as he ran his fingertips upon its smooth, molded contours. He remembered the night he brought the toy home as a surprise from the MSC souvenir counter—as the hour was late, he had placed it quietly on the night table alongside Joey's bed, not wanting to wake his boy.

Oh, son—if only I could have hugged you one more time. If only I could have taught you to ride a bike, could have seen your high school graduation, and could have been there for your wedding—

He closed his eyes, seeing the boy's precious face, seeing him asleep in bed with a love-worn teddy bear clutched tightly to his side, seeing the child running toward him, arms outstretched, wanting to be picked up. Tears tickled Shepherd's temples as they spilled over, wetting his short-trimmed sideburns.

If only I could have been there for you—will you even remember me?

Reflexively, he almost reached as if for his wallet, for the small photo of the boy he carried there. His arm had but twitched when he recalled that the billfold rested safely upon his bedroom dresser—a mere 250,000-odd miles away, right where he had placed it before saying his final good-byes to his beloved family.

He could never have known just how final those good-byes would be.

I miss you so much—a part of me is with you there and always will be—

Returning the astronaut figure to its bedside place of honor, he took its neighboring Bible from the shelf and held it against his chest for a moment, pausing to gather himself and still his frustrations before opening it. Many long breaths and suppressed tears later, he held the old leather-bound book before him and, as he liked to do, flipped to a random page to see what words there would speak to him.

His eyes fell upon a verse he had read before and often, one that more than once had brought encouragement during personal voyages through dire straits, one chiseled into the very rock to which he clung.

A promise.

I am with you always, even unto the end of the world.

He lowered his Bible and considered the words for a few quiet moments, whispered a loving and private good-night to his wife and son, then closed his eyes. With his prolonged inactivity, the lights in the room dimmed.

The deep velvet of inner peace closed in as sleep claimed Charles Shepherd.

The cold wind stung his eyes. They watered, blurring the pale crescent image that filled them, an image that tore deeply into his mind and exhumed memories of two friends he had been forced to abandon.

Vic Kendall stood in his backyard, lost in the sight of the moon as it hung low in the western sky.

Were we really up there?

Steadily it sank, approaching the horizon, beneath which it would soon vanish. Just below, already nearing the vanishing point, the brilliant, jealous orb of Venus tried to wrest his attention away, but to no avail.

All he saw was the moon.

They were up there.

Still.

We're coming, guys—not much longer now—

Something within him wanted desperately to believe that a miracle had kept his friends alive, that they were not sitting frozen and still in the seats of their dead vehicle, wherever it finally had come to rest. Yet, try as he might, the notion would not become real for him. They were gone.

Forgive me—

He barely felt the hand that alighted upon his shoulder. A faint tinkle of ice in a tall glass found his ears.

"Bit chilly for iced tea," he commented, never turning or taking his eyes from the sky.

"I suppose," Katie replied, hugging herself against the cold. Her pink sweater provided little protection from the biting breeze. "But this is Texas and I'm out of cocoa."

She moved to his side and looked up at him. He had been so distant since his return, the distance imposed by pain and guilt and undeserved self-hatred. She too felt it, a profound ache that curled deep within her and pawed listlessly at her being. When he hurt, *she* hurt.

But unlike before, unlike with every other trial they had faced together, *this* pain would not be assuaged. He had shut her out, keeping her from reaching him, forcing her into an exile of loneliness that matched his own.

Blinded by his own agony, he had sentenced her without malice to the same fate.

"You must be freezing. Do you want a jacket or a sweater or—"

"No."

He was there with her, yet he was not.

"Vic," she tried, expecting no more success now than before, "we're all getting together at my sister's place…remember? I told you about it the other day. A nice dinner…just family…"

He didn't respond. She waited a few moments longer than was warranted then went on.

"It, uh…" She glanced down at her watch, its sparkling silver band catching the light of the porch lamp. "It starts in about an hour. Maybe if you came in and took a shower, you'd feel better and—"

"I could see it, Katie," he began, having heard not one word. "During reentry. Filling the window as I hit the air. There it was, right in front of me, staring through the flames like the devil in Hell, getting in a last shot…"

"What was?" Katie asked, taking his arm.

"*That,*" he said, indicating the setting moon, his expression one of loathing.

She shuddered, knowing the depth of his pain. "Come inside, Vic. Let's get ready and—"

He cut her off again. "I should be up there with them. It was my responsibility to bring them home and—"

"No, Vic," Katie said firmly. "You didn't do anything wrong. You did what you had to do. What you were trained to do. Your duty was to come home…to me."

"Three go up; three come down."

"You didn't strand them…that spacecraft did."

He did not hear her. His unblinking gaze remained locked upon the moon.

"Three go up…"

"Vic…please…"

"They're going back. That phone call a little earlier…it was Bruce. He said Congress approved the mission. Twenty is going to fly…they're gonna send her up, through the next window, next month."

A sudden fear filled her, fear that once more he would leave her side and be hurled into a cruel void that wanted only to kill him.

"That signal they're getting," he said, "that was what did it."

"Do you think it's *them?*"

He shook his head. "Can't be. I don't know what it is, but it isn't the guys."

Katie gripped his arm more tightly. "You aren't…"

"I'm not going with them," Kendall said in response to her anxiety, his voice low and slow, the words a labor. "Bruce told me I've been pulled from the rotation altogether. He fought for me, he said, but their minds were made up. No more Skylab, no nothing. Seems they're, uh…*concerned*…about me. I tried to tell him I'm okay…that I just need a few days and I'll be flight-ready. He said he knew that, but Kraft and the others had already made the call and wanted me on the ground for a while. I might get CapCom, but…nothing that…" He trailed off into silence.

"You just came back," Katie said, squeezing his arm. "I don't want you flying off again. I want you *here.*"

"Have you seen the way they've all been toward me since I got home? At the debriefing, at the memorial, even in the hallways at the Space Center…they look away as I walk by. No one knows what to say to me, so they just stay away. I don't know what's worse, the avoidance or the pity…"

He looked down into her wet eyes for the first time in days. "The brass there…they, uh…" He paused, struggling with the words. "They think I'm cracking up, Katie. They think I can't handle it anymore. They're giving me a liaison position…an office with a desk and a window…" His head dropped, looking away from her. "And with all the sharp stuff locked away."

She embraced him, held him hard. She felt his chest heaving as her husband's suppressed sobs began to surface.

"Listen to me. I need you here," she said again. "You've been up there so much…all the fighter planes and space capsules and training missions…you've *earned* this. It's time for you to take it a little easier…to come home for supper every night…to come home to me."

He held her to his chest, feeling her soft, perfumed hair between his fingers. As they embraced, his eyes returned to the mocking crescent that hung in the distance.

"I'm trying, baby," he said.

▣   ▣   ▣

"Is it really true?"

Diane stood staring from the window, watching as the last slender remnant of the moon slipped from sight behind dark, distant trees. The crackling flames of the wide red-brick fireplace cast their glow upon her lovely features as she gazed into the night. Her home, sealed tight against the late winter chill, was warm and pleasant and inviting—yet at the same time cold and empty and forlorn.

Oh, Gary—!

"Yes," Cortney nodded, watching her from his place on the sofa. "It really is. I was in a meeting with Deke and the boys all afternoon...seems the radio signal we're getting made for just enough uncertainty to push it through. They've reinstated the Apollo 20 funding, and she's gonna fly, Diane."

The living room was filled with Gary Lucas. Photos, awards, mementos, wedding pictures, a thousand little things left behind by a man who had lived a vibrant, eventful life. Cortney's eyes skipped from place to place, cutting from one precious object to the next, acutely feeling the man's continued presence, almost as Diane did.

"When, Bruce?"

"There's a launch window in about five weeks. They say it'll be cutting things a little close, but there's no reason the hardware can't be in position and on the pad in time. They've calculated a secondary window for the booster that'll carry the rover up there, and since it really doesn't need the critical lighting conditions a manned landing would, it'll launch only a week before *we* go up. Our booster will already be rolling toward the pad when the first one lifts off."

" 'Our' booster?"

"Since Jim Irwin and I were on the backup crew for Nineteen and already went through the same south pole training, we've been assigned to the flight. I'll be commander, and Jim will make the landing with me...and ol' Deke himself's gonna take the third seat, the one with the penthouse view."

"Deke?" she asked. "Did the doctors clear him?"

"Yup. His ticker is 100 percent and about fifteen years overdue."

Diane allowed herself a slight, almost imperceptible smile. "Well... I'm sure he's happy about that."

"As happy as you might expect, I guess," Cortney said. "Under the circumstances."

Diane turned from the window and crossed to a soft plush chair near the hearth. "Bruce," she began, gently taking a seat, "I haven't told this to anyone else…well, except Carol…" Her words were heavy. "I don't think I could spend the rest of my life knowing Gary's up there…so far away, so cold…so alone. I just couldn't handle it. I want you to know how much it means to me that they're doing this…and I also want you to know how much it means to me that *you're* the one bringing him back."

Cortney nodded. "Wild horses couldn't have kept me off this mission, Diane. I'll bring him home to you…I promise. He and Charlie won't be alone any more."

"The signal…is there a chance…?" Her words died away, but the question danced in her eyes.

"Well," Cortney began, trying to tread kindly, "we don't know, Diane. Their air ran out nearly three weeks ago, so the book says no. We haven't heard a single spoken word from up there, since…just that encoded transmission, and nobody's been able to crack it yet. It's been repeating itself again and again…still is, as far as I know. We *do* know that whatever the call is, it isn't coming from the equipment the guys took up there…the signal is too strong, and the frequencies aren't anything NASA uses."

"On Gary's mission, they launched the rockets a month apart. Now, on yours, it's a week. Why the hurry? Does someone think Gary and Charlie might still be—"

"Diane," he jumped in, "please…don't get your hopes up…"

"Is there a *chance?*" she asked again, her eyes pleading, her fingertips moving gently and lovingly along the familiar contours of her wedding ring.

Cortney looked away for a moment, staring without seeing at the burning logs across the room, nestled there upon their bed of glowing embers. "I *want* to say yes. You know that. But the possibilities just aren't…" He paused and took a deep breath then conceded words the woman desperately needed to hear. "Maybe. A million to one. I'd say the odds are somewhere in that ballpark."

"What will the odds be five weeks from now?"

Cortney let the question hang unanswered as Diane settled back into the chair and pulled her legs up. Curled there like a child, she watched the flames for a few moments, seeing within their dance visions of what might have been and what might yet be. Cortney saw something burning in the depths of her dark, glistening eyes, something far brighter than the fiery reflections upon them.

Hope.

"A million to one," she repeated, almost whispering. "That's one more chance than there was yesterday."

◎ ◎ ◎

"I'm not hungry, Mommy."

"Eat, sweetheart…you like macaroni and cheese."

"I ate that already."

The demanding day had taken its toll on Carol. She had much yet to do—so many loose ends to tie up, so many legal issues to wade through, so many family matters still to be dealt with. Her feet ached, her neck was sore, and only now had her headache finally subsided. She was glad to be home and away from the chaos, away from the well-meaning demands and continual sympathetic queries that in recent days had faced her at every turn. Now off her feet for the first time in hours, she was grateful that her time in the kitchen had been relatively brief.

Thank heaven for frozen foods—

"Did you have a nice time at Grandma's house today?"

"I guess. There was a turtle."

"A turtle?"

"In the backyard...it was big."

"What happened to it?"

"It went in the creek and swam away."

She watched as Joey played with the undesirable vegetables on his plate, their creamy yellow companion long gone. Poking and prodding his Brussels sprouts, the boy was making faces that clearly showed he wished they magically would go away.

"They're good for you, honey," the woman said, sipping from her glass of cold, sweetened tea. "They'll help you grow up big and strong, just like..."

The words died away.

"Daddy!" the boy piped up.

"Yes," she smiled, slightly and bittersweetly. "Like Daddy."

"No...look! It's *Daddy*..." He pointed beyond the kitchen door and into the living room, toward the television news bulletin silently playing there. Carol spun to discover upon the glassy screen a NASA publicity photo of Shepherd and Lucas posing in their training suits, an image she had seen many times both during and after the mission.

Springing to her feet, the woman ran to the console set and turned up the volume.

"...have confirmed that the Apollo 20 mission, previously cancelled just this past December, has now been cleared by Congress and will launch next month. Just what spurred this sudden reversal we do not yet know, but sources in Washington tell ABC News that the primary goal of the flight will be the physical recovery of Apollo 19 astronauts Gary Lucas and Charles Shepherd, seen here on your screen, who will be returned for interment on Earth. We take you now to science correspondent Jules Bergman..."

"What is it, Mommy?" the boy asked, walking up beside her. He tugged at the skirt of her dress, trying to be noticed. "Is Daddy coming home now?"

The dark-haired man on the screen spoke with dramatic flair and with Carol's full attention. "Apollo 19 Commander Gary Lucas and Lunar Module Pilot Charles Shepherd, who were stranded on the lunar surface almost three weeks ago following the catastrophic failure of their spacecraft's ascent engine, will be brought home, if only posthumously. Using a special command module modified to hold five men—a ship originally readied as a Skylab rescue craft—the crew of Apollo 20 will return to the moon and make the recovery. Since Lucas' and Shepherd's last act was to depart the failed lunar module and set out in their roving vehicle, allowing the rover's environmental systems to extend their lives for as long as possible, it will be necessary that the recovery crew make use of such a vehicle as well in order to find them. This means there will again be two launches, those of an unmanned Saturn IB and a manned Saturn V…"

Clinging to his every word, Carol studied Bergman as he went on spouting one scientific point after another, striving to help an unknowledgeable viewing public understand how the mission would unfold. Backing toward a chair, she watched still, even as she sat down and reached for a tabletop extension phone.

"What is it Mommy?" Joey asked again. "Where's Daddy?"

"On the moon, sweetheart," she answered absently, her focus elsewhere as she dialed a number she knew by heart.

A ring sounded in the receiver. Then another.

Be there be there be there be there—!

"Hello?"

"Diane, this is Carol…have you heard?"

"Oh, Carol…yes…Bruce is here with me now. He said he tried to call you earlier…"

"I was out."

"So you know?"

"They're going up again."

"And in a hurry."

"A *hurry?*" she asked, a trace of cautious hope daring to rise within her, carried from one woman to another via a phone line. "Why?"

"Just come over, honey," Diane said. "Right now. Bring Joey with you. We need to talk."

◙　　◙　　◙

A sharp sound awakened the filthy, heavily bearded Lucas from the light sleep he had allowed himself. Weakened from prolonged hunger and many pounds lighter than he had been, he stirred and pulled himself more tightly into an alcove corner of the cell, bringing his dry, weary eyes back into focus as two monstrous men fought viciously only a few feet away.

It was dark, save the light of the fires outside. It was *always* dark in this place, Lucas had noted, as if daylight never came. The pall of smoke that filled the sky outside was so great, so impenetrable, that sunlight apparently could not pierce it.

Hard fists pounded yielding flesh again and again, and tiny droplets of blood spattered the walls and floor. Lucas had lost count of the number of men who had been spared their grisly fate outside, finding death instead at the hands of one or more who shared that fate.

But not this time.

The fight broke up as the chamber door exploded open yet again. Two huge, skull-masked, black-robed figures burst into the room. As they entered, one desperate prisoner tried for the door but fell to the weapons of the guards. Shoving their way through the crowd, the masked men glanced around, seeking a particular man. Their eyes fell upon one after the other, bypassing many with but the most fleeting of glances, until finally they fell upon the object of their search.

Lucas.

At once, the massive figures were upon him. Hauled to his feet as if he weighed nothing, the astronaut was dragged toward the exit as the others in the chamber cowered and parted like the Red Sea.

"No!" Lucas shouted, his voice a harsh croak. "I don't belong here!"

He was hauled away with brute force, his shoulder almost dislocated from its socket. In seconds he found himself in a corridor of wood and stone and metal, all merging in a flowing amalgamation that seemed familiar. The chamber door slammed shut behind him and heavy locking bars were pulled down into place, sealing it until the time of the next sacrifice.

His captors moved quickly. They veered to the right, through and past other doors and down a confusing array of cross corridors, rushing with single-minded purpose. Lucas never found his feet though he tried several times, his weight borne entirely by the two hulking men. His view of the way ahead came only in brief glimpses as the pain in his arms and the roughness of the motion overrode his ability to gain focus. Terror filled him. His heart pounded fiercely.

Finally, just as Lucas thought he would pass out, a final door opened before them and they were outside. The robed men and two guards exchanged words. One of the giants dragging Lucas suddenly paused and dropped his side of the load, then turned to address the guards more directly. The other man lifted the drained and terrified astronaut from the ground altogether and moved quickly away from the massive stone fortress, Lucas draped over his shoulders like a sack of potatoes.

Raising his head just enough to look back, Lucas saw the first man furtively handing something small but weighty to the guards, who laughed in apparent satisfaction and turned away. The robed figure then ran to catch up to his partner.

Where's the altar? Lucas managed to wonder. *This is the wrong place—where are we?*

Sparkles filled his eyes. A whine built in his ears. Blackness descended as awareness began to slip away. The astronaut was only vaguely aware of being dropped into a small, restrictive enclosure of some kind, where in pain he finally came to rest for a few brief moments before feeling a sudden rush of smooth, silent motion.

The deep velvet of inner darkness closed in as oblivion claimed Gary Lucas, and he welcomed it.

29

Thursday, March 20, 1:12 P.M.

It was an old building, a lovingly built structure of great beauty. Hand-chiseled stone lined the walk and steps leading up to its massive front doors, which had been built from heavy oak and were framed on either side by white, vine-covered pillars as ornate as they were functional. Soaring windows of stained glass caught the midday sun, splashing glorious color upon an edifice already magnificent in its piety.

As Carol entered the church, clutching her purse in one hand and her Bible in the other, she drank in the rich, familiar scent of its foyer, a rustic mix of sweet flowers and aromatic wood. The place was silent, save for the steady sound of the biting wind outside. No one was in sight; she would have the solitude she had hoped for. Gliding toward the sanctuary, her high heels clicked on the smooth tile, the sound echoing along the walls.

After pausing to remove her coat and arrange her windblown hair, she pushed open the tall, wide door. On Sundays it always stood invitingly open, welcoming all who would enter, and it had struck her as odd to see it closed.

Soundlessly and slowly she moved along the wide carpeted aisle toward the pulpit and the immense golden cross behind it.

She then realized she was, in fact, not alone. Someone else was already there, sitting on a front-row pew. The nearer she grew, the more familiar the person became, and the curiosity filling Carol rapidly gave way to surprise and joy.

As the blond woman reached the foremost pew and paused, the darkly dressed person turned as if embarrassed to have been found there.

"Oh, Carol," Diane said, allowing herself a gentle smile. "Hi." She quickly pulled a tissue from her purse and raised it discreetly to her face.

"Hi, honey," Carol smiled, setting her coat and purse down and taking a seat beside her friend. "I'm sorry if I disturbed you…"

"No, no," Diane said. "It's good to see you. I just…well, I felt I ought to…" The words came awkwardly. "The church was open, and…"

Carol reached out and they hugged, once again drawing strength from each other. "Don't think you don't belong in this room, Diane. God's house is open to everyone."

"I know," Diane smiled, touched by her friend's devotion. "It's just that I'm not a member or anything…but I wanted to come in and, well…"

"Pray?"

"Yes."

Carol smiled. "Great minds think alike, I guess. I'm here for the same reason."

Diane laughed slightly. Her eyes were still slightly red, still wet—her supplications apparently had come with tears.

"I'm so glad you're here," Diane said.

"Likewise."

"I've been sitting here…talking to God."

"He's a good listener."

"I hope so." Diane kneaded her purse slightly. "I've asked for a lot…not just here today, but…" She looked down at her hands, at her wedding ring. "This last month has been...well, so much has changed... and losing Gary...I talked to God...I've never done that before..."

"He's heard from me a lot too, these last several weeks. I always draw closer to Him when Charlie's off flying somewhere or on a mission...not that He doesn't also hear from me on the way to the grocery store."

"I don't really know the words," Diane said. "I'm not sure how to speak to Him...what to say..."

"Just do it the way you speak with me or anyone else. I tend to have plain old conversations with Him...especially when I'm driving. A closed, moving car makes for wonderful privacy."

"I suppose it does."

The women sat in silence for a few moments, each pondering the burdensome situation they shared. Diane stared for a time at the cross before her, seeing it anew, and began to wonder.

"I don't understand," she said.

"What, honey?"

"Well, when Gary..." The words were hard. "When this all happened...Jeff turned his back on the world. It's as if he hates everyone and everything for taking his father away from him. He says that if there is a God, He isn't worth knowing if He could let something like that happen."

"That's not unusual, when something like this—"

"No, that's not what I'm getting at..." She took a deep breath. "He's gone into a shell...he barely speaks to me. I worried about him so much, worried about how this might affect him...change him... you know? But Carol, *I didn't react that way.* I never got angry at God...never hated Him for what happened to Gary..." She looked down for a moment, gazing blankly at her well-manicured nails as she sought the right words.

"*And* Charlie," she quickly added. "Gary and Charlie." The words came laboriously, and Carol saw her struggle. "Why didn't I get angry? Shouldn't I have? Why didn't I curse God for taking my husband and almost my whole life away from me?"

"A lot of people would have," Carol replied, resting a comforting hand upon Diane's. "Most people."

"And since then, I've found myself praying, which I *never* do…asking Him for…" She placed her other hand atop Carol's. "Well, not for Gary to be alive or to be given back to me…well, not in that way…but I wanted him to have known God. I wanted Charlie to have said something or done something to make Gary realize, to make him…" Words failed her.

"Believe?"

"Yes. Believe."

Carol nodded. "If anyone could reach him, honey, I'd put my money on Charlie…and if God wanted Gary to hear, he heard."

"I hope so," Diane said. "You know, I still can't think of him as 'gone.' I'd *almost* accepted it, I think…almost…but now, after what Bruce said, with that signal and the new mission going up…" She paused. "I just…do you think they could still be alive up there?"

Carol looked toward the golden cross, considering the question. Tears welled in her eyes as her heart again embraced her beloved husband, now separated from her at the very least by the ominous black void of cislunar space.

"I don't know…I'm not sure what to think. My heart and my head aren't seeing things the same way. I *want* it to be true…I want to have Charlie home again. I want to feel him holding me again. I want to dance with him and hear his voice and see him playing with Joey again."

"A one-in-a-million chance…that's what Bruce said."

"God's overcome much worse odds than those, honey," Carol said. "I recall one garden tomb in particular."

Diane smiled at the thought, her head bowed slightly. "That really happened…didn't it?"

"Yes, it did. Just like He promised it would." She took a moment, reminding herself of her Lord's infinite faithfulness.

"Whatever Bruce finds up there," Carol went on, "I know I *will* see Charlie again. Even if he isn't still alive up on the moon, he isn't gone…he's just moved on. In that case, I know exactly where he is and I know he's happy and that he's there waiting for me and for Joey."

Diane nodded slightly, coming to terms with something that recently had become a part of her, something that now lived within the gaping empty place that had always been a part of her life, filling it perfectly and to its limits.

"I want that for Gary…so much…"

She raised her eyes to Carol, who suddenly realized there now was something different in her friend's eyes, something that had never been there before, something behind those pools of crystal blue that burned far more brilliantly than the mere hope Cortney had seen there a few days earlier.

Diane herself could not have pointed to a specific moment, a turning point, an instant of awakening. But no matter. She knew to the depths of her soul that everything had changed, that she was not the woman she had been.

Diane Lucas *believed.*

30

His mind began to work again.

Lucas rolled onto his side, his arm beneath a dense, soft, cool pillow. Only half aware, he smiled—the bed was so comfortable he did not wish to awaken. A gentle sound of trickling water filled his ears.

Just another hour, Annie—

As he started to drift back to sleep, a nagging something refused to lie quietly, refused to let him be. Irritated, he tried to shut it out, but the effort only served to pull him closer to consciousness.

I wasn't home—I was in that cell!

The realization brought him around quickly. Slowly he opened his eyes. The light was soft and welcoming. Music was playing, a gentle, lilting melody of strings and winds intoxicating in its grandeur.

Lifting his head reluctantly from the cool pillow, he braced himself with one elbow and winced as a deep soreness in his back and shoulders stabbed at him. Finding a less painful position, he looked around with sleep-clouded eyes. He was alone in a spacious room of great beauty, an architectural wonder, exquisite both in design and execution. Carved wooden shapes reached outward from the walls high above, seemingly defying gravity as they met in a graceful, stationary ballet directly overhead. Load-bearing structures of dark, polished timber formed rich, soaring arches that joined with a complex arrangement of equally majestic ceiling beams. Wood, in fact, was everywhere, combined aesthetically with stone and glass and other earthy materials. A mural in carved relief encircled the room, a wide band high along the walls, its amazing detail depicting a civilization Lucas did not recognize—unfamiliar beasts and men and flora and technology fought and breathed and lived and soared, surrounding him with a celebrated tale he did not understand. To his surprise, there was no cruelty in the display, no delight in suffering, no pain on the faces those portrayed—only the magnificence of the distant past. It was—*beautiful.*

His hosts were highly skilled woodworkers and artists, that much was certain.

Some twenty-five feet above, a dramatic depiction of great ocean-going vessels and terrible sea monsters crowned the chamber. At the center of the arched expanse hung another of the shallow domed arrays. Now, with better lighting, he could discern thousands of tiny, mirrored facets behind its five-foot glass covering, an intricate apparatus of sparkling blue that filled its rear surface almost from edge to edge.

He got the distinct impression of a vast insect's eye, ever watchful and all-seeing.

Big Brother, maybe?

The bed was much larger than the king-sized bed he had owned back home and even bigger than the huge bunks he and Charlie had discovered within the moon base. Its head was wider than its foot, a trapezoidal form that struck the astronaut as being the norm on this world rather than the exception. The mattress was soft and supportive at the same time and felt as if nothing was beneath him at all. Sheets and blankets of the softest fabrics and purest colors covered it, and as he slid his arms and feet upon the bedcovers, he marveled at how wonderful they felt.

Lucas began to notice that the bed was a bit *too* comfortable and quickly realized he was naked beneath the sheets. More than that, he had been bathed from head to foot and lightly anointed with pleasant, scented oils. *Someone* had taken him in, cleaned him up, and put him to bed.

Why—?

After weeks spent on the hard, hay-covered stone floor of the cell, Lucas was reluctant to get up at all, but he knew he must. Keeping the covers draped over his midsection, he sat up and tossed his legs to the side, scooting with some effort toward the edge. He sat there for a few moments, scratching his beard, letting the momentary pain of movement subside. His feet dangled above the inlaid wooden floor as he studied the room, and he remained astonished by what he saw.

A relatively small table fashioned from a veined, reddish wood stood near the bed, its flowing legs and top bordered by exquisite detail work. Finished to a high gloss, its pearly grain reflected the light of the intricate glass lamp that rested upon it, a piece that, like the table, was as much art as it was practical.

There was one door in the room, towering and wide like those within the lunar base, tooled of dark timber with an intricate pattern of swirling hollows and silver filigree around its edges. Something like a doorknob was mounted at its exact center, the focal point of several radiating inlays created from a lighter variety of wood.

A multipaned, panoramic window comprised one entire wall and was curtained with flowing fabrics of vivid green and lustrous white. Little light spilled through it, however, lending the room the same quality of pseudonight Lucas had known during his captivity.

Is this entire world shrouded in darkness?

A waterfall built into one corner of the room, a living sculpture in stone and water, was both delightful and relaxing. Its soft sound blended with the music that filled the room, creating an ambience of poetic beauty. Moving bands of blue light danced slowly within the falling cascade, making it appear alive. Lush plants on stone terraces surrounded the aquatic display, lending the feel of a tropical paradise. What appeared to be a built-in wooden dresser with several large drawers rested in one nearby wall, on top of which stood several holographic photocrystals of the type Charlie had discovered in the dead man's quarters on the moon. A chair of what appeared to be oak inset with accents of colored glass rested near the bed, upholstered in earth tones.

There was no sign of his soiled cooling garment, but he noticed a purple robe spread across the foot of the bed, just beyond arm's reach. Leaning over, he pulled the clothing closer and draped it around his shoulders, enjoying the luxurious feel of the rich fabric against his skin. It was big for him but not too, and while it swallowed him up a bit, it was still manageable.

He slipped from the bed, his bare feet hitting the floor with a thud. Gathering his robe, he walked around the room, giving closer examination to its many fascinating features. The pictures on the dresser depicted men and women, all robed similarly and seemingly happy, and the display was not unlike the arrangement of family photos one might find in any Earth home. Lucas did notice, however, that there were no children anywhere to be seen—those in the images ranged from the middle-aged to the elderly.

Beyond the grand window, less than twenty yards away, stood a wall of towering trees. It was the face of a dense forest, likely home to hungry monsters like the one that almost caught him upon his arrival.

Who brought me here? What do they want?

He doubted anyone would have bathed him and left him alone had they harbored evil intentions toward him.

Unless they just want a clean sacrifice—

After a few moments of uneasy consideration, he decided to leave the room via the door, the only apparent exit. Drawing near, he paused, his eyes upon the knob, fearing what might lie beyond.

No—if they had wanted to kill me, they would have—wouldn't they?

There was only one way to find out. Gathering his courage, he began to reach for the doorknob.

Then he yanked his hand back suddenly, as if it had been burned. His eyes went wide.

The knob was turning.

◙   ◙   ◙

The dark, inscrutable panel stood silently and still before him, reflecting his own puzzled image but showing nothing else.

Okay, so what's your deal?

Shepherd, hands on hips in frustration, considered the dormant console. For days it had stood defiantly, black and still, an island of darkness in an otherwise vibrant room. It alone, of the many varying panels throughout the base, had failed to awaken at his touch and for no apparent reason.

Did you blow a breaker or what? Do these things even use breakers?

Put simply, it was bugging him.

His forced solitude, combined with the same inherent curiosity and desire for adventure that had driven Shepherd to become an astronaut in the first place, had caused the man to exercise less caution than he otherwise might have. Spending the rest of his life locked alone in an alien cage was not an appealing prospect, although the thought allowed his need for information to override—at least for now—his need for personal safety.

He leaned close, extending his hands yet again. Though he could not feel the sleeping panel beneath his fingers, he knew he had made contact. Pressing both hands against its glide barrier as firmly as he could, he slid his hands back and forth and from side to side, seeking a response.

Come on, baby!

He tried small circles, large circles, sweeping motions, whatever he could think of—moving his arms and wrists like a conductor leading an orchestra.

Come on—show me the sweet spot—

Nothing.

Then, suddenly—it spoke.

"Corsic tylusta creatani," came the words, calmly and in a rich, masculine voice.

Shepherd jumped. He had expected a display of lights and motion as with the other consoles, not a verbal address, and they were the first words, other than his own, that he had heard in weeks.

"Who...are you?" he cautiously asked. "Who are your people?"

"Corsic tylusta creatani," it said again, more firmly.

He could not discern a specific source for the voice. It seemed to come from all around him, as if spoken simultaneously by several identical people standing beside, behind, and before him.

"Is this a radio?" he asked, hoping he had stumbled upon one. "Where are you? I'm stranded here...can you help me? How can I contact Earth?"

Silence.

"Listen...I need help," Shepherd said. "I'm not—"

"Corsic tylusta creatani!" came the words again, insistently this time.

"I don't know what you want from me! My name is Charles Shepherd...I'm an astronaut...from the United States of—"

"Loskeni yanira creatani," the voice cut him off, sounding in a threatening tone. "Kyto fendalia...alitria jialo tosanna!"

Great going, Charlie. You made him mad!

Shepherd stood silently, hoping the system he had activated would respond to his stillness in kind.

No such luck—

In answer to his continued silence, a tight row of bright, angry red circles, each perhaps six inches in diameter, flared to life within the console. Stretching from left to right and from one end of the panel to the other, the lights, all thirty-seven of them, glowed solidly and more brilliantly with each passing second.

"Okay, now," Shepherd said, uneasy and sensing real trouble. "Take it easy…just talk to me here…we can work this out…"

"Merilla doso," the voice said in a very matter-of-fact tone. "Merilla uli. Merilla eristi."

The lights swelled to a peak brightness and remained, unwavering, at that level. Shepherd watched them for several minutes but detected no further change.

"Merilla aldo," the voice conclusively stated before going silent. The worried astronaut slowly backed away from the display, keeping his eyes on the lights. They did not move or otherwise alter their appearance, nor were there any further utterances.

Something occurred to him. He prayed he was wrong.

What if this isn't a radio I'm hearing? What if it's some kind of computer?

With uncertain steps, Shepherd walked across the room and took a seat at the map console, keeping an eye on the enraged lights. He counted them twice and came up with the same number both times, assuring himself that he had done so correctly. His heart was pounding—he had done something he probably should not have, he knew, bringing to life a machine with capabilities he could not venture to guess.

What if this is like one of those space movies? What if this thing went nuts and killed everyone in the place?

He watched the illuminated row for a good while, never moving from the map operator's chair. The lights remained steady as if staring, like unblinking eyes of angry crimson. As far as he could determine, nothing more was happening at the awakened console, and between confirming glances he passed the time by silently reading a few passages from his Bible. He had dodged a proverbial bullet and was thankful.

Close call, Charlie old boy—

After more than an hour of no change, no voice, no apparent threat of any kind, his watch and stomach both told him that lunchtime had come and gone. With a growl from within him breaking the silence, he gingerly rose from his seat and headed for the dining hall.

◎　　◎　　◎

The afternoon slipped away and evening arrived. Shepherd cautiously returned to the war room to retrieve the Bible he had left at the map console—he had been so preoccupied with the voice he had heard and the lights he inadvertently had triggered that, when he left, he had forgotten to take the book with him. By the time he realized his oversight a short time later, he had already decided to avoid the place for a while, to let any hornet's nest he might have stirred up settle down before spending any more time in there. There was plenty to occupy him elsewhere, at least as much as he had found to do in the huge control chamber, and since it was well away from the primary living areas, he thought it prudent to avoid further aggravating a possibly menacing situation.

Entering quietly, he found his Bible right where he had left it. Taking the old tome gently in hand, he turned away again, headed toward his quarters and a bit of welcome, relaxing reading.

Nearing the exit, he glanced across the room at the array of red circles he inadvertently had ignited, and casually counted them.

Wait a minute—

Thinking he had erred, he stopped in his tracks and counted them again.

That's not right—

And again.

Why is it—?

The light at the far right end of the row had gone out while he was away.

What is it doing?

At that moment, even as his gaze was focused upon it, the next circle in line went dark.

Dear Lord, what did I do?

A chill gripped him, its icy fingers clutching his spine as he understood.

A countdown was under way.

31

The door began to open.

Lucas stepped back, bracing for anything. He missed his knife.

A space appeared at the edge of the door and silently grew. When it had widened but a foot or so, it stopped. Its ornamental knob rotated back into position.

Then, soundlessly, the door continued to move.

Lucas tensed, bracing for a fight, knowing his chances were poor should he have to defend himself. In but a second, he scanned the room searching for anything that might be usable as a weapon, but he saw nothing that might make a dent in an attacker.

He turned his eyes back to the door. In moments it was fully open, and Lucas, adrenaline still filling his limbs, could only stare at the sight now before him.

A woman stood in the huge opening, facing him. Her beauty was striking—her dark flowing hair framed a face of sheer loveliness, her colorful green robes draped upon a body of pure feminine magnificence. She was taller than he by a good six inches. Her smile was intoxicating. Her dark, sparkling eyes gazed directly into his.

He knew those eyes, that face. The very image of his Diane's.

"You," he whispered.

Lucas saw a light bruising on her forearms, a fading reminder of the brutal attack to which she had almost fallen. No longer dressed in tatters, her intricately made robes concealed yet emphasized her statuesque form, and a sash drawn at her waist further accentuated the classic lines of her figure. Her hair was arranged in an exacting, flattering style that incorporated small, intricate objects of glass and polished metal. Her angelic facial features were accented flawlessly, brought to perfection by a subtle, elegant use of makeup. Her lips were full and kind. Her nails were long and polished a glossy turquoise, and her open, airy sandals revealed feet that appeared dainty despite their size.

She saw the look of recognition that had crossed his face and smiled, her rose-glossed lips glistening in the light.

"You clean up real nice," he smiled, speaking primarily for his own benefit, knowing not a word was being understood. "I'm glad you got home all right…there are some nasty things living out in those woods. One almost got me…"

"Losira chiraati," she said, stepping closer. She put out a hand and touched his cheek, then drew close and put her arms around him, pulling him into her. Lucas was surprised by the sudden embrace.

"Well, now, Miss…I…uh…"

"Reviata tu letani," she said, the words imbued with meaning. Her tone was one of deep gratitude.

"You're welcome…I think," Lucas smiled, as the woman pulled away. "But I didn't do anything anybody else wouldn't have done."

After backing away a few steps, she held a hand out, imploring him wordlessly to take it. He paused and remained still, considering his options.

"Seliasi," she smiled, wiggling her fingers.

"Okay, sure," Lucas agreed, taking her hand. "Why not?"

She led him slowly through the door and into a wide hallway. As they walked, hand in hand, they passed several open areas, rooms filled with lush plant life and works of art, and Lucas noticed that the soft music hanging in the air filled every inch of the hallway, every room, and every alcove. The perfume of tropical flowers greeted him anew with each step. Beauty filled his every sense.

The hallway soon opened into a room much larger than the bed chamber. From the hundreds of shelving recesses lining the walls, he deduced that the three-story-high room was some form of library. Tens of thousands of bound, booklike items of leather and glass filled the ascending shelves, placed there along with carefully arranged, variously sized scrolls handwritten on rolls of pearlescent paper. Exotic, flowering houseplants of a size and variety Lucas had never seen thrived throughout the room, standing both on the floor and upon small, ornate projections that dotted the walls, mingling emerald and a hundred vibrant colors with the room's rich wood tones. Directly overhead, an immense skylight spanned the chamber, its faceted, crystal panes defying the smoky darkness above by reflecting the warm light of the room. At the center of the ceiling was another of the great domed arrays.

Is there one of those in every room of every building on the planet?

The woman moved aside, revealing to Lucas the center of the library floor. There, waiting within a wide, sunken seating pit, waited the remainder of his hosts, seven in all.

They sat silently and still with all eyes upon their guest, patiently allowing him to grow more comfortable with his surroundings. The woman took Lucas' arm and gently brought him closer to the others, smiling reassurances at him with each step. They stopped a few feet from the edge of the pit, and as the astronaut looked upon the woman's companions, she spoke with them. He saw upon their faces and in their eyes a kindness he had not seen on this world, save for the woman at his side. Their clothing was as hers, consisting of multicolored robes, waist belts, and sandals.

It appeared to Lucas that she was not alone in appreciating his actions in saving her. A silver-haired, clean-shaven man, clearly the eldest of the lot, gave him a smile and a reassuring nod, then gestured approvingly toward the woman with whom Lucas had entered.

There were other women in the room as well, three of them, seated with the men, apparently as couples. Everyone was of great stature, as Lucas had come to expect. Three of the men and two of the women appeared to be in their thirties, while the elder fellow and the woman seated beside him were likely in their sixties. One of the younger men had a short, neat head of black hair, another sported red and the last was blond.

The older man rose and extended a hand toward Lucas in an inviting gesture, beckoning him to move closer. After taking a deep breath, Lucas did so, his steps slow and his way careful as he descended the steps into the pit.

"Thank you," Lucas said, though the words were in vain. "You saved my life." He turned his gaze toward two of the younger men seated there and quickly noticed what it was that was draped beside them on the couch.

Two gruesome masks and two black robes.

"It was you," Lucas realized. "You came for me."

He walked up to his rescuers and extended a hand. Instead of shaking hands, however, each in turn gripped the astronaut's forearm and held it for an affirming moment.

"Deri toloso," one said. "Tufernaan du kerili."

"Well," Lucas guessed, his free hand over his heart, "I want you to know I am most grateful."

As the men watched, he picked up one of the skull-like masks, peering into the darkness of its eyeholes as he recalled his rescue.

"You bribed the guards," he knew. "You risked your own lives on my account."

The woman at his side glided over to the remaining man, her robes flowing gracefully behind her. They held each other for a moment, then kissed as she ran her fingers through his thick auburn tresses.

"You have a lovely home," Lucas smiled, addressing the eldest man, who approached and towered over him. "Very impressive." Extending his hand, the man employed the same forearm-to-forearm gesture as had the others, clearly in gratitude.

"Welia kriestan," he said in a thunderous yet kind voice, tears welling in his eyes. He then bent down enough to embrace Lucas fully, the hug long and heartfelt and inescapable.

"You too," Lucas said as their contact finally broke.

There was a call from across the room. The astronaut turned to see the young dark-haired man open a wide, double door, inviting Lucas closer. As he approached, the displaced commander discovered to his absolute delight that beyond the doorway lay a table set with a bountiful quantity of food and drink of all kinds—fruits, meats, cheeses, vegetables, and lots of delicious-looking things he could not readily identify. His hosts, their expressions joyful, gestured broadly toward the table, clearly inviting the lost soul they had taken in to dig in and make himself at home.

"You read my mind," Lucas smiled in return, his gratitude profound and obvious. "Thank you."

32

Tuesday, April 22, 9:04 A.M.

Clank.

The hatch sealed with a loud, very distinctive, very mechanical sound as its dozens of latches slid home, locking it firmly into place. Cortney could not, however, hear the gentle double pat on its heavily insulated outer surface as Pad Leader Guenter Wendt, as was his custom, silently wished the crew luck in their mission.

It was a perfect morning. The rising sun had found a calm breeze and gentle temperatures as it rose over the cape, casting a long shadow behind the towering launch vehicle and its ruddy orange umbilical tower. The mammoth booster, a layer of frost and ice already covering its outer skin as moisture in the air froze against its supercold propellant tanks, stood ready and waiting. White plumes spilled from vent valves in each of its stages as rising pressures within the tanks was relieved. In time those same pressures would be allowed to build as the time of glory neared.

Apollo 20 was headed for the moon to find two of NASA's sons and bring them back to Earth.

The remaining hours before launch sped by. The crew of three, having completed their final preflight checks, lay still, tied to their couches, waiting for the moment two of them had experienced before. They glanced around, as familiar with the cabin as they were with their own faces, knowing every panel, every switch, every bolt.

Sunlight suddenly found the cabin. The white room had pulled away as its access arm retracted, leaving the spacecraft and its crew utterly isolated. The pad crew had been evacuated now, pulled back to a minimum safe distance of more than a mile from the tower, to wait with the rest of the world.

Of the craft's five windows, blue daylight streamed in through only two, those left unobstructed by the conical, protective shroud that would shield the command module from frictional heating during its mach-nine-plus ascent. Cortney, glancing through the round window of the sealed hatch, saw a seagull soar by, the early sun glistening upon its wings.

"Just saw a gull," he smiled. "Odd that he's up this high. I hope that's a good omen."

"Could be," Lunar Module Pilot James Irwin replied from the right-hand seat. "Can't hurt, anyway."

Now, with only minutes remaining, the three men were as calm as three men strapped to a massive hydrogen-oxygen-kerosene bomb could be.

Cortney angled a small mirror mounted to a panel to his left. Reflected there, he saw one of the two additional couches mounted sideways behind his crew's. In a matter of days, they would hold the lifeless forms of Lucas and Shepherd.

He shuddered.

"So," Command Module Pilot Donald Slayton began, drumming his gloved fingers upon his armrest, "when this baby goes…"

"You'll know it, Deke," Irwin smiled. "Trust me."

"When I flew on Eighteen," Cortney said, his gaze upon the busy console before him, "Freddo had built things up in my mind so much that the ride itself paled in comparison, if you can believe that. Made it sound like riding in a blender. Not that it wasn't still a rush…"

"Which reminds me," Irwin said in mock seriousness. "I'll have to have a little talk with Mr. Haise when we get home…he's taken to 'borrowing' my parking space back in Houston."

"Oh, can't have that," Cortney agreed.

"Nope," Slayton chimed in.

"I told him I'd bring back his mower sooner or later," Irwin kidded. "But he feels he just has to make a point."

"What brand?" Slayton asked, his face deadpan.

"Lawn-Boy."

"Good mower."

"Yup."

"Bag attachment?"

"You betcha."

"Twenty, we're looking good at two minutes," Launch Control announced over their headsets. "Mark."

The metallic groans and creaks of the monstrous Saturn made it seem as if the men sat atop a living creature, a behemoth straining against its reins, anxious to free itself of its earthly bonds.

"We have completed the transfer to internal power," came the voice. "You guys are on your own."

"Finally getting close," Slayton said, recalling his medical dismissal from the Mercury program. He had been one of the original "seven," the men chosen to serve as America's first astronauts. An irregular heartbeat had grounded him before he saw a minute of spacecraft flight time, however, and serving as director of the Astronaut Office since that time had never completely dulled his longing for space. "Fourteen years and counting, now down to—"

"Forty-five seconds," the voice said. "We are go."

"Roger, go," Cortney said. "Looks good up here."

The final seconds ticked past.

"Twenty, you are go…stand by for the ten count. Ten…nine… ignition sequence start…six…five…"

Did it light? Slayton wondered for an instant, his eyes scanning the gray-green interior of the spacecraft. He felt nothing, heard nothing.

"…three…two…one…all engines running…"

The waves of thunder rising from almost forty stories below finally climbed the length of the metal colossus and filled the command module. A roar built within the crew's ears, mixing with the hiss of air in their helmets.

"Launch commit…"

A rolling shock wave swept up and into the spacecraft, shaking it madly, vibrating the men's eyes, blurring their vision, rattling their teeth and threatening to loose them from their sockets.

Outside, Cortney knew, the buildup of ice was falling away from the booster in both great sheets and tiny fragments, melting as it neared the maelstrom below. A tangible wall of heat and sound was sweeping across the surrounding marshland, slamming into and through anything standing in its path. The huge umbilical arms tying their vehicle to its tower were pulling back and swinging away, yanking clear its electrical connections and fuel lines, initiating the release of the great beast, freeing it from its captivity.

Immense lockdown clamps momentarily held the monster immobile, allowing its giant F-1 engines to build up to their full thrust of seven and a half million pounds before setting it free to fly. Almost twenty-five hundred gallons of fuel per second poured through the fuel pumps, igniting in a conflagration second only to the atomic bomb in raw power.

Huge valves opened, inundating the concrete blast channel beneath the pad with a torrent of millions of gallons of water, a flood that instantly vaporized into superheated steam as it bore the brunt of the Saturn's fury. Momentarily, another such deluge would douse the umbilical tower, for without the combined, drenching waters, the rocket might destroy its support structures as it departed, reducing both the pad and its tower to charred debris.

The lockdowns fell back. The monster was loose. The men aboard held their collective breath.

And then they felt it *move.*

Slowly at first, more than three thousand tons of machine, man, and propellant began to rise as if by the hand of God.

"Liftoff," Cortney barely heard within his helmet as the call came, declaring the obvious to the airborne astronauts. The ride was a rickety, cacophonous elevator at first—a slow, shaky ascent that rapidly gained in speed. The spacesuited men were pressed into their seats as the g-forces steadily built, straining the module's couch supports as each man let physical law have its way.

"The clock is running," the commander said, watching the digital display of the mission timer on his console.

"Feels like a freight train," Slayton observed. "On ten miles of bad track."

A new voice came over their headsets.

"Twenty, Houston...you have cleared the tower," Kendall called from the CapCom's seat at the Manned Spacecraft Center. As with every flight, communications with the spacecraft switched from the Launch Control Center at the cape to Mission Control in Houston the moment the booster rose beyond its gantry.

"Roger," Cortney called back over the din. They breathed a bit easier now, for the first and greatest threat to the vehicle had been the only other object within collision distance, the launch tower. Once it fell behind, nothing could touch them.

"Looking good, Twenty," Kendall said. "Good thrust from all five engines."

"Roger, Vic," Cortney acknowledged. The booster spun on its long axis, aligning itself for the ascent. "We've got a roll program."

"Roger the roll."

The Saturn began to arc up and out over the ocean as it climbed ever faster toward the heavens.

Dancing the skies on laughter-silvered wings—

"Two thousand feet," the commander called, as the vehicle took an attitude that would place the astronauts in a heads-down position as orbit was attained. "And we have a pitch program."

"Roger the pitch," Kendall acknowledged.

The seconds ticked by, and with each a hundred thousand separate functions kept the booster flying true. It climbed ever faster, splitting the air as it broke the sound barrier. A boom sounded over the cold waters of the Atlantic.

"Stand by for Mode One-Bravo," Kendall called, announcing the abort method now warranted by the vehicle's increasing altitude. "Mark...One-Bravo."

"Roger...Mode One-Bravo."

"Cabin pressure is relieving," Slayton called out, watching his gauges. As the rocket soared higher, the air pressure within the cabin continued to vent, dropping from sea level until it reached its flight pressure of five pounds per square inch.

"Coming up on Max Q," Cortney announced. The soaring vehicle groaned anew as it passed into the region of maximum dynamic pressure, that time in the flight when its increasing velocity and atmospheric density combined to create the most intense stress it would endure.

"Roger," Kendall confirmed from the ground. "Max Q."

"Two and a half gees," Cortney read aloud.

"Man, this baby's moving!" Irwin said.

"You are go, Twenty...everything is looking good."

"Roger...and we are through Max Q."

Amazing machine, Cortney thought, aware that he was riding the greatest technical accomplishment in the history of human flight, perhaps the only modern creation deserving of a place alongside the great, timeless wonders of the world. Every Saturn V ever launched—all sixteen of them—had performed flawlessly, on time, and on target.

Absolutely amazing!

"Sure could use a window," Slayton commented, peering through his viewport at the dark inner surface of the boost cover outside. "Won't be long now..."

"EDS to manual," the commander said, pressing a switch on his main panel, shutting off the spacecraft's automatic abort system. In case of a catastrophic failure in the booster it would now be up to Cortney, not the computer, to save their lives.

"Inboard engine cutoff in ten seconds," he then announced. The first stage had almost finished its work, and the center engine in its cluster of five would now go silent in preparation for staging. "Inboard cutoff."

"Roger, inboard."

"Counting down to first stage cutoff...ten seconds...eight... five..."

"Hang on, guys," Irwin said, knowing what was to come.

"You are go for staging," Kendall called.

Explosive bolts fired, severing the spent first stage from the rest of the vehicle. As it fell away, the booster's velocity suddenly dropped. The men were thrown forward in their seats by their own inertia, sorely testing the straps that held them to their couches.

"Staging," Cortney said.

Almost at once, the five engines of the second stage flared to life. The kick threw the men backward again, hard into their seats.

"*Really* bad track," Slayton said.

"Houston, we have S-II ignition," the commander called out.

"Roger, Twenty…you are go on all five."

The connecting interstage fell away. "We have skirt sep…looking good."

Through the shudder of the cabin, Cortney reached out, lifted a clear protective cover on the panel before him and pressed the switch beneath it. Daylight suddenly filled all five windows as their now-unneeded escape tower was jettisoned, taking the boost cover with it.

"Tower jett," Cortney called.

"Look at that," an awed Slayton said, peering through his now-unobstructed window at the magnificent Earth below. Cortney cut a sideward glance and smiled, watching the man as one might enjoy the face of a child on Christmas morning.

Slayton thought back to 1961, to the days when men soared alone into the fringes of space in tiny craft they practically wore. *Did it look like this to you, Al? Did you see the world the way I do now—the way I should have seen it so long ago?*

"Coming up on four minutes," Kendall announced. "Still looking very good. CMC is go."

"Roger," Cortney replied. "Computer is go."

"Oh, mercy," Slayton said, his eyes upon his viewport. "That horizon is just gorgeous…look at that!"

No artist's brush could have captured the intensity of color, the sheer beauty of the diminishing atmosphere. Deep blues, falling away into white, ending against a sudden, hard black deeper than any on Earth. A fragile shell of life-giving air, protecting and sustaining the entire world for which it had been created.

"Twenty, Houston. We show you 275 miles downrange…86 miles high…velocity 12,483 feet per second. Right on the money. Looks like a home run."

"Roger that," Cortney smiled. "Next stop, Marlow."

The world fell away. The booster, like its sisters, was working perfectly, two million separate parts all functioning exactly as designed, created for one purpose.

Leaving home.

◙   ◙   ◙

Kendall sat watching the display at the front of the room, a world map crisscrossed by orbital tracks and communications network grids. Centered upon it, a small, moving representation of the Apollo 20 vehicle had begun its first transit of the Atlantic Ocean, well on its way to achieving orbit.

The CapCom console felt cold, even clammy beneath his hands, and though the MOCR was packed, it somehow did not feel alive to him as it had in the past. Controllers as well as dozens of officials and astronauts crowded the consoles, all watching with great anticipation as once again a mighty Saturn V left the Earth, likely for the last time. But still Kendall felt isolated and alone.

As the telemetry numbers continued to flow from the ascending craft, he thought of a morning only two months earlier when he had been the one up there amid the delirious burning blue, the one in the center couch, the one who was headed toward the moon.

And there with him, on that day, had been two others. Like him, they savored the journey, the challenge, the mission. Unlike his, theirs had been a one-way trip.

Again their faces hung before him.

Stay focused!

Maybe they had been right. Maybe he was not yet ready to fly. "Twenty, you are go for staging," he relayed, having just heard the flight director voice the confirmation in his headset.

"Roger that," came the reply from Cortney.

High above the world, out over the ocean, the second stage now was falling away. The trusty Saturn third stage would carry the crew into orbit and would eventually accelerate them toward the moon before being jettisoned itself. It was a standard flight plan that, with few modifications, had been used on every translunar flight.

There was, however, something about this flight that was indeed a first: specialized equipment stowed aboard Apollo 20 that never before had been a part of any lunar mission.

Body bags.

Kendall struggled with the image that dogged his mind's eye—two frozen, pressure-suited men, locked into whatever bodily position had been their last, being vacuum sealed into zippered bags and carried as cargo on a journey home that, for them, had come much too late.

He remained a haunted man.

33

Cinders stung his eyes.

Lucas stood upon a scaffold, spray gun in hand, facing a wall that seemed never to end as it stretched high and to either side. Silently, a resinous liquid in tanks below him flowed upward through long, snaking hoses and found freedom through the precisely machined equipment he held, meeting its final rest upon the massive wooden structure before him.

Smoke, as always, filled the skies, and ash cast upward by a thousand distant fires rained down, spoiling the purity of his work as it insisted on sticking to the tacky russet coating. Banks of brilliant white lights illuminated his work, for the sunlight could no longer pierce the imposed quasi night of the heavy shroud overhead.

While not the largest he had ever seen, the rectangular building that loomed before him was extraordinary, even for this world. For days he had assisted with its completion, standing shoulder-to-ribcage with a dozen other men applying the weatherproofing. Built of precision-cut, heavy timber, it was a storehouse six hundred feet long and sixty feet high, with a foundation as expansive as two city blocks. At that foundation, scattered upon the concrete work areas that surrounded it, rested advanced machines used in its creation—but how they had been used, Lucas could only guess. The edifice dwarfed every other structure in the area, many of which were warehouses filled with supporting shops, heavy woodworking tools, and building materials.

Despite its grand scale and heavily reinforced construction, Lucas was familiar with such buildings. He had spent many a boyhood summer on a family farm that had been home to his uncle and aunt, and their wheat fields, among the largest in Kansas, had filled such storehouses to overflowing come harvest time. The granary now before him was similar to his family's, and he even drew comfort from the fond memories it engendered. Its immense door had remained open the entire time he had worked there, swallowing load after load of crops as soon as they were harvested from the surrounding fields. He had watched in fascination as bizarre threshing machines had razed the artificially lit fields, transforming their bounty from raw growth to usable sustenance in one pass. Grains mostly, the yield had been brought in on transporting vehicles, hauled up the repository's ponderous entry ramp, and deposited into waiting silo bins. Lucas, standing at its vast, open doorway, once stole a glance at the interior, and the brief look had been enough to reveal that the place was filled from end to end with huge storage compartments, some full and others empty, and smaller holds of varying shapes and sizes. Its multiple levels surrounded a central atrium, its interior lit by lamps mounted at regular intervals throughout.

Around the clock, the harvesting had continued. Thousands of acres gave up their bounty and every bit was brought into the storehouse, yet it was nowhere near capacity. Lucas supposed that the building, when full, could supply the needs of hundreds of thousands of people, and that his hosts were the primary providers for their region.

No wonder they can afford to build such an amazing house and hold onto so much prime farmland. This family must feed half the county or kingdom or whatever—they've cornered the local food market, and everybody needs food, right?

Orchards all around him already had been stripped of their fruit.

Vines had yielded their large, juicy grapes. Most of the fields had been harvested before his arrival, and Lucas could only imagine the amount of food that had been stored within the incredible facility.

The main house, where he had first awakened, stood some seventy yards behind him and was connected to the granary by a wide paved road. The soaring manor seemed suited for ancient kings, wondrously crafted of wood, stone, and glass. The elegance of antiquity, melded with a sophisticated use of materials, line, and form, lent the structure an air of transcendent timelessness that spoke of legend and of life. Missing were the hideous gargoyles Lucas had seen elsewhere, as was the inherent, masochistic cruelty that had lurked within the living areas of the lunar base.

The space between the house and the granary was filled largely by landscaped tracts that clearly had been neglected of late—what once had been artfully sculpted trees and bushes had become ragged and random, and grasses in many places grew to waist height. At the center of the unkempt yard, atop a forty-foot tower of bronze and steel, was mounted a glass sphere about ten feet across. Within the crystalline shell, filling it and rotating slowly, was a round, multifaceted array of brilliant, glittering blue like those he had seen before.

My, Grandma—what big eyes you have!

Lucas had been introduced to the storehouse the day after his rescue. His hosts had seen to his every need, feeding and dressing him, grateful in turn for his intervention on the young woman's behalf. He had been happy to trade his cooling garment for the soft, clean robes the family provided. He also had been offered shaving instruments but chose to keep his beard for the time being; he had long wanted to try growing one, but military protocol prevented him.

Seeing the work going on at the vast granary, and still full of gratitude for having been saved from certain, horrible death, Lucas managed to express his desire to help in finishing the construction.

Whether the structure was new or simply being renovated he could not tell, but in any case it surely had been a massive undertaking.

His small stature and apparently odd mannerisms had been looked upon with both amusement and derision as he took his place on the scaffolds among his towering fellow workers. He quickly learned to stay out of their way for the most part, avoiding conflict as much as possible. One man, his black hair long and matted, his face marred by lengthy, heavy scars, had taken a particular dislike to the astronaut, and with harsh words repeatedly had shoved him aside while reaching for equipment. Lucas, not knowing why he had been singled out, but hoping to stay out of sight and therefore out of mind, had taken a place at the opposite end of the scaffold, as far from the aggressor as was possible. Like most of the planet's inhabitants, the brutes' patience was short, their tempers violent. Again and again, fights broke out on the scaffolds over one trivial thing or another, forcing the granary's owners to intervene and sometimes dismiss one or both of the troublemakers.

Those laboring at Lucas' side were hired workers, that much he had figured out. Their muted robes were ragged, their sandals tattered, and it was clear they were there for one reason only: While their love for the work was minimal, their pay apparently was not. After taking their hefty wages in gold coins each evening, they retired to a community of relatively small houses that had been built adjacent to the storehouse. Who knew how long each man had lived there or how long the rotations of work crews had labored in erecting the building, but it appeared to Lucas that the scaffolds soon would be coming down.

The wood of the structure was unlike any he had ever seen. No mere timber, it had the appearance of composite material, one of many interlocking strands of different colored woods, all of the same basic grain and texture. Its strength would be incredible, a product of an advanced technology that utilized organic elements in astounding ways. The linear grain showed through the rich translucent glaze of the resin sealant, which now covered the entire building with its deep, dark amber hue to a depth of a quarter of an inch. Surely, Lucas thought, the coating made its walls and gently sloping roof impervious to the worst the elements could unleash upon it.

He looked out over the darkened countryside as he had again and again, drinking in the wonder of it all from his high vantage point near the roofline. Deep forests, fertile fields, and the glorious architecture of the compound filled his senses with a magnificence that was obvious even in the diminished light. Other than the smoke that blocked the sun, there was no sign here of the shadowed city from which he had been rescued, and he could only guess how far away it lay. Colored birds singing songs of unearthly beauty and small, batlike things glittered like jewels as they flitted from tree to tree, catching the glaring floodlights. Animals sounded in the distance—some roaring like lions or bears, others trumpeting perhaps like elephants, and still others like nothing he had heard. Still wary of the monsters he knew lurked in the nearby forests, he occasionally kept an eye on the tightly packed tree line, fearful of what might emerge. The ever-present aroma of burning wood and falling ash that hung in the still air only served to make the place seem more surreal.

On this day, as Lucas let his spray gun rest by his side for a moment, sudden cries sounded from below. The harvesting machines went silent. Hurried footfalls clattered against the ground. Lucas' attentions were drawn downward, where he saw the elderly man and several of the younger members of the family running toward the house as if in alarm. The others on the scaffolds, ignoring the apparent concerns of their employers, turned a deaf ear and continued apathetically with their work. Certain that something must be terribly wrong, the astronaut-turned-construction worker shut off and dropped his spray applicator, then descended the metal ladder behind him.

Trailing far behind his hosts, Lucas traversed the yard toward the house. After crossing the home's spacious rear portico, he entered the main hall but found no one there. He peered through the broad entrances into the kitchen and library, but they too were empty. All was still. Clearly, there had been an emergency of some kind.

Where did you all go?

The sound of lowered voices trickled down the main hall's wide, curving staircase, and found his ears. Lucas ascended the polished wooden steps and found himself before an open intricately appointed double door on the upper landing. Cautiously approaching the gilded threshold, he paused and peered quietly into the circular room beyond.

The entire family was gathered there, huddled around an ornate, tentlike bed of rich, dark wood draped in luxurious fabrics of blue and green. Warm, gentle light filled the room, a place of elegance. As Lucas stood and watched, he was noticed by the woman whose life he had saved. Seeing his reluctance to intrude, with a slight nod she beckoned him. He slowly entered, drew closer, and quickly understood.

It was a deathbed. An ancient man with dry, papery skin and long white hair rested there, clad in sleeping clothes of vivid red, surrounded by grandchildren and great-grandchildren as he drew his final breaths. His eyes were closed, his deeply lined face one of joyful acquiescence and profound peace. As his loved ones looked upon him, saying their farewells with wet eyes, they knew an abundant life once measured in robust decades had now dwindled to a trickle, a fragile flow of wispy, swiftly fading moments.

Clearly, this man was the patriarch of the family, a man whose rich, vibrant life had been filled with innumerable joys and heartbreaks, whose life had served as a shining example for those who now surrounded him.

Lucas, touched by the sheer solemnity and deep emotion of the scene, felt a lump in his throat as the image of another deathbed flashed to mind. There, many years earlier, Lucas had sat by his father, whose once vital life gave way to a disease no man could conquer. A tear coursed down Lucas' cheek.

And then, with the face of his father still hanging before his mind's eye, he watched as the old man exhaled his last and went utterly still. A weary heart, having worked unceasingly since its birth, was at rest.

His allotted years had finally come to an end.

The family spoke gentle words, good-byes, and prayers. Lucas bowed his head and listened, not understanding a word but feeling their grief nonetheless. After a few minutes, the old man's quiet form was covered by a sheet and left in peace as the family walked from the room. The woman took Lucas' arm, led him down the stairs and back outside, and all immediately resumed their labors.

Talk about a work ethic, Lucas mused with astonishment, watching as his hosts again climbed aboard their harvesters or disappeared into the storehouse. *Can't they even take time to mourn?*

He walked back out to the granary, affected by the death he had seen. After climbing the oversized ladder once more, he quietly resumed his place on the scaffold and picked up his spraying equipment. It would not be long, now—the job was nearly complete, for the rapidly hardening resin he had helped to apply covered almost the entirety of the structure, including its broad, unshingled roof.

A sudden shock rocked the scaffold as an eruption of thunderous voices and brutal motion knocked Lucas aside. Yet another fight had broken out between two workers. As they exchanged shouts and blows, the astronaut found himself in harm's way, with nowhere to hide and no means by which to shield himself. A driving fist crashed into Lucas' left shoulder, sending a wave of severe pain down his arm. With another blow, one of the combatants stumbled into him, knocking the small man backward and off balance. His foot became ensnared in one of the resin feed lines, and with his full weight the astronaut fell hard into the low railing of the platform.

His hand shot out, trying to stop his momentum, but he was unsuccessful. His knuckles cracked sharply against the edge of the metal handrail. Deep red warmth poured from the gash, his arms flailing madly. The instant passed as if in slow motion. Lucas flipped back over the railing and fell some thirty feet onto the ground below, landing hard on a small grassy area bordered on three sides by polished pavement. A sharp crack of breaking bone filled the air as his ribcage slammed into the ground. The impact knocked his breath away and sudden, intense pain wracked his body. He coughed, tasting blood, the spastic movement an agony.

A whine filled his ears. Blackness swirled within him as falling ash gently rained upon his tortured, writhing form.

His senses slipped away, and he went still.

◙   ◙   ◙

Voices.

They echoed in Lucas' head, drawing him back from the void. He opened his eyes and found himself once more in his bed in the residence, surrounded by the towering forms of his hosts. One of them, leaning over him, held a small, glowing metal object near his bandage-wrapped chest. As the mechanism moved over him, tracing the contours of his ribcage and abdomen, he felt energy draining away as if a forced relaxation was claiming his flesh.

"Dori teluia," the man said in a reassuring tone, smiling as he shut off the silvery gadget with a slight sideward motion of his thumb. He rose, stepped back from the bed, and handed the mysterious device to one of the women.

The dark-haired woman who resembled Diane sat on the edge of the bed, lightly mopping his brow with a cool, damp cloth.

"Kelesta," she said with a smile and a gentle voice. Placing one hand behind his head, she put a glass of cold water to his lips.

He smiled, nodded slightly, and sipped of the water, his head pounding. He still felt pain in his back and sides and was stiff and sore all over.

"I took a spill, I think," he said weakly. "Big one."

She gave him something else to drink from a crystal vial, a bitter, emerald liquid that tasted like medicine. The solemnity upon her face made her seem like a nurse at that moment. After he had downed it all, she followed up with more water and spoke to him in a soft, reassuring tone.

"I guess it wouldn't work if it didn't taste like that, huh?" he said.

Gently, she laid his head back upon the pillow. His hosts all smiled, apparently relieved at his return to consciousness, and after a few minutes of cautious observation, words were spoken among them.

"I want to thank you again," Lucas tried. "All of you."

The women, save Diane's near twin, nodded toward the men and left the room, leaving the four gentlemen standing near the foot of the bed.

"Dewila sedi," the younger, red-haired man said to the others, indicating Lucas with a broad gesture, his voice firm.

At that, a debate erupted among the four. The eldest appeared to be taking one standpoint while the other three argued with him, their stance expressed with intense emotion and insistence. The old man, equally rigid in his view, was clearly alone in his position, whatever it was. The woman sitting at Lucas' side, watching silently, placed a hand upon his shoulder as the argument unfolded, as if to comfort him.

Though Lucas did not understand a word being spoken, he was certain of one thing—*he* was the subject of the dispute.

After the heated debate had gone on for a few minutes, the old man raised his deep voice and gestured toward the heavens, crying out in a tone that carried power and authority. At once, the other men went silent, their stand clearly subdued by the old man's words. Looking into Lucas' eyes with sadness in their own, each of the younger men, in turn, approached his bedside and took his hand, said a few words, then silently left the room.

The woman slowly and reluctantly rose from the bedside, then leaned over and kissed the injured man gently on the forehead. Her eyes glistened as she caressed his cheek, and wetness traced her cheeks. Her lower lip quivered, betraying an inner struggle she clearly was losing.

Lucas knew a good-bye when he saw one.

They're going to make me leave—

He lost himself in her countenance, cherishing her beauty, her compassion.

So very like my Annie—

Gliding as if on air, she turned and departed the bed chamber, the drape of her elegant gossamer robe sparkling as it billowed behind her. She vanished through the door.

The white-haired man remained behind. Now alone with the astronaut, he moved closer and, standing at the bedside, spoke in a solemn, even apologetic tone.

"Creatila sestilaam," he said, his voice resonant. "Kessta frela tu kessilac…bilada tensa noraalti."

With that, he reached out and took hold of Lucas' hand, gently yet with great authority and with obvious regret.

"Why are you sending me away?" Lucas asked. "Whatever I did, I'm sorry."

"Verisiala du mortria…kusona detria mei."

The man released his grip and walked away. At the doorway he paused and turned to face his injured guest once more. Their eyes locked. A silent moment passed.

"Kusona detria mei," the old man repeated slowly, through tears. Then he too was gone.

Lucas laid back, staring up at the ceiling, at the domed array that hung there.

They're definitely making me leave, probably the moment I'm well enough—

He remembered he had fallen, though he was unsure what had brought it about. His memory at that point was fuzzy, but whatever the cause he was certain it had been an accident, and he could recall nothing that might warrant expulsion.

What did I do?

He examined the facts solidly within his grasp, replaying in his mind the images of the concerned faces he had just seen and the sounds of the heartfelt words he had just heard.

Where will I go?

The pain still residing in his ribs was sufficient to limit his motion, and he knew he was in no shape to get out of bed, much less climb a scaffold. His weakness now was such that even making a simple fist took great, deliberate effort. He needed to allow his body the time it needed, having endured so much.

The younger three didn't want me to leave, and neither did the woman—but the old man did. Why?

The medicine he had swallowed was taking effect, and a deep, wondrous drowsiness settled in. He relaxed each part of his body in turn, beginning with his toes and working his way upward, letting the pain fade within the stillness of his flesh.

I'll get some rest, and tomorrow I'll be better. Tomorrow I'll be leaving—

Driving from his mind the sudden uncertainty that had descended upon him, he let sleep close in, yielding himself fully to its timeless, healing embrace.

34

Saturday, April 26, 8:42 P.M.

Jeff Lucas went deep, cut to his right, then went deep again.

Turning to look back over his left shoulder, he saw the football arc-ing toward him. Night had just fallen and the first stars were shining brightly, but he could make out the streaking phantom as it sailed into his arms. Without breaking stride, he caught the ball in his out-stretched hands and he pulled it in, securing it against his body. He continued to run a few more yards, the pigskin tucked firmly into the crook of his arm, scoring an imaginary touchdown on an imaginary field, before an imaginary, cheering crowd.

"Good catch," called the passer, a boy named Roger Carroll, who had been one of Jeff's closest friends throughout his years in junior high.

"Good pass," Jeff countered. "Right on the money."

"The Oilers need me," Roger smiled.

"They need *somebody.*"

Jeff jogged back toward his schoolmate, who stood waiting in the middle of the street. At that moment, headlights appeared behind Roger.

"Car," Jeff called out, seeing his buddy was unaware of it. Both boys stepped to the sidewalk, allowing the metallic-brown station wagon to pass before moving back out into the center of the lane.

"I guess it's getting dark anyway," Jeff went on, pausing to lob the

324

ball back in Roger's direction. "Even with the streetlight…hard to see the ball."

"Yeah…I guess you're right," he replied, making the catch. He turned to walk toward his family's driveway. "What do you want to do now? I got a new model…wanna take a look?"

"Another monster?"

"No, this one's a bomber. It's big too…I'm not sure where I'll put it when it's done. I'll be getting a King Kong with next week's allowance, though…he's carrying the girl and everything. Pretty cool."

Jeff joined Roger in the Carrolls' front yard, where he stood waiting, repeatedly and casually tossing the ball up and catching it again.

"Want to come into my room for a while?"

"Better not," Jeff said, "I should be getting home. What time is it, anyway?"

Roger strained to read his watch by the light of the porch lamp. "After eight-thirty," Roger answered. "No…make that closer to twenty till."

Jeff walked over to his bicycle, which lay on its side in the grass next to his friend's. "My mom wanted me home at nine, so I'd better not cut it too close."

"You sure?"

"Yeah."

"Okay. See you tomorrow. 'Night."

Roger disappeared into his warmly lit home. As Jeff began to mount his bike, he paused to look up at the moon. Just rising, silhouetting the distant trees before it, the lunar orb was bright and full.

And hated.

This is supposed to be the night—might be any time now—

He heard the Carrolls' front door open again behind him, and Roger reappeared on the front doorstep.

"Hey…it's about to happen. It's on every channel. You want to come in and watch for a few minutes?"

Jeff shook his head. "No...I'm sure my mom will have it on."

"My parents don't mind."

"Thanks anyway."

Jeff rolled down the sloped driveway and into the street. He pedaled the white ten-speed at a leisurely pace, watching the moon as it continued to rise. Now clear of the tree line, it seemed to be bearing down on him, growing closer.

Any moment now, the Apollo 20 lunar module would be settling onto the Cabean plain, a moonrock's throw from the craft his father had piloted, the craft that had left him stranded.

The craft that had killed him.

He did not want to watch the coverage of the new mission, fearful that he might see or hear something of his father's horrible fate, something that would make the man's death utterly final and painfully real. Yet something else within the boy wanted to be excited at the thought that soon they would find his father, for he held out some tiny flicker of hope that, somehow, the man might still be alive. Those faint embers of optimism, fragile though they were, had managed to survive despite being constantly doused by harsh reality—the reality that there was simply no way his father could still be alive up there with no air, no water, no food, and no power. It would take nothing short of a miracle.

And Jeff Lucas, like his father, had never believed in miracles.

◙　◙　◙

As sleep stubbornly fell away, Shepherd pulled his hands up and rubbed his face. His hands were cold, his fingers painfully stiff. The discomfort had awakened him.

The chill of his own touch cut through the curtain of slumber draped over him. Rolling onto his side, he immediately noticed something odd about his bed, about the way it felt beneath him. He raised himself onto one elbow and scooted to its edge, quite easily. Very easily.

Too easily.

Oh, no—!

He swung his legs over the side of the bed and dangled them for a moment, gathering his thoughts before dropping to the floor. The motion triggered the room lights, but they were much dimmer than usual. The polished stone beneath him was no longer a warm, pleasant surface. Instead, it was icy against his bare feet.

Something's wrong—

The room was colder than it had been by about as much as twenty degrees. The gentle warmth he had enjoyed throughout the base had fallen away drastically, and in only a few hours. While he was not yet in danger of freezing, Shepherd knew the change meant nothing good.

The installation's heating systems, it seemed, had been shut off. The lethal cold of Marlow was creeping in.

The soles of his feet testified that more than the temperature had changed as he had slept that night, and not for the better. Testing as he must, he bent his knees and jumped flatfooted from the floor, finding what he had feared as he came down again, quite slowly.

Too slowly.

The base's enhanced gravity was gone, and all he now felt was the moon's natural one-sixth g. Weighing but the equivalent of a small child, he walked slowly toward the bathroom, hoping to find the water systems still operative. They were, but he suspected that was likely to change too, and quickly.

Fear gripped him, for he realized what the dwindling lights signified. *The whole place is shutting down.*

An hourglass was running. His life, terrifyingly finite once again, was being measured in red light—and would end in a mere span of days, when the last of the merciless circles had gone dark.

35

So sore—

Lucas struggled to sit up in bed, his body protesting. Every joint, every muscle wanted only to remain still, yet he overrode them and forced his legs to one side. Finding the edge of the bed, he allowed himself a few minutes more. It had been a hard sleep.

How long was I out?

He sat up, rubbing his neck, his arms. His ribs ached with each breath, but the easing soreness he now felt was far from the pain he had known immediately after his fall.

Potent stuff, that medicine.

He scratched his beard, thinking back over the unfathomable occurrences that had led to his being there. As he sat, quietly remembering, his eyes aimed absently at the woodgrain of the flooring, he came to realize something.

It was quiet.

No music was playing. No water was running in the sculptured falls across the room. No threshing machines were operating outside.

Silence.

His brow furrowed in puzzlement, Lucas dropped to his feet and drew himself to his full height. Momentary dizziness struck as he raised his arms and stretched, working out the stiffness.

Draped upon the foot of the bed he found not the robes he had been wearing, but his liquid cooling garment and the threadbare socks that accompanied it.

They really do *want me to leave—*

He picked up the one piece article, playing the worn, familiar fabric in his hands. The sweat, blood, and soil with which it had been stained were gone.

Well, at least they washed it—

It was white as when new, though a few small tatters spoke of its earlier exploits. Lucas donned the veteran garment, then pointed his toes and pulled the matching footwear up until its tops embraced his calves. The sandals he had worn during his stay still rested on the floor beside him, so he slipped them on as well and made his way out into the hallway.

All was still.

"Hello?" he called. There was no response. His voice echoed strangely, as if he walked an abandoned mortuary.

He made his way down the hall, peering into each room as he went along. There was no sign of anyone. All of the furniture was still in place, but there seemed to be fewer knickknacks and personal items than he remembered. And the silence—the only sounds he heard were those of his own footsteps against the polished floor. No voices, no music, nothing.

Upon entering the library, Lucas found it, too, was unoccupied. Here and there, throughout the room, several volumes were gone from their shelves, lending an appearance not unlike the smile of a child with a few teeth missing. A small, fragile piece of sculpture lay shattered on the floor, having apparently been knocked from its cherished place above. The room did not appear to have been ransacked, but neither was it as it should have been.

What in the world?

The kitchen had been stripped of foodstuffs and cooking utensils.

Storage compartments stood open, littered by discarded or forgotten items. With thirst and hunger nagging at him, Lucas paused a few moments to drink some water from the spigot and ate from a partial loaf of bread he found on the pantry shelf.

Momentarily sated, he walked out into the main hall, listening for any sign of life.

"Is anybody here?" he called again.

If they left, why did they leave so much of their stuff behind?

As quickly as his aching body would allow, Lucas ran upstairs, toward the bedroom where the old man had passed away. He found the bed cleared of linens, the walls stripped of a few of their hangings. The body was gone.

He rushed back downstairs and passed through the house's huge back doors, which stood open. After crossing the enclosed portico, he burst out onto the grounds.

Things had changed there as well.

In the distance, the scaffolds surrounding the towering storehouse were now visibly bare, unmanned, and stripped of equipment. The harvesters sat silent and motionless in the fields, apparently abandoned where they stood. The workers' simple houses were quiet and empty, their windows dark, their doors standing open.

As he slept, the place had become a ghost town.

Save the light, gentle rain of ash, the world had gone utterly still. No birds sang in the forests. No animals roared. No breezes stirred the trees. No living thing moved or breathed or spoke.

He was *alone*.

All that's missing are the tumbleweeds—

Walking on the paved connecting road, he moved cautiously toward the monstrous granary. His eyes, attracted by sudden motion and a glint of light, rose to the tower-mounted array standing sentinel above, which again had begun to rotate within its thick outer shell of flawless glass.

I must have triggered it somehow—

And then he discovered something new in the landscape, something that stood just a dozen yards beyond, rising from the tall grasses of the yard. Rushing forward, he found a break in the uncultivated growth of the roadside, a wide, fresh clearing scythed into the high, tangled lawn. At its center lay a mound of newly turned soil ten by five feet in size.

It was a grave.

Lucas moved closer, his eyes upon the hand-carved marker of veined red stone that rose at its head. Twelve feet tall and six wide, it was as beautiful as any marble sculpture he had seen.

Chiseling this must have taken years—the death couldn't possibly have been sudden—

He could not read the voluminous words engraved upon its glossy surface nor understand the tale told by its pictographs, but he could guess the story it told.

They buried him. Right here, they held a funeral.

The marker declared the story of the ancient man's life, laid out in full relief, a visual testament of his accomplishments and failures—including, amazingly, one event in which Lucas had taken part. He drew nearer, his eyes fixed upon the last scene etched near the bottom of the stone.

It depicted the man's deathbed, his family gathered around him—with the displaced astronaut standing nearby. Lucas knelt to touch the tiny representation of himself, to feel the smooth, cool marble beneath his fingertips.

"How long *did* I sleep?" he wondered aloud. "A few days? A week?"

He held his right arm before him and flexed his hand, noting the stiffness he still felt.

Surely no longer than that!

More puzzled than ever, Lucas backed away from the grave and returned to the road. He noticed that the massive ramp leading into the great storehouse had been raised, nestling tightly into the periphery of the building's only entryway, serving now as a sealed door. He was again reminded of his childhood by the sight, for often he had seen his uncle's barn after the reaping had ended, brimming with grains and corn ready for market, its door sealed against intruders.

They finished the harvest and closed it up—

As Lucas neared the storehouse, he found the ground there trampled and torn as if by a stampede. Hundreds of small chunks of sod had been torn away by the roots and kicked up onto the concrete.

No—please, no!

The muddled prints led primarily from a wide swath in the face of the forest nearby, where most of the smaller trees and bushes had been flattened. Clearly, as he had feared, huge beasts such as the one that had tried to devour him upon his arrival had descended upon his hosts, likely catching them off guard in the course of their work. Animal droppings lay scattered within the path of attack but he saw no blood, which was a good sign. His hosts might have fled in time. Possibly they were still in hiding nearby.

Perhaps within the storehouse.

"Helloooooo!" he called toward the monumental structure, straining his voice to its limits. "Are you in there? Can anyone hear me?"

As if in response, a vibration began beneath his feet that built rapidly into a deep, piercing rumble that shook the air. Thousands of previously hidden and silent birds and other small flying creatures suddenly took flight as one, mounting to the skies above the forests, the cacophonous beating of their wings like a warning to those who might hear. The distant bellow of a great monster sounded, more from fear than hostility, it seemed. The trees began to sway in unison, the ground beneath them moving in fluid waves.

The intensifying tremor threw Lucas from his feet, its roar now deafening. On hands and knees he crawled away from the storehouse, fearing its collapse. Behind him, the scaffolds rocked and began to fall, toppling into each other before plunging to the ground below. Narrow fissures opened everywhere and the earth beneath him rolled, throwing him toward the main house, which began to suffer as wide cracks appeared in its heavy stone walls.

Lucas, still on all fours, was heaved repeatedly by the undulating ground. He came down hard upon the grave mound, the breath knocked out of him. Looking up through the chaos as he clutched at the soil, he realized that the towering stone marker, broken free of its foundation, was rocking in place. Managing to get his feet beneath him, the struggling astronaut leaped out of the way just as the huge obelisk toppled hard onto the grave, fracturing on impact.

Then, as quickly as it had arisen, the quake was gone. The world again went silent. Lucas, his heart pounding, climbed to his feet in the waist-high grass and began to survey the area.

The storehouse itself, stripped now of its scaffolding, seemed no worse for wear, but the homes and warehouses at its base had sustained substantial damage. Some of their roofs had collapsed, and with such extensive destruction Lucas assumed it would be necessary to raze them altogether and build again.

Maybe they'll still need me—maybe I won't have to leave just yet—

No sooner had he begun to collect himself than a new noise startled him. He spun to see a supporting wall of the main residence give way, collapsing into a chain reaction that reduced a good third of the house to rubble. Wood beams cracked and splintered, and glass shattered with its shrill, unmistakable clamor. White dust filled the air as the debris settled, clouding his vision and choking his lungs.

Another sound rose in the distance, growing louder, deeper, and more ominous with each passing second.

It was a roar he recognized, one he knew from repeated rafting trips on the whitewater rapids of the Colorado River.

Rushing water—and a lot of it.

He strained his eyes, squinting as he scanned the horizon beyond the storehouse. At first he found nothing unusual there, shrouded in the gray, smoke-diminished light, yet the sound grew louder and seemed to come from everywhere.

Then he saw it, perhaps a mile away and rapidly closing, shining white in the distant gloom.

A colossal wall of water, its leading edge some forty feet high, was bearing down on him, destroying forests and fields and carrying in its wake their uprooted remains. Unleashed perhaps by the earthquake he just had suffered, the merciless, unstoppable force would be upon him in seconds.

Panicked, he spun and ran for the nearest anchored object, the array tower. He began to climb it, using its ornate outer structure as hand- and footholds. His sore limbs screamed in protest as he went higher. He cried out with each new movement, each foot of elevation. Finally, as he reached the thirty-five-foot level, his body failed him and he could ascend no more. With all his strength he clung to the tower, hoping it would be enough.

Lucas looked back. The granary lay directly between himself and the brutal face of the onrushing wall.

If the storehouse can hold together and break its momentum—if the current is diverted just enough as it passes—

The waters slammed into the back side of the granary, sending a white spray over its roof and onto the yard beyond. Lucas dropped his head and closed his eyes as the shower of denied destruction struck, drenching him in its fury.

It's got to hold—!

Looking up again as the momentary rain diminished, he saw the torrent forcing its way around the granary, which somehow stood its ground. The roar became deafening as the waters encompassed the structure and flowed past, sweeping the scaffolds, workers' houses, and support buildings from their anchors. Splintering as they gave way, they joined the stripped trees and other sundered ruins already trapped within the churning waters, becoming lethal projectiles.

Again and again, torn fragments of scaffolding and structure debris slammed into the tower and carried past. Lucas held on with all his might, terrified that at any moment he would be shaken loose, fall to his death, and be swept away. With his head tucked down against his forearm, he struggled to keep his grip on the wet metal, renewing it again and again as he was able—but he was growing weaker.

Hard rain began to pelt him, the huge, icy drops driven by a fierce wind that seemingly came from everywhere. The beleaguered man managed to slip one arm through an opening in the decorative bronze framework surrounding the tower's central pole, securing him for the moment against the mounting onslaught.

As he watched, carcasses and human bodies swept past, thousands of them, all caught and broken within a thick, raging tangle of torn woodlands and shattered works of man.

Keeping his balance in the gale, Lucas managed to turn his gaze in the direction of the residence, and with disbelieving eyes could only stare at what he found there.

It was gone.

In moments, it like the forest had been razed, the devastation of walls and the snapping of trunks muffled beneath the flow—and still the waters increased.

The hot, turbulent waves reached Lucas' knees. He swung unsteadily to the back side of the tower, fighting to maintain his grip and to avoid being struck by the waterborne wrackage. Lifting his face in the stinging downpour, he managed fleeting glances at the storehouse. The pounding gray rain had reduced visibility to a few hundred feet—the horizon now was lost to him, and closer objects were but ghostly shadows—but he could see well enough to know that every-thing surrounding the storehouse had been erased from the world. The waters had surpassed half the height of the granary, yet still its rein-forced walls held firm, its shadowy lines unmoving within the mael-strom, its heavy construction seemingly an immovable rock against the brutal surge.

It's still standing—somehow, it's still standing!

A new sound rose from the direction of the storehouse, rising above the din of the driving rain, a roar of groaning timber as if the building were alive and crying out in pain. Suffering under the relent-less stresses of the pounding waters and mounting debris, the massive edifice fought valiantly to protect its precious seed.

Please, baby—hang in there—!

In morbid fascination, Lucas remained fixed upon its splintered remains. If it remained in one piece until the raging currents slowed, he might be able to find safety on its roof and survive there until the waters abated. He would not survive at all, however, if it succumbed to the assault. Helpless to move, he would be directly in the path of its splintered wreckage.

The roar of the waters intensified in the distance. Lucas knew they somehow were increasing, building in depth and power as if to leave nothing standing at all.

How can that be?

He heard a sudden, terrifying screech as the straining storehouse began to yield. Through the stinging rain he saw its shadowy outline begin to shift.

There she goes—she's breaking up!

But there was no splintering of timber, no wrenching asunder, no collapse.

Still intact, it began to *move.*

Its heavily reinforced structure protesting, yet still whole, the storehouse rose slowly from its concrete foundation as the deepening inundation finally swept beneath its underside and bore it upward. With unbelieving eyes, Lucas watched as the titanic structure, carried now upon the waters, moved steadily closer—slowly at first, its speed increasing as its inertia was overcome by the savage current.

And then, finally, he understood.

He watched in astonishment as the great, dark mass swept toward him, riding the tumultuous waves.

There was nothing he could do. The heaving torrent, heated by great geothermal pressures, already had reached his chest and he could climb no higher. It rose steadily, unstoppable and invincible, almost scalding his flesh as it overtook him. As he clung there with all of his remaining strength, the steadfast tower that had been his refuge emitted a grating metallic whine and began to bend, finally surrendering to the hydrodynamic pressures being exerted upon it.

This is it—!

The leviathan grew closer, emerging like a ghost from the blinding rain, its tremendous side filling his vision as it bore down upon him.

God, help me!

At the last moment he closed his eyes, bracing for the impact, for death.

Annie—Jeff—I love you!

The behemoth struck, snapping the tower at ground level, and Lucas was knocked into the hot, powerful flow. Fighting a losing battle to remain afloat, he was tossed like a rag doll before being drawn under. The air burst from his lungs as the searing, muddy waters pulled him deeper, away from the surface. Vertigo swelled, and he no longer knew up from down.

The merciless depths engulfed him, claiming him for their own.

◙   ◙   ◙

Shepherd huddled near the central core of the war room, wrapped in blankets he had dragged from his now-abandoned quarters. It had grown too cold there for sleeping, and most of the remainder of the base was little better.

His breath frosted in the still air, lit by the dancing glow of the arcing white energies beside him. The crystalline matrix channeling power to the place had diminished steadily in its intensity, going increasingly quiet as the base's systems, one by one, had shut down.

Fearing a loss of running water, his first hurried task had been to scavenge as many viable containers as possible and fill them to capacity, ensuring him at least a temporary supply. Gathered near him at the base of the power core was a liquid treasure now more precious than gold, contained within once-ornamental porcelain vases, emptied supply bins, cylindrical glass lighting covers, metal equipment housings, and anything else that could be pressed into service—he even had retrieved and filled the huge helmets from the spacesuit locker as well as those he and Lucas had worn outside on the surface. Carrying the overflowing vessels had been manageable in the decreased gravity, and for that he was grateful. As it turned out, his forethought had prolonged his life, for shortly thereafter the base's water circulation systems indeed had failed. Properly rationed, and accounting for evaporation, the gathered store might last a month or more.

By then, however, the increasing cold might render the water problem moot.

More red lights had vanished from the ominous, otherwise dark panel across the room. As each went out, one major system after another had ceased its function. No longer was the air recirculation system working, but with the vast size of the base it was unlikely that carbon-dioxide buildup would become a problem for him. Some areas had gone completely dark while others remained partially lit, and some items of little relative importance still were fully active—water, heat, and gravity all had failed across the board, yet a small device he had discovered mounted to the wall of the atrium still played music on demand. Fortunately, the food machine also was still operational, though he already had drawn several days' rations from it, just to be safe.

Due to its great volume and the warmth of the power-feed mechanism at its center, the war room was the most accommodating site available. Shepherd set up camp there despite the creepiness of the angry red panel, hoping the place would provide the most comfort as his situation continued to deteriorate. He sat huddled on the floor, leaning against the low wall of the core housing as he bit from an apple and read his Bible. Through the reassurances of its pages, despite the growing fears that now plagued him, he had not panicked.

Not yet.

He read now from the book of Isaiah, drawing comfort from promises made long before to others facing seemingly insurmountable dangers:

> Do not fear, for I have redeemed you; I have called you by name;
> you are Mine! When you pass through the waters, I will be with
> you; and through the rivers, they will not overflow you. When you
> walk through the fire, you will not be scorched, nor will the flame
> burn you.

The words hit home.

Water and fire, he mused. *I hope the same goes for ice—*

Shepherd lowered the book and looked up, his gaze falling upon the deep shadows of the ceiling high above.

"Father," he said, quite conversationally, "I still believe there's a reason for everything that's happened…that there's a purpose behind it all. Finding this place was a one-in-a-trillion shot…I know that. But I gotta tell You…right now I'm hoping part of that purpose doesn't involve me winding up like that fellow outside. I trust You," he paused, a lump in his throat, a wetness in his eyes, "but I'm afraid."

He turned back to the book, flipped to another page. It fell upon the book of Job, upon a passage wherein God emphasized His infinite dominion over all things:

From whose womb has come the ice? And the frost of heaven, who has given it birth? Water becomes hard like stone, and the surface of the deep is imprisoned. Can you bind the chains of the Pleiades, or loose the cords of Orion? Can you lead forth a constellation in its season, and guide the Bear with her satellites? Do you know the ordinances of the heavens, or fix their rule over the earth?

Shepherd sighed, and a slight smile crossed his lips.

"Thank You," he said, winking humbly toward the heavens, his breath hanging white before him. "I'm still scared…but I *do* trust You. So if it turns out they have to take me out of here with ice tongs…well, in Jesus' name, I reckon I can live with that."

His ears perked as a sudden, unfamiliar sound echoed from the corridors. He lowered his Bible, unmoving, listening intently.

Something—or *someone*—was moving within the base.

Gary—!

Shepherd rose, a forgotten hope burning anew within him.

36

There had been a swirl of brilliant white light, a sensation of falling.

Suddenly, beneath him, was hard, cool stone.

Lucas' head spun as the intense dizziness subsided. His chest heaved as he repeatedly gagged, and as he found air again, a series of deep, choking coughs expelled the hot water he had swallowed. Slowly, he began to recover, his face and hair dripping, his clothes soaking wet. Greedily, he drew deeply of the cool air, his heart racing, his body trembling.

What—where am I—?

Slowly, he became aware of the room around him. As the shock abated, he began to recognize the walls, the furnishings.

He was back in his room.

On the moon base.

Weakly, he pulled himself to his hands and knees and climbed up onto the bed. The mattress felt softer than he remembered as it caressed his strained, aching form, and he wanted only to lie still.

I'm back—!

The events of the past weeks suddenly seemed to him a dream, a fleeting illusion that now, finally, had released him.

Did it really happen?

He raised a hand to his face, finding the water that soaked his beard, his sleeve.

I'm still wet—!

He was too weary to reason it through. He was back, and for now that was enough. There was a rational explanation, of that he was certain—but it would wait.

Feels so good just to lie here—

Just a few minutes rest, and he would be good to go.

Give me a minute—

Those words. They rang with eerie familiarity, echoing and nagging until he remembered.

They had been the last words he had heard from—

"Charlie!" he thought aloud. Springing to his feet despite the protests of his battered body, Lucas grabbed his lightkey from its cradle and staggered toward the door. With each step, his ankles, his knees throbbed. Raising the glittering key to its ebony lock, the door slid open to reveal the waiting corridor beyond.

His socks left damp places on the smooth, dark floor, his sandals lost in the turbulent waters. Stepping out into the gloomy passageway, he paused, hearing voices as they resonated along the walls.

Charlie?

Leaning against the wall, he listened intently. It seemed that more than one person was speaking—and whoever they were, they were within the atrium.

Warily, he inched his way toward the source of the muffled sound. As he grew nearer, he discerned the cadence of the speech, the language.

It's them—!

He was hearing the same flowing, lyrical language he had heard spoken so often on the strange, alien planet.

Lucas stopped dead, unsure of his next move. As he stood trying to devise a plan of action, three piercing alarm tones suddenly filled the air, followed a few moments later by a prolonged, earsplitting hiss of escaping air. Startled, he dove into an alcove and crouched behind a large pedestal-mounted sculpture, a winged, dragonlike creature with two heads.

No sooner had he frozen in his place than he heard approaching footsteps, coming from the direction of the atrium. They were heavy and hurried.

A mountain of a man rushed past. His short-cropped hair was white, his clean-shaven jaw firmly set. He wore a jumpsuit of brilliant red.

Lucas recognized the uniform. It was like those he had seen worn by each of the mummified bodies within the base.

"I don't get it," he whispered, breathing heavily. "I don't get it…"

What happened? Did they come back?

His fears turned to his friend. Had the aliens returned to reclaim their base? What had brought them there after so long a time? Did they find Charlie within it? Had he been captured?

"No no no no no," Lucas muttered under his breath. "He's all right…he's *got* to be…"

He emerged from his hiding place, his senses intense. Hugging the wall, he crept along the corridor, away from the atrium, headed toward the war room. As he passed the door of each quarters, he feared it would open to reveal an emerging giant. He knew what these people were, the atrocities they were capable of. Visions of the horrendous prison where he had been held and the sadistic sacrificial rites he had seen filled his mind. Only one family on that entire world, it seemed, had any compassion at all.

He came to the door that had led into Charlie's room.

What if I open it, and one of those monsters is inside? But what if I don't, and Charlie's in there?

Lucas tensed, bracing for anything, fearing the worst.

He raised the lightkey. The door slid open.

The room was empty.

He almost collapsed with relief. Gathering himself quickly, he resumed his perilous quest to find his friend and encountered no one else as he passed through the living area. As he neared the war room, however, he again heard voices. His heart was pounding in his throat as he peered around the edge of the entryway.

Perhaps a dozen people were gathered there, all uniformed, intently watching one of the huge data displays. Their backs were to him, their attentions fixed. One of the men was leaning over a console, speaking into the transmitter of a communications system. His voice loud and insistent, he repeated himself again and again, yet no response came.

Lucas took a deep breath and quickly made his way along the war room wall, to one of the deeper alcoves there. He was grateful for his stealthy, stockinged feet. Ducking into shadow, he peered intently at his unwanted hosts, trying to sort out what was going on. On the screen above them, filling it from edge to edge, a world mottled with black and an odd pinkish white was going increasingly gray, lifelessness spreading like a cancer across its face.

The planet appeared to be dying, its life seeping away before their eyes.

That's their home world—and I was just there—

Lucas discerned that the man in the brilliant red uniform was the commander of the group. The others, all dressed in muted dark greens, reds, and blacks, seemed to respond to his orders, at least at first.

Dissension was growing in the ranks.

Voices rose. Arguments began. The nine men and three women were panicking, clearly in response to what they were seeing on the screen overhead. The disputes continued, rising in intensity as the commander fought to maintain order. Blows were exchanged, and any semblance of stability was quickly disintegrating.

One man suddenly bolted from the room and ran down the corridor leading to the spacesuit locker. A few of the others called after him and gave chase, apparently trying to stop him. The commander manipulated the panel and at once the screen above was filled with a view of the locker compartment's interior.

The man was there. He had sealed the door behind him and was opening the hatchway in its far wall, which Lucas once had chosen not to disturb. Acting like a prisoner on the run, the man did not wait for it to fully open before vanishing through it, into the darkness beyond.

The commander touched the panel again. The display switched to the interior of a vast, well-lit circular chamber.

A hangar.

Of course, Lucas nodded, his eyes fixed upon the screen.

He looked on in wonder. On the flight deck rested two identical spacecraft, born of a technology beyond NASA's imaginings. Each was perhaps seventy-five feet in length, a sweeping, streamlined form that, while thick along the centerline, swept outward into blunt, curved, upswept wings. Their hulls glistened like pearl, their glass-smooth bodies a symphony of pale pinks and blues as they caught the light, hanging motionless some six feet above the hangar floor.

No landing gear, Lucas realized. *They're just hovering there, unpowered—!*

Total gravity manipulation—the dream of the flight sciences.

The craft had no windows that he could see. From bow to stern, each ship was unbroken in line and contour.

The man rushed into view, headed toward the nearest spacecraft, a lightkey in hand. At once, a squarish portal opened in the ship's side— he leaped through it then vanished from sight as the hull behind him sealed itself once more.

Several in the war room began to panic at the sight, crying out in angry, frantic words as the instinct for self-preservation took over. The commander's already tenuous influence over his crew had now vanished, and any remaining stability among the ranks had broken down entirely. Utter chaos swept the room.

On the screen, a portion of the spacecraft's forward hull faded into transparency, becoming a view port. High above the craft, pinpoints of brilliant light began to appear in odd lines, increasing in number with each passing moment. Lucas, puzzled at first, realized what he was seeing.

A great, circular door was opening, its retracting segments revealing the sparkling stars above.

Before the wide portal was fully open, and with no sound or light or visible thrust of any kind, the craft rose and disappeared from view, accelerating at a rate that should have killed the pilot.

Lucas' mouth hung open.

We're like infants—they're so far beyond us—

He allowed himself the luxury of a moment's thought, bewildered by a point raised by the military lobe of his brain.

Why haven't they attacked Earth? In five minutes, they'd own the whole planet—!

Those in the war room were more frenetic than ever, running in different directions as the angry commander, now ignored, shouted orders after them. In moments, the frenzied war room had been abandoned and was quiet once more.

Lucas, knowing the base's crew had become more volatile and more lethal than ever, feared for Shepherd's safety. He struggled to devise a plan of action that might save both their lives.

Think, Gary, think!

He envisioned what he knew of the base's layout, mentally searching for anything he had overlooked, anything that might help him to survive long enough to find his friend.

There has to be some way for us to get out of here—

He returned his gaze to the screen, to the image of the hangar, of the lone remaining spacecraft waiting there. His pilot's ego *knew* he could fly it, if only he could get the chance.

If we could reach that ship—

Gathering his resolve, he emerged from the shadows and inched along the walls of the empty room, headed toward the primary corridor.

If I were Charlie and I'd been captured, where would I be—?

He paused before the entry to a small storage room he recalled finding and opened its door with his key. Slipping inside, he closed the door behind him and began to search for something that might serve as a weapon. Surrounding him were bins of oddly shaped spare parts and thousands of things he could not identify at all, but nothing that looked as if it might provide some measure of defense.

Come on—give me a metal pipe or a sharp stick or something—anything—

He froze as horrifying sounds exploded in the corridor outside.

Listening through the door, he heard screams and the repeated concussion of what could only be some form of gunfire. Angry words. Pleading words. The loud crash of toppling furniture and the breaking of glass carried again and again along the hall. The shrill clatter of colliding blades filled the air. Explosions rang out in succession, shaking the walls. More screams. More gunfire.

The conflict went on for several minutes.

Then all went terribly silent.

Lucas pressed his ear to the door, straining to hear, holding his breath that its sound might not cover those from outside.

Running footsteps of several people echoed past. He heard hushed, breathless words. The sounds faded. All went silent again.

He waited for a few minutes and heard nothing more.

Here goes nothing—

He held up his lightkey. The door slid open. He peered around the door facing.

The corridor was empty. The entire base was silent.

Lucas stepped out into the hallway. He expected to see drops of blood upon the floor, but there were none. Down the way, the supply room door stood open, from which emanated a light pall of smoke that hung stratified in the still air of the corridor. He smelled burning flesh.

No no no no no—

He crept closer, forcing each step.

Not that room—!

Reaching the edge of the door, he shook his head, wanting to go no further. After pausing to gather his fragile wits, he stepped forward and looked inside.

It can't be—it can't be—that's impossible!

The dead lay strewn where they had fallen, their flesh torn and mutilated, their bodies contorted in horrifying, agonized poses. Unseeing eyes stared from battered sockets. Blood and splattered tissue covered much of the walls, the floor, the ceiling. What had been furniture lay toppled and broken, hurled in combat or crushed beneath falling bodies. The deep, violent char of concussion charges scarred the walls of the room, once lined with heavy shelves that had been pulled from their mounts and toppled. The oppressive quiet was wildly discordant with the sheer devastation of the scene. The stench of death was heavy in the murky air.

All who had fought there had died there.

They lay just as he had found them—*thousands of years later.*

It just can't be—!

Lucas spun, nausea rising within him. He fell to his hands and knees in the corridor as the spasms wrenched his abdomen and burning acid seared his throat.

His legs weak, his knees shaking, he struggled to his feet and moved away from the grisly scene. His breathing labored, he made his way back to the living area and his adopted quarters, to his refuge there. Reaching its still-open door, he entered the darkened chamber and sealed it behind him, then he crossed to the bathroom.

He drank from the faucet, the cool liquid soothing his burning throat. After rinsing his mouth a few times he splashed his face, hanging over the basin as the water dripped from his nose and beard.

How? How?

The impossible gripped him, shook him hard. He feared for his sanity.

How did it happen? How—?

The years had vanished as if they had never been, separating him from his home, his family by insurmountable time as well as by distance.

Charlie must be back here too—he has to be—

He forced himself to believe it. The alternative was unthinkable.

He paced, clinging to the safety of the room. His thoughts became a jumble of discarded strategies and imagined fates. After half an hour of wearied reasoning, he had collected himself, knowing despite his bewildering circumstances that he no longer had the luxury of time. He had to go back out there to find Shepherd, and he had to do it quickly.

I've got to find a weapon—something—anything—!

Lucas searched his room and found in the bathroom storage cabinet what appeared to be a straight razor. Its sculptured handle felt good in his hand and, much as with the panels in the war room, he could not feel the side of its blade as he lightly ran a fingertip there. It was a bit oversized, but so much the better.

Now armed, at least to an extent, he reentered the corridor. Slowly, he made his way along, fearing every sealed door, every shadow.

The low drone of voices drifted from the direction of the atrium, a rhythmic chanting that was very, very familiar.

No—not here—!

He found the atrium empty, its central fountain flowing freely. A door on its opposite wall stood open. The voices grew louder as he approached.

He paused, pressing himself into the wall next to the doorway, his razor at the ready. Then, slowly, he dared to take a look inside.

It was a sacrificial temple, a horror-in-the-round.

The rotunda was lit only by the light of a fire pit that burned beneath a towering idol of gold, one representing the deity Lucas had seen worshipped on their home world. At its feet, a large goat lay stretched upon a stone altar, pinned there by two men. A half-dozen of the base's personnel sat on low stone benches before the ghastly display, their arms upstretched, their voices raised in the eerie intonation.

A robed priest in a death's-head mask raised a glinting blade, and as the gathered few chanted, down it flashed again and again.

Lucas watched in revulsion as the priest cut the beast's heart from its carcass and tossed it into the fire behind him. The two men holding the animal dragged it from the altar and dropped it into a pit dug into the floor to one side. The priest motioned toward another man far across the room, who responded by pressing his hand against a small black panel on the dark, arching wall.

A section of the wall glowed and became a large display screen, filling with an image of the dying planet Lucas had seen in the war room.

It was still dying, still gray, still lifeless.

The chanting ceased, and a murmur rose. The priest raised his arms, the bloodied knife still in his hands.

"Koranda selicu!" he cried out, his voice deep and menacing. "Dorlen tu soriac!"

The two men at his side rushed the audience, who appeared surprised. Seizing a woman seated there, they pulled her from her place on the pew as she screamed and struggled to free herself. No one around her lifted a finger to help, but rather began to chant again, raising their arms in supplication.

She was lifted from her feet and placed atop the altar, her continual shrieks filling the chamber.

Lucas stared in grim realization. It was evident that the priest considered animal sacrifice no longer sufficient to overcome the global devastation of their now-dying home world.

Not that it had helped there.

Sickened, Lucas turned away. As he quietly moved along the perimeter of the atrium, resuming his search for Shepherd, he heard the woman's screams go suddenly, horribly silent.

Please—tell me Charlie wasn't in there—

If he had been, Lucas knew, he was now dead. He refused to consider the possibility.

We have to get to that ship and get out of here—

He cautiously explored the atrium's other chambers, discovering what seemed to be an athletic court and a dining hall. He had not eaten in days, but had no time to decipher the operation of the food service, not now. Another room, filled to the brim with a mass of complex machinery, struck him as oddly familiar, but a quick look from the doorway revealed that his friend was not there either.

You have to be here somewhere, Charlie—you have to—!

Everyone still within the base had been gathered in the temple chamber behind him, it appeared, for the remainder of the base was devoid of personnel. After searching every room, every corner, every possible hiding place that Shepherd might have found for himself, Lucas reached an inescapable conclusion.

He isn't here.

He was seized by despair, facing the facts that clutched at his soul, stripping away all hope.

I'm back here—in the past—and Charlie—

He closed his eyes.

Charlie isn't.

He breathed deeply, struggling to compose his thoughts. Finally, he stopped dwelling upon his own situation for a moment, long enough to realize something else.

Charlie's safe, sitting in this same base, a jillion years from now—he has to be.

He drew comfort from that.

Take care, buddy—I hope you get home somehow—

One astounding question still nagged at him.

How did I get here? What was the last thing I did, the last thing I saw, the last thing I touched before I—before I—what?

The memory would not come.

He walked the corridor, almost aimlessly, and found himself near the war room once again. Pausing at its entrance, he found it quiet and unoccupied.

He glanced up at the big screen, at the image of the hangar that filled it still.

Only now, that image had changed.

The hangar was empty. The last remaining spacecraft was gone, surely headed out across the galaxy, desperately seeking to return to a world that might now prove no haven at all.

His head dropped, as if in defeat.

No—!

He was marooned again.

They took it—they stranded their crewmates here and left—!

That explained the urgency of the sacrifices. Those in the temple were as stranded as he, begging their god for deliverance.

As if they were heard—

Those who had died in the main supply room had been fighting for seats home. Instead, the combatants had nearly wiped each other out, leaving but an injured few to claim the remaining spacecraft for themselves.

They're beasts, all of them—

He left the area and returned to his quarters, needing no longer to search, needing rest. Dead on his feet, he knew that his fatigue was clouding his judgment and that was not a handicap he could afford. It was his hope that, since his room had remained unassigned, none of the few remaining crew would have reason to enter and find him there.

"Mirabelle," he smiled weakly, remembering—and missing—his friend.

37

Sunday, April 27, 10:10 A.M.

"Houston, we've got their tracks."

The rover, its batteries and environmental systems at capacity, neared the rim of the Marlow basin. Cortney, at the controls, gazed ahead, his stark shadow stretching into the distance before him, his course retracing the wheel ruts left by Lucas and Shepherd. The tracks led directly into the engulfing darkness that waited just ahead.

"Roger, Bruce," came Kendall's voice.

Irwin flipped a few switches on his console. "Heaters and floods on. The gauges look good."

"Okay, Vic, we're about to drop over the edge," Cortney reported. "Rover systems are nominal."

"We're with you," came the reply. "All the way."

Just ahead, the first of the comm relay units planted by Shepherd stood in the harsh light, its powerful but short-lived power cell now depleted. Cortney and Irwin carried such relays themselves, but many more of them—which would allow them to travel deeper into Marlow than the men who had passed that way before had been planned.

"Man, but it's dark out here," Irwin said, his eyes searching the apparent void ahead. "Looks like the moon just *quits*."

354

"Yeah," Cortney agreed. "Now I know how Columbus must have felt…or his crew, anyway. I don't think we'll be falling off the edge of the world, though."

"Here's hoping."

Cortney pressed forward on the control handle, an odd combination of exhilaration and trepidation filling him. He knew his mission and what he would find, waiting frozen and lifeless in the shadows ahead.

He did not want to find it.

◙　　◙　　◙

Lucas opened the door of his quarters and moved onto the shadowy, gothic corridor, carrying his lightkey and armed with the razor. Two days' rest and a bit of unthreatened sleep, however uneasy, had done much to settle his nerves and soothe his body, and he was hungry.

He had been awakened more than once by a trembling in the floor and walls, a lingering, mild succession of tremors that had gone on and on with only intermittent pauses. The motion was barely noticeable, but his sleep was light, his mind troubled. His first thought had been that some form of support equipment was malfunctioning and sending the vibrations throughout the base, but their prolonged presence seemed to demand a different explanation.

He saw no one as he entered the atrium. The door to the sacrificial temple stood open. It was dark beyond—and hushed. Pausing to listen, Lucas heard nothing but the water in the fountain, and as he approached, careful not to enter and thereby activate the room lights, he determined that no one was inside.

For now, at least, the horrors had ended.

He entered the dining hall and approached the food dispenser. After about ten minutes of trial and error, he discovered its secrets and produced a meal for himself of steak, fruits, and bread.

The odd tremors continued still. Their intensity remained the same, wherever in the base he had gone.

The meal sat heavily. As he left the dining hall, he took an apple with him, using it in lieu of a toothbrush as he had learned to do as a Boy Scout. He walked the corridors of the base, hearing no one, seeing no one.

Where are they?

And then he remembered.

He paused at one of the doors near his own quarters, the room that had been the first entered by Shepherd and him during their second day in the base.

Slowly, unsure if he was doing the right thing, he raised his lightkey to the black disk. The door opened.

The room was dark. Lucas lifted one arm, breaking the plane of the door, and lights rose in response.

Inside was a dead man, slumped in his chair and lying across a table. Naked save for a small waistcloth, one of his arms dangled limply over the side, hanging where it lifelessly had fallen. Blood covered much of the tabletop beneath him and had dripped onto the polished stone floor, forming a puddle that flowed almost all the way to the door. Beneath his hand, resting where it had fallen, was an outsized knife.

It was the one Lucas had carried with him—*would* carry with him—in his journey to their home world.

He closed his eyes and backed away, sealing the door again.

They're all dead.

I'm alone.

Fearing nothing now but isolation, he proceeded toward the war room. Not for any particular reason, but simply because he had nothing else to do, nowhere else to go.

Quite casually, he walked into the cavernous command center, biting from his apple. His mind was far away, focused on the family, the friends he had lost.

Only when he had walked well into the room did he realize it already was occupied.

One man remained alive.

The base commander, sitting quietly in his bright red uniform, turned and looked upon the small, white-clad man. His face showed no surprise, no bewilderment, no hostility. Their eyes locked, each man too weary, too beaten to act.

The giant's eyes returned to the screen above him, and Lucas' gaze followed. Upon it was an orbital depiction of the moon, an image apparently being captured by a monitoring satellite. Bright flashes of light flared again and again upon the gray orb, thousands of them, some larger and more brilliant than others. The lunar surface Lucas saw filling the screen was cratered but much smoother than it should have been, which puzzled him. Enormous, scattered pools of cooling lava glowed a dull red, lying in areas that should have been lunar seas.

The embattled moon, from pole to pole, was suffering a massive barrage of meteors, its plains and hills sustaining a pounding that would leave it forever and deeply scarred.

In short, it was becoming the moon Lucas' world knew.

The tremors—

Lucas dared to approach, feeling no threat from the giant at the console. The man moved his hands upon the panel, playing it with trained precision as if it were a musical instrument. The scene above shifted, becoming a surreal glimpse of another place, one Lucas all too intimately had known.

It was a nightside view of the alien home world. Thunderstorms of an intensity neither man could ever have imagined flashed white hot as they boiled across the entirety of its turbulent face, devastating the world beneath them, erasing all that had dwelled there, all that had been built, all that had breathed. Meteorites left brilliant, golden scars in the chaotic skies, striking the distant planet as violently as they were the moon beneath him.

What's going on? Is the whole universe raining death and ruin—?

The base commander's eyes glistened as he looked upon the besieged image, his hands trembling, his face a mask of disbelief and resigned horror.

His home was gone. Everything and everyone he ever had known, every dream he had ever had, his every reason for living—*gone.*

Lucas shared the pain the man felt, the loss. The two orphaned commanders stood in the stillness of the moment, the floor gently trembling beneath them.

"I'm sorry," Lucas quietly offered.

The base commander dropped his head for a moment, his thoughts obviously in conflict.

"Selia tocliana creaatu," he said, his voice deep and anguished. "Creaatu."

He rose from his seat and headed for the corridor. Lucas set his apple on a neighboring chair and followed, keeping a modest distance.

The man entered his quarters. Lucas approached the open door, standing in the entry, watching silently. The man picked up a photocrystal and held it as if it were a treasure, his wet eyes drinking in the image imprisoned there. After a few long, sorrow-filled minutes, he slipped the crystal into a pocket of his uniform and headed back into the corridor, brushing past Lucas almost as if he were not there.

"It's just you and me, now," Lucas said, trailing behind as the grief-stricken man moved through the maze of passageways. "I know you don't have a clue what I'm saying, but—"

"Durian tu bellatriaca," the base commander said, his voice breaking, cutting him off. He waved his arms dismissively, as if wishing Lucas away.

Lucas stopped, allowing the space between himself and the other man to widen. Not wanting to press his luck, he veered down another corridor and took a seat in the war room, where the stormy view still loomed.

In mournful silence, he watched the awesome display, remembering the family who had freed him from his prison and taken him in, who now likely had perished as their world, falling victim to a nature gone mad, turned upside down.

"Thank you," he whispered, his eyes reflecting the glaring light of one lightning flash, one meteor strike after another. "For all you did for me. I owe you my life."

As if those words are sufficient, he thought. *But what words would be?*

His attention was drawn elsewhere as the sound of heavy boot steps echoed in the chamber. He spun in his chair to see the base commander, encumbered now in a brilliant white spacesuit and carrying a helmet, crossing the war room on his way to the main airlock.

The man we found outside!

Lucas sprang from his seat, moving as if to cut him off and prevent his exit. Maintaining a safe distance, he tried to implore him not to do what Lucas knew he was determined to do—not merely for the man's sake, but for his own.

He did not want to be alone.

"Don't do this," he insisted, sidestepping quickly to match the pace of the base commander, who continued on, adjusting a few of the controls on his suit as he moved. "You don't have to—!"

The man ignored him, headed still for the towering airlock door.

"You never know what might happen…trust me on this one. Charlie and I found a miracle when we should have died…!"

A miracle—

"There's a reason for everything that happens—"

It was useless. The huge white-haired man pushed past Lucas, who fell back and watched helplessly as the airlock door responded to the lightkey. As the door knifed downward behind the man, Lucas saw him don the helmet and lock it into place.

There was a solid, final thud as the heavy door sealed shut.

Lucas stood there, stunned by what had happened.

I should have stopped him somehow. I should have tackled him or shoved him aside or something—!

As if he could have.

Lucas turned and slowly walked back into the heart of the base, feeling more alone than at any other time in his life. His steps were slow, his heart heavy, his mind clouded by a deep gloom that grew deeper by the minute.

He was doomed to spend the rest of his life caged in a forgotten, lonely prison, where his only companions were the dead.

In utter desperation, his heart cried out. He dropped to his knees, lowered his head.

God—dear Jesus—if You have one more miracle up there for me—!

He was heard.

38

Monday, April 28, 6:12 A.M.

"Come on, baby...one more time for Charlie..."

Wrapped in his glass-cloth blanket, Shepherd slapped at the food dispenser, fearing the worst. The machine had gone dark and quiet, and as he repeatedly hit his palm against the activator plates with no effect, his fears were realized. Like the water system, the food supply had been shut off too.

"Well," he sighed, his hair still tousled from sleep, "I still have air, anyway."

He had withdrawn enough food for a short period of time, but unfortunately everything the machine produced was perishable, intended to be eaten right away. The increasingly cold conditions within the base would help the food to last a bit longer, and if it got cold enough to freeze—which it might very soon—it would last a long time indeed.

Unfortunately, so would he—in an equally icy state.

"What I wouldn't give for a few cases of C-rations and some Sterno right now," he muttered, his breath fogging the surface of the dormant machine. "I never thought I'd hear myself saying *that*."

He turned from the dispenser and took a seat in the dim light, pondering his situation.

"About time to go out and chop some firewood," he said, rubbing his hands together. "The deep backwoods of Marlow…"

His hope that Lucas might have rejoined him faded quickly as he sought the source of the sound he had heard. A brief search revealed that his creative hunt for water storage vessels had unsteadied an equipment mount as he had pulled one possible container free, causing an adjoining mechanism to loosen and eventually topple.

The image of the diminishing red circles on the war room console haunted him.

You had to go and slap the panel. You could have left well enough alone, but nooooooo—!

He was startled by three shrill, piercing tones, coming from the atrium.

He rose and hurried to the door. Across the way, he saw new light and motion amid the heavy machinery in the chamber beyond the now-dry fountain.

An emergency alarm!

He feared the worst.

No, please—not the life support, too—

Fearing that he now would lose his air as well, he crossed the atrium, his eyes focused on the gigantic cylindrical machine that dominated the room. The glowing blue strip near its top had dimmed. Its many radiant conduits, too, now had gone dark.

It was shutting down, for sure.

I guess I really was on borrowed time.

As he approached the open door, there came an explosive, prolonged burst of white, escaping gases that jolted him and forced him to cover his ears.

With the deafening sound, the huge cylinder began to *open,* its entire front face pulling away, sliding forward. Unnerved, Shepherd cautiously entered the room and neared the gleaming, towering mechanism, holding his blanket tightly around him as if he were a child wrapped in an oversized comforter.

He moved past the machine's steely outer shell and peered inside. At once, his heart leaped. He dropped the blanket.

"Gary!"

⬚　　⬚　　⬚

The screens had gone dark. The lights had dimmed. The entire base had taken on an unreal, illusory quality, dancing at the outskirts of his senses as if the fog of dreams had descended. He thought he heard the faint, distant barking of a dog.

I'm going insane—

Lucas sat in the war room, huddling in a chair. One minute, one hour, one day—they all would pass the same way, empty and without purpose. It had been hours since the base commander had departed, and Lucas knew that, by now, the man had taken his own life.

He considered joining him.

There was no hope, no chance. No reason to go on.

How did it feel? What was it like when that lethal cold took him, and his body froze before his heart even had time to stop beating?

"Charlie…wherever you are, I wish I were with you. This place was bearable when it was the two of us, but now…"

His head swam as a dizziness rose. His hands flew to the arms of the chair, a sensation like that of a sudden upward rush casting his equilibrium aside.

After a few moments, the feeling passed. Returning to his thoughts, he envisioned the faces of his wife and son, remembering the good times, the times he had managed to squeeze family considerations into his frenzied, demanding training schedule. They had been too few and too far between, and regrets swelled as he began to punish himself for missing so much of Jeff's life.

I never saw you take your first steps—I missed all those birthdays and Christmas mornings and baseball games—

"Gary?"

The voice came from everywhere. He looked up, as if to see someone standing nearby, then spun, searching.

No one was there.

Did I really—?

"Gary, can you hear me?"

"Charlie?!" Lucas called out. "I hear you!"

He leaped from the chair.

"I'm in here!" he shouted, moving slowly across the room, spinning slightly with each step. "Where are you?"

"Skipper?"

Lucas moved hurriedly into the corridor, following the ethereal voice. No matter where he turned or how far he traveled, it remained elusive and maddeningly out of reach.

"Charlie! I'm here! Can you hear me? Can you see me?"

"Come back to us—"

Lucas ran through every corridor, every room, desperately searching for his friend. The base's layout seemed to have changed, becoming a maze of chambers and hallways that led nowhere and shifted from one moment to the next.

"I'm trying! I'm here!"

Lucas struggled forward, fighting a building vertigo that forced him to lean into the walls for support as he moved. Finally, the corridor spun madly and the lights faded away, and he dropped hard to the floor—and missed.

He plummeted through the darkness, his senses all but closed to him.

Then there came a light. The sense of falling ceased.

He opened his eyes.

Blurred but coming into focus was the smiling face of Shepherd, just a foot or so away, leaning over him.

"Charlie?" Lucas asked weakly.

"Right here, Skipper...welcome back."

Lucas looked around, trying to get a handle on where he was. His mind, still muddled, took a moment to come to terms with the evidence of his reawakened senses. Angled forms in blue-gray, white, and silver hung before his eyes, shapes familiar to him. He was in a zero-gravity environment, Velcro straps around his chest and waist holding him in place.

A command module—!

"Quest?" he asked, his eyes darting around.

"No, no, Skipper," Charlie said, his face radiating joy. "Vic went home without us, remember? You and I caught another ride."

"And wait till you get the bill," came another voice, one Lucas knew.

The smiling face of Cortney appeared, leaning around the edge of the seat beneath which Lucas' rescue couch had been mounted. "At ten cents a mile, it adds up."

"Bruce?"

"Right here, Gary."

"How...?"

"The bigwigs changed their minds and let us launch Twenty. Seems they thought you guys were important enough to come after. Go figure. Don't go getting a big head, though."

Lucas found the faces of Irwin and Slayton as well, all obviously quite pleased that they had not, after all, needed the body bags they had carried.

"But how...? What happened...? I remember being in the base... being alone..."

"You spent almost two months inside some kind of machine," Shepherd said. "I looked everywhere for you…finally gave up. I must have walked right past you a thousand times, and never knew it…not until the base shut down and the thing spit you out."

With a grimace, Lucas moved his arms and shoulders, finding them stiff and sore. Weakly, he reached up and felt his beard, having noted Shepherd's clean-shaven appearance.

"You stop off at a barber's, Charlie?"

"Oh, that," Shepherd smiled, reaching for a storage pocket. "I found an interesting little razor in my room…works like a charm."

"Large, with a carved handle," Lucas added. "Like a straight razor. With a blade you couldn't feel with your fingers."

Shepherd, surprised, nodded and pulled the razor from its place. "Yeah," he said, stretching to hand it to Lucas. "You found one in your room too?"

"Long time ago." Lucas twirled the ornate relic in his hands, smiling knowingly. "I was back there, Charlie. I saw it all."

"What?"

"I saw them…met them. The people who built the base…"

"Skipper, you were in that machine the whole time, surrounded by tubes and gizmos and who knows what. You had to be. Somehow, it was feeding you and keeping you alive. I guess it still would be if it hadn't—"

"No, no," Lucas quietly insisted, releasing the razor to float gently back to Shepherd. "I was on their world…I saw it die…"

Shepherd cut a glance toward Cortney, who looked concerned. "Well, Skip…I'm sure we'll get this whole thing figured out. For right now, just lie back and take it easy."

Lucas looked to his rescuers. "How did you guys find us?"

"Well," Irwin said, "actually, all we had to do was follow your rover tracks, at first. When those ran out at the edge of the ice sheet, we used a radio tracker to pinpoint the source of the signal we'd gotten."

"Signal?"

Cortney nodded. "Seems Charlie accidentally set off some kind of automatic beacon. That's just a guess, though. What it is exactly, we never figured out. Just a repeating, coded signal, coming from the base. Led us right up to the front door. You should have seen Charlie's face when we came waltzing in."

"Which reminds me," Irwin cut in. "I was wondering about that. We had the signal to follow, but you guys didn't…and the odds of finding that base by chance, in the dark, out of the entire Marlow basin, would be astronomical. How did you know it was there?"

"We didn't," Lucas admitted, something new rising within him. "But God did."

Shepherd smiled at that. "God, Gary?"

He nodded. "Had to be." He looked over at his friend and crewmate, then reached out and took his hand firmly. "I was wrong, Charlie. Dead wrong. There's no fence…and no such thing as chance. Can't be."

Shepherd returned the grip, seeing the spiritual life blazing behind Lucas' eyes.

"You were right," the man said. "About everything."

"The last thing we expected was to find you guys alive," Cortney said.

"Last thing we expected was to be found," Lucas replied, putting his hands to his face and rubbing his dry eyes. "But now that I look back…" He went silent.

"What?" Shepherd asked. "What is it?"

"Let me…" He paused, his mind obviously considering possibilities. "Let me mull a few things over. Ask me again later, after we get home."

"Anyway," Irwin continued, "we found you guys just in time, I'd say…it was getting pretty cold in there. Used the buddy hoses to get you back out to the rover, then got the heck out of Dodge while the groceries still held out. We even managed to bring back one of the rock boxes you and Charlie had left aboard *Starlight*."

"Dr. Silver will kiss you smack on the mouth," Lucas grinned.

"Hope not," Irwin laughed.

Lucas looked up at the panels and storage compartments around him, embracing their welcome familiarity. He realized the cabin bore five couches, not the usual three. "Skylab rescue craft, huh? Kind of crowded in here."

"No kidding," Cortney agreed. "Consider yourselves lucky…Deke voted to strap you both to the outside of the spacecraft."

"Nice view from out there," Shepherd grinned.

"Actually," the man went on, "just so you know, that was the plan for getting you both back up into orbit…strapping you to the sides of the LM. No way we could have gotten you through the hatch if you'd been…" He let the thought go silent.

"Frozen?" Lucas offered. "Yeah, that would present a problem."

Cortney nodded. "Yup. But fortunately, you guys got upgraded from coach to first class."

"Does Houston know?" the bearded astronaut asked, his tone more serious. "About everything?"

"Uh…no. Not yet. They know we found something on the surface and that we're bringing you home, but they don't know you're alive. Jim and I went off comm on the drive back…kept it local so we could talk to Charlie and not be overheard. Made a couple of guarded announcements during the launch and docking…but nothing else."

"I figured," Lucas agreed. "Can't go broadcasting the existence of that base on an open channel…not with the whole world listening."

"And," Slayton added, "even telling the world you're alive opens up a can of worms we can't account for yet. You shouldn't be…and the fact that you are raises way too many questions."

"We've been running on radio silence since leaving lunar orbit…

shut off the transmitter just after we told CapCom we were headed home okay. By now, the world's been told there's something wrong with our little Heathkit here, but Houston knows better."

"How do they know?"

"For this flight, they made a special arrangement…we weren't sure what we might have to tell them about you two, and we didn't want the whole world listening in if the details got rough. So if we started running silent, they knew to expect word of your status on the dump tapes. I sent the recording on down almost half an hour ago, so I figure the boys in the trenches are getting an earful about now. We'll be hearing from them at any time, and they'll give us the code for a secured live frequency."

"I'd love to be in the MOCR right now," Slayton smiled. "To see their faces…"

"Think of it," Cortney said, his face filled with wonder. "You guys discovered the first hard evidence of extraterrestrial life…I just can't wrap my brain around that. Who knows how long ago, someone walked the moon before we did…someone from another world."

"I hate to admit it," Shepherd said, "but you're right."

"Twenty, Houston," sounded an urgent voice. "Radio check three-two-two bravo. Do you read?"

Smiles crossed all of their faces, the triumphant beam of men who knew they bore good news indeed.

"Showtime," Cortney said, plucking his drifting headset out of the air. "Oh, by the way, Charlie…I almost forgot. Where's my pecan log?"

"I knew I forgot something," came the reply, spoken through a huge grin.

Irwin hurriedly flipped through a procedures manual, then adjusted their high-gain settings for the frequency specified by the coded request. "Roger, Houston," he said, now speaking freely. "We've got you five-by-five. Got a couple of fellows with me here who'd like to say hello."

◙   ◙   ◙

In the dark, frigid stillness of the war room, a faint red glow spilled upon the chamber's now-sleeping central core. Its source was an angry, unwavering disk of brilliant crimson, the sole point of radiance in the pitch blackness that now pervaded the entirety of the base.

A wide pool of ice coated the floor nearby, its source water spilled there as a pair of pressure helmets, needed once more, had been emptied of their gelid contents.

The last of many, the disk maintained a lonely, mandated vigil, waiting patiently for what must now be, lest the installation fall into unfamiliar, hostile hands—its fate decreed by an artificial mind, the technological spawn of a world that existed no more.

Its final moments ticked inexorably away.

Then the light went out. For but an instant, the console went as dark as the once-forgotten base around it.

Then, for the first time, came the dawn.

The sun rose over Marlow.

◙   ◙   ◙

Shepherd, sitting in the spacecraft's right-hand couch, shielded his face as a blinding white light suddenly filled the side window.

What the—?

Cautiously, he looked back at the receding moon, the ashen orb still occupying most of the view port. As he watched, its southern basin, engulfed by the fury of a swelling fireball as intense as the solar core, simply ceased to be. Iron, glass, stone, and water all vaporized, swallowed within the silent, glaring violence.

Shepherd felt the heat upon his face from twenty thousand miles away.

The radiance reached its peak and began to fade. In its place remained a vast, uneven bowl of molten glass and rock, its reddish glow darkening as the material rapidly cooled.

Millennia of pent-up energies, released as a single, raw, uncontrolled eruption, had consumed the very mechanism of their birth and much more. In moments, the ancient base, the lake of ice, two hundred cubic miles of lunar bedrock, and the faithful *Mirabelle*—all were gone.

"Did you see that?" Shepherd animatedly asked of his companions, his voice breaking. "Did you?"

"What was it?" Cortney asked, having seen only the momentary throw of light that splashed the main console. "You had the only window facing that way."

Shepherd felt a deep, sinking knot grip his stomach as the thought of what might have been bombarded him.

The red lights—!

"Guys," he said slowly, his voice grim with realization, "when you said you showed up just in time...you weren't kidding."

39

Wednesday, April 30, 8:53 P.M.

They were alone together, watching the reports as they came down, their hopes long faded, the fervent prayers of one seemingly unheard.

Diane and Carol sat in the Lucas' living room, their eyes on the television screen, following the coverage of the mission. They had just finished a light dinner of chicken, green beans, and corn, and as Joey Shepherd sat playing with a few toys in another room, the two women tried to cope with the silence coming from space.

They knew what the world knew. Before them, filling the screen, a trusted voice accompanied an artist's conception of the engine burn that earlier had broken Apollo 20 free of the moon's gravity, sending it homeward.

"We believe the spacecraft is performing well," Walter Cronkite announced, adjusting his glasses as the camera came back to him. "The radio malfunction that occurred just after the journey earthward began continues still…though we are told that NASA is still receiving good telemetry, and the data shows the craft to be in good shape. We have no evidence of a major malfunction such as that which plagued the Apollo 13 mission, nor do we believe the crew is in danger of any kind. They are headed back, their mission a success, for they have recovered their fallen comrades and are bringing them home to their native soil."

"I'm not up to it, Carol," Diane said, turning away from the set. Barely healed wounds were being reopened. "I'm just not up to it."

Carol turned down the television and placed a reassuring hand upon her friend's. "I know, honey…"

"I'm worried about Jeff…he's still struggling, and to throw a burial on top of everything else…"

"Maybe the finality is something he needs."

"I don't know…"

Diane rose from her seat on the couch and walked to the window. There was no moon in the starry sky; it had not yet risen.

"At least we'll be able to look at the moon again," she said, wrapping her arms around herself. "Mostly…"

Carol waited, seeing a struggle in the woman's eyes as she gazed up into the darkness.

"I prayed and prayed, Carol. I know I shouldn't have, but I held out hope. I prayed for that one-in-a-million chance. All day, every day, ever since Bruce told me…told me they might…" She paused, the words coming hard. "I hoped somehow…that some way Gary might still…" She trailed off into pain.

"What purpose could there possibly be in losing my husband?" she went on. "Or in losing yours? Or in our children losing their fathers?"

Their eyes glistened as their bond deepened still.

"Faith," Carol said softly. "Trust. We have to believe that He knows what He's doing, even when we don't understand."

"I guess I don't have any faith in God, after all," Diane said, her head dropping. "I guess I never did…I never believed enough. I wasn't really saved. Otherwise, I wouldn't question."

Carol put an arm around her. "No, no, now…it doesn't work that way. We *all* doubt. We all question."

"*You* don't."

"Oh, yes I do. When Charlie died, I questioned. When my sister died, I questioned. That's one of the ways faith grows…when we're tested and we look for answers and we turn to Him and learn to trust. It's a process. No one on this planet has a perfect faith…but that isn't what being a Christian is about."

Diane looked into Carol's eyes, silently questioning through tears.

"We aren't expected to be perfect. That's God's job. The last perfect man died on a cross and rose from the dead almost two thousand years ago. That was why He died for us in the first place…because we *can't* be perfect, not in this life. We're not even expected always to do the best we can…none of us are capable even of *that*. Our job is to let Christ live through us…to let Him make us what He would have us be. We will doubt and question and do wrong and mess up in a thousand ways, all our lives…but we're *forgiven*. That's the wonder of the Christian faith…the burden is not ours, but *God's*."

Diane smiled, an inner joy cutting through the grief. *How can it be?*

"It sounds too easy," she said.

"No, no. Our salvation isn't easy. It was paid for at the greatest cost of all…death. The difference is that its price was paid *for* us by someone else. We can't earn eternal life, we can only accept it. As I once heard it said, 'salvation is a gift, not a paycheck.'"

Headlights shone through the front window, giving the curtains a brilliant glow.

"Someone's here," Diane said, wiping the tears from her face. "Look at me…I must be a mess."

Carol crossed the room and peered outside. In the driveway was a black sedan, an official car bearing the NASA emblem and a carpool number on its front doors. The driver's door opened and a man climbed out, but in the darkness she could not tell who it was.

That did not matter. She knew already.

The Angel of Death.

"It's someone from the Space Center," she said. "He must be here to give us the official word."

"Let's get this over with," Diane nodded, gathering herself as she reluctantly started for the entry foyer.

The doorbell rang.

A darkly clad figure stood just outside, his image obscured by the cut, frosted glass of the door. Diane took a deep breath then flipped on the outside light, and after a moment reached for the knob as Carol hung back, waiting at the entrance to the living room.

The door opened to reveal Vic Kendall.

"Diane…" he began, the harsh light of the porch lamp casting half his face into shadow. Looking beyond her, he spotted another familiar face. "Carol…I'm glad you're here."

"Oh…Vic…come in," Diane said, her tone serious.

Kendall entered, an emotional torrent masked beneath his somber face. She closed the door behind him and followed as he moved into the living room. The women looked upon him with stern, readied faces, waiting for the blow.

His face broke into a wide smile, catching them both off guard.

"They're alive," he said simply. "Both of them."

As the words soaked in, the wives stared in stunned silence, their eyes going wide. Their minds longing desperately that it be true, they fought nonetheless to believe.

"We don't know all the details yet," Kendall added, "but Gary and Charlie are alive and well and headed home."

Carol closed her eyes in tearful, jubilant praise.

Diane gasped and put a hand to her mouth.

I must be dreaming—!

Happy tears flooded forth, wetting faces of joyous disbelief. With a squeal, Diane rushed forward and embraced her visiting angel, letting the moment last as long as possible.

If I am dreaming, please don't let me wake up—

Kendall held her, his burden also finally lifted. No longer did he wear the unjust, largely self-imposed mark that so severely had afflicted him.

"I'm here to help you get ready for a little trip," he smiled, as the woman pulled away and reached for a tissue. "You'll be meeting them in Hawaii, day after tomorrow. I assumed you'd want to go…"

"Yes!" the overjoyed women cried in unison, sniffling and laughing and crying all at the same time.

Joey walked into the room, having overheard Kendall's words and the resulting flood of blissful excitement.

"Is Daddy coming home now?" the young boy asked.

"Yes, baby," Carol replied tearfully, reaching for her child. She knelt and cradled him tightly, loving him, cherishing him. "Daddy's coming home."

"Good," the boy smiled, holding up a little plastic astronaut. "I need my other spaceman back."

Epilogue

On a clear, April morning in 1975, three men left Earth, headed for another world.

Almost two weeks later, five came home.

The jubilation had been palpable as an amazed populace looked upon two who had been given up for dead on a world so far from their own, yet walked again.

It was—*a miracle.*

Of course, the truth behind that miracle could not be revealed to the masses. The risks for public panic were too high, should the fact of a race of ancient astronauts become known. At least, that was the consensus in high places. Worse yet, there remained the possibility of another, yet undiscovered lunar base—what if an unfriendly nation were to seek it out and use its advanced technology against the United States?

Most of those at NASA did not know the truth, and those who did had been sworn to secrecy, under penalty of treason.

Still, the world had to be told *something.*

In a carefully crafted press release, it was "disclosed" that an unmanned Russian spacecraft dubbed *Priyut,* disowned by its government after what mistakenly had been thought a failed landing, had provided shelter and sustenance for the two men. The radio signal heard by those on Earth had been a desperate call for help, made by a system not designed for voice communications. The USSR responded by insisting that the experimental survival module, launched some two years earlier, had crashed at a location nearly a thousand miles from where NASA claimed its men had discovered it intact.

In short, the Soviet Union flatly denied the American statement. But then, as everyone knew, they always denied *everything*.

Besides, Lucas and Shepherd were alive. The story *had* to be true.

The press demanded as many details of the astounding tale of survival as they could get, and NASA complied with reams of creatively and carefully compiled documents. The two astronauts were heroes, and the free world was hungry for their story. It had been almost three months since splashdown, and nine weeks since the chaotic rush of ticker-tape parades and honorary dinners that had swept the triumphant pair from one laudatory venue to the next. Sending the men out among the masses had been a dangerous but necessary public relations move on the part of NASA, one calculated to implant more solidly the seeds of revisionism so carefully sown by the agency. Beyond that initial seven-day whirlwind countrywide tour, Lucas and Shepherd spoke little and rarely about their ordeal on the lunar surface, claiming the need for privacy and family time now that they had been reunited with their loved ones.

Even the universe had given an assist to the deception, it seemed. Due to a fluke in orbital positioning, the brief though brilliant detonation at Marlow had not been witnessed by a single earthly observatory. At the moment of the event, the moon had been out of position for viewing from any of the world's major telescopes, resting either too low on the horizon or almost directly overhead. Immediately following the reports of a few, scattered eyewitnesses who had seen the momentary flash of light, experts assumed that a massive meteor strike had taken place, a hypothesis that could not be confirmed or denied without seismic data. Unfortunately, no seismometer had been placed by the crew of Apollo 19, and the equipment left by the previous mission had failed after only four months of operation. Nor did any of the delicate units carried to the moon on the first flights some three to six years earlier still function, having long since exceeded their designed life spans.

A tree had fallen in the forest, and no one had heard.

■ ■ ■

Shepherd sat alone in a briefing room in the Washington, D.C., headquarters of NASA. Models of rockets and spacecraft stood within a display case behind him, and the walls were covered with framed photos taken over the course of a dozen successful missions. Not far away, down halls abuzz with news of a fully restored spaceflight budget, a committee of NASA, Defense Department, and NSA officials were gathering, preparing to hear closed, exhaustive testimony from the four men who had walked the surface of Marlow and, in so doing, had encountered a technology beyond any Earth had to offer. There was great uneasiness about that, a concern for national security, a fear that discovery of further installations—but by Soviet forces—might be forthcoming. First, Lucas and Shepherd would testify, then, later that afternoon, Cortney and Irwin would be asked to do the same.

Shepherd sat quietly, pondering all he had experienced during his stay on the moon. The evidence of extraterrestrial life he had witnessed disturbed him, shaking his deeply held convictions concerning the place of man in God's creation, and since he had not yet had time to sort things out for himself, he had been all too happy not to disclose the truths he knew about what he had seen.

Father—what did it all mean? Why in the world did you show us that place—?

He had begun to wonder if it had been wise to bring his lightkey back with him. With no choice but to turn it over to an NSA official while still aboard the recovery carrier, he had done so. Their intent, he quickly learned, was to bury the device along with any other evidence of the base's existence, to make Shepherd complicit in an intricate cover-up that ultimately would haunt them.

There was one piece of evidence Shepherd had hidden away, however, not sharing it even with NASA. An intangible doubt had nagged at him as their return voyage had grown to a close, demanding that some form of substantiation remain out of the hands of those who would hide the truth. Just before splashdown, he had taped his razor securely to the inside of his calf, allowing him to smuggle it safely away and ultimately to a secret place, where it rested still. He felt guilt over the purposeful concealment of such evidence, but also felt he had little choice, at least for the moment.

His Bible, too, had been locked away for safekeeping, its note pages filled with the journal entries and diagrams of the base he had set down during his stay. For so long, the worn book had been at his side almost everywhere he had traveled—and now, being without it felt as if he had lost a dear friend.

Am I doing the right thing? Is such a truth withheld a blessing, or a curse?

The base he had seen was no longer there—he was certain of that—but there was no such guarantee that others did not exist. He fully understood the need for national security, and if there was any great scientific or technological discovery still to be made on the moon, he wanted his country to make it. Still, he was troubled, his mind unsettled by hard questions demanding answers.

Somehow, shouldn't the truth be told? Doesn't the world have a right to know? Can't Christianity withstand the revelation of truth, whatever that truth may be? Indeed, mustn't that truth confirm the fact of our faith and not deny it?

As he sat pondering these things, the door opened and in walked Lucas, a briefcase in one hand, a Bible in the other.

"There he is," Shepherd said, rising from his chair as he greeted his friend.

The well-rested, fully recovered astronaut walked up to him and they embraced, patting each other firmly on the back.

"By the way," Shepherd said. "I meant to tell you. You look better now...without the beard."

"Annie was rather insistent about that," he grinned. "She wanted the husband who went to the moon...not Jeremiah Johnson."

"Well, she has a point there." He patted his friend and former crewmate on the shoulder. "It's been good seeing you two in church these last few weeks," Shepherd smiled.

"Wouldn't miss it. You know how close Annie and Carol grew while we were away...they're like sisters now. Apparently, she found the Lord about the same time I did."

"Or, He found *you*," Shepherd said. He noted the book in Lucas' hand. "I see you picked up a Bible."

"Yup...first one I've ever owned, I'm ashamed to admit."

"Well, as the great Freddo Haise would say, 'better late then never.'"

Lucas smiled. "I suppose."

"You ready to talk to these guys?" Shepherd asked, returning to his seat at the dark, polished conference table. His friend lowered himself into an adjoining chair.

"Nope."

"Me neither. What can you say after you go through something like that? We don't even understand it ourselves...but I hate its implications."

Lucas seemed unusually ill at ease, and his friend saw it.

"What?"

Lucas looked down at the book in his hands, its cover of rich burgundy leather.

"I've done a lot of reading these past few months, Charlie," he began, indicating the Bible. "Not just this...but a lot of things written by a lot of people. When I started into this book, I just thought I ought to get to know its author a little better...spent a few nights in bed reading before turning in. Started at the beginning, with Genesis."

"The beginning's always a good place to start," Shepherd smiled gently.

Lucas stared hard at the book, as if reluctant to go on.

"Gary...?"

"That machine I was in...I told you it sent me somewhere. I never told you exactly *where.*"

"You said you saw the aliens' home world," Shepherd recalled. "I think you filled me in pretty well. But I'm telling you, Gary...you were inside that thing the whole time. You had to be. Somehow, it was creating the things you saw...making them real for you."

"Why would it do that?"

"I don't know. Maybe it was a recreation machine of some kind...their way of getting away and taking a vacation. As isolated as they must have been up there, I'd say that's a good bet. It's not like they could get a weekend pass or anything."

"Charlie, I'm telling you...it was all as real as you and me here now. The same way I can reach out and touch you or this book or this table, I could do it there, too. The sights, the sounds, the smells, everything...it was real. I'm telling you, *it was real.*"

"Okay," Shepherd conceded. "For the sake of argument, let's say it *was* real. Let's say the machine sent you back to their planet. How did it happen? Did you climb into it or push any buttons or anything?"

"I can't remember. One minute I was standing at the door to your quarters and then...nothing. I have no memory at all, after that."

"Hmmmm..."

"What?"

Shepherd thought back. "Just before that thing opened up and I found you, there were these weird alarm tones. Three of them. I almost jumped out of my skin. Do you remember anything like that? I mean, it had to have opened for you, right?"

A memory suddenly shone in Lucas' mind. "Alarm tones..."

"Ring a bell?"

"While I was back there," he began, "just before the bottom fell out...I heard tones like that while I was standing in the corridor. I hid, and then the base commander came running by. *He must have been using the machine.* If he left it open, or never reset it or whatever it was they'd do when they were done..."

Lucas nodded to himself.

"Somehow, I wound up inside it," he concluded. "And it sent me where *he* had been."

"Through *time,* you mean?"

"I know it sounds crazy," Lucas said, shaking his head.

"Well, I guess we'll never know," Shepherd said. "Won't know what that planet you saw was or *where* it was, either...it's a big universe."

Lucas went quiet. After a weighty pause, he spoke.

"No...I *know* where I was. I didn't then...but I do now. You were right all along. Aliens didn't build that base."

"Then who did?"

"*We* did."

Shepherd was caught off guard. "Say what?"

"That's what I was getting at before..."

Lucas opened his Bible and began to read.

"And God looked on the earth, and behold, it was corrupt; for all flesh had corrupted their way upon the earth.

Then God said to Noah, 'The end of all flesh has come
before Me; for the earth is filled with violence because of them;
and behold, I am about to destroy them with the earth.'"

Shepherd's brow furrowed.

"*Noah*, Charlie," Lucas said, his voice calm and certain. "I slept
under his roof…ate at his table…"

He went on.

"Make for yourself an ark of gopher wood; you shall make the ark
with rooms, and shall cover it inside and out with pitch. And this
is how you shall make it: the length of the ark three hundred
cubits, its breadth fifty cubits, and its height thirty cubits. You shall
make a window for the ark, and finish it to a cubit from the top;
and set the door of the ark in the side of it; you shall make it with
lower, second, and third decks.

"I had assumed it was a storehouse, but it wasn't. I didn't figure that
out until it began to *move*. The size, the material, everything matches
this description. Everything. I even helped apply the pitch."

He took a deep breath and went on as Shepherd listened in
stunned amazement, wondering if it really could be true.

"And behold, I, even I am bringing the flood of water upon the
earth, to destroy all flesh in which is the breath of life, from under
heaven; everything that is on the earth shall perish. But I will
establish My covenant with you; and you shall enter the ark—you
and your sons and your wife, and your sons' wives with you. And
of every living thing of all flesh, you shall bring two of every kind
into the ark, to keep them alive with you; they shall be male and
female."

Lucas lowered the book. "That was what they were arguing about...it *has* to be."

"Huh?" Shepherd managed.

"Remember what I told you, about after I'd fallen...when I was laid up in bed? The argument they had...I thought they were kicking me out, but I was wrong." He paused, the memory vivid and clear. "I know now...Noah's sons wanted to take me aboard with them. They felt they owed me something for having saved the life of his daughter-in-law. But the man made the hard call...he put his foot down because God had told him that *only* he and his family were to enter the ark."

He still could hear their voices, see their faces.

"They weren't asking me to leave...*they were leaving me behind.*"

Shepherd sat silently, staring across the room. *Is it possible—?*

"And the man I saw on his deathbed wasn't just old, he was the *oldest* man who ever lived..." He tapped his Bible. "*Methuselah,* Charlie...according to this, he died right before the Flood hit."

"Gary, I'd be the first to stand up for the truth of the Deluge. You know that. But they didn't have spaceflight and moon bases in Noah's day. They didn't have the advanced technology you said you saw while you were there. The machines, the tools, the physics, all of it...they just didn't have those things."

"How do you know that?"

"Well...because there's no sign of it."

"An absence of evidence is not evidence of absence," Lucas said. "Their world was *utterly* devastated. Any physical remains of that civilization lie broken and buried under miles and miles of mud and rock, beneath the sedimentary layers we see everywhere." He held up his Bible. "But there *is* a record of it all...right here."

"Of *that* kind of science?"

"A vessel six hundred feet long, Charlie...ships only got that big again within the last century or so. Imagine the structural technology it would have taken to conceive and build a ship that immense…the sheer *genius* of its design. Do you think a culture such as we've been taught existed then could have pulled that off? Imagine the stresses it must have withstood…it endured a hydraulic cataclysm powerful enough to destroy everything else ever built."

"So why was it wood, then, if they were that advanced? Why not steel or—?"

"It was a *symbol*. I've talked to our pastor and a few others about that. Symbolism means *everything* to God…that's why He always had things built just so. He was always very explicit in His instructions.

"Wood was a symbol of man, just as gold was a symbol of the Lord. Take the ark of the covenant…it was made of wood overlaid with gold, inside and out, a picture of the coming melding of God and man through Jesus Christ. But the ark of Noah was wood overlaid with *pitch,* inside and out, and the Hebrew word used for 'pitch' in that verse of Genesis is the same one used for 'atonement' everywhere else in the Old Testament. Wood covered by pitch…man and his sins covered by *the blood of Christ*."

Shepherd paused to let it all soak in. "But, Gary…*spaceflight?*"

Lucas considered his theories, formulating an example.

"Just think about it," he continued. "Where was the world sixteen hundred years ago, as far as technology goes?"

"Not too far along," Shepherd replied.

"Right. We were smack in the middle of the Dark Ages. Not much happening. There had been great wonders built way back when, the pyramids and such, but around A.D. 400, *squat*. And since then, mostly in the last few centuries, we've developed the sciences and flight and lasers and medical miracles and engineering feats that were impossible not long ago…not to mention TV dinners and landings on the moon."

"Okay, I'm with you so far."

Lucas held up his Bible. "Tell me…according to this, how many years passed between the creation of man and the Flood of Noah?"

Shepherd realized and nodded slowly. "About *sixteen hundred years.*"

"And those men lived to be well into their eight and nine hundreds…huge men, brilliant men, men who, though fallen, were just two or three generations removed from *the very hand of God.*" He was awed at the thought. "Just imagine…a world filled with minds beyond that of Einstein, even as demented and evil as they became, with those kinds of life spans to work with. If we could achieve all that *we* did in sixteen centuries, think of what *they* could have done in the same amount of time."

Shepherd was astounded.

"So…why didn't they resume that level of technology after the Flood?"

"Just because they were brilliant doesn't mean every person knew how to do everything," Lucas said. "It's a good bet they took things for granted the way we do…it's only natural." He indicated his wristwatch. "I use this every day. But if you asked me to make one, or just to *tell* you how to make one, I couldn't do it. They lost *everything* and had to begin again from square one…and no one lived as long after that. Man's life span dropped by more than ninety percent, and in a hurry."

"Okay," Shepherd spoke softly, nodding almost imperceptibly. "Okay…"

Lucas held the Bible tightly, wondering at its veracity. "This explains everything, Charlie…even why the race who built that moon base never attacked Earth, despite their advanced science, despite their cruelty. It was because they were *from* here."

He considered the written miracle in his hands. "And if this book is right even about the Flood, it's right about everything else. God *did* come down to Earth as a man. Jesus Christ *is* the only way."

Shepherd smiled, relishing the new life he saw within his friend.

"*Now* who's the old preacher man?" He had seen Gary Lucas happy, sad, angry, bitter, and pensive throughout the years, throughout their training, throughout their ordeal. But this—this was something altogether new.

Something wonderful.

"You know," Shepherd wondered, "ever since we got back you've been telling me about this place you saw, but you never said a thing about all of *this*. Why did you wait until now?"

"Because I wasn't sure, and I wanted to *be* sure before I brought the whole thing up. Now I am. And since we have to testify this morning, I thought you might draw some comfort from knowing that it wasn't a contradiction of the Bible we found up there on the moon...it was *proof* of it."

Shepherd smiled, shaking his head.

There's always a reason—

He thought back in light of all he had just heard, his mind returning to the huge star map they had seen in the war room.

"The fifth planet...and oceans on Mars...and rings on all the gas giants..."

"I bet they're still there, or evidence of them, anyway. The rings we just may not have seen yet. Mars is a desert now, but thousands of years ago...who knows? And as for the fifth planet—"

"The asteroid belt," Shepherd said. "At least, that's what's left of it."

"That would be my guess."

"Wow," Shepherd said in quiet awe.

The two men sat silently, knowing they shared a deep truth unknown to the rest of the world.

"Boy, Gary," Shepherd finally said. "When you get saved, *you get saved.*"

Lucas was humbled by it all. "The blessing I've been given...it's so *big*. To actually have been there...to have seen it all firsthand...to have found eternal life because of it. What a *gift.*"

"I'll have to call you 'Thomas' from now on."

"Why's that?"

"Because," Shepherd said, reaching out to turn the man's palm upward. "You, my friend, put your finger in the nail holes...*and believed.*"

Put out my hand, Lucas thought with a nod, *and touched the face of God.*

"I wish it hadn't taken that. You were right all along, Charlie, but I wouldn't listen. Everything in our lives, however great or small, is a part of the outworking of God's plan. Nothing happens by chance." He smiled. "You know...the guys at Grumman will be thrilled to know that it took divine intervention to keep *Starlight* from lifting off. If that engine had fired the way it should have..."

"We would never have found the base."

"And Annie and I would never have found God."

A knock sounded at the door, and it opened to reveal a government official in a dark suit, wearing a security badge.

"Colonel Lucas, Colonel Shepherd," he said, "they're ready for you now."

"One minute," Lucas asked. The man turned and took a few steps down the hall, leaving the door open behind him.

"It still sounds nice, doesn't it?" Shepherd smiled. "'Colonel.'"

Lucas closed his Bible and rose from his seat. "Rank does have its privileges. Maybe the promotion will help them to hear us in there. It's going to be a tough climb, convincing the committee of what we saw."

"So," Shepherd quietly said, standing as well. "What *do* we tell them? They'll never believe us."

"I know."

Shepherd's brow suddenly furrowed. He looked away, clearly troubled.

"What, Charlie? What is it?"

"I just thought of something," he answered, his tone grave. "The last days…the 'end times'…Christ said they'd be 'as it was in the days of Noah.' What you saw…by the grace of God, Gary, it was a *warning*. We can't let this be covered up. We have to tell *everyone*, not just the committee. The world has to hear."

Lucas nodded and put a hand on his friend's shoulder.

"It will."

They gathered their things and walked from the room.

◈   ◈   ◈

It stood watch over the dusty plain as it had for almost five thousand years, unaffected by the shifting dunes or the bitter cold or the harsh, driven sands.

Cut into the jagged stone of a cliff face, it stood open, ten feet wide and fifteen high. Beyond lay a darkened, circular chamber, half-filled now with dust deposited there by centuries of icy winds.

A door.

As it had for so long, it greeted each new sunrise, watching as the pale skies brightened each morning, waiting as they darkened to star-studded black each night. Almost two million times the sun had come and gone and still the gleaming sentry stood, glinting a ruddy silver in the soft light, awaiting the passage of its builders.

Its world was a lifeless desert. It had not always been so.

The sky grew dark as night descended, and the white caress of frost settled upon the rocks and in the hollows. Amid the myriad stars overhead hung a bright, shining orb, a pinpoint of crystalline blue, slowly crossing the heavens as it beckoned a distant few who could behold its beauty no longer.

They were no more—yet they would be heard.

Afterword

This novel presents an alternate history of American spaceflight, shortly after the time of the first lunar landing, that deviates from actual history. In reality, the last manned mission to the moon—Apollo 17—landed and returned to Earth in December 1972. It was not originally intended to have been the last, however, for the initial plan had been for *twenty* lunar flights, a plan cut short by public apathy and governmental shortsightedness.

It was my desire to maintain the unique flavor of the Apollo era as much as possible, despite the fact that *Ice* is set in a year well after the actual program had ended, when the space agency had moved on to other projects. To this end, I have retained some designations that in fact changed prior to the mid-1970s—for example, rather than referring to NASA's primary Houston facility as the "Johnson Space Center" (as it was known in 1975, and is today), I used the name "Manned Spacecraft Center," which it carried during Apollo's heyday. A few of the NASA personnel presented herein as background characters, who in actuality retired from the agency in the early 1970s, are portrayed as having remained in their jobs until the time of the story's conclusion. Any actual persons or corporations mentioned in the story were added for purposes of authenticity, and all such individuals and corporations have been used fictitiously in the telling of this story.

The *Aurora* probe described in chapter 1 is fictitious, as is its creator, Artemus Marlow. Similarly, none of the events depicted regarding the flights of the Apollo 19 and 20 missions ever really happened, and any resemblance to actual occurrences is purely coincidental.

The water ice located at the lunar south pole was not known to exist until the flight of NASA's *Clementine* probe in 1994, a discovery confirmed a few years later by the unmanned lunar satellite *Lunar Prospector*. The exact nature of this ice is not yet known—it may be frost embedded in the lunar soil, for example—but whatever form it takes, it is known that there is a *lot* of it. The deep, southern lunar basin, itself an actual feature of the moon, was also discovered in the 1990s and is in reality named Aitken—not Marlow. For the purposes of this novel, it was necessary to devise a method for detecting this basin some twenty years earlier than actually occurred, hence *Aurora*.

All of the American hardware and mission parameters described in this story were derived from actual concepts, conceived by NASA, Boeing, Grumman, and North American Rockwell for use in an extended Apollo program that never materialized. The LM Truck and heavy rover featured in this story might actually have been utilized on the moon if not for budget cuts. In contrast to *Starlight*, the lunar module depicted in the story, the spacecraft built by Grumman performed flawlessly in all of its missions, and all of the scenes involving the company and its personnel are entirely fictitious. The Soviet spacecraft *Priyut*, mentioned near the conclusion of the story, is fictitious but is based upon that nation's discontinued L3M lunar vehicle concept, proposed in 1972.

The radio address given by the president of the United States in *Ice* is closely based upon one written on July 18, 1969, by White House Speechwriter William Safire, a contingency prepared for then-President Richard Nixon. While it was not likely that the men of Apollo 11 would fail in their mission, the writing of that speech (written even as the spacecraft neared the moon) only served to underscore the dangers of such an undertaking and the apprehension behind the pride felt by a watching nation. Even then, despite the successful flights of Apollos 7 through 10, NASA's astronauts were threatened by many unknowns, any one of which might have proven catastrophic. When asked before his flight which single threat to the mission was greatest, Apollo 11 CMP Michael Collins replied, "the one we failed to prepare for."

This novel paints a picture of the antediluvian world that lies well outside the more conventional notions generally held today. The idea of pre-Flood man having known spaceflight is indeed speculative and is derived primarily from the extraordinary nature of man as he likely existed at the time. Living in an era so near the time of his original creation, it is probable that he was physically superior to modern man. Despite his fallen nature, he had not yet suffered the crippling effects of long-term solar radiation, one of the primary causes of skin cancers, genetic damage, and many other cumulative disorders known today. This radiation would have been screened completely by the protective canopy that, according to the Bible, enshrouded the Earth before collapsing as precipitation during the second phase of the Flood of Noah.

At that time, man and all other living things, both plant and animal, were much larger and had much greater life spans, as evidenced by the fossil record and written of in Scripture. Given the extended lives and yet undamaged physical nature enjoyed by mankind in those days, it is reasonable to assume that he was smarter, faster, larger, and more advanced than we are, and if that is true, since *we* could perfect the science of flight and use it to go to the moon, pre-Flood man *certainly* would have been capable of doing the same. Whether or not he chose to do so is quite open to debate.

It is interesting to note that, according to the book of Genesis, man's life span dropped dramatically immediately after the Noachian Deluge, from an average of almost eight hundred years to a mere seventy in just a few generations. And it is important to remember that the Jewish people held it as a sacred duty to record the deeds of their God and the history of their world both *reverently* and *unwaveringly* throughout the centuries. No one writing an account of the early Earth under these restrictive conditions, who expected to be taken seriously, would make the apparently outlandish claim that men lived to be as much as nine hundred sixty-nine years old—*unless it was true.*

The Ark of Noah is described in the Bible as being three hundred cubits long by fifty cubits wide by thirty cubits tall. This traditionally has been taken to imply a length of four hundred fifty feet, given an eighteen-inch cubit. However, the cubit was a *biological* standard of measurement, based upon the distance from a man's elbow to his fingertip—and if man was larger in those days, *the cubit would have been longer* as well. A human physical size of seven or eight feet, as described in *Ice,* would lend a cubit of approximately twenty-four inches, making the Ark some six hundred feet long, increasing its already great interior volume dramatically.

Following the recent, world-changing events in New York City and Washington, D.C., many have turned to their faith for reassurance. It is important to remember that however evil an act of man may be, our all-knowing, all-powerful God is not surprised by its occurrence and uses it for the outworking of His own plan, turning even the most heinous evils back upon themselves, causing good to rise from the ashes. We must draw comfort from this. *God is in control.*

The inerrancy and trustworthiness of the Bible must be the cornerstone of our faith, for it is the *one* rock to which we moor our witness as we struggle to live in this turbulent, ever-changing, revisionist world. Truth is not determined by society, or our feelings, or our opinions, or our desires—*truth is truth,* and it does not change. However we feel, whatever our perceptions, there is only *one* true history of the world, *one* true manner in which we came to be, and *one* true answer concerning the nature of God and of salvation.

We must focus upon the Creator, not the Creation, and upon His Word to us.

That Word is the Bible.

Do not be deceived. We cannot choose to believe one part of the Bible and not another, or reject any part as "unreliable," or consider this verse or that to be but parable or allegory unless the Bible itself claims it to be such. One cannot dismiss the Creation account as mere poetry, for example, while taking the account of the Crucifixion as fact. We must not try to fall back on the common excuse of supposed translation errors made "down through the years." If our God can bring the entire time-space continuum and all the worlds and stars within it into existence by a sheer act of will, He *certainly* can see to it that His Bible remains intact and valid despite the limitations or tamperings of man. The Bible is God's Word to *you,* and He does not mumble, nor does He mislead, nor is He an author of confusion. The evidence for the Bible's continued veracity and astounding uniqueness is overwhelming, as elucidated in such works as Josh McDowell's *Evidence That Demands a Verdict,* the *Reformation Study Bible,* and the *Ryrie Study Bible.*

There is no fence. When it comes to the Holy Scriptures, we must believe *none* of it—not one verse, not one word—or believe it *all,* every jot and tittle.

Christ did. And His Word should be good enough for us.

Shane Johnson
December 2001
http://www.apollo19.net

Acknowledgments

I would like to thank the following people, all of whom took the time to help make this novel better than it otherwise might have been:

Ret Martin, who spent many hours working with me to preedit the text and in many ways helped make the writing of this novel possible.

Kathy Johnson, my wife, who put up with months of my spending overnight hours pounding away at the keyboard, somehow puts up with me in general, and offers all the love and support anyone could ask for.

Daniel Johnson, my son, who already is a better writer than I was at his age and is a constant inspiration to me.

Ron and Nina Johnson, whose words of encouragement mean more to me than they can ever know.

Shirley Johnson, whose profound impact upon my youth brought me nearer to the Lord, and whose words have spoken to my heart as only a grandmother's can.

Reg Martin, a wise man who first opened my eyes to the possibility that the world is not as old as some would have us believe.

Erin Healy, my editor, whose encouragement and expertise once again have proven invaluable to me—in working with her, I am truly blessed.

Alan Beckner, Craig Ligon, Mark Vinson, Scott Bell, Mike Okuda, Steve and Verna McClellan, Debbie Dennis, Phil Lublin, Ron Gross, Joel Tavera, Barry and Roberta Smith, Gene and Maudie Lam, Tim Vanderkolk, Peter Landrey, and *John Hopkins,* who took time out of their busy lives to read the story and offered the fine feedback I needed in the crafting of this novel.

I would also like to express my gratitude to the late Martin Caidin, author of dozens of books, including *Marooned, Golden Wings,* and *By Apollo to the Moon,* whose brilliant work has inspired me for more than thirty years and made me believe that I might be able to write this novel after all.